DRAGON LORD

Book II of the
Shattered Worlds Trilogy

By

MICHAEL ANTHONY CARIOLA

ISBN-13: 979-8-9956483-1-4

Prologue

An excerpt from the Atlantean Book of Magickal Creatures

Written and Compiled by Master Nicodemus the Immortal

What can be said about Dragons? In my early days as a student of the magickal arts, I was determined to understand the nature of the first creatures to inhabit Earth before it was violently split apart from Aralia. The texts concerning dragons written by the old masters were either vague or incomplete. Thus, I set out on a journey to the Mountains of Paranak, which separated eastern Atlantis from the west. There, it was rumored, that Maragog, that dragon of Paranak, dwelled deep within those mountains. I was unwavering in my desire to interview the ancient beast and learn at her feet. My master tried to discourage me from what he deemed a fool's quest. So many others who undertook quests for dragons either sought to kill them or were slain by the great beasts. Maragog would perchance not understand, and most likely scorch me to ashes. With sword and shield in hand, I undertook a journey of many days fraught with peril to reach her mountain, and then many days more in the bowels of the earth to locate her lair.

Let me begin by saying that dragons are terribly misunderstood creatures. In truth, they would prefer to be left alone. Only encroachment by man has given dragons such a terrible reputation. It also might be said that either ignorance or folly saved me from a most unpleasant death, for dragons are, as is their nature, wary of man. Truth be told, when I finally, by chance, located and entered the dragon's lair, it was either my naïveté or intuition that saved my skin. The jury on that is still out. Nevertheless, I left my shield and sword at the mouth of the cave and faced Maragog. I planted my feet firmly and startled her to wakefulness. I said to her, "Ancient Maragog, I wish to ask some questions!"

She reared up at her full height and it was then that I realized the fullness of my folly. At that moment, I expected to be scorched to cinders. But to my astonishment, Maragog began to laugh, and to my embarrassment, she continued to laugh for a good five minutes. Finally, when she caught her breath and was able to calm herself enough to speak, she said, "Pardon me but I haven't had a good laugh for several centuries."

Unable to resist a good repartee, I responded most indignantly, "So glad that I could oblige you, madam!"

Maragog chuckled for a few more minutes and finally addressed me.

"Little man, are you not aware that it is in the nature of dragons to scorch first and ask questions later?"

"Perhaps that's the reason why men know so little about dragons," I answered.

"Good point." She acquiesced. "Little man, are you even remotely concerned for the fact that you are completely defenseless?"

"No," I answered, "I left my shield and sword at the entrance. I did not wish to alarm you, Ancient Maragog, nor threaten your peace. I only wish to engage you in conversation and learn at your feet. I fully expect you to be civilized."

Somewhat bemused, she finally asked, "Who *are* you?"

"I am Nicodemus—a sorcerer, and fully at your service, madam."

She chuckled again. "So, Young Nicodemus, you traveled half the countryside for many days seeking me out. Why have you chosen me for this, er—honor?"

I answered her. "It is known among all wizards and sorcerers that you are the oldest and the wisest of dragons."

"Hmm, flattery—a most human attribute, and quite effective in appealing to a lady's vanity." She laughed again. "I haven't had a good conversation for a great many years. I would be glad to fill your head with the nonsense of the universe, but first you must do something for me."

"And what would that be, madam?"

"Bring me a cow. I'm famished."

I departed forthwith and returned a few hours later with two cows, which she devoured in my presence. It wasn't a pretty sight, but I held my tongue, and she was gracious enough to charbroil a haunch of meat so I could join her in the feast.

The Teachings of Maragog

First came the Egg. It lay nestled and dormant within the bosom of the Great Mother Dragon, who has no name. Man vainly has given it many names, but the Great Mother Dragon was there from the beginning, content and without title, since she was One and had no need for a moniker. She was the Eternal and the First without substance and form, but embodied all that would be.

Proceeding from her was the Egg formed of ethereal matter. There, for untold eons, it waited, rested, and grew within the Great Mother Dragon, waiting for the nest to be formed. When finally the nest was completed, the Great Mother Dragon cast out the solid nest into the universe and deposited the Egg so her children, once born, would have a place to rest their feet. It was that great event, vibrating throughout the stars, when the Egg finally cracked and began the procession of life across the universe. The first to emerge from the Egg was the Elemental Dragon of Earth. Of Spirit and Substance, she created the first foundation of all that is, the solid places to walk and the rugged mountains to call home.

The next to emerge from the Egg was the Elemental Dragon of Water. Of Spirit and Liquid, she flowed to the low places of solid ground and rained on the mountains. Together, Earth and Water formed the foundation from which all life would pour forth.

Next to be released from the Egg was the Elemental Dragon of Air. Of Spirit and Æther, he surrounded Earth and Water and filled the high places with the will to combine with Earth and Water; together they took the first breath.

Finally, out of the Egg, there emerged the Dragon Elemental of Fire. Of Spirit and Heat, he provided the impetus of motion. In the final commingling with Earth, Water and Air, it was Fire that provided the final spark from which all animate creatures of the Earth would have life.

When their work was done, the four Elementals guarded the four corners of their creation. To the north, the Elemental Dragon of Air stood guard to protect the winds, his great wings buffeting the air and cleansing the planet. His color is yellow.

To the east, where the sun rises, the Dragon Elemental of Fire spreads his warmth to nurture the earth, and his color is red.

And to the south, the Dragon Elemental of Earth nurtures the soil and delights in the growing things of the fields; her color, green.

The west anchors the Elemental of Water, her wings set over the seas to wash over the land and bring its nurturing rains. Her color is blue.

The Great Spirit Dragons stood over the four cardinal directions in balance and in wisdom, watching over life as guardians of all that is good.

It was at this time that the Great Egg heaved forth yet another Dragon, and the Elemental Dragons watched in dismay for it was dark—black—the absence of color. It immediately began to devour that which they had created. It twisted the air into the destructive forces of tornadoes that leveled cities. The gentle rains it perverted into killing hailstorms and destroying floods. Heat was bent toward the earth to scorch the plains to become deserts and to invoke wildfires that consumed the great forests. The Dark Dragon ravaged Earth, melting rock and heaving forth lava that destroyed all in its path, and it burrowed underground to instigate earthquakes that leveled mountains.

As one, the Four Elemental Dragons confronted the Great Mother Dragon and asked, "Why have you brought this evil upon us? Why have you afflicted us with this dark one that destroys what we create and kills those who dwell upon the Earth?"

She answered them gently saying, "Do not spurn what I give you as a gift, but embrace him as your brother. Without him, you would stagnate and your creation would be without meaning and devoid of hope. If not for the destruction, your creation would be finished and you would be without purpose. With the Darkness I've given you, my children, you may always create, shaping and forming that which is in your will. When the Darkness destroys, you may build again, for that is joy. When the Dark One brings death, you can bring renewed life. It is the balance I sought from the beginning. What I have given you is not evil, but goodness so life may ever change in shape and splendor in the kaleidoscope of colors from which you were created. It is conflict which keeps you strong and hones your skill. It is that which gives life meaning. It is the Dragon of Death which allows your creations to cherish the life you have given them. Be not therefore dismayed, my children." The Great Mother Dragon consoled them. She added, "One more Dragon has yet to be born of the Great Egg. He will be the fusion of all colors, the Luminance of life and the Dragon of Peace. All your labors will reach their fulfillment at his coming."

The Dragon Elementals resumed their places at the four cardinal directions and welcomed their new brother. They agreed to give him dominion over the dark places, and all that is profane, for the abyss was without law and required a ruler. Thus the balancing laws of nature formed as equal and opposite. Growth and decay therefore lived in harmony.

When all was right with the Elementals, they each created their own race of magickal beings to populate the world. For the Air Elemental, he created the Sylphs to protect the skies. The Earth Elemental was pleased by the birth of her Dryads to protect the forests and nurture the green things. The Dragon Elemental of Water created her Naiads to inhabit the oceans and rivers, and the Fire Elemental created the race of Drakes, the elusive fire Faeries to protect hearth and home, and to ensure safety and good fortune.

They also created the mortal dragons, each as a reflection of their own kind. Mountain dragons are the most abundant, living in the earth, dwelling in the cool of the caves. In oceans dwell the leviathans deep in the watery abyss, the great wurms of the sea. To the dizzying heights of the highest peaks, where the air is rarefied, dwell the wyverns. In the caverns of lava, where the blood of the Earth flows, lives the race of great Salamanders who are most comfortable where the earth is hottest, thus, each to their own environment as a reflection of the elements that gave birth to them.

A word on Gargoyles

Gargoyles are very distant cousins of Earth Dragons. They are clever and omnivorous, having a tendency toward gluttony. A gargoyle can generally understand any language, though they themselves cannot speak any human tongue. They only vaguely resemble dragons in that they can fly, which is a deep mystery since in physical terms their wings are too small for their body mass. It can only be assumed that their ability to fly occurs because they think they can, and nobody has hazarded to tell them otherwise.

Chapter 1

A week had passed since Abelene's abduction. Azriel was baffled and frustrated by Nicodemus' lack of action. Azriel itched for vengeance against the Clave and in particular Altais, who had somehow managed to defeat Abelene in magickal combat. It was inconceivable to him that Abelene could have been so easily taken. How was it that one who could stop time at will, one who could cross through the dimensional barrier of space, could have succumbed to the will of the Clave?

He missed her. As long as she was absent, the great hole in his heart was a piece misplaced—a chasm of emptiness. He lay in bed staring out the window looking at the moon. He was awakened again by Abelene's voice. Always the same. He would jolt awake hearing her call to him, muffled—distant, as though speaking from the other side of a thick pane of glass. And then reality would set in.

Abelene was gone, hidden far away where she could not be reached. Out of sight, but never out of his mind. Azriel couldn't help but blame himself, even though the thought lacked logic or reason. But he could not banish the feeling of responsibility for her abduction. If he had not been the One, the destined Son of Luminance, she would have never been taken. Assuredly Abelene was being used to get to him, to pull Azriel off course.

In the darkest dungeons of irrational thought, Azriel imagined horrible tortures set aside by the Clave for Abelene, but his hands were tied, unable to do anything about it.

For the past several days, Azriel even began hearing Abelene calling to him in his waking hours, a phantom voice in his head pleading for acknowledgement. But Azriel refused to give in to it. He was afraid he was starting to go mad. Once over that line, he knew it would continue as a steady plunge into insanity. And thus, he resisted, shutting the voice out. He needed to remain focused and strived to resist any extraneous thoughts.

Both Eltanin and Nicodemus assured him that though captured and perhaps even imprisoned by the Clave, the likelihood of Abelene ever being molested or mistreated by the Clave was remote. Eltanin assured him with certainty that although Rastaban and the Clave had been warped by their lust for power and their foray into darkness, they were still bound by a code of ethics practiced by all wizards and sorcerers. One can harm, even kill, in magickal combat, but to harm an opponent while defenseless still binds that sorcerer to the first and second laws of High Magick. Harm none, Eltanin repeated several times. He also reiterated the second karmic law of threefold reciprocation. The only time the laws didn't apply was in combat and then, to put it in layman's terms, all bets were off. But otherwise, whether on the side of darkness or of light, those laws were foundational, binding, and adhered to with religious zeal. No, Abelene would not be harmed. The Clave wanted her for a different reason that had yet needed to be clarified.

Azriel continued to stare up at the moon. Full and bright, unclouded on a pristine night, it was comforting in a way. Slow, steady—always there. When his whole world seemed to be on the verge of tumbling into a deep pit of sorrow, the moon was an absolute, an unwavering force that would always be there, like the sun, fixed and immutable.

He looked at the clock on his nightstand. Two-thirty. The insufferable mechanical click-click-click was beginning to get on Azriel's nerves. He had a good mind to dash it against the stone walls of his bedchamber.

Nicodemus had a love for mechanical things, be it alarm clocks, old automobiles, wind-up phonographs, but he had no use for electricity, not that it was even remotely possible to bring power to Caer Wylusung. It was secluded from any civilization and far off the grid, which as far as Nicodemus was concerned, pleased the old wizard immensely.

Azriel reclined on the oversized bed trying to recapture sleep, but the perpetual ticking of the clock and the full moon blaring through his window kept him awake. He looked up at the wall behind him. Mounted on heavy brackets, the sword, Errin-lil brooded down at him. It burned with purple fire in the moonlight, and it seemed to be regarding him as if it had consciousness.

"What are you looking at?" Azriel snarled.

Though obviously the sword didn't respond Azriel couldn't help feeling that Errin-lil was laughing at him, amused at some cosmic joke.

"All right, keep your secrets then," he muttered. Azriel rolled to one side with his back to the moonlight still seeping in through the window. He closed his eyes hoping sleep would come, but as always, his thoughts kept him awake. Like a hamster on a treadmill, each thought cycled through and returned to the same place over and over again. *Abelene, the Clave, Alchemy, Camille, Nicodemus, Eddie, Errin-lil, Magick, Abelene, the Clave, Alchemy...* Azriel growled in frustration and punched his pillow.

His thoughts then turned to Eltanin. At least in that regard, some things were beginning to make sense. The ancient sorcerer had disguised himself as Pog, the annoying little troll who seemingly lived somewhere hidden underground near the faerie bridge. But it had all been an elaborate ruse. Azriel certainly understood the reason behind it. Eltanin, for twenty thousand years was a hunted man, reviled by the Clave and thoroughly misunderstood by his own people. Even in the book of Aralia, Eltanin was deemed the arch villain, responsible for shattering the world. Blame was heaped upon his head when indeed, he bore the blame with nobility, sacrificing himself and his future for love of his people. Outcast, defiler, destroyer of worlds. Though guiltless, he had borne the shame and guilt with dignity for untold eons, waiting for the Son of Luminance to arrive, the one who would heal the rift and cleanse the worlds, restoring them to one.

Azriel now understood why Eltanin, disguised as Pog, had refused to meet Abelene. As a powerful sorceress, she would have seen through his masquerade before he was ready. In retrospect, a good call. Abelene, being held by the Clave, could not reveal under interrogation what she didn't know. As far as she was concerned, Eltanin had disappeared into the pages of history never to resurface again. *Better she believes that than the truth.* In Abelene's present situation, the truth could be detrimental to her very existence.

Son of Luminance, the Awaited One, Prince of Aralia—all responsibility now rested on Azriel's shoulders. Would he break under the enormous weight and responsibility? A year and a half—that's all the time he had to right the wrong, to restore two worlds into one. An impossible task and too great a burden to bear. But bear it he must; otherwise, all would come to ruin, plunging both worlds into darkness. Azriel held on to the fragile hope that somehow he would find the strength to meet the challenge head-on. So many had already put their faith in him, relying on fortitude Azriel was having trouble finding within himself.

He was about to lower the wick on the oil lamp beside his bed when he heard a gentle tap on his door.

"Azriel, are you awake?" Camille's voice was muffled.

"I am. Come in," he answered.

She slipped through the door dressed in a flannel nightgown and wrapped in a terrycloth bathrobe.

"Couldn't sleep?" he asked.

"No. Too much on my mind," Camille answered.

"I know the feeling."

She slipped next to him, under the covers, and snuggled up to his shoulder, shivering.

"So cold!" She whispered. Just then, Mortimer pushed the door open and flew in, landing at the foot of the bed, perching on the footboard. He noticed Camille shivering and flew over to the hearth at the other side of the room. He threw a few logs on the remaining embers, then flew back to Azriel, gesturing with his hand, pointing at the fire.

"Good idea, Mortimer." Azriel smiled and scratched the gargoyle at the nape of his neck. He then directed his attention to the hearth and spoke a word of command. "Fiero!"

The logs burst into flames and soon the room became warm and toasty. Mortimer grinned and found a spot on the chair by the fire. He tucked his head under a wing, quickly falling asleep.

Camille didn't need to ask why Azriel couldn't sleep. She, too, was kept awake by her thoughts. So much had happened over the past week that she was still sorting it out. With the kidnapping of Abelene, they both felt as though the wind had been knocked out of their sails. Abelene had always been the solid rock, the foundation when events threatened to capsize their lives. She had always been there with sage advice or just a listening ear. Camille, over the past three years, had come to think of Abelene as her second mother. Certainly she could always speak with her Aunts Pen and Daffie, but there were some things she couldn't share with them, too secret or painful to burden them with. But Abelene always understood. Camille had not yet told Azriel of the portentous vision she had seen of her own death when scrying the future. She debated whether she should tell Azriel of what she saw, but knew in her heart that the mere mention of this possible future would pull him off course, perhaps even cause him to quit the quest for love of her. What was one life in comparison to the millions who would suffer at the hands of the Clave if the future was not repaired? She opted to keep the dark foreboding to herself.

Azriel watched Camille's face as she contemplated her future. He saw the subtle changes of expression, though she tried hard to mask her emotions.

"You seem troubled. What haven't you told me?"

"I…" Camille grimaced. "No, it's nothing." She smiled.

Azriel glanced at her suspiciously. "Are you sure?" he probed.

"Yeah, I guess everything's fine, well, under the circumstances." She looked sadly at Azriel. "What about you?"

Azriel sighed heavily. "I keep hearing my mother. It's far away, like just outside my range of hearing. I wake up from my dreams with her voice ringing in my ears and even throughout the day. It's maddening!"

She touched the ring on Azriel's middle finger, and then looked at her own. "Maybe it's the ring," she suggested. "Maybe she's trying to communicate with you."

"Not likely," Azriel sighed. He removed the leather pouch from his nightstand and emptied it on the bedspread. Among the few magickal items sat Abelene's ring. "She left this on her dresser before going to confront Altais."

"But why would she have done that?" Camille's eyes became moist. "Now there's no way of reaching her."

Azriel glowered at the ring. "Sometimes my mother does things that make no sense, at least initially. I only find out later that there was some logic to her actions. Problem is I have no way of asking her."

Camille sniffed and buried her head in Azriel's shoulder. "I'm sorry. This is all such a mess."

Azriel wrapped his arms around her, but didn't respond. There was really nothing to say. All he could do now was to pay heed to the instructions Eltanin and Nicodemus had laid out for him. The first thing would be the completion of the Lapis Occultus—the Philosopher's stone.

"I tell you what's making me crazy, Camille. Doing nothing! It's hard to complete what I'm supposed to do when all I can think about is my mother. What if she's injured? What if she's dead?" Azriel flopped back on his pillow, looking up at the vaulted ceiling. Camille snuggled closer and said with assurance. "That's not what Eltanin and Nicodemus said, remember? They said that the Clave would never harm her. They would do so at their own peril." She kissed him tenderly. "No, Azriel, they're trying to distract you. Keep you from releasing the Dragon Elementals. Don't you get it? They fear you, or at least what you will become!"

"Yeah, they should!" Azriel said with more bravado than he felt. "All I want to do right now is kick Altais' ass!"

Camille giggled. "You're probably not ready for that yet, Azriel. But I'm sure you will be."

Azriel smiled and kissed Camille on the lips. "And I sure hope you'll be there to see it!" he grinned deviously.

Camille's smile faltered. "I will be, Azriel. I'll go wherever you go." She kissed him again and rested her head against his chest. Comfortable and warm beside him, her weariness began to overtake her. Camille yawned and began to doze off. Azriel's eyes grew heavy as well.

The door swung open, and Azriel bolted upright, nearly throwing Camille off the bed.

"What is going on here?" Nicodemus demanded. He stood in his robe, arms crossed over the broom he held in one hand, scowling at Azriel.

"Um, nothing." Azriel stared guiltily at the old sorcerer. "We were just talking."

"Talking, indeed!"

"Uncle Nick," Camille said, somewhat cross, "Azriel's a perfect gentleman!"

"Yes, but the question remains whether you're a perfect lady!"

Camille's jaw dropped, and she stammered, lost for words. "Uncle Nick!" she shot back, blushing indignantly.

Nicodemus scowled a few more moments then broke into a broad smile.

Azriel glared at him. "Are you having a good time?"

"An immensely good time," he riposted. "Camille, out with you!"

"But..."

"Now, young lady!"

She grumbled as she climbed out of bed, then stuck her tongue out at Nicodemus as she walked past. He wound up and swatted her on the backside with the broom.

"Ow!" she giggled, scampering out of the room. Nicodemus watched her go, amusement in his eyes.

"That is one dangerous little vixen, Azriel—and quite lovely. I fear she has captured your heart."

Azriel looked away and smiled.

"But as to this other thing..." Nicodemus looked suggestively at the bed. "You should wait for a more appropriate time."

"Uncle Nick, it was nothing like that." Azriel's cheeks flushed.

"You know, son, waiting always enhances that wonderful commingling. Candlelight, soft music, good wine..."

Azriel fidgeted, embarrassed.

Nicodemus continued. "Why, I remember one moonlit night in the south of France, nearly four hundred years ago—a lovely stable girl had been caring for my horse, and she'd been giving me the eye all day, but I kept avoiding her—not really, of course. I was a bit of a rake, back then and recognized good flirting when I saw it. Now, what was her name?" Uncle Nick mused, tapping a finger against his beard. "Ah, yes—Clarice! Her name was

Clarice! Lovely girl! Rich, lush golden locks of hair; tall and lithe. Quite a buxom figure, too…”

Azriel squirmed. “Uh, Uncle Nick…”

“Well, toward evening, with the moon full, I found her, quite by accident, bathing in the stream behind the stables. I had brought some wine, a blanket, and a wonderful book of love sonnets, so I could woo the damsel. Let me tell you, Azriel—she looked like a goddess, her naked body glistening in the wondrous moonlight.”

Azriel’s cheeks turned crimson. “Uncle Nick…” he pleaded.

“Then she turned and noticed me watching her. Oh, she didn’t scream or anything like that, and she was far from shy. She came to me, and we had a most glorious night.” He sighed, remembering. “And the pleasures we gave each other…”

“Uncle Nick! That’s disgusting!”

“What?” Nicodemus said, feigning innocence.

“I didn’t need to hear that!” Azriel grumbled.

“Hear what?”

“Please stop—please stop right now and spare me the details!”

“Stop what, Azriel?” Nick suppressed a smile.

Azriel sputtered, “Too much information, Uncle Nick—please! My ears are bleeding!”

“Azriel,” Nicodemus said, folding his arms and suppressing a smile at the boy’s discomfort, “are you suggesting that you’re a prude? I’m so disappointed!”

“Look, Uncle Nick, I *really* don’t want to know about your— conquests!”

“Well,” Nicodemus coughed to mask a laugh, “when the right moment occurs for you and that lovely girl, I want to know all the details.”

Azriel stared at Nicodemus in shock and disgust. “Uncle Nick, you’re a lecherous old bastard!”

“No, son—just an awful tease. Really had you going there.”

Azriel rolled his eyes and sighed. “You’re disgusting. Now I know where Pog gets it from.”

“You mean Eltanin. And the truth is, I learned it from him!”

“Ugh! Abelene would so kick your ass right now.”

There was a moment of uncomfortable silence as they locked eyes, but they both suddenly burst into riotous laughter.

Camille opened the door and stood with arms crossed. "Hey, I'm trying to sleep! What's so funny?"

"Er—nothing." Azriel caught Uncle Nick's innocent look, and suddenly they both burst out in laughter again.

Camille had the impression that somehow the joke was on her and glared at them both. She clucked her tongue and stormed out of the room.

Since the arrival of all his guests, breakfast had become a loud, boisterous affair. Nicodemus had been accustomed to quiet mornings in the solitude of his castle. The addition of five enthusiastic teenagers, four adults, two mountain lions, and one gargoyle was all confusion he could bear. It wasn't necessarily the guests themselves, but the noise. He glanced sourly at what amounted to organized confusion. He grabbed his cup of coffee with a few waffles and exited to the courtyard table for some peace.

Eltanin seemed to be having a wonderful time. Having remained in isolation for so long—hiding out as Pog and masking his true identity—Eltanin welcomed the attention and was often as troublesome and wildly unpredictable as Nicodemus' younger charges. Not that Nicodemus wasn't aware of Eltanin's propensity for chaos. It was his old mentor's way of disarming both friend and adversary. Now among youngsters, Eltanin was having an enormously good time. He enjoyed telling stories and demonstrating spells that haven't been seen in thousands of years. Worse, the children learned quickly. What had once been a place of peace had, at times, become a house of horrors.

The Cunningham children seemed to take particular delight in rattling their mother. Two days earlier, during breakfast, they plotted an elaborate illusion with Azriel and Camille. Maggie arrived at the dining hall, voiced a cheerful good morning, and then headed to the kitchen to serve herself a plate of eggs and sausage with toast and butter. Meanwhile, with his mom out of sight, Jasper transformed himself into a wolfman with drool slathering from his hideously gaping maw. Not to be outdone, Albert morphed into a monstrous troll with gnarly green skin. Exploding pustules oozed onto the table. Julia's transformation was just as hideous. She appeared as a headless ghoul. Blood gushed from her gaping neck, and her head rested on a platter. She shoved food into the head's mouth. Camille couldn't resist a good gag and joined in the insanity. She morphed into a toothless old hag. Putrid, tattered clothes hung off withered limbs, and one of her eyeballs had flopped out of its socket. Azriel opted for a gelatinous blob of shapeless protoplasm. His brain was exposed and maggot-infested. To finish the Illusion, they skillfully transformed the platters of food into half-eaten, body parts. They gleefully tore them apart, flinging bloody guts and viscera as they spattered the walls and ceiling.

Maggie returned to the dining room; her tray filled with breakfast. She took one look and screamed in horror. Her breakfast flew into the air and splattered the floor and walls as she ran screaming out of the hall.

They all laughed hysterically until they cried. Maggie, however, returned with a sizable wooden spoon and began beating them on their backs, arms, and shoulders. She didn't know who she was beating, and it didn't matter. They all deserved it. Whack! Ow!—laughter. Smack!—more giggles.

"All right, we give!" Jasper hollered as Maggie continued to pummel him with the spoon. They all reconstituted into their own forms taking the pus, worms, and blood splatter with them. They hunched over, laughing.

"You're all horrible brats! Horrible!" Maggie stormed out of the room in hysterics, her head full of steam.

After the incident, and after calming Maggie down sufficiently, Nicodemus firmly ordered that no such shenanigans would ever be permitted again. The last thing he needed was to have poor Mrs. Cunningham to keel over with a heart attack.

Azriel worked in the laboratory with Eltanin. The old wizard was well acquainted with the alchemical arts, having sustained his life for more than twenty thousand years. In the ancient days of

Aralia, alchemy was required learning for all Aralians. The knowledge was passed from generation to generation. It was Eltanin's fear, however, that as Aralian society deteriorated, the exacting discipline had most likely been lost over time. Many misconceptions surrounded the arcane science, not the least of which was the idea of immortality. Certainly, immortality was a side effect of mastering alchemy, but it wasn't intended to be the end result—merely a benefit. The true purpose of alchemy was the annealing and purification of the spirit. Once that was attained, the Lapis Occultus was well within the wizard's reach. The disciple would need to commit long hours of study, which required fortitude and wisdom. Many tried and failed—not for any lack of skill, but through impure motives. If immortality was the only goal, the wizard was doomed to failure.

Many alchemists, having perfected the science, rued partaking of the Lapis Occultus, as it was a gift as much as it was a burden. One must know himself well enough to determine whether he is suited for immortality. It is the nature of all things to die eventually. The fear of death, in Eltanin's estimation, was the worst reason of all to ingest the magickal substance.

Immortality required the total transformation of the self to become a teacher and servant to others—one who would elevate human and Ferrishyn alike from a lower to a higher state. But those who partook of the Lapis Occultus with selfish motives, only seeking personal gain and wealth became hollow and filled with unattainable desire—never satisfied, never fulfilled. Immortality became a curse—a bane to all around them.

"Rastaban is such a man," Eltanin said gravely. "At first his motives were pure, his heart chaste, but he was swayed to the darkness and took the Clave with him. His lust for power betrayed his soul to everlasting emptiness."

Azriel digested the thought and remained silent. Finally, he spoke up. "Grandfather, if that was indeed the case, how was it you didn't recognize the flaw in him?"

"That's a good question." Eltanin nodded sagely. "Rastaban was like a bucket with a pinprick hole in the bottom. At first you barely notice the leak, but over time corrosion sets in, and then the rust crumbles. The leak becomes a stream then a torrent and soon the bucket is useless— fit only for the trash heap.”

“But couldn’t the bucket be repaired?” Azriel asked, keeping up the metaphor.

Eltanin glowered. “Son, some things are beyond repair.”

Azriel contemplated Eltanin’s words as he helped the Arch Wizard set up a series of prisms on various stands and tripods. A small window had been covered with black cloth and before it stood a focusing lens. A crucible had been set over an open forge to liquefy some lead to the consistency of quicksilver. However, Azriel was still in the dark concerning the purpose. In another glass vessel ran a tube much like a thermometer. In the bottom of the vessel was a small amount of mercury.

“Grandfather, what are we doing?” Azriel asked.

“We are combining the properties of Æther, liquid—that which is in between, and solid. From there you will see a marvelous thing!”

“I don’t understand.”

“It’s in seeing that you will understand. First, you must contemplate light. Light breaks down to its base values when you separate them. It is the combination of all colors that create pure light. But even within that light, there is darkness. Separate the darkness from the light, and you create the Æther necessary for transformation. Now observe.”

Eltanin yanked the black cloth from the window. However, the pane of glass was covered by a black plate with a single hole.

“Now, if you don’t mind, extinguish that lamp.” Azriel did as instructed and lowered the wick until the flame went out. Now the only light in the room came from the small hole in the window. Eltanin focused the sunlight through the lens, adjusting it until it formed a tight beam that struck the prism several feet away. As the old wizard had predicted, the light split into beams of color representing the full spectrum.

“Now, what do you see, Azriel?”

“It looks like a rainbow.”

“Indeed. There are the three primaries, yellow, red, and blue. They are pure because they cannot be split further to any other color, but in between, you also see green, orange and indigo. They are the secondary colors because any combination of the primaries creates every other color known to man. They are also pure because they consist of prime colors. But then there is this." Eltanin pointed to another prism beyond the violet. It seemed to be emitting no light at all.

"Now this one emits the darkness beyond human sight. The ultraviolet, in alchemical terms, the *nigredo*. Though part of the light, it is darkness and must be removed.

"Now watch and learn." Eltanin focused the remaining colors of red, orange, yellow, green, blue, indigo and violet onto a single prism. He adjusted each split prismatic color until they aligned as a single beam of blinding light. The pure beam, he focused with a mirror onto the glass vessel filled with mercury. In turn, the mercury heated and rose in the narrow tube, purified. It took on the ethereal glow of the light, and a single drop emerged from the top of the tube and fell into the crucible of molten lead.

"What you have witnessed is Æther transforming the mercury, which is neither liquid nor solid, into its spiritual form. Transformed, it is given to the lead, which, though solid, is transformed to liquid through intense heat, the element of fire."

Azriel stared into the vessel of lead and noticed it had begun to glow slightly, a shimmer almost beyond sight.

"Now it requires one more thing!" Eltanin's eyes glowed with passion. He took a small amount of sulfur and potassium chloride and mixed them together. From the mixture he extracted the smallest amount, and dropped it in the lead.

"Now behold!"

Azriel's eyes widened with wonder as the lead began to transform. It started to bubble and changed color until it glowed gold. With heavy leather gloves, Eltanin removed the crucible from the furnace and carefully poured the molten metal into a circular mold.

"Now when that cools, you will see a most amazing thing! You can light the lamp now, Azriel."

He quickly lit the wick and raised the flame on the oil lamp, then removed the shield from the window. He watched, amazed, as the metal solidified. In the final process, Eltanin lifted the mold with a pair of tongs and dropped it in a tub of water until it was safe to handle. He then pried the piece from the stone mold and handed it to Azriel.

"Is this what I think it is?" he stared down at the disk. It was fashioned into a perfect pentagram with all the alchemical symbols arranged in a circle around the border.

"Yes, Azriel. It is the purest gold! It is the next step toward achieving the Lapis Occultus. Now, what I'd like you to do is repeat the experiment on your own. Here is the formula." Eltanin handed him a scroll of parchment.

"*Azriel, where are you?*" He winced and shook his head. Azriel then stuck a finger in his ear and wiggled it a few times.

"What's wrong, son?" Eltanin asked, concerned by the boy's odd behavior.

"I'm not sure. Every few hours I keep hearing my mother's voice. It's faint, like a memory—barely audible."

"Then why don't you answer it?"

"Because it's not real. She left her ring of communication on the dresser before leaving the house to confront Altais."

"That's a shame," Eltanin mused. "It will make locating Lady Abelene all the more difficult."

Azriel grimaced at the truth of Eltanin's words.

"Now, Azriel, I must depart for a few hours. Continue with your studies and recreate what you have just learned. I will return later. Something I must see to."

Eltanin exited the laboratory. Azriel continued his experiment. He readjusted the prisms and placed the shield over the window.

Nicodemus sat before his charges, giving a lecture on the proper use of the Ignotus spell. Daphne and Penelope took notes, even though they were adept witches. There were always more things to learn.

"The whole point of the spell is to hide something in plain sight," Nicodemus explained. "It is not for making something disappear, but for keeping it from being noticed by others."

"But what's the purpose of all this?" Jasper inquired.

"Oh, the Ignotus spell has many uses—some benign and some quite sinister. Some creatures have a natural ability to hide when they are nearby. Take the common moth for example. Its wings are mottled brown and gray. It rests on a tree, blending in with the bark and making it nearly invisible to the crow, who considers it quite a tasty treat."

"Yeah, but that's simple camouflage," Albert countered. "It's found in nature everywhere. Really not that remarkable."

"True." Nicodemus retorted. "But what about a creature like Mortimer?"

The gargoyle, having heard its name from across the courtyard, flew in through the open window and alighted on Nicodemus's desk. He held a hand to his chest and bowed. Camille giggled.

"Now Mortimer, would you mind assisting me with a small demonstration?"

The creature shrugged and gestured with open hands.

"Good!" Nicodemus grinned. "Let's start with something easy." He pulled out several posters from beneath his desk. He held one upright behind Mortimer. It was a simple photo of grass. Mortimer held a hand to his mouth and yawned with boredom. His skin quickly shifted to a vibrant green striation to match the grass.

"How about this?" Nicodemus held up a poster of zebra striping. Mortimer spread his wings and stood still. His skin shifted to black-and-white patterns that blended with the poster, making him nearly invisible. The class clapped enthusiastically, and Mortimer bowed, clearly enjoying the attention.

"And this!" Nicodemus held up a poster of multicolored river rock. Mortimer eyed the picture and tapped a finger against his cheek, thinking. He stood before the photo, and soon different shades of browns, reds, and greens formed in various patterns to blend in with the rock. To add to the effect, Mortimer rippled his wings, giving the appearance of water.

"Quite impressive, Mortimer," the old wizard complimented. "Why don't you try this?" Nicodemus displayed a poster board covered in a stark tartan plaid over its surface.

Mortimer turned to look at the pattern and immediately began gesturing and growling angrily. He grabbed the poster out of

Nicodemus's hands and quicker than anyone thought possible, shredded it into hundreds of tiny pieces. As the fragments settled on the desk, he began stomping on them, just in case the class hadn't figured out what he thought of the whole affair. To complete his tantrum, he stormed out the room grumbling—but not without farting noisily before slamming the door.

"Geez, Nicodemus, I think you hurt his feelings," Camille snickered.

"Perhaps I pushed him too far," the wizard chuckled. "But the point is made. There are some things even a magickal creature like Mortimer cannot camouflage."

"I still don't understand the point." Julia said, shrugging.

"Consider this," Nicodemus said. "You've all mastered the illusion spell as Mrs. Cunningham would attest."

Maggie glared at Jasper knowing he was the ringleader behind nearly scaring her to death. Nicodemus silenced the laughter.

"But the Ignotus spell is a bit different. Perhaps you have the need to hide in plain sight for a bit of spying, or you need to mask an object to keep it from being stolen." Nicodemus removed a crystal ball from his pocket. "Let's just say, for the moment, you don't want anyone to see this beautiful gem. Now observe!"

Nicodemus waved his hand over the object. "Ignotus!" he intoned the incantation with a flourish. The crystal ball suddenly changed into an apple.

"See now—place that in a bowl of fruit and no one would ever suspect, unless, of course, they bit it. You can even change yourself, but with one restriction: whatever you change into must be of roughly the same weight and mass. You couldn't become a mouse, Camille, since there are no one-hundred-and-thirty-pound mice."

"A hundred and thirty pounds?" Camille shot back, insulted. "Perhaps you need glasses, Uncle Nick. I'm only one-hundred and *ten* pounds!" Her voice was acid.

"Hmm..." Nicodemus eyed her critically. He gestured with an upturned hand and Camille floated off her chair. He motioned up and down with his outstretched hand, and Camille bounced with the motion.

"No dear, perhaps it is time for you to lay off the chocolate cake. One hundred and fifteen would be more accurate." She floated back onto the seat, her face reddening with embarrassment.

"Creep!" she muttered.

Nicodemus coughed to mask his laugh. "You could, however, transform yourselves into trees or shrubbery. Why, you all could be standing in a field and no one would be the wiser—not even the dog, which might use you as a convenient latrine. There is a downside to everything, after all."

Eltanin had been absent for a few hours, then suddenly returned, popping into view with Lady Rosaluna. Most of Nicodemus' guests were seated at the table, eating an early lunch while studying, immersed in their lessons. Camille picked at her food every so often, glaring at Nicodemus, who sat at the head of the table.

"Now dear, stop looking at me like that. You must know I was only teasing. You're a bit too skinny and could use a few pounds," He said gruffly.

"Humph!" she snorted and went back to her book.

"Good to see you, Rosemary," Nicodemus said affably.

"Likewise, Master Nicodemus. Now, if'n ye don't mind, where is that boy? I need to speak to Azriel immediately!" she sounded a bit cross.

"Would you mind telling me the problem?"

"That's between him and me!" she snapped.

"He's still in the lab." Nicodemus pointed and shrugged.

Rosemary stormed out of the dining hall and pounded on the laboratory door.

"Just a minute." Azriel's voice was muffled from the other side, but Rosemary let herself in.

"No—Don't open the door. Crap!"

The light from the adjoining room invaded the darkened lab, and the transformation Azriel had been so painstakingly performing suddenly fizzled into an unidentifiable blob and crumbled into blackened powder.

"Well, so much for that!" Azriel grumbled.

Rosemary faced him, arms folded. The exasperated expression on her face told volumes.

"What?" Azriel gestured with his hands, clearly annoyed by the interruption and the failure of his experiment. He was so close!

"Are ye deef as well as blind, boy?"

"What did I do?" Azriel retorted defensively.

Rosemary exhaled sharply. "Yer mother's been tryin' to reach ye fer three days. Why haven't ye replied?"

Chapter 2

Abelene awoke from a troubled sleep, disoriented, and her body ached. It took only a few moments for her to remember the last thing that had happened before she lost physical consciousness. She had been in formal magickal combat with Altais. He had put her in a chokehold, depriving her of air, and she had blacked out. At least, that was what she wanted him to think. Abelene found it ironic that Altais had fallen for such a blatant deception. Before her body went limp, she released her spiritual energy to watch over her mortal body. Should any harm come to it, she could immediately respond and return to her corporeal state. She was therefore fully aware that Altais had trapped her in a spectral pyramid and transported her elsewhere. The transformation was instantaneous, and she wasn't surprised that her prison had been prepared ahead of time. She also considered herself fortunate that Altais practiced the old formulas of magick, garnered from the ancient laws of Aralia. That could be to her advantage and prove useful later. For now, she would store that handy piece of information away. Altais had underestimated Abelene's powers. She had led him to believe he had bested her. For now, let the Clave believe she was weak and no match for them. She had them right where she wanted them.

True, her prison was inescapable. Abelene assessed her surroundings. She was encased in a crystal force field. It was roomy, square at the base, and met at an apex sixty or so feet above her—a nearly transparent pyramid of force. The Clave had afforded her privacy, with a curtained bed and a separate concealed area with a laving bowl and commode for her personal needs. Beside the bed, a writing desk and a small table sat neatly on the stone floor. Beyond sat a shelf of books, scrolls, and volumes of magickal texts. They even had provided her with any magickal item she might require to amuse herself. As she walked the perimeter, Abelene opened the doors of a wardrobe filled with beautiful clothing. Beside it, on a night table, perched a sizeable chest packed with exotic jewelry.

Nonetheless, it was still a prison. She had read about such creations in the legends of Aralia. They had been used to incarcerate only the most powerful sorcerers, but were considered dark magick and were forbidden. Magick worked within its walls; Abelene would lack for nothing, but it was impervious to destruction. No spell would penetrate its walls; no sorcery would function beyond its perimeter. Inescapable, Abelene would remain trapped within the forcefield.

Abelene was at least comforted by the fact that the Clave practiced the old forms of protocol. Though a wizard or sorcerer may be on opposing sides, unless formal combat is declared, neither may cause harm or molest the other. For whether one walks the path of light or the path of dark, both powers proceed from the same eternal source.

The prison itself was formed of the most potent magick. In a sense, its barriers transcended time and space. For example, Abelene could not shift to a time before she was captured. She would still be trapped. The pyramid would always be there, from the beginning until the end of time. From within, it was a separate dimension with its own rules, yet paradoxically, it remained adhered to the normal space-time of mortal men. For those reasons alone, the Carcer Eternis was forbidden magic and the purest evil, for once cast, not even the sorcerer who wrought it could ever break the spell.

There was one thing, however, that the prison could not control—simple thought. And Abelene's was well developed beyond the normal realm of men—the one advantage she had over the Clave. They could control her movements and her location, but they could not control her mind.

She sat at the table. With a gesture of her fingers, a tea set appeared. She poured a cup of breakfast tea and sipped it thoughtfully as she considered her situation. She focused her attention on what lay beyond the pyramid.

The pyramid rested within an enormous underground cavern. Abelene could not determine how deep into the earth the cavern lay, but judging from the length and breadth of the stalactites and stalagmites, the chamber was incredibly ancient. The continual seepage of calcium-laden water through the damp cave had, over millennia, formed rich deposits of calcite along the walls, ceilings, and floor of the chamber. Beyond her prison, a set of carved steps—some natural, others shaped by man—led upward to an iron door. From its contour and size, Abelene determined it to be a more recent addition—twenty thousand years or so.

On one side of the ethereal structure, however, her view was blocked by an elaborately woven arras draped over a freestanding frame. It seemed oddly out of place or deliberately set up to shield her from something. Abelene considered the design. It depicted two world side by side, a sword plunged through them like two olives skewered by a toothpick. She frowned at the odd choice of décor and decided she didn't like it at all. What message was the Clave trying to send her? With disdain, she yanked it off the frame—then suddenly stopped cold.

Another pyramid sat beside hers. Imprisoned within, a black iridescence assaulted her eyes. It took her a few moments to realize she was staring at the flank of an enormous creature. Its spade-tipped tail wrapped the length of his body, with his head resting on folded forelegs, tucked under a massive wing. One leg was shackled by a chain, another manacle clamped around his neck, but they glowed with magickal power. His enormity evoked awe at his size; he was beautiful in a frightening and grotesque sort of way.

"By Shenach, what have they done to you, sad creature?" Abelene whispered. Tears formed in her eyes, for she could feel the creature's sadness, pain, and outrage.

Roused by her voice, the creature moved a wing and raised his head. He regarded Abelene with mere curiosity. His venomous yellow eyes considered her with mild interest. He yawned and stretched, then sat on his haunches. He tilted his head, examining Abelene. She looked up at him with tears flowing down her cheeks, her hand held to her mouth.

"Do you weep for me, Lady?" His voice sounded almost tender.

"I would mourn for any creature so wrongly mistreated."

"Hmm," the dragon lifted his clawed wing and scratched behind his ear. "You may be the first living thing on this world to feel anything other than fear and contempt for me."

"Why should I feel contempt for you?"

"Don't you know what I am, Lady?"

Abelene regarded the black dragon, examining his height, the breadth of his wings. Her eyes rested on his broad chest. Only one thing marred his perfection. A single scale had been blasted from the region over his heart. The wound still bled, a deep scarlet trickle of blood staining his otherwise perfect body. She stared up at him in awe. "Yes Dark Lord of Dragons, I do know you."

"Are you not afraid of me?" he asked.

"Should I be?" Abelene pushed a black tress of hair behind her ear. "Dying is just as natural as living. Without you, my Lord, people would suffer. There would be no relief from pain, illness or old age—no renewal of the spirit. I would be a fool to fear you."

The dragon chuckled. "You have much wisdom for one so young, Queen Regent of Aralia. Aren't you a mere three hundred years old?"

"Then you know who I am?"

"I know every life and death that ever was, is, and will be, Lady Abelene."

"I see." Abelene paused to consider the enormity of his knowledge. He knew the future of her son—and of herself. But she also knew that knowledge of the future doesn't change it—it only creates fear.

"Interesting." The great dragon shifted his weight and grunted. "You do not ask the obvious question."

"It would serve no benefit or purpose." Abelene smiled graciously.

"You speak the truth, Lady Abelene. I am bound by nature never to reveal the time of one's passing. It would alter reality with undreamed-of consequences that could not be undone. Though I take life with impunity, I judge neither goodness or evil. I am the Law of Death itself—unalterable and intractable."

"Actually, that brings me comfort in a strange sort of way."

"You have much wisdom indeed, Lady. I can tell you this—you have a great many years ahead of you." He smiled in the fashion of dragons. "I think I like you. I will regret the day of your passing."

"I promise I will not fear you, Dark Lord, when that day arrives," she said solemnly.

"That would bring me joy, Lady Abelene."

Abelene touched the transparent wall of her prison. It crackled with impenetrable power. She winced as it slightly drained her life force.

"Lady, you would be wise not to touch the walls. I would prefer taking you later rather than sooner."

"Thank you, my Lord. It would seem that, for better or worse, you and I are companions here."

"For better, I think. Rastaban and the rest of the Clave are tiresome." The dark dragon yawned. "I look forward to our next conversation."

"As do I." Abelene smiled.

The Dragon Lord bowed his head graciously and tucked it beneath a wing to resume his nap.

Abelene strode to the small table and resumed drinking her tea. She was hungry and conjured a plate of biscuits. A jar of honey appeared beside them. She glanced at an empty corner and rued the loss of her kitchen. She had always disliked magically creating food. Though delicious, it always felt somehow like cheating, but in her present circumstance, it was the best she could do.

Now for the task at hand. Abelene regretted not telling Azriel what was to occur before her abduction. She had looked into the future and known she would be captured and held by the Clave. It was for that very reason she had left the ring of communication on her night table. She only hoped that Azriel would find it and understand the message. Within the pyramid, it would have been useless anyway. Worse, if Rastaban had taken it from her, he would have had access to Azriel. Now Abelene berated herself for never teaching Azriel the silent art of telepathy. He certainly had the ability, granted to him by Krinaea, Queen of the Sylphs. But that had been in the magickal realm between worlds, and Azriel hadn't had much time to hone his abilities. He had not yet used his telepathic powers in the world of men and lacked the practice he needed.

Abelene lay comfortably on the sumptuous bed, cleared her mind of all distraction, and slowed her breathing until she accomplished the near-dream state she had learned from an Indian yogi when Azriel was a baby. She had traveled the world with Nicodemus to learn human magick. This was the advantage she hoped would trick the Clave. They had made it well known that they considered human magick inferior to Elvin Magick. Their arrogance was their flaw. Human magick was nearly as potent and in some cases even surpassed Elvin magick. Nicodemus and Camille were perfect examples of that human potential. Abelene had learned remarkable things in the remote regions of India and Tibet, exploring many levels of human spirituality.

Once Abelene achieved the astral state of consciousness, she projected her thoughts outward to reach Azriel. It was best to do this when he was asleep or just waking.

"Azriel." She projected her thoughts, seeking his unique frequency. There was a flicker of connection—but then a sudden withdrawal. She tried again, strengthening her projection into his mind. *"Azriel,"* She said more firmly. Without Azriel completing the telepathic connection, she began to tire. Abelene withdrew her astral projection and severed the link. She would try again later.

The queen sorceress suddenly felt she was being observed. She rose from the bed and walked to the edge of the pyramid to face Rastaban. Her manner was cool as she stood before him, examining his appearance. His handsome features were finely chiseled, framed by a close-cropped beard and striking blue eyes. Graying hair was tied back at the nape of his neck. He had used his immortality well, appearing no more than fifty years of age. Rastaban wore the formal robe of his office—dark purple velvet with magickal Aralian symbols, finely stitched into the brocaded border.

Rastaban bowed respectfully. "I am very pleased to finally make your acquaintance, Lady Abelene."

"Likewise, Master Rastaban. Your legend precedes you."

He smiled pleasantly. "I trust your new home is… comfortable?"

"Home?" she replied with a caustic smile. "A home is only pleasant when one can leave it and return at will."

"A well-spoken riposte, Lady." He nodded imperiously. "Let's just say you are being held for your own protection. I wish no harm to come to you. Besides, I have need of your help."

"Hmm." She held a finger to her lips, tapping gently as she thought. "The Crocodile and the Scorpion."

"Pardon me, Lady?" Rastaban smiled at her enigmatic reply.

"Ancient wisdom, sir. As the story goes, a scorpion came out of the desert to the banks of the Nile, whereupon he addressed a crocodile. 'My friend,' he said to the crocodile, 'could you perhaps help me get to the other side of the river?'

"The crocodile answered, 'Do you think me a fool? I would be at your complete mercy. You could sting me and kill me at any time during the crossing.'

"'Of course I wouldn't,' said the scorpion. 'I promise not to sting you, for if I did, wouldn't I drown as well?'

"The crocodile thought for a moment and then agreed this made perfect sense and allowed the scorpion to crawl onto his back. About midway across the river, the scorpion became agitated and stung the crocodile.

"As the two were about to go under, the crocodile turned to the scorpion and said, 'Now we will both die. What possible explanation or logic is there for such an act?'

"'I am sorry,' said the scorpion, 'but I cannot change what is in my nature.'"

"Bravo, Lady Abelene." Rastaban nodded formally. He was about to say more when deep, rumbling laughter interrupted him. The dark dragon glared down at him gleefully from the adjoining pyramid.

"You are a fool, Rastaban," he chuckled. "For all your so-called wisdom, you have allowed the wolf into your sheepfold. Meet your nemesis, Rastaban—the Lady Abelene!" The dragon continued to laugh in open derision at the old wizard. "She is stronger than you, old man. And I will revel in the day that she and her progeny utterly defeat you." The dark dragon continued to chuckle. "And something else to consider, Rastaban," he spat the name with scorn. "There will come a time when I break free of my bonds, and when that day comes, you will die! Oh, not the sweet, gentle death of peace, but a special one set aside just for you, wizard. I will consume your soul and the last eternal emotion you will feel is fear and despair." He chuckled darkly.

Rastaban scoffed. "That may be so, though unlikely, my lord enemy. But there is one thing you will never forget for the rest of your eternal life: You will always remember that I bested you and held you captive against your will. That bitter morsel will forever roil in your gut. My name shall be a bitter thorn in your side. In that, I am comforted."

The dragon roared in anger and yanked uselessly at the manacles binding his leg and neck. Abelene looked with pity at the struggling creature, and back at Rastaban. She did not hide the contempt on her face.

"You wear your flaws like a blemish, Rastaban."

"More verbal sparring, Lady?"

"I haven't even begun, wizard. Isn't it enough that you capture? Must you torture as well?" She stood erect and recited softly: "'In order to get power and retain it, it is necessary to love power; but love of power is not connected with goodness but with qualities that are the opposite of goodness, such as pride, cunning and cruelty.'—Leo Tolstoy."

Abelene coldly turned her back on Rastaban and walked to the table. She poured herself tea and took a slow sip. She glanced up at Rastaban. "The next time you wish to engage me in conversation, it would serve you well to be civil—if the word is even in your vocabulary."

Rastaban did not flinch. "You speak of cruelty. Tell me, Lady Abelene. Which is more cruel: Is it the snake that devours the innocent mouse while the poor creature is still alive—or the woman who allows her son to believe he is invulnerable, when surely he will die?"

Abelene clenched her jaw, her face turning to stone. Rastaban smirked and climbed the stairs, sealing the iron door behind him.

Once he was out of sight, Abelene allowed her tears to fall. Her shoulders shook as she wept.

"Please do not weep, Lady," the dragon said tenderly. "Rastaban is an arrogant fool. Do not succumb to his wordplay. Here—this is for you." He bowed his head gently and a scarlet rose appeared on her table.

"How did you do that?" she sniffed.

"Oh, I still have all my powers of influence. I can still destroy and take lives as is my purpose. The rose is beautiful, but alas, it already has begun to die."

"Then why haven't you broken free of your prison?"

The Dragon Lord lifted his shackled leg and shook it. He shrugged in the manner of dragons.

"Lord Dragon, do you have a name?"

"I have many. In ignorance, some call me Lucifer, the Angel of Death, the Devil. Others call me Azi Dahaka. They are false of course, for I am neither evil, nor good. I merely serve a purpose. Perhaps you may call me Charlie. Any name will do."

"Charlie?" In spite of her distress, Abelene giggled. "You're a magnificent dragon. Charlie doesn't seem grand enough."

"What is in a name, Lady?"

"Well, all right—Charlie. As long as we are on a first name basis, please call me Abelene."

"That would please me."

"Charlie?" she bowed her head pensively. "Did you imply that Azriel wouldn't die?"

"Abelene, all creatures die."

"That's not what I meant."

"I know," he said with remorse, "but I cannot tell you."

"You cannot because you are forbidden from telling me—or you won't?"

"The truth is, Abelene... I don't know."

"But..."

"Hear me, Lady. It was destined from the very beginning of creation that Azriel and I must face one another. Even I do not know the outcome of that great event. In a way that you cannot understand, Azriel and I are brothers. The moment we meet will be a time of decision when all things change. In the end, he and I must stand face to face. The outcome of that event lies not in my hands, but his."

"Then there is hope?" she replied.

"Abelene, there is always hope."

She looked up at him and smiled. "There is kindness in you, ancient one."

"Kindness, Lady? I'm merely being practical." He sounded faintly offended.

"No, I think not, Charlie. If people knew your true nature, perhaps they would not fear you as they do."

The dark dragon chuckled. "Perhaps—but don't let the secret out just yet. There is still one who *should* fear me."

"Rastaban?"

"Indeed. He—and the Clave—will someday feel my wrath."

"And mine." Abelene glowered. "It must have been very lonely for you being trapped here."

"It has, Lady." Charlie lay back down with his chin resting on his crossed forelegs. "Though I rue your imprisonment here, I am grateful for your company." The ancient dragon yawned and closed his eyes, drifting into a deep slumber.

"Good night, Charlie," Abelene whispered affectionately. She returned to her bed and drew the curtain. Resting easily, she again attempted to reach Azriel, but as before, her efforts were thwarted by his inability—or unwillingness—to complete the connection.

Abelene decided to change her tactic. She projected her thoughts to the small shop tucked into a narrow alley in Castleton.

"Abelene, is that you?" The voice rang clear in her mind.

"Yes, Rosemary. I suppose I've created quite the stir," Abelene replied.

"Are ye harmed?" Rosemary asked with deep concern.

"I am well tended, though imprisoned."

"Where are ye, Lady?"

"I am deep within the enemy's camp," Abelene responded.

"Then our plan worked?" Rosemary asked.

"It has. If Nicodemus only knew, he would be quite cross with me. I trust you haven't said anything to him."

"No Abelene, I haven't."

"Is Azriel well?"

"I've been in communication with Nicodemus. Azriel is angry and frightened for ye. There's something else ye should know. Eltanin has come out of hiding. He is helping Azriel."

"That's an unexpected boon. Then our gambit worked."

Rosemary laughed. *"Ye are a master of manipulation, Lady Abelene."*

"Keep that to yourself, Rosemary. Now I need you to do something for me."

"Anything ye ask."

"Good." Abelene smiled. *"I need you to contact my forgetful son."*

Michael Anthony Cariola

Chapter 3

Nodus set the snifter of cognac down on the conference table with less finesse than he intended. He took a moment to compose himself, and forced back his anger.

"My Lord Rastaban." Nodus' words were clipped. "There's only one question I have." He rubbed his temple and inhaled a steadying breath. Through a clenched jaw, he said, "Have you gone mad?" His hands trembled with a faint palsy. Of the six members of the Clave, Nodus was the most ancient of the wizards, and his health was beginning to fail. Only the Lapis Occultus had staved off death a while longer, but no more would it restore his years. The remaining five were mystified by his decline. Once hale and strong, Nodus had begun to wither over the past one hundred years,

"Why don't you simply express your concern, Nodus?" Rastaban said with feigned respect.

"My concerns?" he retorted caustically, "My concerns lie with the state of your mind—your power to reason. What were you thinking bringing that woman here?"

Rastaban laughed quietly. "Allay your fears, brother. The Lady Abelene is hardly in any position to do us physical harm. The spectral pyramid has kept the dragon imprisoned; it will do no less for the Lady."

"I'm not concerned with anything physical, Rastaban. Her powers are far more subtle."

Altais came to his master's defense. "My brother, I engaged in formal battle with the damsel. True, she *is* powerful, but she was no match for me. Your fears are unfounded."

"By Shenach—twenty thousand years and you both have learned nothing!" Nodus raged. "Though the Lady Abelene is of House Gorlyn, she is still of Eltanin's lineage. That makes her quite the powerful sorceress, and there is one thing—the most obvious thing you both have missed."

"Oh, and what would that be, Lord Nodus?" Altais didn't hide his amusement.

"She's a woman, you fool. Crafty. Conniving. Deceptive—a woman." He spat.

"And your point, Nodus?" Rastaban poured another inch of cognac for the decrepit old wizard. Nodus took a sip, nurturing the fine crystal in his hand.

"My point," he muttered. "Are you both so readily seduced? The Lady Abelene should not have been so easily taken."

"It was anything but easy, my brother." Altais shot back defensively.

"What can you possibly hope to accomplish by all this?" Nodus enunciated, "Send her back!"

Rastaban smiled. "Nodus, she is the mother of the One, the Avatar. Her son, Azriel, is destined to restore the worlds to one. But time is running out. I am using the Lady Abelene to lure him here, to draw him off task. Either he joins us—or he dies!"

"Just like that! And do you think he will fall for such a blatant ruse? There are things I know that you don't." He cackled at the irony. "I was right, then. You *have* lost your faculties."

"No, old wizard. It is you who have. Your mind is clouded with atrophy, and you have become weak."

"Oh, have I, Rastaban? I still have a few tricks up my sleeve. What you fail to see, my young friend, is that there are prowlers circling the gates—held at bay, and yet you let one in right through the front door!"

"Nonsense." Rastaban growled.

"Truly you are blind, brother. My body may be weak, but my mind is as sharp as yours is clouded by the lady's beauty."

For once, Rastaban did not respond. Nodus smiled, but his expression was grim. He, in fact, had information vital to the Clave, the one thing that gave him power over Rastaban.

Eltanin had returned.

Nodus had felt it, sensed it. He stroked his beard thoughtfully. What had blinded Rastaban and the others? Altais had even been given the cube of discernment and failed to see the obvious. Now to add to their total blindness, they had missed another critical piece of information. Nicodemus was alive as well. The Clave had assumed when they had destroyed the human wizard's castle some five hundred years before that Nicodemus had been buried in the rubble. Only recently did Nodus discover the truth. The crafty sorcerer had escaped his assumed demise and remained hidden for five centuries. Nodus had discovered the truth by mere happenstance.

As was his habit, Nodus, an adept shape shifter, had assumed the form of a vulture. Out for an afternoon hike, he was attracted by the sound of thunder resounding through the mountains, only there were no clouds in the sky. Following the rumbling, he discovered hidden deep within the secluded Canyonlands, a castle of very clever design blending in with the native rock. If not for two young people practicing the hurling of energy balls at boulders, he would have missed it altogether. Perching high on a rocky escarpment, Nodus continued to observe. And there he was, emerging from the castle to instruct his students—that renegade sorcerer, Nicodemus accompanied by none other than Eltanin!

"Rastaban, you are truly blind." Nodus drained his snifter of cognac. "You are blinded by beauty, blinded by power, and blinded by your arrogance."

"Oh am I?" Rastaban smiled, but his eyes were hard.

Nodus suddenly lurched and gasped. He clutched at his chest and pitched forward again, stumbling out of his seat. His body began to spasm as he lay sprawled on the floor.

"Poison?" Nodus laughed through the pain. "That is beneath even you, Rastaban."

"You have outlived your usefulness, old man."

"Have I!" Nodus laughed heartily even though he was dying. "You should have waited, you fool." He laughed as though he held onto some private joke. "Now you will never know, and your shortsightedness will spell your doom." His laughter came in gales. He laughed at Rastaban and Altais and the remaining Clave. With one final tremor, Nodus heaved forward, his mouth hanging open in a shudder of pain. With an excruciating gasp, Nodus collapsed and died.

Rastaban stared down at his dead brother and shook his head. "I shall miss him," he muttered.

At the moment of Nodus' death, the third star of the constellation Draco—the serpent—an ancient red giant known in the small circle of astronomers as Nodus Secundus went nova. The third-magnitude star, at its final moment of life, also took out the remaining planets of its solar system. Its fourth planet had just completed the next stage of its evolution. The creatures inhabiting that world had recently discovered fire and were only beginning to use simple tools. The eight-legged creatures—descendants of arachnids and part of a collective hive mind—looked up in the sky as the destruction descended. They had time for only one thought. Its human equivalent would have been something like: "huh?"

As it is the nature of light to travel, the destruction of Nodus Secundus—its dying blaze of glory—would not be visible on Earth for another hundred years.

Abelene sat in a comfortable chair, writing in a leather-bound journal. Her feet rested on an ottoman. She saw it fit to record everything she sensed, her impressions and conversations with Charlie. The ancient dragon was far different from what she would have expected from the guardian of death. He was friendly, guileless and not without humor—an enigma, really. She smiled as she wrote. One would expect the creature to be somber and frightening, but he was paradoxically charming and witty. Even the choosing of his name, Charlie, showed a whimsical sense about him.

Her impression of Rastaban, however, was very much in line with what she would have expected. Despicable. She was able to see through his external charm. Hidden beneath his cultured exterior dwelled a monster without scruples and a soul utterly corrupted by an egotistical nature. She sensed the Arch Wizard of the Clave saw himself as invincible. Good, she thought—he showed his Achilles' heel early in the game. White queen to Black queen's knight—check! Let him believe what he wanted. It will serve to unseat him. She had much information to convey to Azriel, that is, whenever her errant son would answer her summoning. She wrote a few more lines in her journal and shifted her weight to a more comfortable position.

Across from her, in the adjoining phantasmal pyramid, Charlie bolted upright. He sat on his haunches and scratched his head.

"Now that's interesting," he mused.

"Charlie, what is it?" Abelene looked up from her journal.

"The Clave has been reduced by one. Fascinating," he said with wonder. "I must be getting distracted—or senile. I never saw this coming."

"Well, are you going to tell me, or do I have to beg?" Abelene bantered.

Charlie chuckled. "Nodus is dead—betrayed, murdered by Rastaban. Strange… I never saw it."

"I thought you had foreknowledge of every death that would occur."

"I do, Lady Abelene. That is why I am so thoroughly mystified. Perhaps your beauty and friendship have dulled my senses."

"Oh, you're such a charmer, Charlie." Abelene smiled.

The ancient dragon laughed. "It's no great loss, of course. Nodus was ready for death." Charlie thought and cocked his head this way and that. "Hmm, now that I think about it, I can't see the deaths of any of the five Arch Wizards."

"It actually makes sense, when you consider it." Abelene reasoned. "You are being held prisoner by the Clave. They have used your power for twenty thousand years. It's possible their dominion over you has prevented you from knowing their demise."

"I suppose that's possible." Charlie mulled the concept over in his mind. "It's actually rather entertaining—refreshing , even. I get to sit back and watch."

"It does raise a question, though." Abelene frowned.

"Lady?"

"Why would Rastaban kill his own man? It seems counterintuitive."

"Not really. Nodus was always on the fringe. His goals were never truly in line with those of the Clave. That made him a liability. It does have a more serious implication, however."

"Oh, and what would that be?" Abelene asked.

"Merely that Rastaban has become more dangerous than ever— and unpredictable. I would suggest caution when speaking with him, Lady. His infatuation with you could easily turn to malice. For my sake, Abelene, tread lightly. Do not provoke him. I would rather not see you harmed."

"Charlie, you've developed a soft spot for me."

The ancient dragon sighed tragically. "Alas. It is as you say."

"Charlie, I need to see about reaching my son. I must beg leave for now." Abelene smiled apologetically.

"Of course, lady. One thing I would ask, though."

"Yes?"

"Do not tell him about me—not just yet."

"Why, Charlie?"

"It's better for both our sakes right now. You might not believe this, but your son is a danger to me."

"Then I will do as you ask. No harm will come to you."

"Thank you, Lady Abelene."

Azriel sat across from Rosemary and shrugged. "I'm sorry. I thought I was going nuts. I kept hearing my mother's voice in my head. I didn't think it was possible since she left this behind." He removed the ring from his pouch.

"With good reason, Azriel." Rosemary leaned forward. "She knew if she was taken, it would have been a liability. The Clave could have used it to get to ye."

"My mother thinks of everything, doesn't she?" Azriel said, a hint of humor in his voice.

"She's yer mother, and that has nary a thing to do with her sorcery. Call it woman's intuition."

"Yeah, you're right. Growing up with her, I couldn't get away with anything."

Rosemary smiled knowingly. "Now when yer mother tries to reach ye again, just answer her as if she were in the same room."

"Won't Rastaban know what she's doing?"

"It's not likely. For all his perception, he can't conceive that Abelene would use human telepathy. He can't detect or sense it and he's blinded by his own prejudice. He reviles human magick."

"That's good to know." Azriel nodded.

"Indeed. Now young master, when yer mother calls, don't be a wanker. For pity's sake, answer the call!"

"Yes ma'am." Azriel smiled sheepishly.

Abelene drew the curtain to her bed giving her privacy. As before, she prepared herself for astral communication with her son. Deep breaths, the slowing of her heartbeat, the semi-conscious state between, she readied herself to contact Azriel. This time she hoped her son would be receptive. One thing that made it difficult was the lack of sunlight. Her time sense felt askew. She wasn't sure whether it was day or night. Nighttime would be easier, but alas, she could only guess.

Abelene released her spirit energy and thought herself to Nicodemus' castle. She sensed Azriel's presence and was fortunate he was just retiring to bed. She projected her thoughts into his mind.

"*Azriel?*" she probed gently. Abelene sensed the sharpening of his awareness.

Azriel answered tentatively. "*Mom? Is that you?*"

"*Yes, son.*" An onrushing flood of relief washed over her, radiating from Azriel's heart.

"*Mom, I was so worried. Where are you?*"

"*I'm not sure—somewhere underground. The Clave has me imprisoned.*"

"*Are you hurt?*"

"*No, I am well attended to.*"

"*Why Mom, why did you do it?*"

Abelene could feel his hurt. "*It was necessary, Azriel. I am deeply entrenched in the enemy's camp. Here I can be of value to you.*"

"*Mom, you were always of value to me.*"

"*That's not what I meant.*" She smiled. "*I can provide you with useful information. It is not Rastaban who captured me. I captured him!*"

"*Mom, do you think you can manage to be just a little more vague?*"

"No need to be sarcastic, Azriel. Let's just say that I am your personal spy."

"Okay, so what can you tell me?"

"For one thing, Nodus is dead. Rastaban murdered him."

"How do you know that?"

Abelene hesitated. She promised Charlie she wouldn't reveal his secret just yet. *"I sensed it,"* she lied.

"Was it in formal magickal combat?"

"No son. Rastaban poisoned him."

"Then how can you be so sure you will not be harmed? He's already broken one of the most fundamental rules of magickal conduct."

"True, Azriel. He has damned himself and the Clave."

"Then you're not safe."

"I assure you, Azriel. He will not harm me. I think he is smitten."

"Smitten? What do you mean?"

"He likes me, Azriel. I can use my feminine charms to our advantage."

Azriel hesitated. *"Mom, that's disgusting."* He shuddered.

Abelene giggled aloud. *"I promise to be a good girl, Azriel. I just need to get into his head. Find out what he is planning."*

"Just be careful—please." He paused. *"Mom?"*

"Yes, Azriel."

"Something you should know."

"What is it, son?"

"Eltanin has returned. He is here with me and Nicodemus."

Abelene nodded. *"Yes dear, I know. Rosemary told me."*

"There's more. Eltanin is Pog. Pog is Eltanin. He's been here all along."

"I had my suspicions. Your friend always seemed somewhat elusive."

"Eltanin is instructing me in Alchemy. I think I'm close to my goal."

"Good. I don't need to remind you that time is getting short."

"I know, Mom."

"Well, we should break contact for now. I'll speak to you tomorrow."

"Mom, I love you. Please be safe."

"You too. Good night, Azriel."

Finally, the first night in a week, and Azriel slept soundly. He awoke refreshed and ready to tackle any obstacle placed before him. As usual, the breakfast table was alive with chatter and the usual Cunningham chaos. This time, Julia had flown into a rage against Jasper. He was taken by surprise at her wrath.

"What did I do?" He held out his hands helplessly.

"What did you do? Nothing! Except you're the one who's supposed to keep Mortimer on a tight leash," she seethed.

"What's your problem?"

"I found Mortimer camouflaged against the wall in my bedroom!"

"So? That's what he does."

"He saw me naked!" Julia sputtered and raged, her face red with embarrassment.

Jasper snorted trying desperately to keep from laughing. "Aw, come on, he's just a gargoyle. It's not like he's human."

"He's a lecherous little creep! Keep him away from me!" Julia stormed off grumbling as she headed to the kitchen.

"Mortimer, come here." Jasper ordered. The gargoyle flew over and perched on the table."

"Did you spy on my sister?"

He looked and struck an innocent pose.

"Mortimer." Jasper scolded him firmly.

The little creature began to chortle, thoroughly pleased with himself.

"That wasn't nice, Mortimer, and you got *me* in trouble."

Mortimer hung his head in shame and did his best to look remorseful.

"Don't ever do that again, okay? Now go apologize to Julia."

The gargoyle brightened and flew off to the kitchen. He wasn't in there three seconds before Jasper heard Julia's muffled scream. Terrified, Mortimer darted out of the door followed by a bowl of oatmeal that grazed his head. It crashed to the floor as Mortimer cowered behind Jasper.

Jasper stared at the broken shards of ceramic with wonder. Julia charged out from the adjoining room. "Keep him away from me, Jasper," she growled, "or I just might turn him back into stone!" She returned to the other room in a huff.

"Mortimer, you might be better off letting her cool down. Give her a couple of days—maybe longer."

There was another crash of broken china coming from the kitchen and a string of curses directed at Jasper and Mortimer.

Jasper pursed his lips. "Better make that a *lot* longer.

After several abortive attempts at transmuting lead to gold, Azriel finally had his eureka moment. He had come to a vital realization. Transmuting wasn't merely a physical formula of elements and light, but required something more than just the setting up of apparatus. It required Azriel to be in the proper state of mind. Once he attuned his heart to the experiment and cleared his mind of all extraneous thought, focusing only on the supreme transformation, did he arrive at his goal.

Azriel repeated the transmutation successfully another three times. On his fourth transmutation, he had a sudden flash of intuition. Azriel fashioned a mold to form the components for a tiny golden chest like the one he had seen Nicodemus use to house the Lapis Occultus. He remembered Amaryllis' transformation when they first met. A tiny amount of the substance had restored the ancient woman's youth.

Lid, clasp, hinges and a tiny spoon were already poured. For the chest, he had anchored a smaller box within a larger and carefully poured the molten gold between the spaces separating them. While they cooled, Azriel examined the third object he had fashioned, a gift for Camille. He tried not to be filled with pride, but Azriel was surprised at his own craftiness. He had been secretly working on a custom mold for a few days and had carved into stone a negative imprint of a magnificent dragon with his wings outstretched. Having released it now from the mold, he carefully hammered the wings back until it formed a clever bracelet.

Azriel assembled the tiny chest fitting the hinges and clasps onto the lid and attaching it to the tiny golden chest. He now stared thoughtfully at the four objects before him. The first two were merely a repetition of the pendant Eltanin had made. After the third time transmuting lead to gold, Azriel was amazed at how easy it was to accomplish once he knew the secret.

He sat now, contemplating the four objects before him when he heard a gentle tapping on the laboratory door.

"It's safe to enter.' Azriel answered.

Eltanin strolled in and studied Azriel's creations. He couldn't help but be impressed by the craftsmanship, though he downplayed his admiration. Pride was not the lesson he needed to convey. Azriel's reaction to his achievement would be crucial to the young man's future. Much would be determined by how he answered the questions Eltanin was about to ask. If he answered with wisdom, Azriel would be allowed to proceed. If he answered poorly, Eltanin would prevent him from creating the Lapis Occultus until he was ready.

"Hello, Grandfather." Azriel spoke, still studying the four objects he had fashioned.

"Deep thoughts, son?"

"Yeah, sort of."

Eltanin tested. "You must be quite proud of yourself for such an accomplishment."

"No, not really." Azriel stared pensively at the tiny chest, turning it in his hand. His words came slowly. "Actually, I'm somewhat disappointed. This whole exercise feels—anticlimactic. I've always thought gold was something to be desired. Look at the world and the greed attached to gold. People go crazy around it and do terrible, evil things to attain it. But now that I can create it, it's just like any other metal. I know it sounds strange, but it's lost its sparkle."

"Ah, but look at all the things you could have with gold in your possession," Eltanin cajoled.

"Like what? A new car? Fame? women? I don't need or want any of it! I can go anywhere I want with the dream orb. I have as much use for fame as I would for a bag of horse manure. And women? I already have the best girl I could ever hope for."

Eltanin said enticingly, "Yes, but there are things you could acquire—art, rare antiquities… power!" his eyes gleamed.

"Power?" Azriel retorted. "If a man has to buy power, then he has little or no power at all."

"Great quote," Eltanin mused. "Who said that?"

"I just did," Azriel said with annoyance. "Whose side are you on anyway?" Azriel was becoming cross with the ancient wizard.

Eltanin chuckled and shook Azriel by the shoulder. "Enough, my young adept. I had to be sure you were ready. Everything you said is true. You see, Azriel, wealth can have a dark allure. It has its benefits, yes. But one can become so immersed in attainment, so insulated by power, that it becomes easy to settle for less—and lose your soul in the process. You have learned a valuable lesson," he laughed quietly, "more valuable than all the gold you can create. Some people strain their entire lives and never attain the wisdom you gained in the past five minutes."

"Eltanin, I don't think it's all that profound, it just seems like common sense."

"Azriel, something I've learned in all my thousands of years is that sense is not at all common."

"Really?" Azriel grimaced.

"Really!" Eltanin intoned. "I have seen men amass fortunes and never be content with their lives. And I have seen a hungry man be thoroughly content and filled with joy over a simple bowl of rice. Contentment is the greatest thing you could own, for it's the one thing that can never be taken from you."

"I think I understand. But I won't be totally content until my mother is back home and safe."

"That's different." Eltanin replied. "One should never be content when another suffers. But at least be comforted—be content—that you have the power and fortitude to change that. It will take time, however. Abelene is another matter altogether, and I must commend her for her teachings. They are strong in you. She must be a remarkable woman."

"Yes, she is." Azriel said solemnly.

"You are ready for the next step." Eltanin smiled candidly. "Tomorrow you will begin the final lessons of creating the Lapis Occultus. Now you should rest from your labors." He picked up the golden bracelet Azriel had fashioned. "And you should present this to that lovely young lady who seems to shine every time she is in your presence."

Michael Anthony Cariola

50

Chapter 4

During one of those rare times when the castle was free of noise and constant activity, Nicodemus slept soundly in his chambers. Each of the guests rested easily in their rooms. Camille and Julia shared one, and the brothers shared the adjoining room. Mortimer, as was his habit, perched upon the stone sill of the open window opposite Jasper's bed, staring out into the night. Though no one officially charged Mortimer with watching over the castle, he deemed it his personal duty to guard over everyone and keep them safe. Not that it was much of a burden. By nature, Mortimer was a creature of the night. His nocturnal ways allowed him the luxury of hunting for a few snacks unseen by the others. With his excellent night vision, he noticed a tasty-looking desert hare dart from one boulder to another beyond the courtyard walls. Mortimer slipped out the window and soared soundlessly toward his quarry. With one perfectly timed swoop, he sank his claws into the unsuspecting rabbit and began to feast. About halfway through his meal, Mortimer sensed a presence. A vague shadow passed overhead, momentarily blocking out the moonlight. He jerked his head up, craning his neck, and caught a glimpse of something just beyond his vision. True to a gargoyle's curious nature, he grudgingly left the remains of the rabbit behind and followed the presence. Whatever it was, it disappeared into a cave opening about two miles beyond Castle Wylusung. He was about to fly further to investigate when a commanding voice suddenly sounded in his mind. It was in no way threatening. If anything, it sounded weary… and in pain. The voice said, "Little cousin, bring Nicodemus to me. You know where I am."

Mortimer bristled at the urgency of the voice and circled back with all speed to Nicodemus' window. Nicodemus lay in his bed snoring noisily, muttering in his sleep. The gargoyle glided down to the foot of the old wizard's bed and grabbed at his ankle, giving it a firm shake. Nicodemus grumbled in his sleep and responded with a violent kick, sending Mortimer sailing off the bed. He shook himself off and pumped at Nick's shoulders a few times, trying to rouse him, but the old man refused to awaken. Mortimer sighed with frustration glancing around the room when he spied the laving bowl on Nicodemus's dresser. Snatching it up, Mortimer hovered above the wizard's head and emptied the contents, dousing him squarely in the face.

Nicodemus awoke with a start sputtering and cursing. Mortimer cowered sheepishly on the footboard of the bed and gestured apologetically.

"Now what couldn't wait until the morning?" Nicodemus grumbled. The little gargoyle perched onto the windowsill and pointed to a spot beyond the courtyard. He tugged at the wizard's arm and then flew back to the window. Sensing the urgency, Nicodemus quickly dressed and followed Mortimer to the main hall and out the front gate of the castle. Tailing Mortimer, it took him only a half an hour to locate the mouth of the cave. A ruddy glow emanated from the cavernous opening. Within the low-roofed chamber, a small fire burned, and Nicodemus stepped into the inner recess, peering into the darkness.

"Enter, my old friend. I've been expecting you." A weakened voice rumbled, the speaker hidden in shadow. The creature shifted and moved her massive head so Nicodemus could see her.

"Maragog, is that you?"

She chuckled weakly. "Yes, little brother, it is me."

Nicodemus said with wonder, "This is truly an unexpected pleasure, my old friend."

"Yes, I am your friend, and yes I have grown very old." She sighed heavily.

"I haven't seen you for many, many years. I thought you perished in the great deluge."

"So it would have seemed. It's how I wanted it. The less seen, the safer I am. This world has become dangerous for one such as me."

Maragog inched closer to the fire. Nicodemus could now see in the light how her condition had degraded. Her once-lustrous scales were now dulled with age and patchy in places. Her wings were scored with deep scars and festering sores. It was obvious the old dragon was in pain, yet she bore it stoically. He stared at Maragog with pity.

"Do I look so wretched, old friend?"

"Er, no, Maragog. You look as grand as ever."

She chuckled. "You were never a good liar, Nicodemus."

"No, I suppose not, at least not to you. How did you find me?"

"Oh, I always knew where you were. I was merely waiting for the right time to see you. I wish to speak with you one last time."

Nicodemus stared at her with compassion. "Is there anything I can do to ease your suffering, great lady?"

"Still the charmer you are. Hmm… no, old friend. The last few thousand years have been a long, hard road for me. Once it was that the world of men believed in dragons, but like my legend, I have faded into myth. Thus, it is my time to die."

"I can restore your years," Nicodemus offered as he removed a tiny wooden box from his pocket. "I have the Lapis Occultus."

"You're a dear man, Nicodemus, but let things be as they are. Now I must ask you. Has the Son of Luminance arrived?"

"Yes he has."

"That is well. His appearance is timely, but alas too late for me. Does he know yet who and what he is?"

"He knows who he is, but has not come into the knowledge of what he is, although I believe he is beginning to suspect."

"The time is short, Nicodemus. He must come into that knowledge soon."

"Indeed, it is as you say. He has learned three of the four names, but he still must solve the riddle of the Lapis Occultus. This is not something I can give him, nor can Eltanin do so. This he must solve on his own. When he does, he will truly know what he is. It is only in this way he can free his brothers and sisters. What he does at that crucial time must be a choice made without coercion otherwise what is meant to happen will never be. There is one thing in our favor, however."

"Oh?" Maragog shifted her massive weight.

"His mother, the Queen Sorceress is held captive by the Clave."

"And how is this in any way fortunate?"

"She is imprisoned in the same place the Clave holds the Dark Lord captive. I have been in communication with her. It is indeed fortunate that she is learning the true nature of the immortal lord, something the Clave has not done. It will be their undoing."

"Then I am pleased, little brother." She sighed wearily and rested her head on the ground. "Now, my friend, the time grows short. Something I must ask of you."

"Anything, great Lady."

"It's funny," Maragog mused. "I have lived for the entire history of civilized man, that is, if they can be called civilized." She chuckled. "And yet now I haven't enough time left to complete my final task."

She shifted her great tail and gently moved an object to rest against Nicodemus' feet. "This is my last egg. I won't be alive long enough to see him hatch. If the Son of Luminance cannot complete his task, then my hatchling will be the last of his kind."

Maragog coughed painfully, and a wisp of sulfuric smoke escaped her lips. "He will hatch soon. Please take care of him. Keep him warm and safe."

Nicodemus stroked Maragog's head gently. "This I will do, dear friend. I have a castle. Now it will be complete with a dragon to guard it. He will also have five young sorcerers to pamper him."

She smiled weakly. "Oh don't spoil Magador too much. You don't want him to become belligerent."

Nicodemus patted Maragog with affection. "Magador! It's a good and noble name. All right then, not too much spoiling. You have my promise to take good care of him."

"Then I am content." Maragog's eyes grew heavy.

Nicodemus gently lifted the egg and wrapped it in his cape.

Now, old friend, it is my time to die. Goodbye... and farewell." She fixed her eyes on Nicodemus and smiled. Her massive chest heaved and a gentle sigh escaped her lips. She slowly closed her eyes and passed into the beyond.

Nicodemus stroked the great head of the old dragon affectionately and whispered, "Goodbye, dear Maragog."

He took one last look and exited the cave. Before departing, he raised his hand and spoke an incantation. "Maxima Obstructo!"

The mouth of the cave suddenly shuddered and shifted as if alive. The massive stone caved in, sealing Maragog's remains from mortal eyes for all time.

Abelene was startled awake by a great mournful roar erupting from Charlie's prison. She rose from her bed and turned toward the Dark Lord to see what was wrong. His huge shoulders were hunched in sorrow, and if she didn't know better, it appeared as if tears were welling in his eyes.

"Charlie, what's wrong?"

"A Great One has just died. She was the last of her kind. Her soul just passed through me to the immortal gate."

"Who, Charlie?"

"It was Maragog the Ancient. Her magick has left this realm. This world is now diminished."

Abelene stared at Charlie sadly. "I see now that your duties can be difficult for you."

"At times, yes, Lady Abelene. I took no pleasure in it, for she was a child of the earth. Lagina-Tierra shall mourn for her daughter, as I will."

"But it is the way of life, is it not?"

"True, but it is a difficult burden to bear. Maragog simply gave up. There was not enough magick left in this world to sustain one as great as she. Lady Abelene, your son must complete his task. The Elementals must return."

"There is still magick in this world, my lord. I can feel it."

"Alas, it is as you say, but she gave her life so enough magick would survive to nurture her son. He will hatch soon."

"But who will care for him?"

Charlie chuckled, "Don't you know, Lady? It is your son, Azriel, with the help of Nicodemus."

"Oh my. It's not like Azriel doesn't have enough on his plate."

It's an easy burden, though. Dragons are quite self-sufficient and there is much Azriel can learn from the youngster. The hatchling has all of Maragog's knowledge in his head."

"That is good to know, Charlie. It would indeed be a pity if all that knowledge was lost." Abelene mused and changed the subject.

"My Lord, you've been trapped here for twenty thousand years. Do you have any idea where *here* is?"

"No, my Lady. Although my power reaches throughout this planet and beyond, my prison prevents me from seeing past these damnable walls."

"It is as you say, Charlie. I can stretch my consciousness to speak with Azriel and others who have the talent, but I have remained blind. I can't tell them where we are."

"You must be patient, Abelene. Your son will find you—and me."

She hesitated thoughtfully. "Why does that frighten you, Charlie?"

"Azriel is learning fast. He is close to solving the riddle of the Lapis Occultus. Soon he will have power over death. When that happens he will have the ability to destroy me."

"Yet I don't believe he will, my lord. He may be young, but he has gained in wisdom."

"That he has, Lady, but his love for the human girl will blind him. Sometimes passion can overtake wisdom."

"You speak of Camille."

"Yes."

"Then her visions…"

"Are fated to happen, Abelene. Azriel believes that destroying death will prevent the inevitable. What your son doesn't understand is that I do not cause death. I am merely the gateway."

"Must she die?"

"It is fated to happen. It's her death that might save the worlds."

"I don't understand."

"Her death is the nexus point. What Azriel does at that moment of decision will determine what course the future will take. If he chooses to destroy me, then humanity and elvinkind will be set on a course from which there will be no return—and all will be lost."

"Why, Charlie?" Abelene's voice cracked with emotion.

"Great Lady, it is because I bring balance, set forth from the very beginning. My demise would spell the doom of both worlds. Life, without the balancing force of death, would continue its growth unchecked. Without decay, all living things would crowd each other out. There would be war upon war and pain upon pain, but no release from suffering. Your worlds would become a place of torments. A Hell worse than anything humanity has ever imagined. The immortality that men seek would indeed become a curse."

Abelene wiped at her tears. "Your existence is a sad one, my friend."

"It is as you say. But I cannot be anything other than what I am."

"Perhaps Azriel will choose a different path."

"It is my hope, Abelene."

"Then I will tell him what he needs to know, my lord."

"You cannot."

"Why not? I am his mother."

"His moment of decision must come freely and without coercion. The events must play out as destiny would have it. Besides, he will never believe you. He must arrive at this truth on his own."

"What will happen if he succeeds?"

"My lady, even I don't have an answer for that. There are many futures, but he can only choose one."

"I fear for him, Charlie."

The dark dragon tilted his head as though thinking, or listening to a suggestion. "He has made friends along the way. Help will come from unexpected sources. If he is wise, he will take heed. I am not his enemy. I am his brother."

"It is not the first time you have said that, Charlie. I don't understand."

"Nor will you until the time when all things will be made transparent."

"More riddles." Abelene sighed.

Charlie laughed quietly. "I can only reveal what I am permitted. I do not mean to cause you vexation, my lady."

"I understand. But I am still vexed." She crossed her arms with disapproval.

Charlie, however, could not hide his amusement. "Yes, it is quite disagreeable to be kept in the dark."

Azriel took the afternoon off from his usual time in Uncle Nick's laboratory. Studying alchemy was becoming tedious and its exacting disciplines taxed his brain in ways he never could have imagined. Although Azriel had succeeded in transforming lead to gold, creating the Lapis Occultus still seemed so far out of reach. The time off would be a welcome respite—one he wouldn't have missed for the world. The center of his attention was a bronze-and green-mottled egg that had been strategically placed before the blazing hearth in the great hall. Three times the size of an ostrich egg, it was carefully attended to by Azriel, Camille and Nicodemus, each giving it a quarter turn every hour on the hour. Mortimer also seemed to be quite protective of it and would allow no one near it other than the chosen caretakers. This day, however, when it was Azriel's turn to turn the egg, he felt a shifting and a gentle tapping from within the shell. Thus, with great anticipation, everyone gathered around the hearth for the momentous occasion. Prepared for the event, Nicodemus had a large serving of raw chicken ready. He was well schooled in dragon lore and knew Magador would be extremely hungry when he hatched.

As they all watched with eager anticipation, the egg suddenly began to rattle and shake. Camille held her breath as a fissure appeared at the narrow end and spread to the base. The egg shook violently as the youngling struggled to free himself. First, a wing jutted out from the crack, then another fragment of shell scattered as the other wing emerged. Finally the dragon's head appeared as the remainder of the shell shattered into pieces. Only the top of the egg rested like a tiny beanie on Magador's head. Amid cries of awe, he shook himself off and unsteadily took a few steps before flopping face first onto the floor. Maggie took a few steps back, still not quite comfortable with some aspects of magick.

Magador spread his wings and shook them out, then yawned before squealing pathetically. His golden scales shone in the firelight and the tiny ridges on his head and neck, as well as his wingtips, shone a deep crimson. His eyes were striking, bejeweled like finely faceted rubies.

Camille stared wide-eyed at the magnificent tiny creature and cooed. "Oh my! He's beautiful!"

Azriel smiled broadly. "He is quite a handsome little guy, isn't he!"

Magador, however, began to stomp his feet with agitation and opened his mouth wide emitting grunts of frustration.

Nicodemus chuckled. "Our newborn is hungry. Azriel, feed him." Uncle Nick handed Azriel the massive bowl of raw chicken, chopped into dragon-sized bites. Taking charge, Azriel held out a chicken leg to the fledgling. Magador sniffed at it before lunging, nearly taking Azriel's fingers with it.

"Ow—crap!" Azriel yelped.

Magador tried to attack the bowl, but Nicodemus snatched it away. "Azriel, this is a most crucial time. You must show Magador who is in charge."

"Yeah? I think *he* is!" Azriel rubbed his hand with annoyance.

"Now hold it out to him. If he lunges, pull it away. Magador will understand after a few times that he needs to be gentle."

As Nicodemus had predicted, the tiny dragon pounced again at the chicken breast Azriel held out. But he snatched it away and then gently held it out again. Magador whimpered, but then let Azriel drop the tasty morsel in his gaping mouth. Camille then took a piece and held it out. Magador took it gently from her open palm. The little dragon learned quickly and soon everyone took turns feeding him. Three chickens later, Julia held out the last piece, but Magador, his belly full, burped and turned away to warm himself by the fire. He stretched out and fell asleep contentedly.

Mortimer, spying the raw chicken leg in Julia's hand inched closer to her and looked up with a pleading expression.

"What do *you* want?" She glowered down at the gargoyle.

He pointed sheepishly at the delectable piece.

"I'm still mad at you!" Julia said with a scowl.

Mortimer hung his head with shame and rubbed pathetically at his eyes.

"Oh, all right. You can have it." She smiled. "I forgive you."

Mortimer brightened and accepted the offering. He tossed it in his mouth and crunched noisily, bones and all.

"Wow, this is a milestone," Jasper taunted. "It only took you three weeks to give the little guy a break."

"Shut up, Jasper." Julia grumbled.

Within a month, Magador outgrew the main hall. Soon he would not be able to pass through the front gate. To accommodate the growing youngster, Nicodemus cleared out a section of the courtyard and raised an overhang to shade Magador from the midday sun. Azriel and Camille had all they could do rubbing down Magador's hide with lard to keep his skin from cracking and to quiet the incessant itching that plagued the young dragon.

It seemed Magador had grown attached to Azriel and Camille and even came to think of the human caretakers as his parents. Often, when they arrived in the morning, he would appear sulky and indignant at the audacity of being left alone at night. But soon he would forget his disappointment and rub his head affectionately against Azriel's chest, nearly knocking him to the ground.

As Camille anointed his back, Magador tried desperately to scratch behind his neck, but couldn't quite reach the spot. Azriel kept a stiff bristle brush nearby for just such a purpose.

"Is it bothering you again, Magador?" Azriel asked and smiled.

The dragon nodded.

"Would you like me to scratch it for you?"

He nodded again.

Azriel attacked the troublesome spot with the brush and Magador sighed with contentment. "Ahhh, that feels so much better."

Azriel stepped back, puzzled. "Did you just speak?"

"Well of course I did. I'm not stupid, you know." Magador spoke with an aristocratic, if not adolescent, voice.

"Then why haven't you spoken before?"

"Probably because I didn't feel like it. And besides, I'm feeling rather put out, left here all by myself most of the day." He brooded.

"Oh, quit complaining. When Camille and I aren't here, Jasper, Albert, or Julia stay with you. And when they're not, Mortimer always keeps you company."

"It's not the same, cousin Azriel."

"Cousin?"

"Why yes. You're the closest thing I have to kin, you being a dragon and all."

"Uh, Magador. I think you're confused. I'm not a dragon; I'm Ferrishyn."

Magador laughed lightly. "Maybe *you're* the one who's confused."

"Whatever." Azriel rolled his eyes.

So what's your problem with Albert and Jasper?" Camille asked.

"Don't get me wrong. I like them just fine, but they never stop talking, bickering and arguing. It's tiresome."

Camille giggled. "And Julia? What's your problem with her? She's very sweet."

"Yes, a lovely girl. Sometimes I wish she were a dragon, but her constant stroking, fawning, and smothering me with kisses— it's getting on my nerves. I'm not a pet, you know."

Azriel suppressed a laugh. "Then why don't you just tell her that it annoys you."

"I don't want to hurt her feelings."

"Well that's pretty big of you, but you should still tell her anyway. She'll understand. What about Mortimer?"

"He's a fine little guy, but not much of a conversationalist."

"Good point." Azriel replied wryly.

"Nevertheless, he did offer to give me flying lessons when my wings are stronger."

"That's great, Magador. Once you have that mastered, Nicodemus has a great place set aside just for you."

"Oh, and where would that be?"

"Up there!" Azriel pointed to the turret high above the castle walls. "You can see the entire countryside from there."

Magador nodded. "That would be acceptable. After that, you must teach me to chew rock."

"Excuse me?" Azriel responded, utterly confused.

"Well I'm never going to be able to breathe fire unless I learn to chew rock. I understand good coal deposits are quite abundant here."

"You're probably too young for that yet, Magador. I can't have you blowing yourself up. I've heard that happens sometimes. And who told you about coal, anyway?"

"My mother—Maragog. I have her memories." He sounded somewhat indignant. "In fact I have all the memories of every dragon who ever lived, including yours."

"Stop saying that. I'm not a dragon."

"I give you a high compliment, cousin. As a matter of fact, I'll make a deal with you, Azriel. You teach me to chew rock, and I'll help you solve the riddle of fire. Deal?"

"If you say so." Azriel mumbled unenthusiastically.

"Cousin, your lack of faith offends me."

"Begging your pardon, Magador, but I don't see how you can help me. Alchemy is a pretty exacting discipline. How could you possibly..."

Magador interrupted. "Just who do you think taught alchemy to Eltanin? It was my grandfather, Maladon, who gave him the knowledge he needed to complete his task. Do I need to remind you that I have all his memories? You're not very bright for a dragon."

Azriel sighed with frustration while Camille giggled.

"Why do you insist that I'm a dragon?" he grumbled.

"The question should be—what *is* a dragon? What magick makes a dragon what he is? Is it the flesh, the heart, the very meat of his existence? Or is it something deeper perhaps, beyond the heart and bones of your body. Only you can decide who you are and what is within."

"You're speaking in riddles, Magador. Can you be more concise?"

"Actually, cousin, I speak quite plainly. You're just not listening."

"You're starting to sound an awful lot like Nicodemus. Maybe he's your father."

"Maybe he is." Magador chuckled. "Now if you don't mind, I have this terrible itch above my left flank I just can't reach. It's quite troublesome. Would you mind?"

"Not at all." Azriel picked up the bristle brush and scratched Magador's back with gusto.

"Ahhh—Ahhh—ah, yes! Thank you, thank you, thank you!" The golden dragon purred with contentment.

At the usual predetermined time, Abelene made contact with Azriel. He lay in his bed when he heard his mother's voice in his mind.

"How are you tonight, son?"

"It's been a busy day. Magador is growing rapidly. He's already two heads taller than me! And there's something else, Mom. He's started talking and hasn't shut up since." Azriel heard his mother giggle.

"He's young yet, Azriel. Give him time. He has so much knowledge in his head; he just wants to share it."

"So how much do you know about dragon lore?"

"Some. But Nicodemus knows much more. Why don't you ask him?"

"I would if I could locate him. He said he had urgent business to attend to and has been gone for the past three days. He wouldn't say what it was."

"Hmm, just like your uncle to be secretive. So what would you like to know?"

"What's the connection between dragons and alchemy?"

"That's a difficult one to answer, Azriel."

"How so?"

"The best way I can explain is that dragons are the embodiment of magick and alchemy. Dragons owe their existence from the very beginning to the alchemical merging of the Elementals. That they exist at all is a great mystery. By all rights they shouldn't exist. They are a paradox since they have no equivalent in nature. They subsisted for thousands of years but most people couldn't see them."

"Why not, Mom?"

"Because they weren't trained to. In fact, most people are taught at an early age that dragons are a myth. Their lack of belief has brought dragons nearly to extinction, at least on this planet. Magador is the last one. Perhaps it's the reason he talks so much. He's lonely. I've heard that long ago, dragons were said to speak across great distances—much as you and I are doing right now."

"That makes sense. Mom, there's something else though."

"Oh?"

"Magador insists that *I'm* a dragon. I really don't know what he means by that. Any thoughts?"

Abelene hesitated before answering. "Well, if you *are* a dragon, it's certainly not from my side of the family." She chuckled.

"Mom, I'm being serious."

"Then perhaps you should ask Eltanin. He is after all, the dragon's head."

"I don't understand. Can you speak more plainly?" Azriel's ire rose.

"Now don't get snippy, Azriel."

"Mom, please!"

"All right, I'll speak plainly. It's about Draconis—the Clave of Wizards. Rastaban is not the head, although he pretends to be. Altais, Giausur, Thuban, and Edasich are all that remain of the body. There were many more at one time, but they were loyal to Eltanin and were murdered by Rastaban. Now Nodus is dead as well. Understand that Rastaban is *not* the head. Although Eltanin was deposed as Arch Wizard of the Clave, he is still the legitimate head of Draconis. Should the lave ever be defeated, Eltanin will take his rightful place as its head."

"But what does that have to do with me being a dragon?"

"Don't be dense, son. You are Eltanin's heir just as your father was. Legend had it that Eltanin was able to transform into a dragon, though that remains an unsubstantiated rumor. But if you remember, your spirit is of the dragon just like Camille's is of the lioness. Perhaps that's what Magador was referring to. All I know is that Eltanin's blood flows in your veins."

"Then I guess I have questions for Eltanin." Azriel sighed.

"That would be a good place to start, Azriel. And don't forget the Book of Aralia. There's more information in there for you to learn."

"It's just too much to absorb. I've kind of skipped around to the more interesting parts."

Abelene checked her temper. Sometimes her son's vagueness boiled her blood.

"Azriel, this is not a game. Time is getting short. You must learn who you are. There is a section on your genealogy. Read it. Study dragon lore. The Book of Aralia has little to say on the matter, but I know Nicodemus has volumes on it. For some reason, your uncle held a particular fascination with dragons. I don't mean to be cross with you, son, but you have many resources available to you. You need to start using them."

"I am, Mom, I am!" Azriel growled. "I just don't know how I'm going to complete everything I have to do." His heart felt heavy in his chest as he made the admission.

Abelene softened. "One thing I know of you, Azriel, is that you have excellent instincts—and your heart is in the right place. Remain true to that and you will not fail."

Chapter 5

The undulating sand impeded Nicodemus's progress from the jutting spire called Devil's Leap to the oasis, home for Habib's tribe of Bedouins. The desert wind tore viciously at Nicodemus's robe, and he covered his mouth with a flap of cloth from his turban. The night sky felt dangerous and the moon, low on the horizon, cast a deathly pall over the dunes. His camel seemed skittish, as if sensing a disturbance in the air. Nicodemus felt it too. A dark presence seemed to pursue him just beyond the periphery of his vision. The purpose of his visit was now all the more urgent. The day before, he had sensed the old seeress, Jezeera, calling him. The time of her death was approaching, and she needed to speak with him one last time. This was a dangerous time. It was not unusual for desert demons to rise from the earth to wrest the souls of the dying from their bodies, particularly one of such magickal power as Jezeera. It was the duty of Halimah to protect Jezeera in her time of transition, but she was young and inexperienced in dealing with the dark forces of nature. Worse, the demon trailing Nicodemus seemed unnaturally dark and virulent.

Nicodemus sensed the hand of the Clave at work here. This was no ordinary demon trailing him but *Ahl Alard*—a monstrous ogre, a supernatural from the depths. Only powerful magick could raise such a demon. It was obvious to Nicodemus that the Clave was tightening their grip, seeking to squash any form of magick, human or otherwise, from the earth. Why, however, were they interested in Jezeera, unless they sought to prevent the passing on of her power to Halimah?

He was halfway to the Bedouin encampment when Nicodemus felt his hackles rise. The demon was near and he whirled around to confront it.

"Ahl Alard, return to the pit, whence you came!" Nicodemus motioned with his hands, momentarily stopping the ogre in its pursuit. Though the demon was invisible to his eyes, the swirling sand and dust created an outline of a hideous monster. It stood twice the height of a man. It moved not on legs, but on the tail and carapace of a scorpion. Its torso and head, however, seemed to be formed of native rock. Jutting from its shoulders were four arms with fists clenched like mauls.

It laughed, its voice like gravel scraping against stone. "Do not impede me, wizard, or I shall be forced to destroy you. I must follow my master's wishes."

"Who is thy master, demon?"

The monster laughed again. "You are weak, old man. I will crush you."

The demon launched himself at Nicodemus, knocking him from his camel. In response, Nicodemus removed the talisman from around his neck and thrust it toward the demon's face. The monster shrank back from the powerful amulet. With a voice of command, Nicodemus shouted, "By the power of Azi Dahaka, Dark Dragon of Death, I command you to reveal thy master's name!"

The demon struggled against the compulsion but could not resist the command. Malice surged within the creature of the dark as if the words burned in his mouth. "He is the shoulder that supports the head of the serpent."

Nicodemus shouted triumphantly, "Altais!"

The demon shrieked in pain as the speaking of his master's name broke the summoning. The desert wind began to swirl, and a vortex rose from the ground, capturing and enveloping the hideous creature. Trapped, it railed against its bonds.

"Ahl Alard, return to the pit and to Altais, thy master!" Nicodemus shouted the command. With a great roar of frustration, the creature was dragged down into the sand by the raging vortex.

Nicodemus sighed with relief and mounted his camel. The reprieve bought him a little time, but he knew the creature would return. However, the summoning spell was broken and Ahl Alard released from his bonds would now return to his summoner, seeking to destroy Altais for having the audacity to raise it from its slumber. It would take Altais some time to bring the raging creature back under his control or be destroyed by it. But the implications were troubling indeed. The Clave's reach was growing even longer. Soon, Nicodemus may not be able to hide his whereabouts and that of his charges.

Now able to travel freely, Nicodemus was soon met at the perimeter of the Bedouin encampment by Habib, the chieftain.

"As salaamu alaykum." Habib offered the traditional greeting.

Nicodemus responded, "Wa alaykum as salaam."

The required formalities complete, Habib bowed. "Master Nicodemus, I've been expecting you. She told me you would come. Please follow me. Jezeera's time grows short."

Nicodemus allowed himself to be led to an airy tent lit by lamplight. The ancient woman was being tended to by a few women. She rested on the carpeted ground, reclining on a woven sleeping mat. One woman gently lifted Jezeera's back while the other propped her up with beautifully woven pillows.

Jezeera smiled as Nicodemus entered the tent. He looked down at her with pity as he kneeled by her side. She had grown frail since the last time they had spoken. Though unseeing, she grasped his hand.

"How are you, old friend?" Nicodemus asked with compassion.

"I've been better," she answered with a smile.

"There's still time, Jezeera. You can still accept the gift I offered you so many years ago."

"No, dear wizard. Immortality is not for me. You could not accept the gift I offered you, thus I can't accept yours." She trailed off and muttered, "Ah youth—so fleeting." She rallied, her strength waning. "No, I will pass my powers to Halimah."

Nicodemus remembered. Eighty years earlier, Jezeera had been young and beautiful. From across the continents, he had sensed her power rising. A mere girl, she had already mastered some of the mystical spells her grandmother had taught her, but quite suddenly, the old woman died without passing on her power. Nicodemus felt it was his responsibility to complete her training. The final aspect was to use necromancy to raise her grandmother's shade so she could impart her knowledge to Jezeera. But when Nicodemus sought to leave after Jezeera's transformation had been completed, she offered herself to him, vowing that she loved him. He loved her too, but he was bound by his quest. He needed to remain free.

He offered to keep Jezeera young by giving her the Lapis Occultus, but she refused.

"Still stubborn to a fault, Jezeera?"

She chuckled. "I used to be beautiful once. Do you remember? Now I am skin and bones—old and ugly."

"I remember," Nicodemus said gently. "I wish things had been different." His voice was thick with regret. "I could not marry you, not while there was the possibility that the Clave would learn of my existence. It would have endangered you. And you knew I awaited the Son of Luminance."

"I would have made a good wife."

"Indeed, Jezeera." Nicodemus' eyes welled with tears.

"Do you weep for me, old friend?"

"I think I weep for myself. When you are gone, the world will become smaller."

"I will not truly be gone. I will be within Halimah. So tell me, Nicodemus—how is the Son of Luminance?"

"He waxes strong. Soon he will be equal to his task. I thank you for the gift you gave him. You kept it safe all those years, but you must have known it also prolonged your life. Giving the scale of Azi Dahaka to Azriel has taken your strength away."

"Scale or not, I could not prevent the inevitable. Now there is something I need you to do for me."

"And what would that be?"

Jezeera sighed. "I need your promise, old man."

"Looking to trap me again, Jezeera?"

She chuckled, then began to cough weakly. "Your promise!"

Nicodemus sighed in resignation. "You have my word."

"Good!" she said, smiling. "Here is what I ask. You must take Halimah with you and complete her training."

"Jezeera, you're a treacherous old hag."

She cackled. "I know."

"With all that's going on right now, how could you ask me such a thing? I have more responsibility than I can handle."

"She will be a blessing to you, Nicodemus. Besides, there's one more thing you don't know."

"Oh? And what would that be?"

"She's your granddaughter."

Nicodemus paled.

"Yes, dear one. I kept the birth of your daughter secret from you. I knew what it would cost you. Unfortunately, she died when Halimah was but a child, and I helped Habib raise her daughter. You see, Nicodemus, her four other siblings are her half-sisters from Habib's second wife."

"And this you kept secret from me?" Nicodemus struggled to control his temper. "How could you?"

"Please don't let our parting be in anger, Nicodemus."

His fury quickly melted into tears. "Don't you know I would have been here for you, had only told me?"

"Of course. That is why I never did. How could I have taken you from your work? It would have been selfish. Besides, you gave me a most precious gift—our daughter."

"What was her name?"

"Nawal." Jezeera smiled serenely. "Her name meant *'gift'*. Now Halimah will be my parting gift to you. You must protect her, my love. Her life is in terrible danger if she remains here. I have sensed it."

"And I have seen it." Nicodemus said. "I have sent it back to the pit, but it will return."

"Then we shouldn't delay this any longer. I feel Azi Dahaka calling to me." She turned her blind, unfocused eyes to her servant girl. "Please bring Halimah to me."

Once the girl left the tent, Jezeera reached for Nicodemus's hand. "Now, my old friend, I have already spoken to Habib. He knows you must take Halimah with you. It is the only way she can be protected."

"You have my promise."

"Then I am content."

Halimah let herself into the tent where Jezeera lay. A vision of beauty, she approached and knelt beside the old woman. Jezeera reached her hand up to touch the girl's face and noticed the moisture on her cheeks. She smiled sadly. "Ah, granddaughter, you knew this day would come."

"Too soon, Grandmother."

Jezeera chided her. "Too soon? Dear child, I have lived over a hundred years! I'm tired of life. It is time for me to pass my legacy to you."

"I know, but I will miss you."

"Ah, but I will be inside you. You can call upon me any time you wish." Jezeera said. "Put your fears to rest. Now take the talisman from around my neck. It will protect you."

The amulet that Jezeera wore was festooned with ancient mystical symbols and inscribed in Arabic. Halimah carefully slipped the chain from around her grandmother's neck and clasped it around her own neck.

"It is time, child. The demon will come against you. It will want my spirit. I have taught you what to do. Your grandfather is here to protect you. Trust him."

"Yes, Grandmother." Halimah now openly wept.

"Come close to me so I may breathe my last." Jezeera turned her face to Nicodemus. "Goodbye, my old friend." She smiled weakly. "Come, child, do as I ask."

Halimah bent low, her face close to Jezeera's. With a shuddering sigh, Jezeera released her breath into Halimah's mouth. The girl suddenly gasped and arched her back as Jezeera's knowledge coursed through her body. Her eyes were filled with awareness, the mysteries now opened to her as the next holy woman of her tribe.

She smiled sadly at Jezeera. "I release you, Grandmother."

"It is done," Jezeera whispered, then slowly closed her eyes, releasing her spirit to the stars.

A howl of rage echoed from across the desert. It rose in pitch to an ear-splitting keening that sent shivers through Halimah's body.

"It has returned," Nicodemus said gravely.

"I know what to do. We must meet it halfway, otherwise, it will destroy the oasis and my people." Halimah left Jezeera's tent and peered toward the south, where the spire of the Devil's Leap pierced the sky. "There!" she pointed to a speck in the distance. It approached with frightening speed, a whirlwind of sand surrounding it as the fell creature moved. Fearless, Halimah set out to confront the demon before it could harm her people.

"You must be careful, Granddaughter. It will seek to sting you with its tail. If stung, the venom will transform you into a demon. Ahl Alard will take you as his own and try to possess that which is within you."

"Do not fear for me. Grandmother has taught me well."

"It is powerful. Don't underestimate him."

"I am a desert creature, Grandfather. I will not be harmed."

"How can you be so sure? If you break his summoning, he will only return."

Halimah's dark eyes flashed with her resolve. "I do not intend to return him to the pit. I intend to kill him!" She removed a curved dagger from her sash and stood her ground. The amulet around her neck seemed to glow as the whirlwind containing the demon drew near.

Nicodemus stood by her side and scooped up a handful of sand, ready to hurl it at the offending monster. Quickly, he muttered an incantation into his clenched fist. "Reveal yourself, Ahl Alard, creature of the darkness!" He cast the sand at the creature, and it suddenly became visible, breaking the spell of concealment. It stood before Nicodemus and glared down at him. "My issue is not with you, wizard. It is with her." He pointed with his two left hands. "Give me what is mine, sorceress. Jezeera's soul belongs to me."

"You can't have her." Halimah stood firmly. "By what right do you make claim to Jezeera's soul, foul demon?"

"Her power derived from the darkness—from me, little fool."

"Liar!" she hissed. "My grandmother's power came from generations before, passed down from daughter to daughter. You are nothing more than a thief. Every time the power passes, you, or one like you has attempted to take it and has failed. This is the last time, demon. Go now or be killed!" Halimah's face darkened with fury.

Ahl Alard bellowed contemptuous laughter down on the girl. "You, a mere child, will destroy me? I see Jezeera failed to teach you wisdom."

"Enough of this! Either return to your master or be destroyed."

"Prepare for battle then. I shall consume you and the soul of your grandmother." The demon suddenly whirled around and struck out with his tail, nearly knocking Nicodemus to the ground while attempting to sting Halimah. Nicodemus, quickly drawing the power of the stars into himself produced a plasma sphere and hurled it at Ahl Alard. It struck true and blasted an arm from the monster. It howled with pain and rage. Acid blood seeped from its ravaged stump and spilled onto the sand. Acrid smoke rose from the ground, nearly choking the old wizard.

"Grandfather, stand back. This is not your fight!" Halimah ordered.

"To hell, it's not!" Nicodemus shot back.

"I'll not be having my grandfather killed on the first day I meet him!" she snarled.

The demon advanced again and whipped his tail overhead, nearly striking Halimah on the shoulder, but she lashed out with her blade, slicing at the stinger.

Nicodemus stared at her with wonder. From whom did she receive her training? No ordinary girl, Halimah was a dangerous weapon with all the honed skills of a killer.

Ahl Alard drew back and sized her up, his bearing not quite as confident as before, he feinted and lunged at Halimah, his remaining three hands extended and clawed with the full intent of tearing her limb from limb, but she suddenly erupted with power. When the flash subsided, Halimah was gone. In her place stood an impossibly huge meerkat. It hissed and snarled at the fiendish creature.

Nicodemus stared in shock. Not much surprised him, but this was extraordinary magick. The only reason he knew the meerkat was Halimah was that the creature still wore the talisman and gripped the blade in its clawed hand. He had never seen one so young so adept at shape-shifting. The demon from the pit advanced warily and struck out again with its tail, stinging the meerkat squarely on the hip. She whirled around and lunged. Her gaping jaws closed around the demon's throat. Clamping down with all her strength, Ahl Alard struggled against her weight and dropped to the ground, its tail whipping furiously as it tried to wrestle her away. But she bit viciously into its carapace, refusing to release her hold on its throat.

Nicodemus heard the crunch of bone as the meerkat crushed the demon's neck. With one final rending she tore its head clear off. The body twitched a few times and then remained still.

Another flash of light and Halimah returned to her true form. She sat by the dead creature and regarded it with disdain as she absently picked at her teeth. Nicodemus sat beside Halimah and smiled broadly with awe. "That was outstanding, granddaughter!"

She grinned back. "I told you. I am a desert creature."

"Indeed! But why a meerkat?"

She stared at him with a level gaze. "How old are you?"

"Hmm, about 10,000 years give or take."

"And in all that time, you never learned that meerkats are immune to scorpion venom?"

Nicodemus bellowed with laughter, delighted at Halimah's effrontery.

"Besides, grandfather, a meerkat will viciously fight to the death to protect its own ends."

"Granddaughter, I don't need protection. What you did was courageous and foolish. This monster could very well have killed you."

"But you would have intervened."

"True, but why refuse my help?"

"Every time the legacy is passed on to a new seeress, this foul demon has sought to wrest away the soul of the departed. I have trained for this since Grandmother discovered that I would receive her power."

"But who trained you?"

"Al Haddah. He is my uncle and the most highly regarded assassin of my tribe."

"Well that would explain your battle skills, but not your magick."

"True," Halimah smiled. "Most of it came from Jezeera, and then there was the traveler who came every year to instruct me. He would spend a few months with me, and then disappear. One time, about a year ago, he brought Azriel here to restore our water. I never let on that I knew him. Our meetings have always been in secret. It has always been the way of the sorceress to keep her sources hidden from the tribe."

"Does this traveler have a name?"

"I never knew his name. I only referred to him as master, but he was a foul little man with a strange sense of humor. He ate and drank like a pig, had rude manners and put me through hell!" Halimah smiled ruefully, yet Nicodemus sensed that Halimah held a deep affection for her mentor. He chuckled to himself.

"Do you know of this man?" Halimah asked sincerely.

"Something tells me, dear Granddaughter, that I do." Nicodemus thought about this for a while. It would seem Eltanin had furtively been doing his own manipulations. Halimah must have an important role to play in the celestial endgame to be staged in the near future.

Halimah stood and removed a vial from the pocket of her desert robe. She gathered the venom seeping from the demon's tail and sealed it with a cork. She might have need of it later.

"Shall we go, Grandfather?"

He nodded, and they headed back to the oasis and her father's tent. The Bedouin encampment was already in mourning as the body of Jezeera was being prepared for burial. In the desert, it was important that the dead be interred quickly to prevent the spread of disease. When Halimah entered the tent, the expression on Habib's face showed immediate relief.

"Ah, daughter, I feared for your life." He smiled, pleased that she was still alive.

"Ada, you know I prepared many months for this day. Jezeera taught me well."

"Alas, what you say is true."

"I believe I'll be well taken care of, Ada."

"But what of marriage, daughter? Soon you will be past the age of eligibility."

"My path has taken a new direction, Ada. Marriage is no longer a priority. However, it does not preclude love. It is still in my future."

"But what of your sisters? You are the eldest. It is against tradition for them to marry before you do."

"Then tradition will have to change, Ada."

"You were always one to travel against the wind." Habib sighed with a hint of humor. He turned to Nicodemus. "I never liked you, old man. Not that I blame you for what you didn't know, but Nawal deserved better. She never knew her father. Nevertheless, take good care of my daughter. If she is mistreated, I will hear of it."

Halimah's four sisters waited outside the tent. Habib opened the flap to let them in. Nicodemus hung back as they made their tearful goodbyes to their eldest sibling. She said firmly, "Now all of you behave yourselves and don't aggravate Father, at least not too much. You don't want to wither his pancreas!" She smiled slyly at Habib as he chuckled.

"It's time, Halimah. We must depart," Nicodemus said gently. He lifted two embroidered satchels containing Halimah's things and hefted one over his shoulder. He handed the other to Halimah. They exited the tent and headed outside the perimeter of the oasis amid goodbyes and the well-wishers of the tribe. When out of visual range of her people, Halimah finally asked, "You surely don't intend for me to cross the desert without a camel, do you?"

"Quit complaining. A little toil builds character," Nicodemus said.

Halimah belligerently tossed down her bag and stopped. She faced her grandfather with her arms crossed. "If you intend for me to plod along without protection, then perhaps I should turn *you* into a camel and ride you all the way!" Her eyes flashed dangerously.

Nicodemus chuckled at her petulance. "I have no intention of making you suffer, young lady." He removed the dream orb from his pocket and fixed an image into the sphere. "Now take up your pack, my ill-tempered granddaughter and follow my lead."

As instructed, she touched the orb and found herself at the gates of Castle Wylusung.

"A remarkable way to travel." Halimah commented as she shielded her eyes from the sun, looking up at the naturally formed spires that seemed to blend into the native rock.

"Hmm, cozy." She said tartly.

"Like it or not, Granddaughter, this is your home for the next few months."

She looked into the courtyard beyond the gate and noticed Azriel and a few others gathered around eating lunch, and chatting amiably. Her face lit up with happiness at seeing him. She strode up to the group and beamed at Azriel. Surprised, he rose to greet her.

"Halimah took his hands in hers. "Azriel, it is so good to see you! What are you doing here? I've missed you!"

"This is Castle Wylusung. It's Uncle Nicodemus' home."

Camille hung back a bit and examined the newcomer. Halimah was stunningly beautiful. Her dark hair cascaded down her back in thick curls, covered only by a thin veil. Above her dark eyes, a crown of golden bangles kept the veil in place. Her face was an exotic shade of golden brown with full lips and a small defined chin. She stared at Halimah and then glanced at Azriel, but kept her poise.

Azriel made introductions. "Halimah, these are my friends. This is Jasper, Albert, and Julia." They all nodded in greeting. "And this is Camille." She approached and purposely took Azriel's hand.

"Pleased," she said, though her tone was less than amiable. She strode off to the main hall, but not without shooting Azriel a sour look. He looked back at her somewhat perplexed by her behavior, and shrugged. Julia ran after Camille and caught up with her as she entered the great hall.

Halimah suddenly felt a nudge from behind. Whatever touched her was huge. Her eyes widened as she spun around. She was face to face with an absurd impossibility. The creature smiled in the fashion of dragons and bowed cordially.

"I'm so very pleased to meet you, Princess Halimah."

Azriel completed the introduction as Halimah backed away in fear. "Don't be afraid, Halimah, this is Magador. He's really quite harmless."

"Harmless, you say, cousin? Friendly, yes, but not harmless—at least to my enemies." He craned his neck, trying to scratch a troublesome spot. "Er, Princess would you mind? Molting is such a bother."

Halimah giggled and scratched Magador behind his crest while he writhed with pleasure.

Albert spoke up. "Halimah, I think you just made a friend for life."

She beamed at Albert, but then straightened as she sensed a powerful presence. She turned around to stare into a pair of gentle, ancient eyes. She lowered her gaze in humility.

"Ah, I've been expecting you, Seeress Halimah. We have some unfinished business, you and I."

"Do I know you, ancient one?"

"Only in legend. Your people know me as At-Tinnin. I am also known as Eltanin."

"Yet you seem as one familiar to me, my Lord."

"Aye, and it is well that ye should remember me, lass." He suddenly morphed into the troll she had known for years.

"Master!" she said. "Have you returned to torture me again?" She wrapped her arms around Pog in a familiar and somewhat undignified manner.

"Wait a minute." Azriel stared at them with wonder. "You know each other?"

"Well, of course. Master has been my teacher for years."

Azriel stared at Pog with barely concealed annoyance. "What other secrets do you hold, Pog?"

"Now, don't ye be lookin' at me like that, laddie. Yer not the only fish in the sea—or in the sand—fer that matter." He winked at Halimah, then transformed back to Eltanin.

"Well, my young apprentice, I can only assume that since you're here, you were successful in slaying the demon?"

"Yes, my lord. Your lessons in shapeshifting were useful and effective. I think I scared the devil out of Grandfather, though."

"Grandfather?" Azriel and Jasper said in unison, and stared at Nicodemus. He smiled at them sheepishly and shrugged, gesturing helplessly.

"This just gets better and better by the moment," Azriel sighed.

Eltanin chuckled and placed his hand on Halimah's shoulder. "Now perhaps, young lady, you should get settled in. I will speak at length with you later. Albert, would you mind showing Halimah to her room?"

"No problem," he said, a bit too enthusiastically.

"Oh, and Albert." Eltanin warned. "Mind your manners with the lady. Halimah is quite adept. She could easily turn you into something repulsive."

Albert glanced at the Arch Wizard and paled, then turned to Halimah, putting a bit more space between them. "Come on, there's a great room on the second floor next to my sister's." He picked up her bags and led the way.

"Well, that should keep Albert occupied for a while." Magador spoke with nonchalance. "Quite a lovely young lady, don't you think, cousin?"

"Yeah, I suppose. I wouldn't mention it in front of Camille, though. I have the distinct impression things are going to get interesting around here. I think she's jealous."

"Would you like me to talk to her?" Nicodemus said.

"No, I think you'll only make it worse. Best that Camille and Halimah just get to know each other. And I think it best that she doesn't know that Halimah asked me to marry her the last time we met."

Nicodemus chortled, "Yes, that would be wise, Azriel." He patted Magador on the flank. "How are your wings today, friend dragon?"

"Feeling stronger daily." He flapped his massive wings and flew to the top of the tower, then back again.

"Impressive, Magador. Why don't you meet Azriel up on the tower? I think he has a surprise for you."

"Are you sure he's ready, Uncle Nick?"

"Ready for what?" Magador asked.

"He can fly now, Azriel. Now's as good a time as any."

Azriel shrugged and headed into the main hall. He climbed the spiral stairs that led into the turreted tower. It was large enough to house Magador even when he eventually reached his full size.

Azriel grabbed a sack that rested by the door and climbed to the top, where Magador eagerly awaited.

"What do you have for me, cousin?"

Azriel smiled and upended the sack, pouring a pile of coal onto the stone floor. "There it is. Do you know what to do?"

"I think so," Magador said doubtfully.

"I'm no expert in dragon lore, but to my understanding, you have two stomachs: one is for food, the other for storing methane. You need to chew the coal, but make sure it goes into the right chamber. The coal will mix with the acids to create methane. You should know when your furnace is primed." Azriel said. "Now once you have enough, you must breathe it out and click the igniter at the base of your jaw. Just a little cough should do it. You got that?"

"Sounds easy enough."

"Oh, and one other thing. Make sure you aim outside the tower. I'm in no mood to get charbroiled today."

"Cousin, I would never harm you—at least not intentionally." Magador said, his feelings slightly bruised. He scooped up a few chunks and began to munch thoughtfully. "Hmm, not bad." He said with his mouth full. A few crumbs dribbled out the side of his lips. "Pardon me," Magador mumbled, embarrassed. He swallowed and took another mouthful.

"Er, Magador, perhaps you should slow down."

"I know what I'm doing!" Magador's voice took on an air of cockiness. He swallowed and took yet another mouthful. "I think I'm ready."

Magador reared back and craned his neck, ready to belch out a roaring flame. Nothing happened except a pathetic puff of black smoke. It smelled of sulfur.

"That was a good start. Try again," Azriel patted his flank with encouragement.

This time Magador belched with even greater enthusiasm, but the flame fizzled out and backfired. Magador swooned. "Um, cousin. I feel sick. Actually, I must correct myself, Azriel. I feel violently ill!"

Magador suddenly heaved up all the coal he had consumed into a sodden heap. The stone floor began to smoke as the acid hissed and ate into it.

"Oh dear! Nicodemus will be quite unhappy with me." Magador hung his head in shame.

Azriel patted Magador on the neck affectionately. "Aw, don't worry. Just try again—but not too much this time, okay?"

Magador smiled sheepishly and took only a single mouthful, crunching it into a fine powder, then swallowed noisily. He felt a rumbling in his stomach and belched involuntarily. In surprise, he produced a rather weak but respectable flame.

"That was awesome, Magador!" Azriel clapped. "Do it again!"

This time Magador reared back and produced a twelve-foot flame that shot out from the tower. Azriel, however, was standing a bit too close and the sleeve of his robe caught fire. He quickly tore it off and stomped out the flame.

"Sorry, cousin." Magador said contritely.

"It's all right. The next thing we need to do is work on your aim!"

Chapter 6

Over the next few days, the castle carried a faint strain beneath the usual chatter. Azriel noticed it at lunch.

Camille was already seated in the courtyard when he arrived, her tray neatly arranged, food barely touched. She wasn't sulking—just waiting.

"You're late," she said, calm but cool.

"Sorry," he replied. "I lost track of time."

"Let me guess," she said lightly, not looking up. "You were giving Halimah the grand tour again."

He hesitated. "She keeps getting turned around in this place. I was just showing her to the library."

Camille nodded once. "Of course."

Something about the way she said it made his stomach tighten.

"You could've started without me," he said.

"I didn't want to," she replied. "We said we'd meet."

He sat down. "It's not a big deal."

"No," she agreed. "It's not."

But the words carried weight.

They ate in silence for a moment.

Then she added, carefully, "You've been busy a lot lately."

"I've just been helping her get settled. So has Albert."

"I know." She kept her eyes on her plate. "You don't have to explain."

That stung more than if she'd yelled.

"Camille—"

"I'm not saying don't spend time with her," she said quickly. "Just... don't forget I'm here too."

Frustration, sharp and sudden, got the better of him. "Why do you keep acting like she's some kind of problem?" Azriel snapped. "You treat her like a disease. You've even been short with Julia just for talking to her."

Her head lifted at that.

"I'm not being cruel," she said quietly.

"No—you're just being jealous."

The word landed harder than he meant it to.

Camille's jaw tightened. "Maybe," she said. "Or maybe I just don't like watching you drop everything the second she calls your name."

Albert, who had been feeding Magador nearby, wandered over.

"Hey," he said, "she's pretty far from home. Halimah could use a few friends." Albert tossed another slab of meat to Magador.

"I'm not stopping you," Camille said coolly. "You seem to have volunteered for the job."

Albert frowned. "What's that supposed to mean?"

"It means you trail after her like a lovesick puppy. It's a little obvious."

"So what if I do?"

"So maybe don't act like I'm a villain for not doing the same."

"I didn't say you were—"

"You didn't have to."

Azriel rubbed his temples. "Can we not do this right now?"

"No," Albert said. "Because everyone keeps pretending nothing's wrong."

"Nothing is wrong," Camille shot back.

"Who are you kidding. You've been snapping at people since she got here!"

"I have not."

"You snapped at Julia yesterday!"

"That was different!"

"How?"

"It just was!"

"Stop it," Azriel said sharply. "Both of you."

Albert turned on him. "Don't talk to me like I'm the problem. You've been impossible lately too."

"What's that supposed to mean?"

"You vanish all day, show up late, act like everyone owes you something—"

"That's not fair."

"Neither is the mood you've been in!"

"Stay out of it," Camille snapped.

"You stay out of it," Albert fired back. "Every time Halimah walks by, you look like you swallowed a lemon."

That one landed. Azriel shoved Albert away from her.

Albert shoved back harder.

"Stop it!" Camille grabbed Albert's sleeve.

He jerked loose too fast and Camille stumbled.

Azriel saw it and swung.

The punch barely clipped Albert's shoulder.

Albert answered on instinct and caught Azriel square in the cheek.

"Hey—HEY!" Julia rushed in.

Jasper grabbed Azriel around the chest. While Julia pulled Albert away. "Stop it, both of you!" she hissed.

"Let go!"

"Back off!"

"Are you crazy—?"

Camille shoved Albert again.

Albert shoved Jasper by mistake.

Julia got knocked sideways.

Magador recoiled and leapt for the safety of the turret.

Now everyone was shouting at once.

"Stop it!"

"Get off him!"

"Quit shoving!"

"Watch it—!"

Hands grabbing. Feet slipping. Someone swore.

Someone swung.

It wasn't even clear who was fighting who anymore.

Then—

"ENOUGH!" Nicodemus's voice cracked across the courtyard like thunder. Everything froze.

Halimah stood beside Nicodemus.

At first no one noticed her.

Her hands were clenched so tightly her knuckles had gone white.

"I didn't ask for this," she said.

Her voice was steady—but only barely.

"I didn't come here to take anything from any of you."

She swallowed hard.

"I only wanted to be safe. That's all."

She was answered by guilty silence.

Her eyes shone, but she refused to let the tears fall.

"If my being here makes you hate each other..." Her voice faltered. "...then perhaps I shouldn't be."

She turned before anyone could answer and walked away too quickly—almost running.

Nicodemus's face flushed crimson with suppressed rage. When he spoke, his voice was low—far worse than a shout.

"Are you proud of yourselves?"

No one answered.

"She buried her grandmother three days ago," he said. "Three days... and this is what she walks into."

His gaze moved from one to the next.

"All she needed was kindness. Instead, you gave her this."

Silence pressed down on the courtyard.

"I expected better. From every one of you."

His jaw tightened. "I am ashamed."

The silence resounded through the courtyard. Nicodemus glared at all of them. "Now, get out of my sight."

They stood with their heads down not daring to look at each other.

"Now!" Nicodemus growled.

They all scrambled to get away, each finding shelter in their private rooms.

For the first time in a month, Castle Wylusung was quiet.

Azriel shut himself in the laboratory for the rest of the day, avoiding Camille even when she tapped gently on the door. In the kitchen, Maggie held a raw steak over Albert's blackened eye, haranguing him with a severe tongue-lashing for ever getting into a scuffle with his best friend.

Camille, searching for answers to her own behavior, locked herself in her bedroom and removed her scrying mirror from beneath the bed. In the darkened room, lit by a single candle, she focused her thoughts on the mirror, letting its images speak to her. It only took a few moments for the visions to reveal themselves in rapid succession.

The first was one with which she was very familiar—and dreaded. Camille saw herself struck down in the heat of magickal combat. She knew not whom she battled, only that in the end she would die. In the vision, Azriel knelt beside her, weeping with grief.

Before she had time to consider the portent, another image swam into view. It too was familiar—a dream she had once shared with Azriel. In a bountiful meadow surrounded by many well-wishers, they were married and then crowned as king and queen of Aralia. Their friends and family stood with them—Albert and Jasper, Julia, Maggie, Nicodemus and Abelene—they were all there. Oddly, Halimah stood closest to her side as her bridesmaid.

Camille frowned. Halimah, standing beside her? After today? It seemed improbable that Halimah would be there. It was more likely that the girl would never speak to Camille again after the way she had been treated.

The scene shifted yet again. Camille stood upon a peak overlooking an encampment of gaily decorated tents. Behind her, a white-crested dragon spread its wings in a protective stance. She sensed an intimacy between them—something natural and unspoken—as though the dragon loved her.

After that, the mirror went dark.

Camille wiped her eyes, frustrated. None of it fit.

Death. Marriage. A dragon.

How could all three be true?

If she was to die, how could the others come to pass? Would not the first preclude the rest? Camille wept, frustrated by her inability to comprehend what it all meant.

How she wished Abelene were there to answer her questions.

Instead, the room felt very small and very lonely.

Azriel climbed the spiral stairs leading up into the tower where Magador now liked to roost. Mortimer perched on top of the turret sleeping with his head tucked under his wing. He seemed to spend most of his time with Magador now, considering him the closest thing he had to kin.

"Magador, would you care for some company?"

The dragon yawned and stretched, shaking out his crimson-tipped wings. "Of course, cousin; I always have time for you."

Azriel sat down next to Magador and sighed heavily. He stared up into the night sky. The air was clear and the full moon shone down from a pristine star-encrusted expanse, bringing a strange sense of comfort.

"You seem troubled, cousin."

"Oh, you don't know the half of it."

"Actually, I do, Azriel. I heard everything." Magador shifted his wings and settled beside him. "Humans fascinate me. You are so clever, yet so poor at speaking what is in your hearts. You bury your fears, and then you are surprised when they grow teeth."

Azriel huffed a weak laugh. "Yeah, I suppose."

"This quarrel was not really about Halimah," Magador continued. "It was about silence. You left Camille alone with her thoughts for too long."

"My fault?" Azriel retorted.

"Of course. You knew she would worry. You know her nature better than anyone."

"It seems that's her problem, not mine."

Magador turned his great head slowly. "When you care for someone, their troubles become yours. That is the price of love, cousin."

Azriel stared at the stones. "I still don't understand."

"Jealousy is not complicated," Magador said. "It is fear. Fear of losing what one treasures most. Humans dress it up with pride and anger, but at its heart it is only that—fear."

He flexed one claw against the stone.

"A creature that feels threatened will lash out, even at shadows. Camille does not doubt you, not truly. She doubts herself. She looks at Halimah and sees someone stronger, braver... and wonders if she is enough."

"That's ridiculous," Azriel said. "I love Camille. You know that."

"I know," Magador replied gently. "But she cannot hear what you never say."

Silence settled between them.

"She needs reassurance, not logic. Warmth, not arguments. Speak plainly to her, Azriel. Humans forget their fears when they feel safe."

Azriel nodded slowly, the tension easing from his shoulders. "Magador... how did you get so wise for one so young?"

The dragon lifted his head, a low rumble of pride in his chest. "You misunderstand, cousin. Dragons do not become wise."

A faint curl of smoke escaped his nostrils.

"We are born so."

Azriel smiled. "Well... I'll take your advice. It's the most sensible thing I've heard all day."

It was late and most people in the castle were asleep, but Azriel had amends to make. He found Albert in the main hall reading a book of spells. He glanced at Albert's face and winced at the sight of his black eye. Azriel felt terrible for losing his temper. Albert glanced up and noted that he had landed a pretty good right hook based on the nasty bruise below Azriel's left cheek.

"This got out of hand, didn't it," Azriel scrunched his face with regret. "Hey, I'm sorry I lost my temper."

"Yeah, me too." Albert smiled ruefully.

"We're good then?"

"Yeah, we're good. But I think you need to find Camille. She's not talking to anyone. I tried to apologize for what I said to her, but she wouldn't answer. She just stays holed up in her room."

"She can be bad tempered and stubborn sometimes. She'll come around."

Their conflict now past, Azriel shook Albert's hand and headed off to the laboratory to retrieve the golden bracelet he had fashioned for Camille. He had not given it to her yet and now hoped that it would be a suitable peace offering. From there he headed up to the second floor and gently tapped on Camille's door.

"Go away," she said, her voice ragged with crying.

"Come on, Camille. Please, I just want to talk."

It took a few moments, but she finally opened the door. She stood before him, eyes red-rimmed with spent tears. Azriel felt terrible.

"Look, most of this was my fault. You know no one could come between us. I love you, Camille.

Camille's tears began anew. "But she's beautiful—and smart—and it's obvious she likes you…" She sniffed once, tried to speak, then finally wailed, "And she's a princess!"

"Camille, you're beautiful and smart too. Halimah's just a friend. I'm not going to be swayed by a pretty face. There's more between us than that. And besides, you haven't forgotten that you're my queen, have you?"

"No…" she sniffed.

"Don't you trust me? Should I be jealous if I see you talking to Albert or Jasper?"

"But that's different."

"How so?"

"They're just friends. I have no interest other than that."

Azriel stared at Camille with a wry expression so her own words would sink in.

After a few moments she clicked her tongue with exasperation and sighed. "You're right. I was wrong, too. And I've been really mean to Halimah. She didn't deserve it, nor did she give me any cause to be jealous." She slipped into Azriel's arms and leaned her head against his shoulder. Their lips met in a gentle kiss as Camille's eyes welled with remorse. She looked down at her feet, unable to meet his eyes.

"Here, I have something for you." Azriel reached into his pocket and removed the bracelet. He slipped it onto her wrist. "I made this for you."

Camille looked at the beautifully wrought piece of jewelry with wonder. The golden dragon's wings wrapped gently around her wrist and gleamed in the dim light.

"It's beautiful, Azriel."

"It will protect you. I've imbued it with magick to keep you safe."

She couldn't help but think of the third vision she had with her scrying mirror, the one in which a white dragon stood behind her in a protective stance. Camille wondered if there was any connection. It made the vision even more mysterious.

"Thank you, Azriel. I'll treasure it forever." She gave him a long lingering kiss. "I love you, Azriel. I won't forget that."

He stroked her glossy black hair and stared into her deep blue eyes.

"There's something I need to do before I go to bed." Camille said wistfully. "I'll see you in the morning."

Camille had to tap a few times on the door before Halimah finally answered.

"Enter." she said quietly.

Camille slipped into the room. Halimah sat by the open window, staring at the moon. She was stroking something on her lap absently, and two embroidered bags rested at her feet.

"You got what you wanted. I'm leaving tomorrow. Grandfather's taking me home." Halimah looked up at Camille. Her dark eyes were red-rimmed with tears.

"You can't leave—you mustn't." Camille's eyes brimmed over with remorse. "I was monstrous to you, and I'm so sorry. I—I was jealous of you."

"You have nothing to be jealous of. I knew his heart already belonged to someone long before I knew it was you."

"I don't understand." Camille wiped at her wet cheeks.

"I knew even before he did, before he would admit it to himself. You see, Camille, the first time I met Azriel, I threw myself at him—offered to marry him."

"Oh, you did?" Camille's voice took on a hard edge.

"You have nothing to worry about. He rejected my offer. That's when I knew he loved someone else—you, Camille. And tomorrow you will be free of me."

"No, you can't." Camille pleaded. "I don't know why, but it's important you stay. You're needed here, and much as I hate to admit it, I think Azriel needs you here, too."

Halimah looked up puzzled. Camille averted her eyes. "It's something I've seen in my scrying mirror, though it doesn't make sense."

"The mirror always tells the truth. My grandmother taught me that."

"Your grandmother may have been wrong." Camille looked down at Halimah's lap. "Good gods, what the hell is that!"

"It's called a glossy snake. He's very friendly." She gently stroked the colorfully patterned creature on the head as it hissed with contentment. "Now what have you seen in the mirror?"

"It's not easy to talk about."

"An uncomfortable truth never is."

"It's not just about what I saw, Halimah, it's that both visions can't possibly be true."

"Maybe you should tell me about it. I'm not bad at such things."

"I don't want to burden you, besides, Azriel doesn't know. It would break his heart, and he wouldn't complete what he has to do—to protect me."

Halimah frowned thoughtfully. "My grandmother taught me that the future is never set in stone, and what we think we know is never quite what the future truly is. Clarity usually comes after the fated event."

"Well that may be all well and good, but chances are that I won't be around to appreciate the clarity. I'm going to die, Halimah. I saw it in the mirror."

Halimah paled. "How?" she asked.

"I'm not sure how and when, all I know is it feels certain—and Azriel will be with me when it happens. Pog—Eltanin once told me that love is a powerful force, sometimes more powerful than Magick. In the end, Azriel will need me. There's a reason I must be there."

"So you've already consigned yourself to fate?" Halimah bristled. "You can change it, you know. You don't have to be a martyr."

"But there's more, Halimah. In another vision from the mirror and a shared dream I had with Azriel, I am being married to him. We are in a beautiful countryside overlooking a magnificent white castle. Then Azriel is being crowned as king, and I, as his wife, Queen of Aralia. Everyone I know was present—even you!"

"Me?"

"Yes, you were my maid of honor and stood by my side."

"Strange. Isn't that an honor reserved for best friends? You don't even like me." Halimah said blithely.

Camille glanced at her with a bruised expression. "I deserved that. I was awful to you!"

Halimah shrugged. "You were just defending your territory. I suppose I'd do the same." She smiled and steered the conversation back. "So your visions, what do you think they mean?"

"I don't know. One says I will die. The other says I will live to marry Azriel. They can't both be true."

"Why not?"

"Well Azriel certainly isn't going to marry a corpse, is he?"

"Gross!" Halimah muttered as Camille giggled in spite of her tears. "Maybe you're just mistaken."

"Not likely. It seemed like I was in magickal combat of some kind. I fell with a hole blasted through my chest."

"And the wedding? Could that be wishful thinking?"

"No," Camille mused. She quickly explained about the magickal place that she and Azriel had seen. Pog had called it a place in-between. There the sylph, Paralda, had told her that this was the future awaiting them, should they complete what was required of them. "So you see it appears there are two possible futures."

"No Camille, only one. The one you will choose, in fact, have already chosen. You've already decided that you will not shy away from your fate. You will die, yet somehow you won't, as little sense as that might make. You will also marry Azriel, as the mirror has shown, and I will be your lady in waiting."

"It still makes no sense."

"Does it have to? Would you have predicted two days ago that you and I would become friends?"

"Are we friends?" Camille asked sheepishly.

"Yes—if you want to be."

"Does that mean you're not leaving?"

Halimah smiled. "I guess not."

"Good. I'm happy you don't hate me for how I treated you. Albert will be pleased you're staying, too."

"Albert?"

Camille glanced at Halimah with a twinkle in her eyes. "I've known Albert long enough to tell when he's smitten. He generally is a thinker and hates conflict of any kind. Yet it came to blows between him and Azriel when I spouted off. He defended your honor." She sighed wistfully, "And Azriel defended mine."

They caught each other's eye and shook their heads.

"Boys," Halimah sighed. "We do bring out the best and worst in them, wouldn't you agree, Camille."

"Sadly, yes."

There were a few moments of silence before they both burst out in laughter.

Chapter 7

Typically, the Canyonlands offered a forbidding landscape and inhospitable weather—either unbearably hot in summer or frigid in winter—but as the days grew shorter and September gave way to October, Azriel found it pleasant to spend time in the courtyard of Castle Wylusung. Next to him, piled high on the stone bench, was a stack of old manuscripts containing dragon lore. To his left, the Book of Aralia lay open to a chapter on dragon physiology and the most effective ways of slaying the magickal beast. Azriel grimaced and closed the book. He found that segment particularly distasteful.

As he sifted through the piles of documents, Mortimer flew over to him, scattering the pages on the ground with the turbulence of his wings.

"Mortimer!" Azriel snapped. "Please be careful."

The gargoyle threw the book he was holding at Azriel with indignation and grumbled as he flew off.

"Wait, Mortimer!"

He flew back and hovered before Azriel with his arms crossed.

"Hey, I'm sorry. I didn't mean to get irritated with you." Azriel said.

His anger abated, Mortimer gathered up the scattered papers and stacked them back on the pile.

Azriel continued. "It's just that most of this information on dragons is useless or downright wrong. At this rate I'll never achieve the Lapis Occultus." He sighed. "I'm screwed."

Mortimer didn't hide his impatience. He snatched the book he had just delivered from Azriel's lap and held it inches from his face. It was titled, *The Atlantean Book of Magickal Creatures*, and a section had been bookmarked.

"Where did you get this, Mortimer?"

The creature shrugged noncommittally.

"Did Eltanin give it to you?"

The little gargoyle shook his head.

"Then it was from Nicodemus."

Mortimer hunched his back and spread his hands, trying his best to look innocent.

"Mortimer," Azriel said firmly. "Did you steal this from Uncle Nick's private library?"

The creature rocked from side to side with a sheepish grin.

"You're going to get me in so much trouble," Azriel sighed and opened the book to the dog-eared page. The chapter heading read: *Understanding the Relationship Between Dragons and Alchemy.*

Azriel glanced at Mortimer. "Actually, little friend, I take it all back. You're brilliant."

The creature bowed dramatically and flew off to find some scraps from the kitchen. Azriel began to read.

To understand *the dragon, one must also understand the alchemical disposition of the creature. By its very nature, a dragon is both physically and spiritually a fusion of all four elements. It is a given that all creatures, including men and dragons, are derived from the earth. And so it is also that the egg or the womb contains the waters of birth in which all life grows. And as all creatures need air to breathe, so does the dragon. It is air that also raises the dragon aloft. Yet it is the element of fire that truly defines the dragon, for no other creature can produce fire from the pit of its bowels. It is the unique gift that Pyrrhos bestowed upon the creature from the beginning, and it was this ability that allowed the dragon to combine the essence, or spirit of the four elements, to give it near immortality. It is also this gift—this quintessence— which is passed on to the dragon on the day of its hatching.*

It has been said that dragons receive their wisdom from their progenitors, but it is my opinion that dragons are the embodiment of wisdom through the perfect merging of the four elements within them. Thus it is from this wisdom that the science of Alchemy came to be. Therefore, in all endeavors, the wizard must seek to emulate the dragon before he can gain perfection.

Only one, in legend, is said to have achieved the perfection required to become a dragon, though it has never been proven or substantiated.

Hence, a wizard must keep his mind on higher things and meditate on the elements of life, experience them to the fullest, and allow the elements to manifest in his soul. In this way he will earn immortality.

Azriel gaped at the paragraph, nearly breathless. The answers were here before him. There on the page was the name of the Fire Elemental.

Pyrrhos.

Azriel dare not utter the name—not yet. Not until he was among the Order of the Ankh. Only then would he reveal the name. Azriel felt a surge of joy welling in his chest. Now he knew he was on the right track, and the Lapis Occultus was within his reach.

"Nicodemus is quite the scholar, wouldn't you say, cousin."

Azriel nearly jumped, startled by Magador's silent approach. The dragon apparently had been reading over his shoulder.

"Brilliant, actually."

"Yes, cousin. Mortimer found the book open to that page you just read. I think perhaps it was meant to be found." Magador mused.

"Then why didn't Nicodemus just give it to me without all the subterfuge?"

"Ah, but isn't joy found in the discovery, even if it requires a little burglary? When one searches diligently, shouldn't he use every resource available? Azriel, you're not alone in this. You have friends willing to help, and that is why I am here. The time grows short when you must face your enemies. You have yet to create the Lapis Occultus."

"I try, Magador, but it still eludes me." Azriel sighed with frustration.

"That's because you're not thinking like a dragon, cousin."

"Well, how do I do that?"

"I can't tell you. I must show you. Eltanin suggested that I should teach you to fly."

"That would seem impossible without wings, Magador."

"You must get your mind out of the physical and begin to think in the mystical. Mortals are blinded by the world they see. They cannot see through the many dimensions that exist side by side. Once you see them, you will know the secret to immortality and the Lapis Occultus."

Magador crouched lower to meet Azriel's eyes. "Now, if you would, cousin, climb on my back."

"Are you sure? I don't want to hurt you."

"Are you really that uninformed or maybe just being naïve? A dragon can bear ten times his weight!" Magador stated proudly. He lowered his shoulder to give Azriel access. "Now get on board."

Magador lifted Azriel onto his back. He flexed his golden wings a few times until Azriel was situated in the proper place. "Are you ready?" he asked.

"I guess so—whoa!"

In moments Magador was aloft and quickly caught a thermal draft that carried him high above the castle. Azriel's breath caught in his throat when he looked down and realized how high up they had climbed. Magador beat his wings harder to gain another thousand feet and then dropped into a dizzying descent while Azriel clung on for dear life. He swooped low to the ground and pounced on an unwary jackrabbit, swallowing it in one bite.

"Hmm, delicious," he said. Magador flew back up and leveled into a gentle flight. "Are you feeling more comfortable, Azriel?"

"I think I'm getting the hang of this!" Azriel laughed. When Magador banked to the left, Azriel didn't fight it, but shifted his weight, flowing with the turn.

Magador chuckled. "Yes cousin, I think you are! Now I would like to take it a step further. You must allow me into your mind. It's easy, really. It's just like when you speak to your mother telepathically. Once you join with me, you will be able to see through my eyes and everything will become clear to you."

"What will I see?"

"Everything!"

Azriel was nervous at first when he felt a prickling at the base of his skull. The powerful energy Magador released felt as though it would overwhelm Azriel's senses. He resisted.

"Don't be afraid, cousin." Magador said jovially. "I just want to open your eyes."

Magador caught another thermal and soared higher. The sun reflected off his gold and crimson scales nearly blinding Azriel, but the warmth of the sun felt good on his face. Azriel relaxed.

A sudden surge of energy washed over Azriel's body, and like crossing an unseen barrier, his vision suddenly altered. Colors swirled before his eyes, and he realized he was surrounded by a fleet of dragons flying alongside with Magador.

"Where am I?"

"You are here, cousin!" Magador laughed.

"But where is here?"

"Where you were in the first place!"

"I don't understand."

"You are seeing the world in the way it is seen by dragons, all the dimensions gathered into one. You see, Azriel, the dimension of mortals is a narrow place with diminished vision. The thought-forms of human and elf are powerful, yes, but though men and elves create with their minds, often they cannot see the outcome of what they put into motion. That is why humans are dangerous creatures—they lack mental discipline. When humans began doubting the stories of dragons, elves, the beasts of the earth and air, those creatures could no longer dwell in your dimension, so they moved on to the next. This is the realm of possibility."

"Well spoken, son!"

Maragog was suddenly flying alongside Magador.

"Good morning, Mother!" Magador laughed with joy.

Azriel looked to his right and noticed another magnificent dragon flying alongside. She wasn't quite as substantial as Magador, but her skin glowed bronze and silver-blue.

She smiled in the fashion of dragons. "Well then, I finally meet young Lord Azriel."

"Pleased to meet you, Madam Dragon!" Azriel replied cheerfully.

"Ah, a charmer, just like Nicodemus!"

As they soared even higher in tight formation, four glowing orbs of light appeared, two at each wing flanking Magador. As the light waned, Krinaea, queen of the dryads, and Paralda, queen of Sylphs, were at his left. To his right Maera, queen of the naiads beamed at Azriel. Next to her, however, was another faerie he had never met. She glowed with crimson and orange, her skin shining like a burnished brazier. She remained aloft on spiked wings, the ribbing between like alternating bands of copper and iron. As they fluttered, sparks and bolts of electricity emanated like a webbed network keeping her aloft. Brilliant red hair flickered behind her like flames of a torch.

Maera made introductions. "Azriel, this is my sister, Fieré. She is queen of the Drakes!" Maera switched positions with Fieré so the fire queen could speak with Azriel.

"Greetings, Master Azriel."

"Hello, Fieré. I'm glad to finally meet you. You have been most elusive."

Her pure laughter evoked memories of sitting around Amaryllis' open hearth with Abelene, Nicodemus and Felisa; as warm and cozy as a fire on a snow blanketed evening. She was the comfort of friends and family. Fieré responded. "No young master, you just took a long time to learn the name, yet you haven't spoken it. Why not?" She frowned and her wings shot out a shower of sparks.

"I must speak it before the Order of the Ankh to complete my task."

"That is well, but it must be done soon." Fieré smiled winningly and flew toward Magador. She alit, resting gently on his neck, facing Azriel. Like her elemental sisters, Fieré was beautiful and graceful, only half the height of a woman.

"As my sisters have done, I wish to present you with a gift. With it you will be able to summon me when you are in need." Fieré produced a perfect cube cut from flint, then a tiny rod of iron. She handed them to Azriel. "You need only strike the stone with the rod to produce the spark, and I will come to you." Fieré beamed a smile.

"Now I must be off to prepare."

"To prepare for what?" Azriel asked.

Fieré just laughed and flew off. She, with her elemental sisters, suddenly vanished.

"Remarkable!" Azriel stared at the empty air with wonder.

Magador laughed. "It is the way of Faeries. You never know where they might turn up." He gained speed, flapping harder, and remained aloft for what seemed a long while. Azriel noticed they were flying toward the craggy peak of a mountain. Finally Magador alit at the summit.

"There is something you need to see, cousin." Magador suddenly loosed a great roar and breathed a sizeable flame. "Now look, Azriel. See a marvel."

Faintly at first the rarefied air around him seemed to shimmer across the horizon. Then the outline of four images emerged, spanning the sky. They were locked wingtip to wingtip, the most magnificent dragons Azriel had ever seen. They surrounded him at the four cardinal directions, filling the sky with their splendor. Though virtually transparent, he could see their ghostly forms facing him. He felt the potential of their power pass through him like a blessing. Overwhelmed, he stared in awe at their magnificence.

"Magador, I don't understand. I thought the elemental dragons were imprisoned."

"True, cousin. Their physical forms are held captive, but that doesn't negate the laws of nature. The elementals still retain their power and exert their influence over the earth. The dark dragon of death is also imprisoned, yet people die every day, yes? Their magick has waned, bringing this world, and the world of Aralia to the brink of ruin. Now there is one more thing you need to see."

Magador faced west and Azriel's breath caught in his mouth. Beyond the blue transparency of the water elemental, a planet much like Earth filled the western sky.

"Is that Aralia?"

"Yes, cousin. In a little over a year, the dimension of Earth and that of Aralia will overlap and align. In that one moment, you must repair the fracture that Eltanin caused twenty thousand years ago. When that occurs, both worlds will become one again."

Azriel stared at the approaching planet. An enormous disc in the sky, it revealed rivers, lakes, oceans, and continents, and within the land masses, grand cities, but quite different from Earth. He pondered the enormity of what he had to do.

"It's quite dissimilar from Earth, Magador."

"Of course it is. The Ferrishyn took a different path than their human counterparts. They work *with* their planet. Humans seem to work *against* theirs."

Azriel pondered the implications. "Has anyone given thought to what such a merging will do to the Ferrishyn and humans? Has anyone even considered that merging the dimensions may not be such a good idea?"

Magador responded. "On the surface it seems like a bad idea, but what Ferrishyn and human alike fail to comprehend is that both worlds are dying. Magick must be restored by revitalizing both planets into one."

"Yeah, but have you considered that humans can't even get along with each other. How are they going to coexist with a new race of people?"

"To use a human expression, I guess we'll have to see how the chips fall."

"That's not very comforting."

"No. I suppose it's not." Magador shrugged and leapt from the craggy peak of the mountain. He folded his wings and plunged at a dizzying speed, then swooped just above the treetops. Exhilarated, Azriel emitted peals of laughter. This was what freedom felt like! Azriel had been sequestered in the castle so much that it felt like a wonderful release from his studies.

They flew for the remainder of the afternoon and approached Castle Wylusung as twilight blanketed the desert. Magador gently released their mental link, and Azriel's vision returned to normal. It had filled him with such elation that Azriel regretted severing the link.

"Yes, your sight does seem rather ordinary now, doesn't it, cousin."

"It's so limiting. It's like being blind."

"Of course. But now that you have experienced dragonsight, all you need do is remember the elation of flying with me. Keep those feelings within and you'll be able to evoke the dragonsight at will."

"Will it aid in producing the Lapis Occultus?"

"Without question, cousin."

Azriel couldn't hide his elation. "Then I am close?"

"Very!" Magador chuckled as he glided toward the castle. As Azriel looked down, he noticed activity in the courtyard. He saw flickers of torchlight scurrying, lining up at the gate. Magador didn't land in the courtyard as Azriel expected, but flapped his wings steadily and alit just beyond the gate where Eltanin waited.

Azriel slid down from Magador's back and faced the Arch Wizard. He felt a sudden chill. Something important was taking place. Magador nudged Azriel forward and spoke gently. "Go Azriel; go and embrace your destiny."

Outside the gate, Eltanin met Azriel halfway. He held his black-orbed staff imperiously with an air of command, and handed his grandson a light-gray robe.

"You must now wear the robe of the wizard and take up its office. As of today, all present here have been elevated in rank to adepts in sorcery. You, however, have been elevated to the office of Wizard Primus and now must take your place among the league of wizards."

Eltanin led Azriel to the open gate of Castle Wylusung. He noticed the path into the castle was lined on each side with members of the order by rank, from apprentice to adept and to master.

He was greeted with formal bows from Penelope, Daphne and Maggie on the left. To his right stood Billy, Muriel, and Mr. Parkins from the Isle of Man. Further along the column, Jasper, Albert, and Julia; opposite them, Halimah, Amaryllis, Felisa, and Camille. Azriel noticed in the courtyard that Kita and Hermes, now nearly full-grown, reclined near Magador and Mortimer. They seemed to be engaged in quiet conversation.

Upon entering the great hall, Azriel saw that a change had taken place. The massive room was now empty of all furniture save for one ornately carved table serving as an altar. The only light came from the hearth and from candelabras scattered throughout the stone-carved floor.

Lady Rosaluna waited by the altar with Nicodemus, and at the four corners of the table, the elemental faeries—Paralda, Maera, Krinaea and Fieré—hovered. The altar had been ceremonially set with Azriel's four magickal tools: his Athame, Pentagram, Wand, and Chalice. But central upon the altar lay the sword, Errin-lil.

Speaking for the faeries, Paralda blocked the altar and faced Azriel. "Son of Luminance," she began. "I greet thee in the name of all my kindred, the realm of Faeries. Hast thou completed thy task?"

"I have, Milady."

"Then proceed and embrace thy fate." She smiled and moved aside. Meanwhile, Eltanin took his place beside Lady Rosaluna and Nicodemus. The remaining members of the Order of the Ankh took positions behind Azriel and the sacred space. As this would be a high ceremony, Eltanin removed a silver sword from a scabbard belted around his waist. Bowing, he handed the sword to Lady Rosaluna, High Priestess of the Order. She began to scribe a circle around the altar, weaving a spell of protection to keep everyone safe from outside influence or from attacks by dark forces. The reach of the Clave was growing stronger, and one could not take enough precautions. As she scribed the circle clockwise from the head of the altar, there seemed to be a faint release of light from the tip of the blade. She alone remained inside the protective circle as she spoke the words of empowerment.

"I conjure thee, O circle of power that thou beest a meeting place of love, joy, and truth, a shield against all wickedness, a boundary between the worlds of men and the realms of the mighty ones, both holy and profane. I raise a rampart of protection that shall preserve and contain the power we shall raise within thee. Wherefore do I bless thee and consecrate thee in the name of all that is good and holy."

Using the sword, she scribed a gateway, admitting Eltanin and Nicodemus into the circle of protection. Azriel passed through, then the remaining Order into the sacred space. Lady Rosaluna then sealed the portal shut by scribing the doorway with the sword in the opposite direction from which she opened it. Solemnly, she handed the sword to Eltanin and bowed formally.

As one, Sylph, Dryad, Naiad and Drake faced the four cardinal directions. To the north, Paralda produced a censer that released a cloud of heady incense. She spoke the summoning words.

"Ye watchtowers of the north, Great Dragon, Lord of the Air, I dost summon thee. I call thee up, Anvindr, to bear witness to our rite and to guard this circle."

Next Krinaea facing south, magically released a spray of flowers from her hands, and, like her sister, summoned Lagina-Tierra, Great Dragon of Earth. In turn, Maera, facing west, produced a mist of water from her hands that washed over all present and summoned Salacia, Elemental Dragon of Water. Finally, to the east where the sun rises, Fieré lifted her arms, releasing two gentle flames from her cupped hands. She called upon the protection of the Fire Elemental Dragon over all assembled within the circle.

The summoning complete, Lady Rosaluna faced Azriel and spoke with authority. "Son of Luminance, produce the amulet."

He obeyed and removed the heavy chain and amulet from around his neck, placing it on the altar.

"You may now speak the name." Rosaluna smiled.

"Lady, before I speak the name, I'd like to ask a question," Azriel stated nervously.

"You may ask."

"It is true, I have learned the name, but I hesitate to speak it since I haven't yet created the Lapis Occultus."

"You haven't?"

"No, Milady. I learned it from a book that Mortimer… sort of borrowed from Nicodemus's study."

Azriel's uncle nonchalantly glanced up at the ceiling. He covered his mouth and coughed to keep a chuckle from escaping. Rosaluna turned and glared at Nicodemus for his obvious breach of magickal protocol.

"Thank you, my young lord Azriel, for your honesty." Rosaluna leveled her gaze at him. "But I must say that this development is indeed troubling. I must think on this for a moment."

Magador had been observing the proceedings from the courtyard and entered partway into the great hall, since his body no longer fit through the door.

Magador cleared his throat, and a wisp of sulfur escaped his lips. "Pardon my intrusion, Lady, but in his defense, Azriel now has all the knowledge he needs to accomplish creating the stone of immortality. To his credit, today Azriel learned dragonsight. He needs only to use it, and I'm certain he will succeed."

Rosaluna sighed heavily. "I see. Very well then. Azriel, speak the name."

There was a hush of anticipation, then Azriel called out with command.

"Pyrrhos!"

As expected, the fourth and final dragon on the amulet began to glow and transform. It reared up and loosed a roar of fire. With its roar it transmuted its color from inert purplish-grey to a brilliant red copper. With the final transformation, all four Dragons represented within the amulet shifted their positions, becoming interwoven with one another. The final merging created a rainbow burst of color, and each dragon produced a sound that became a brilliant musical fanfare, resonating throughout the chamber.

Azriel placed the glowing amulet around his neck.

"Now, young Master, take up Errin-lil, the sword of your inheritance!"

When Azriel lifted the sword from the altar, Errin-lil suddenly erupted with power, bathing the walls in garish light. Most shielded their eyes against the brilliance. Azriel held it aloft and noticed that the stone in the pommel, normally a blackened orb, now radiated the same rainbow of color that his amulet had displayed. The sword also imbued Azriel with the full knowledge of his ancestry. He now knew with certainty that he was destined to ascend the throne of Aralia.

With the euphoria that came with empowerment, Azriel placed the sword back on the altar. Upon releasing the sword, the brilliant light waned into quiescence. But as he turned to face Eltanin, the room suddenly grew cold. Emerging from the floor, a dark phantasm began to take shape. Though it lacked substance, it seemed to absorb all the light from the room, until the beast towered over Azriel. The ghostly dragon spread its wings and bowed cordially to Azriel.

"Well done, my brother!"

Azriel glared at the dragon. "Be gone! You are not welcome here."

"Oh, now don't be that way, brother. I just want to talk."

"We have nothing to talk about, Dark Dragon of Death."

"Of course we do. You cannot avoid your future." The dragon surveyed the room, searching each face until his eyes rested on Camille. She stared up at the Dark Lord with fear and awe. For a moment, however, the dragon's expression changed. If Azriel didn't know better, it seemed the dragon gazed at Camille with sadness and pity. Azriel stepped in front of Camille, shielding her from the dragon's scrutiny.

"What is it you want, Lord Dragon?"

"I want what you want, brother. Our time of meeting draws close. You must release me from my eon's long prison."

"It seems you can go anywhere you want. Why don't you just return to the abyss whence you came?" Azriel glowered.

"Alas, this is only my shade. I would return to my realm if I could, brother." The dragon sighed tragically.

"Stop calling me that. We are not brothers."

The dragon stared beyond Azriel and met Eltanin's eyes. He nodded cordially. "I greet you, Arch-Wizard Eltanin."

Eltanin nodded a greeting in return.

"I must ask you, Wizard, have you taught the boy nothing? Does he still not understand who he is? You opened the gateway that allowed my capture. We have a score to settle, you and I, and yet I have kept your presence secret from the Clave all these years."

Eltanin spoke with regret. "Lord Dragon, you know I raised you from the depths in order to save Aralia from destruction. It was not I who captured you."

"That is true ancient one, but it was your blindness, your shortsightedness, that led to this end. You never considered future events. You never determined the origin of the human race. That is your flaw." The dragon did not soften the blow of accusation. "You were a fool then, and you still remain a fool." He turned his attention back to Azriel.

"You now have the power to find me, even the power to destroy me. You will release me, brother."

"Don't count on it." Azriel grimaced.

"You offend me. I am telling you the truth. Our goals are the same!" The dragon smiled.

"Not likely."

"We are not foes, Azriel. My enemies are your enemies, are they not? We both seek to destroy the Clave. Does that not make us allies—friends? You need me, brother—and I need you."

"Then why don't you just tell me where you are?"

"I cannot. The prison that binds me also blinds me. The location is hidden from my sight, just like it has been for your mother, Abelene."

Azriel felt as though he had just been struck a blow. "What are you saying, Dark Lord?"

"Yes, Abelene is here with me, Azriel. In a sense, we are cellmates."

"If you harm her in any way, I will kill you!" Azriel raged.

"Oh, relax, brother. My prison prevents me, and I would do no harm to Abelene even if I could. The truth is," he shrugged, "I like her."

Azriel bristled with disgust.

"And I also protect her from Rastaban and the Clave in my own fashion. I protect her in the same way your mother shielded you from your father."

"You lie. She fled Aralia to escape the same fate as my father. She protected me from the mob that wanted to depose the throne. They killed my father, and they would have killed my mother as well. It's all in the book of Aralia."

"Is it now?" the dragon snickered. "Perhaps you need to read it again—but this time, remove the blinders. Use your dragonsight. It will open your eyes, brother."

"If all you're saying is true, then why didn't my mother tell me you are there with her?"

"Because I asked her not to. The time wasn't right for you to know. But now you do know, so the next move is yours, Azriel. Soon we will meet."

The Dragon of Death bowed formally and vanished in a wisp of smoke.

With the dragon's departure, light and warmth returned to the room. Lady Rosaluna looked nervously at Eltanin, then at all present. Fear had entered the circle. Camille stared pensively at her feet, thinking. She did not feel fear, only sadness. She had just stared into the face of her doom. What baffled Camille, however, was that when the dark dragon made eye contact with her, he seemed almost compassionate, even regretful in the role that he would have to play in her demise. Oddly, she didn't feel quite as afraid of the dark specter as perhaps she should. Others in the room were not as logical and had allowed fear to consume them. Muriel wept on Jasper's shoulder, but Halimah had instinctively drawn a blade she had secreted in her robe. She stood ready to defend.

Rosaluna held out her hands. "Peace, my friends. Do not allow your fears to cripple you! Have courage."

"Courage?" Jasper stammered. "How do you fight something like that?"

"You don't!" Eltanin interjected. "That creature is the immutable law of death. He cannot be slain, just like one could not destroy an elemental. The dark dragon is bound to the higher laws of nature."

"Then the whole thing is hopeless?" Azriel asked.

Eltanin shook his head. "No, son. The dark dragon is the least of your problems. The Clave is your true enemy. Fearing the Dragon of Death blinds you to the truth. He is held captive by the Clave. They have been feeding off his dark energy for millennia, using it to distort and control for the lust of power—power which

Rastaban covets beyond anything else. It is not enough that you must reunite the worlds, but it is all the more imperative to defeat the Clave." Eltanin spoke now to the entire order. "You all must understand that the Clave will do everything in their power to thwart the inevitable, will use every trick, every deception to keep Azriel from doing what he must. It is now time that the Order of the Ankh must rise to fulfill its purpose. That is, to battle the Clave with every magickal weapon at your disposal. You must be wary at all times. Test your senses; do not always trust what you see."

Eltanin spoke softly to drive the point home. "Keep this in mind. All of you, from the greatest to the smallest are vitally important to the Order. If Azriel fails to unite the worlds into one, magick will be lost for all time and both worlds will fade into chaos and ruin."

Lady Rosaluna looked up at Eltanin and he nodded. As required in closing the ritual, the high priestess thanked the watchtowers—the elemental dragons—for their presence and released the summoning. In closing, she banished the circle of protection, giving leave to all present. Azriel, however, stayed behind and scowled at Eltanin.

"We need to talk," he murmured.

"Indeed," The arch wizard spoke quietly. Eltanin performed a subtle motion with his fingers, and two sumptuous chairs appeared by the fire. He offered a seat to Azriel and pulled his closer so they could speak privately.

"You have questions?"

Azriel stared at him incredulously. "Are you kidding? I'm utterly confused! So far I've heard at least three different accounts of you raising the Elementals—one from the Book of Aralia, a different account from Nicodemus that you told him, and then an even more bizarre story told to me by Jezeera. That's the one of you battling the Dark Dragon and wounding him. Now the Dark Dragon has just implied that you summoned him. They can't all be true! So, grandfather, what is the truth?"

"Ah yes—the truth," he mused. "It's a bit complicated."

"Grandfather, please. No more deception. I need to know what happened. Did you summon the Dragon of Death?"

"Yes—and no."

"How can it be both?" Azriel grimaced.

"Azriel, you know the account written in the Book of Aralia."

"Yes, but it's all a lie."

"Not all of it." Eltanin sighed. "You see, Azriel, when I performed the ritual to raise the Dragon Elementals, I summoned Earth, Air, Fire, and Water. I was blind to the machinations of the Clave. I could not conceive of the fact that Rastaban, my closest friend, had a dark purpose in his heart and had planned to betray me. He knew that by summoning the elementals to one place, it would weaken the very firmament of Aralia and leave an opening to the abyss where the Dark Lord dwelt. He had been bound to the underworld for many eons and was happy enough to be where he was required to be. But, poor creature, the moment he was unfettered and came to the surface, the Clave immediately cast the most powerful binding spell upon him, thus enslaving him to their own purpose."

"It sounds like you feel sorry for the demon."

"I do—and he's not a demon. Azriel, he is not evil, as you wrongly believe. He serves a purpose vital to the existence of all life. Without death there can be no life, and vice versa. It is the perfect balance of the One, and the very heart of Alchemy."

"Is it true that you battled the Dark Lord?"

"Yes. And it almost killed me. The Dragon was furious to be so quickly captured after having been assigned to the abyss for so many eons. Being now controlled by the Clave, he rightly assumed that I was the head and was responsible for his sad demise. He attacked me and we fought. He could not kill me, nor could I vanquish him. I drew Errin-lil and struck a mighty blow at the heart of the beast. The scale over his heart was blasted away from him. If he had any chance of returning to his own realm, that hope was now shattered, because it had weakened him. The Clave tightened their grip on the Dark Lord and imprisoned him with the evilest spell known to wizardry, one forbidden to all wizards who follow the path of light. They created the *Carcer Eternis*, the prison from which there is no escape."

"I don't understand."

"The creation of such a prison distorts the laws of nature. Imprisoned there, one cannot die, nor can one live free; the most powerful wizard or sorceress could not escape it."

"Why not?"

"Because the creation of such a prison transcends time and space. If one were to, let us say, shift time to before the moment the Carcer Eternis was summoned, one would still find himself bound. If one were to move forward in time, even a million years into the future, that person would still be imprisoned. The Carcer Eternis has no beginning or end. It is a dimension all of its own, which is why the creation of it is forbidden. Even if one had committed a horrible crime, an eternity of punishment is inhumane. Better the criminal be killed and be done with it. The Dark Dragon is imprisoned in one of these abominations. Your mother is imprisoned in the other."

Azriel paled. "Yet the Dragon of Death has implied that I could free him."

"Yes."

"Is that all you're going to say?"

Eltanin chuckled softly. "There is one thing that can break the spell."

"And what would that be?"

"You."

"Me?" Azriel bristled. "Why me?"

"Because you are the rightful heir to Errin-lil."

"The sword belonged to you. Why can't you do it?"

"Because I have lost much of my power." Eltanin sighed heavily at that admission. "And I was only Errin-lil's caretaker. The sword was never created for me, but for you—the Son of Luminance."

"I don't get it. I thought you forged the sword."

"That's what the legend says, but it's not entirely accurate."

"Another deception, Grandfather?"

Eltanin smiled slightly. "It's not what you think, Azriel. It is true that I did indeed fashion the sword in all its detail. I inscribed the spell of power and protection on the blade. I forged the hilt and pommel. But even for all its beauty, it was as ordinary as any other sword. To complete it, I searched Aralia for the perfect, flawless stone for the pommel to empower it, but my search was fruitless. I journeyed for days until I climbed Mount Shenach in hopes of finding an answer. There I meditated and fasted for days until I was weak and at the end of my endurance. Then a most remarkable thing happened.

"Resting my back against a tree, tired, hungry, and bitterly cold, I was prepared to die up there at the peak of Mount Shenach, when from out of nowhere a young boy-child appeared before me. Radiant, he shone like the sun."

"I asked him through my delirium, 'Who are you?' and he answered me."

"I am the one who is yet to be." He smiled, sat down and started playing in the snow.

"Child," I asked, "do you not fear death? This mountain will surely take you."

"No." he said and laughed. "I will not die, and neither will you. I bring a message and a boon!"

"A message from whom?" I asked. Intrigued, I suddenly felt stronger, as if in the child's presence, life and warmth had returned to my body.

"the child then said, 'The Lords of Earth, Fire, Air, and Water have observed you and are pleased. They know you have created the sword to protect your people, for already you have sensed a darkness growing in the land.' The child answered solemnly. As the boy spoke, he fashioned a perfect, tiny ball from the snow and cupped it in his hands. Gently blowing on it, the ball of ice transformed before my eyes into a perfect black crystal.

"'This is a gift from my brothers and sisters. They, the great dragon rulers of earth and sky, of starfire and oceans have entrusted this power to you.' The boy then ordered me to give him my sword. I handed it over to him and he carefully placed the stone into the pommel. It immediately erupted with power.

"The child beamed a smile at me and then said, 'I shall name the sword Errin-lil, but alas, Eltanin, it is not for you.'

"I didn't understand, and asked the boy to explain. He replied, 'You are to keep it safe and use it with wisdom, but it will pass from your hands to one of your bloodline. Each generation must also keep it safe to be handed down father to son, and thereafter, father to son, until it finally rests in the hands of its true master.'

"And who would that be?" I inquired.

"'The One who is yet to be!' the child giggled impishly and said, 'You, Eltanin, shall hereafter be known as the most powerful of wizards and are hereby granted the title of Arch Wizard.' He then removed a staff from beneath the snow and presented it to me." Eltanin motioned with his head to the staff he held in his left hand.

"So this mystery child gave you the stone and this staff?" Azriel rubbed his chin, trying to absorb it all.

"Yes, Azriel, but there's more. The child then touched me on the forehead and released a small amount of his power. It nearly bowled me over. He laughed, thinking it exceedingly amusing."

"What was that?" I inquired.

"'It is the prophecy—all the knowledge you will need that, in time, will reveal itself.'

"The luminous boy arose to leave, but I stopped him. Overwhelmed, I asked him again, 'Who are you?' and, like before, he answered, 'I am the one who is yet to be!'

"With that, he spread his arms and suddenly transformed before my eyes into a small, brilliantly white dragon. He smiled again. Laughing, he flew off into the sky. As I watched, he faded from view and disappeared."

Azriel stared wide-eyed at Eltanin, breathless. "That's quite a story, Grandfather."

"Yes, and you are now the only one who has ever heard it. You must keep it secret. No one must ever know from where Errin-lil gets its power."

"Why not?" Azriel queried.

"It is the one weapon that can break through the Carcer Eternis. It is the one thing that can destroy the foul plans of the Clave, and it is that which will reunite the worlds."

"But why me?"

"Because it was preordained by the one who is yet to be."

Azriel rubbed his temples. All these convolutions, deceptions within deceptions, made his head hurt.

"Grandfather?"

"Yes Azriel."

"Let's just say that I am successful in finding the Clave's lair, and, in doing so, release the Dragon of Death, as he has insisted I will. What will happen?"

Eltanin mused. He thought for a while, searching for an answer. This was difficult, for it would add an additional burden to Azriel's already troubled shoulders.

"The first thing the Dark Dragon will do is utterly destroy Rastaban. His rage will be all-consuming for the indignity he has suffered at the hands of the Clave."

"And what else, Grandfather? What are you not telling me?"

Eltanin sighed. "The next thing the Lord Dragon will do, in all likelihood, will be to destroy me."

"Then he must remain where he is. I will not release him."

"That would be your choice to make," Eltanin said gravely.

"Grandfather, it seems to be the only choice. I will not lose you."

Chapter 8

The hour was late, and Azriel enjoyed the quiet of the castle. Alone in the laboratory, he had time to think and sort out all the events of the day. A single candle illuminated the room; its golden light lost in the vaulted ceiling above. Only one window allowed additional light from the full moon, casting ghostly shadows through the open shutters.

Azriel stared at the crucible containing molten gold. It had been purified in the furnace seven times. As he watched it liquefy, he thought of the previous day—a day filled with unfettered joy on the back of Magador—and the culmination of finally awakening his amulet and Errin-lil, Lightbringer, the sword of power. But as all joy has its equal and opposite counterpart, Azriel sat in the misery of despair, for the destruction of Rastaban and the Clave could also spell doom for Eltanin. It was now in his power to rescue his mother and release the Dark Dragon of Death—and ultimately it was his choice to make. But to do so would consign the Order of the Ankh, indeed the whole world, to a path Azriel did not care to tread upon. No, he would have to find another way to defeat Rastaban and the Clave.

It seemed a problem too big for Azriel. His shoulders could only bear so much.

"Why does the fate of both worlds have to lie with me? Why?" Azriel whispered to the night.

"Because you are the destined one from the very beginning, that's why!"

Surprised, Azriel spun around, not expecting an answer to his rhetorical question. "Oh, hello Magador."

The dragon clung to the outer wall of the castle and had his head through the open window. "You're up late," he said.

"I have much to think about." Azriel scowled.

"Don't think so hard, cousin. Sometimes it's better to let events unfold as they will. You have power, yes, but that doesn't necessarily mean you have control over what will be. The currents of time and space are convoluted and complicated."

"But what if…"

"There are no what-ifs, Azriel, only what is!" Magador chuckled at his own wordplay.

"You complicate matters."

"No, cousin, I am only clarifying matters for you. Time and space exist; past and present are reality, and the future only exists as probability. In fact, it is all One. The present and future are only determined by what choices you make. That is what defines reality."

"It seems I don't have much choice in anything. If I try to defeat Rastaban and the Clave on my own, I could fail. If I release the Dark Lord, he can destroy the Clave, but Eltanin could die as well."

"Yet it is still a choice," Magador said gravely. "You do have an advantage, Azriel. You have the dragonsight. In fact, that's why I am here right now."

"Oh?" he replied casually.

"What I'd like you to do right now is clear your mind of all your burdens and sorrows. Remember yesterday morning when we flew together?"

Azriel smiled. "It was wonderful, Magador."

"Now try to recapture the bliss you felt when seeing the universe as it truly is, and you will find the answer to the Lapis Occultus—the stone of immortality."

Azriel thought for a moment, then spread his arms. As he did, he remembered the many layers of dimensions overlapping each other, yet they seemed to be bound together. His vision cleared, and he saw them again. But what was the binding force that kept it all together?

"Good, Azriel! Very good!" Magador said with encouragement. "What do you see?"

"Everything!" The surge of joy filled him again to overflowing as he felt the ebb and flow of life's currents passing in and through him. He looked at his hands and noticed they had taken on a soft glow. More so, everything he saw had the same nearly transparent emanation—an aura of light. Azriel marveled.

Magador laughed. "You see it, don't you?"

"I'm not sure, but I see something, like a glowing mist surrounding everything."

"And what do you suppose that is, Azriel?"

"I don't know."

"Think, cousin, think! What is everything made from?"

"All matter is made from a combination of all or part of the four elements: Earth, Fire, Water, and Air."

"And what would you get if you had the perfect melding of the four?"

Azriel thought for a while and then his expression brightened as he knew the answer. "You would get the Quintessence—the fifth element."

"And what is the fifth element?"

Azriel peered at the glowing energy around him. "It is the purest element there is—the very life-force of the universe itself—the very glue that keeps it all together!"

Azriel's heart suddenly swelled with understanding. Everything in the universe was connected by the common thread of life-energy. From the subatomic particle to the supergiant star, matter was interconnected by this cosmic glue called life-force.

"I understand." Azriel nodded.

"Not fully, cousin. There's one more thing. What creates matter?"

Azriel scowled as he thought long and hard but seemed to be missing some vital piece of knowledge.

"Cousin, go back to your first lesson in Alchemy. From where does One proceed?"

"From Zero!" he answered correctly.

"And is Zero nothing?"

"No. It is pure potential."

"And what is that potential?"

"Anything you can conceive of in your thoughts."

Azriel's breath caught in his throat. The answer was before him.

"So what is *thought*?" Magador continued.

"It is potential turned to energy, which can take any form!"

"And there you have your answer, Azriel." Magador said proudly.

In awe, Azriel stared at the crucible containing the refined gold, then considered the glowing life-force surrounding him. With a sudden leap of intuition, he conceived of the life-force as a tangible form, shaping a part of it into a glowing sphere. When it formed before his eyes, he willed the nearly transparent mass to pour itself into the crucible of gold. Eyes wide, he watched the gold transform. First it exploded into light separating into the prismatic colors he had once witnessed before. They painted the walls of the laboratory with radiant luminescence. But then the beams coalesced back into pure light, and the gold began to change. It no longer appeared as a solid, but more as a white, powdery liquid, nearly translucent, finally transmuting into a soft, brittle stone. In the aftermath, a subtle glow remained on the altered gold. But the transformation was not merely localized in the Lapis Occultus, but had also annealed a change in Azriel. He felt an electric charge pulsing through his body, changing him, infusing him with secret knowledge. He finally understood power and wisdom.

Azriel released the dragonsight, and his vision diminished, yet the subtle glow still remained on the Lapis Occultus and upon his own flesh.

When the light waned, he was also surprised to see Eltanin and Nicodemus standing before him. Eltanin clapped softly. "Bravo, Azriel. Well done!"

Nicodemus also nodded respectfully. "You are now master of your own destiny. What you decide, what you create, is binding and forever." Nicodemus turned to Magador. "And thank you, Master Dragon. Your help was invaluable."

Magador chuckled. "Hmm, flattery. Maragog warned me about you."

Azriel looked at his hands and turned them this way and that. They still glowed with the power of the Lapis Occultus. "Uncle Nick, will this fade? I don't want to freak out all my friends."

"Don't worry, Azriel. They can't see it. Only we can."

"Why is that?"

"Because we're immortal."

"Yeah, but I didn't ingest any of it."

"You didn't need to; at least you won't need to for some time. In creating the Stone of Immortality, you were also transformed. Only one who is immortal can recognize a brother—or an enemy."

"You mean Rastaban?"

"Yes. Let's just say that you would not be invisible in a crowd."

"Perfect," Azriel muttered. He removed the small golden chest from his pocket and carefully poured the Lapis Occultus from the crucible into the container. He then sealed the lid shut.

Eltanin spoke. "Now that you have created the stone, there is one rule you must always obey. The Lapis Occultus is not to be given to one who has not earned it. I endowed someone thousands of years ago—a mistake for which I have paid," he said regrettably.

"But who is truly worthy? That's kind of a grey area, isn't it?" Azriel challenged.

"Nicodemus answered gravely. "That decision must always be approached with wisdom. You must learn to see all possible future results of your making another being immortal. I've only given the Lapis Occultus to one other person."

"Amaryllis, right?"

"Yes."

"Why?"

"Because she was necessary. I needed her."

"Is that the only reason?" Azriel asked suspiciously.

"It was reason enough. For now, that answer must suffice."

After breakfast, Azriel took Camille's hand and decided to take a walk outside the castle walls. By now, most of the guests had departed for their homes. Aunt Pen and Daffie returned to Ireland. Billy, Muriel, Rosemary, and Mr. Parkins returned to the Isle of Man, all by way of Nicodemus's dream orb.

The early hours in the desert were chilly but swiftly warmed as the sun rose higher. Azriel and Camille were not too far from the main gate when Kita and Hermes strode up beside them.

"I must return to the forest," Kita said. "There has been some prowling around your house and I need to investigate. We also need to hunt. I'm not too particularly fond of lizard." She chuckled.

"What's going on there?" Azriel stopped, suddenly nervous.

"Nobody has broken into your home, Azriel, but it seems as though someone keeps walking your property. Whoever it is, lingers there for some time and then leaves. I can smell it."

"Do you have any idea who it might be?" Camille asked.

"No, but it's certainly human. I don't feel any magick," Kita replied.

"And something else," Hermes interjected. "Once, I thought I heard crying. When I went to investigate, the person was already gone."

"Interesting," Azriel mused. "Please keep an eye on my home. Arrange it with Nicodemus to return in a week."

Kita and Hermes both rubbed their heads affectionately against Azriel and Camille, then abruptly turned and returned to the castle gate where Nicodemus waited.

Azriel and Camille continued to walk. The canyon was surrounded by lofty spires towering over their heads, the sun casting a ruddy golden glow over the peaks. Azriel strode on in silence, lost in thought. It wasn't, however, an uncomfortable silence. He was oddly at peace, and Camille smiled, enjoying his company. As of yet, Azriel had not told anybody that he had succeeded in creating the Lapis Occultus, but Camille suspected something had changed. It wasn't just the empowering of Azriel's amulet and the awakening of Errin-lil. Instinctively, she knew that something important had transpired.

"You seem different today, Azriel." she probed.

"Do I?"

"Yes. You seem more confident, more at ease with yourself. What changed?"

Azriel didn't answer. Instead, he asked, "Camille, have you ever given any thought to what it would be like to be immortal?"

She stopped in her tracks and stared at Azriel. A slight grin came to her face in realization. "You did it, didn't you!"

"Yeah, I did. I transformed gold into the Stone of Immortality. But what I didn't know was that the sheer act of creating it also changed me."

"That's wonderful, Azriel!" Camille beamed.

"Is it?" he quickly replied. Camille's smile faltered.

"Think about it. I will remain young while everyone I love and care for will eventually grow old and die."

"Couldn't you just give…"

Azriel cut her off. "No. There is a law surrounding the Lapis Occultus. Eltanin told me that giving immortality to others is forbidden unless they have earned it."

"What does that mean?"

"I haven't a clue." Azriel sighed. "Camille, I love you. I don't want to be immortal. I've always figured that you and I would someday get married, have children, and grow old together. This changes everything. I don't want to stay young if you have to grow old without me."

Camille rested her head on Azriel's shoulder and wept silently. It wasn't just for the pain Azriel felt, but for the one thing that he didn't know. Camille would never have the opportunity to grow old, but she could not tell him. How could she?

"I know we'll figure it out, Azriel, regardless of the outcome. I do love you, and I will never willingly leave you—never."

Azriel cupped her face in his hands and wiped the tears from her cheeks. He did, however, get a strange sense of foreboding as if Camille was hiding something.

"What is it you're not telling me?"

"Nothing. I'm fine," She said sadly and smiled. "I'm just being girly and sentimental. I don't want to think about being without you."

"Me neither," Azriel assured.

Charlie slumbered in his prison. Next to him, in an identical containment, Abelene sat in a comfortable chair and amused herself working on an intricate tapestry. She had designed it to reflect the prophecy that defined Azriel's life. She drew the images from memory and from portents she had seen in her scrying mirror. These, she projected into the rich cloth, burning the outlines onto its surface. A triptych, it depicted three scenes of the future. The first image was of Azriel leading the Order of the Ankh into battle against the Clave. On one side, Rastaban was combining his magickal powers with Altais, Giausur, Edasich, and Thuban. With them was a woman whom Abelene couldn't identify. In the clash, Azriel, protecting Camille, has Errin-lil raised to deflect the blast, and behind him are faces Abelene recognized. Jasper, Albert, Julia, and Maggie fought valiantly, Nicodemus was there as well, but oddly, Eltanin was missing from her vision. Something else didn't make sense, either, but she had to be true to her visions. The boy who had caused Azriel so much trouble, Eddie, was among them and seemed to be aligned with Azriel's side—very strange indeed.

The next panel also made little sense. In this image, the Dark Lord faced off with Azriel, his prison having been shattered. Rastaban lay trodden underfoot by Charlie. Azriel faces Rastaban with Errin-lil ablaze ready to strike him down.

The final depiction was, in Abelene's estimation, cryptic and undecipherable. Six dragons faced each other in a circle. They are the four elementals of Earth, Water, Air and Fire. With them are the Dark Dragon and a gleaming white dragon. But strangely, in her vision, directly in front of each dragon were six children with their hands locked in a circle, and from the center of the circle a beam of light pierces the sky. These images Abelene recorded with tiny needlepoint stitches in a fine tapestry. With each stitch, she poured her magick, empowering the arras like a talisman. She hummed quietly to herself when, suddenly, in the containment next to hers, Charlie bolted upright from his sleep. He scratched behind his crest and chuckled.

Abelene placed the cloth down and stood facing the dragon. "Charlie, what is it?" she smiled with amusement.

"Now this is quite remarkable!" Charlie responded in awe. "Amazing! Oh, this is wonderful indeed!"

"Well, are you going to keep me in the dark?" Abelene put her hands on her hips.

"Pardon me, Lady Abelene. I'm just astounded. It's your son!"

"Yes?" she answered, agitated.

"He's done it, Lady. He has created the Stone of Immortality. He has earned his dragon wings, so to speak."

"What do you mean, and how do you know all this?"

"What I mean, Lady Abelene, is that your son is now an immortal. Like me, he's become a god. I know this because of dragonsight, which, by the way, Azriel now has as well. You should be proud, Lady."

"I am," she smiled.

"It also means that soon he will release my brothers and sisters. Then he will release me!"

"Are you sure of that?"

"I have seen it—as you have. Do you think I don't know what is keeping you so occupied? It's beautiful, by the way. You seem to have captured my magnificence quite accurately!"

"Charlie! Is that conceit?" Abelene asked with a hint of disapproval.

"Not at all. A dragon by nature is magnificent, is it not?"

"I suppose..."

"Even better, I'm sure your artwork will irritate Rastaban to no end, which, of course, pleases me."

Abelene giggled.

Charlie was silent for a while then cleared his throat. "Er, lady Abelene, I do have a confession to make."

"What is it, Charlie?"

"Well," he hesitated, "As you've probably figured out by now, Azriel has awakened his Amulet and Sword."

"You seem to have taken quite an interest in Azriel's life."

"I can't help it, Lady. I find him fascinating. Well, anyway, I spoke to him through my shadow and told him."

"Told him what?" She didn't hide her agitation.

"I told him that you are here with me, wherever *here* is."

"But I thought you didn't want him to know."

"At first, I didn't, but now I am leading him here. I trust he will figure out how to find us."

Abelene suddenly felt afraid. "That might have been foolish, Charlie. He may not be ready to face the Clave."

"Perhaps. Of course, he threatened me. He said he would kill me if I harmed you in any way," Charlie said glibly. "But I tried to assure him we are on the same side!"

"Did he believe you?"

"Probably not." Charlie shrugged. "There's something else you should know."

"What is it, Charlie?"

"My brother's life becomes more imperiled by the moment. As he gains in power, the more visible he becomes to the Clave. They will seek every opportunity to destroy him to prevent him from fulfilling his destiny. They will come against him with what he loves most. That places you in danger, his friends, and that lovely girl who has captured his heart."

"I think I can take care of myself, Charlie."

"Of course, but the next time you speak with Azriel, you must warn him of the danger. He must be wary at all times."

Charlie suddenly perked up his ears. He growled, "They are coming."

An unmistakable squeal resounded from above, followed by footsteps leading downward to the cavern.

Rastaban led Altais, Giausur, Thuban, and Edasich before the massive prison of the Dragon Lord. Charlie smirked, goading Rastaban. "Your doom draws close, old man. This I have seen."

"Your arrogance amazes me, dragon. It is not I who has been imprisoned for twenty thousand years."

"As you have always maintained, Rastaban."

Abelene stood and watched the exchange with interest. She wondered what purpose Charlie had in antagonizing the wizard.

Charlie continued. "You seem to forget, Rastaban. I have lived since the beginning of time. In the scheme of things, twenty thousand years isn't that long to wait for my vengeance against you. Twenty thousand years is nothing compared to the eternity of torments I have prepared for you and your Clave. You imprison, enslave, torture, murder. All you have ever done is to bring misery to the world." Charlie laughed with derision, "An irony indeed that people throughout the ages have viewed me, the Angel of Death, as the great evil of the world when it is you, Rastaban; you're the quintessential demon in these matters. I bring peace to people who suffer. You are the cause of suffering."

"Etcetera, etcetera," Rastaban said, and shook his head with sarcasm.

Charlie observed the features of Altais, Thuban, Edasich, and Giausur. Fear was etched on their faces, particularly Altais's. The dragon laughed and spoke directly to Altais. "It is good that you're afraid, wizard. You bound yourself to the wrong master. There is still hope for you, but mark my words, time is running out for all of you."

It was Rastaban's turn to laugh. "Do you think you can cow us into submission? Do you think your words have any effect?"

"Hmm, yes," Charlie mused and sat on his haunches. His voice took on a more reasonable tone. "Rastaban, do you know that I can see every death, past, present, and future? Beware, wizard. Yours is imminent."

"Just words, I think. Enough of this empty rhetoric." He turned to Altais. "Brothers, it is time."

Rastaban faced Charlie's prison with Altais and Giausur on his right, and Thuban and Edasich on his left. Each held a staff in hand and began chanting in a guttural language Abelene had never heard. Their voices created a horrible dissonance that resounded through the chamber. Suddenly, Charlie began to bellow, roaring his agony. Abelene could see, with mounting alarm, that the Clave was draining Charlie of his life-force, stealing his energy. The great dragon writhed in anger and frustration at his own powerlessness, and his eyes reflected his hatred towards these wizards.

Abelene shouted in anger, "You monsters! Stop it! You're hurting him!" She cursed them, drawing on the most potent spell she could muster. But it merely glanced off the wall of her prison and fizzled out. "You bastards! Stop this!" Her tears welled at the abuse of her friend.

"The Clave finished recharging their life-force from the dragon. Charlie collapsed to the ground. Rastaban turned to the adjoining prison. Abelene noticed that years seemed to fall away from the wizards. Her eyes blazed with indignation.

"Do you object, Lady Abelene? Perhaps I should bend you to my will, as well."

"Then it is fortunate that the prison you create for me also prevents you from touching me."

"Yes, a pity. You are quite lovely, my lady." He smiled lasciviously as he glanced up and down at her body.

"You disgust me." Abelene spat. "Mark my words, Rastaban. Your cruelty shall be returned with cruelty. You know the magickal law of returns, and you ignore them. Such retribution is being gathered and mounting in the stars, waiting for the time when you will reap your reward."

"You are naïve, sorceress. I *am* the ultimate power. I bend the universe to my will."

"You're a fool, Abelene laughed lightly. "The loftier one's power, the more abysmal the plunge will be. Trust me in this, Wizard. If the Dragon Lord doesn't kill you when these bonds are broken, I will kill you myself!"

"Like you killed your husband, the King?" Rastaban countered.

Abelene paled.

Rastaban chuckled. "Yes, Lady. I do know of that tasty little detail. You plan and plot, and then you murder. We're not so different, are we?"

"That all depends on what side of the fence we're on," She said darkly.

"Lady Abelene, the ends don't always justify the means. You committed murder. And do you know the best part? Your son will soon find out!"

She gasped.

"Oh, yes, Lady. Azriel has produced the Lapis Occultus. He is now more visible to me. His dragonsight will open his eyes to the past and your crime will be exposed."

In anger and frustration, Abelene picked up a vase of flowers that rested on her table and hurled it at Rastaban. It shattered against the force field of the prison.

Laughing, Rastaban turned with the clave, following behind and exited the chamber.

Abelene collapsed to the floor and wept. From the adjoining cell, Charlie stood weakly and stared with pity at Abelene.

"I am sorry, Lady. Is there anything I can do?"

"If only you could, Charlie. If I had my way, I would see Rastaban cooked over a slow fire, boiled in oil, torn limb from limb!"

"Lady!" Charlie said with surprise. "You have a very fertile imagination and a dark side that I can appreciate, but trust me. The tortures I have set aside for our friend will be far worse."

Abelene sobbed. "Charlie. I don't know what to do. If Azriel finds out that I murdered his father, he will hate me!"

Charlie's voice became soothing. "Abelene, contrary to what Rastaban said, the ends *did* justify the means. What you did was necessary. I would never fault you for your actions. You saved yourself and your son."

"True, but Azriel will never understand."

"I think you're wrong. In time he will. You will just need to be patient. My brother is a bright young man, and in time he will know the truth. Not all dark deeds are evil. Sometimes they serve a higher purpose."

Exhausted, Charlie slumped down and sighed heavily.

"Are you injured?" Abelene asked as she wiped her eyes.

"Not permanently. I am immortal. My life force is everlasting. It will renew as it always does. The clave takes what is not theirs. Their punishment will be severe."

Abelene smiled ruefully. "Somehow, that brings me comfort." She paused, thinking. Something didn't correlate. "Charlie, why do they need your life-force? They have all created the Stone of Immortality. They shouldn't need your energy."

"Haven't you figured it out, Abelene? The answer is quite obvious."

"No, I don't understand."

Charlie, in spite of his exhaustion, chuckled. "The Lapis Occultus no longer restores their vitality."

"I still don't understand. Shouldn't the Stone of Immortality restore their years? I thought it was an absolute."

"Actually, it's rather a two-edged sword. Rastaban and the Clave have become so corrupted by their evil that they are like a bottomless chasm that can never be filled. The more they try to maintain their immortality, the greater the emptiness becomes. They hunger, but can never be sated."

"So what you're saying," Abelene reasoned, "Is that the Lapis Occultus can either be a blessing or a curse, depending on how it's used. If one lives in the light, being upstanding, true and unselfishly serving others, then it will grant immortality, but if one is corrupted by power, greed and control, it will only grant eternal emptiness, a living death of sorts."

"Yes, exactly." Charlie said wearily. "Now, if you don't mind, Milady, I need to sleep."

"You do that, Charlie. Rest now."

Chapter 9

Azriel was ready for the next phase of his task. With the awakening of his amulet and the empowering of Errin-lil, the stage was set to free the Dragon Elementals from their bondage and undo the damage done to the twin worlds—but where to begin? Azriel scratched his head thinking. He hadn't a clue to their whereabouts. Whatever held them had to be powerful indeed to keep the elementals captive. Yet something else was in the forefront of his thoughts.

His birthday had just passed. Nicodemus had thrown an elaborate party at Caer Wylusung. In Azriel's eyes, however, the celebration of his seventeenth birthday was flawed in two respects, though he kept his thoughts to himself. For one, Abelene was absent and unreachable, which left him feeling hollow, but worse, it now meant that Azriel had less than a year to release the Elementals, confront the Clave, rescue his mother, and finally restore the shattered worlds to one—a monumental undertaking.

So where to begin? Azriel perused Nicodemus' library for any information he could find on the Elementals. Perhaps, he thought, knowing in detail about their properties could unravel the clues as to what it would have taken to keep them captive. He had books precariously stacked on the desk in the study along with the Book of Aralia and readied himself for an evening of study. His only company was Mortimer, who was amusing himself by roasting walnuts over the open flames of the hearth and cracking them open with his teeth. This, Azriel began to find quite annoying as he tried to concentrate. The belching and farting didn't help either. Mortimer seemed to delight in it. After one particularly obnoxious belch, Azriel finally lost his temper. With little ceremony, he pushed Mortimer out into the hall amid the gargoyle's protests and slammed the door.

Sitting back at the desk, he opened several volumes and scanned the pages for any mention of Elemental Dragons. Page after page was written concerning their fundamental properties. Each one emphatically stated that the Elementals were the very definition of natural law. Each embodied the qualities of what they protected. So, for example, Salacia, Dragon Elemental of Water, maintained all that water provided to sustain life, the saltiness of oceans, the sweetness of the rivers, and the extremes of ice and vapor. Likewise, Lagina-Tierra also maintained the function of life-sustaining soil. The all-encompassing Earth spirit, she governed the mountains and all that anchored the world together. Equally, Pyrrhos and Anvindr had their place, to maintain Fire and Air. Yet, interestingly, though they all operated in light, they also worked in a strange juxtaposition with the unnamed dragon of darkness. Though each maintained orderly law within their elements, providing sustenance to all that encompassed the world, each element could be turned to chaos, wreaking destructive power to obliterate life and cause death. Yet, it was also the destructive path that shaped and renewed the world, allowing life to thrive and continue. To cite an example, Azriel read that a volcano can remain dormant for age upon age. But then Pyrrhos removes his constraint, and the mountain explodes, raining fire and ash down on the surrounding forest. The trees explode into flames. The pyroclastic cloud scorches and kills all life in its destructive path for miles on end. And though it might seem tragic, even cruel, to the observer, new life will always emerge from the cleansed and purified earth.

This thought gave Azriel pause. He had always thought of nature as dualistic, light and dark—good and evil. Certainly, there was true evil in the world brought about by the selfish desires of men. But perhaps nature was more of a fusion of opposites. What seems terrible at the time, like an erupting volcano or a torrential flood, in the end could yield positive results. This paradox led Azriel to the germ of an idea. Was it possible that, to keep an elemental captive, would require an equal but opposite force to contain it? This idea seemed to make the most logical sense.

Azriel sifted through the volumes of magickal lore, also examining the pile of ancient scrolls. As he pushed one aside, the stack of books tipped off the lip of the table and landed, scattered onto the floor. Azriel sighed and stopped to gather them up. The Book of Aralia had also tipped over and landed face up. It had opened to a troubling page. He was about to close it when he suddenly remembered something Abelene had once told him. There are no accidents, she had said. Always examine an incident with different eyes.

He arranged the stack of volumes back on the table and lifted the book of Aralia. Smoothing out the creased page, he began to read the passage. It was one in which he was familiar and had spent many an hour trying to understand.

The last few paragraphs written in the book explained, from a certain point of view, that Queen Abelene had been involved in a plot to depose King Berrill, Azriel's father. For her treason, she had been imprisoned in the East Tower. Then the writings stated that Berrill had been murdered, but it was unclear who had committed the act. From what Azriel had seen, it was likely that he had been murdered by his own men.

He stared down at the page and noticed the ever-present symbol of the mystical eye. This was the part that created the most confusion and aggravation for Azriel. It always projected the scene of Abelene's escape from Aralia to Earth. And as always, there were three minutes in which the vision was hidden from him. No spell penetrated the clandestine part. It was as though a vital piece of information was being purposely concealed from him. Azriel knew he had to somehow see past the veil.

He placed the crystal plate over the enigmatic symbol of the eye to let it play out the scene. As before, it displayed Lady Abelene's imprisonment in the tower. Her cousin, Elsinore, had fooled the guards into believing she was the chambermaid. As always, the guard would sift through the food to ensure nothing was hidden within. Knowing the routine, Elsinore had laced the food with a powerful poison that threw the guard into a fit. He collapsed and died. The other guard would have killed Elsinore for her treachery, but she was protected by a complement of soldiers loyal to the queen. The other guard collapsed with an arrow in his back.

Azriel was familiar now with Abelene's escape as Elsinore and Elrid, captain of the guard, led her to the throne room to gather up Errin-lil and the Book of Aralia. She also saved the Amulet that had been fashioned for her unborn child. But oddly, Abelene saw it fit to confront her husband, the king—in fact, sought him out. This was the troubling part that Azriel was never able to see past. As always, her meeting with Berrill grew dark, masked with shadowy static. And as expected, the scene shifted to Abelene's final, heart wrenching escape from Aralia to Earth, where Nicodemus and Eltanin awaited her arrival.

Azriel sighed with frustration and rubbed his chin, grumbling to himself. "How to see through the enigma—how?" He removed the dream orb from his robe and fiddled with it as he contemplated the problem. There didn't seem to be any spell that would break through the darkness. Then he remembered. He whispered to himself. "No accidents. You must see things with different eyes!" He could almost hear his mother's words resounding through his head. He thought, *Different eyes! Dragonsight!* Azriel spoke aloud with wonder. "Could it be that easy?"

He removed the crystal plate and placed it back on the scribe page, effectively resetting the vision back to the beginning. As he watched, he invoked the dragonsight.

It indeed created a difference in how the vision was viewed. It seemed more substantial, almost as if he wasn't merely an observer, but part of it, watching the events unfold. Again the incidents replayed as he remembered, but then he came to the part that had always been hidden from him. Abelene had escaped from the tower and sought out Berrill. When she strode down the corridor, Berrill hurriedly approached, pursued by a band of soldiers.

Abelene raised her hand, fingers clawed to cast a spell.

"Fiero!" she intoned, and the soldiers burst into flame, consuming them amid their desperate cries for help.

"My *Wife*!" Berrill exclaimed with surprise, though his eyes held a murderous rage.

"My *Husband*." She replied with uncharacteristic flint in her voice.

Here was the part that eluded Azriel. Again to his dismay, there was a gathering of dark clouds beginning to mask the exchange between Azriel's mother and father, but with a flash, it suddenly cleared away.

Abelene stood her ground. "I will not allow you to take my son!"

Berrill retorted. "His birth will usher in the end to Aralia. It cannot be permitted."

Another band of soldiers rounded the corner, and approached their King and Queen, but Abelene did not flinch, for they were loyal to her.

Berrill continued, "The child must be sacrificed, otherwise Aralia will come to ruin."

"You fool!" Abelene seethed, "Are you so blind to prophecy? Do you covet your power with such an iron grip that you fail to see that Aralia will be restored? The worlds will be brought together, and all that was torn asunder will be made right again!"

"That is one interpretation." Berrill replied, "Come, Abelene, let us reason together. Give me the child upon his birth and I will look past your treason." Berrill took Abelene by the shoulders. "I still love you, my wife."

"As I love you, my husband." She said quietly.

He took Abelene in his arms and kissed her. Not a desperate kiss, nor angry—tender and familiar—the kiss of two people who had once built a life together.

As the kiss lingered, Abelene stealthily removed a blade from her pocket and thrust it up into Berrill's chest. The steel flashed once in the torchlight. It slid below his sternum and pierced his heart.

He gasped—a small, stunned sound, more confusion than pain —as he collapsed onto the stone floor, looking up at Abelene with shock.

"You will never take my baby! Never!" She screamed, and wept her outrage as Berrill died in a pool of blood.

Azriel fell back into his chair, stunned, gasping for breath. This was the part that had remained hidden, and the only one who could have hidden it, he reasoned, was Abelene. She had deliberately masked the truth so he wouldn't know that she had murdered his father. She had committed regicide!

Azriel wept in the knowledge that his mother was a murderer. She had denied him his father, killing him in cold blood, killing him while they kissed! Azriel felt nauseous, bile rising in his throat, with the rage building up in his heart, a white-hot that seemed to sear his very breath, at his mother's dark deed. What kind of monster was she?

"How could she?" he shouted, "HOW COULD SHE!"

Azriel was so blinded by fury that he swept all the books and scrolls off the table along with the Book of Aralia, the crash of wood and parchment echoing through the study as though the room itself recoiled from the truth, as he wept his outrage.

There was a sudden pounding on Azriel's locked door. "Are you all right in there?" Nicodemus' voice was muffled behind the door.

"Leave me be!" Azriel raged at his uncle.

"Azriel, open the door this instant," Nicodemus said firmly.

"NO!" Azriel could not staunch his tears. He still held the dream orb in his hand and peered into it, implanting an image—the first one that came to mind, desperate and unfocused, anything that would take him away from that room and from the vision still burning behind his eyes.

Nicodemus' first instinct was to begin pounding on the door, trying to break it in. But the door was solidly built. He waved his hands with arcane sigils, and the lock began to crumble. The door blasted open just as Azriel vanished from the room.

Abelene closed the curtain around her bed and prepared to speak with Azriel. It had become their habit to communicate every few days to exchange information. She needed to explain to him her omission concerning Charlie. She initially had her reasons. Azriel certainly had enough on his plate without having to think about yet another detail. The issue was compounded by his lack of understanding concerning the Angel of Death. He still thought of it in terms of light and dark, good and evil. How could she explain to him that Charlie was not evil, but a defining force to sustain life, in essence, a divine paradox.

She now knew that Azriel had awakened his amulet as well as Errin-lil. His success in creating the Lapis Occultus also would now set him on the next phase of his purpose, to release the four Elementals from their captivity. Only then could he reunite the shattered worlds. But now there was a vital piece of information she needed to convey. The Clave no longer had the ability to maintain their immortality. They used Charlie to restore their strength and years. That tidbit could be useful.

Abelene cleared her mind and slowed her heartbeat to begin the process of connecting with Azriel's thoughts. Her spirit hovered in the *between* place of consciousness and sleep. She felt the link begin to form when it was suddenly severed, like a phone taken off the hook. Again she tried, sinking deeper into the trancelike state. Abelene touched Azriel's mind and began to address him when her link was violently disengaged and thrust away, like a door being slammed in her face. She gasped at the brutality of his refusal. With the severing, she also felt Azriel's anger and outrage. It was painfully clear that he would not allow her into his mind.

Dazed, she left her bed and collapsed into the brocaded chair by the reading table. Feeling as though she had been struck through the heart, she began to cry bitterly. Charlie was roused from his slumber by her weeping and stared at her with pity.

"It saddens me, Lady Abelene, that you cry so often lately."

"He knows, Charlie, he knows." She said in a panic.

"Of course he knows. It was only a matter of time."

"Azriel won't talk to me. He's shut me out!"

"Did you expect any other reaction?" Charlie asked glibly.

"You're not helping, Charlie," she shot back.

"Of course I am. You're just being immature!" he snickered.

"Immature?" she glowered at him. "That's not very nice."

"Nice?" Charlie laughed. "When has the word *nice* ever been used to describe me, Lady?"

"Charlie, I'm really beginning to get angry." She fumed.

"Good!" he purred. "You have gone from sad to mad. Don't you feel better?"

She hesitated and thought, then, she smirked. "Yes. I suppose I do."

"Abelene, all this is really your fault."

"Is it, now?" she simmered.

"Well of course it is. You really should have told him a long time ago. You were so afraid of conflict, so afraid of hurting your son, that you made it far worse. If Azriel had heard the truth from your lips instead of having to break through your concealing spell, he no doubt would have been angry with you, but you would have at least had the chance to explain yourself instead of trying to deceive him. Then he would have understood why you did what you did. Azriel's quite reasonable when presented with all the facts."

"But this has nothing to do with facts, Charlie. This is a matter of the heart. Now my son will only see me as a murderer."

"Be patient, Lady. Had you not acted, Azriel would have been killed. Any hope for the future would have been destroyed. I think you acted with instinct and with valor, Abelene."

"Why do you say that?"

"Because, Lady, you were protecting your son. Your actions were strictly animal instinct. In nature, a mother will face an adversary twice her size to protect her young. You know that."

"I know, but Azriel won't see it as such."

"Of course he will. Just give him time to cool down. He'll come around."

Nicodemus entered the room and glanced at the books and scrolls left in disarray on the floor, the result of Azriel's tantrum. One by one, he picked them up and placed them in a neat stack on the reading table. The Book of Aralia he carefully lifted before him and rubbed his beard with vexation. What had Azriel seen that caused such a reaction? Nicodemus had a suspicion, but needed to be sure. Clearing his thoughts, he placed his hand on the cracked leather of the massive tome and invoked a spell. "Reveal!" he intoned. The book opened of its own accord to the last page Azriel had viewed.

He sighed sadly. He didn't need to use the crystal plate to view what was recorded there. He already knew. This was unfortunate that Azriel should find out now—not so much for him finally knowing the truth, but for the timing. Nicodemus slumped in the chair and pondered the dilemma. Of all moments for the boy to vanish, this was the worst possible time.

Camille tapped on the door, searching for Azriel. She was surprised to find Nicodemus in the study.

"Uncle Nick, where's Azriel?"

"Sit down, Camille." She looked at him oddly as she took a seat.

"Azriel has run off."

"But why?"

"Because he couldn't face the truth."

Her voice took on a hard edge. "What truth, Uncle Nick?"

"Azriel discovered what was hidden in the book."

Camille became silent and introspective, wondering what could have set Azriel off. "Was it bad?" she asked quietly.

"Well, that would depend on your point of view." Nicodemus replied.

"Uncle Nick, please don't be so evasive. I'm a big girl. I can take it."

Nicodemus glanced at Camille with a hint of a smile. "Yes, of course you are. All right, I'll lay it out for you. I think it's time for a meeting." Nicodemus whistled sharply and within moments Mortimer flew into the room.

"Mortimer, I need you to round up everyone and bring them here."

Nicodemus strode to the corner of the room and removed a bottle of brandy from the cabinet and poured himself a drink. He downed half of it in one swallow before pouring another. Soon everyone began to file in and seated themselves. Jasper, Albert and Julia arrived together, then Halimah and Maggie.

Once they were settled, Nicodemus addressed them.

"I'll come straight to the point." He began. "Azriel has disappeared."

There was a stirring in the room and Nicodemus quieted them. "Not to worry. I'm sure he will be back once he reasons things out in his mind. Sometimes the truth is unsettling."

"Uncle Nick, what happened?" Julia asked.

"As you have been made aware, the Book of Aralia contains many secrets. Azriel finally unlocked what had been hidden. You've all seen Lady Abelene's escape from Aralia and also know that three minutes of the visual had been wiped from the record."

"What could be so bad that would send Azriel packing?" Jasper scowled.

Nicodemus sighed. "It had always been assumed by all of you, Azriel included, that King Berrill had been killed by his own men, but the truth is much darker. It was Abelene who thrust the knife into Berrill's heart."

They all gasped with shock. Camille was the first to speak. "And you knew this?"

"Of course I did."

"And yet you hid this from Azriel?"

"He wasn't ready to know yet."

"How could anyone be ready to learn something like that?" Jasper snapped. "It's awful!"

"Yeah, Abelene is so kind and gentle. Who would ever expect that she is a murderer?" Albert interjected.

"Don't be such an idiot, Albert," Julia snapped with annoyance.

"Idiot? Are you kidding me? Abelene's a killer!" Albert shot back.

"No she's not!" Halimah joined in the debate.

"How can you say that? You don't even know her." Jasper replied.

"I don't have to. You consider me a lady, right?"

"Well, yeah. I suppose."

"Hmm," she mused. "Yet none of you have considered that I could kill you within seconds and you wouldn't know what hit you. I've had training as an assassin."

"That still doesn't make you a killer until you actually do the deed!" Albert argued.

Surprisingly, Maggie spoke up. "You are all missing the point. As a mother, I wouldn't hesitate to kill anyone who would threaten my children regardless of the consequence. Abelene did the right thing. If she hadn't, Azriel quite possibly would have been murdered by his own father."

"Still doesn't make it right." Albert grumbled.

"Nor does it make it wrong." Nicodemus countered. "I haven't summoned you here, nor have I given you this information so that we can have a debate on morality. Azriel is angry and confused. His logic right now is conflicted with his heart. The truth often does that. Meanwhile there is one thing you can do."

They became silent, waiting for Nicodemus to continue.

"All of you must hone your skills even further, not only magickal, but physical. Sometimes magick is not enough. Often the unexpected thing will defeat your enemy. That is why I am asking you to put logic and morality aside and learn what can save you. I assure you, the Clave is rising and growing more powerful. Even now they gather strength in the shadows. Soon, it will rear its ugly head to strike. If you are not prepared, the serpent will consume you."

Nicodemus observed their faces. Cold, crippling fear had swept through the room.

"I haven't said this to make you afraid. But it is good to know what fear feels like so you may defeat it. You conquer fear by being prepared and confident in your skills."

Nicodemus stood behind Halimah and placed his hands on her shoulders. "My granddaughter is adept in both magick and combat. She will train you all in the use of blade, sword, and whatever else makes an effective weapon."

Halimah twisted around and shot her grandfather a crusty look. "Thanks for the warning!"

"Halimah, it is well within your abilities to teach them." His voice softened. "I need your help."

She glowered up at him. "You have it, but it would have been nice if you had just asked me first."

Nicodemus suppressed a smile at her petulance. "Please," he whispered.

"All right." She groused.

"Good. I'll provide anything you need. Just put together a list of supplies."

"Yes, Grandfather."

The study faded from view as the dream orb shifted time and space with the image Azriel had implanted inside its perfect surface. Transported to the opposite side of the world, Azriel stood on a cliff overlooking the ocean. The locals here called the place Cronk Karren. They had many explanations for the circle of stone, all but the real one. After the worlds were split in two, the circle of stones was all that remained of the Great Temple of Aralia. The Isle of Man had been torn from the continent as a result of the powerful ritual performed by Eltanin. The Isle, all that remained of what was once the Heart of Aralia, had been the most potent and magickal place of the old world.

Azriel wasn't sure why this was the first place he thought of to flee Caer Wylusung, but he needed to escape. The walls of the study felt like they had closed in around him and he couldn't breathe. He slumped to the ground in despair and wiped the remains of tears from his face. The weight he felt was almost unbearable and the burden placed upon him was suddenly too real.

Anger built within his soul, an anger so consuming that the clouds above him suddenly congealed into a massive rainstorm as his magick leaked from his body. The resounding thunder and lightning reflected Azriel's rage as the rain drenched him to the bone. He didn't care. His chest heaved with fury as he thought about his mother's deception. She had deliberately lied to him. Azriel wasn't sure whether it was the lie or the murder that had him so outraged. He thought he knew Abelene. He never would have suspected that she was capable of such a heinous deed.

Resentful, Azriel lost all ability to be rational. It didn't matter that the king had sought the demise of his son. What mattered was that Abelene had blood on her hands that could never be washed away.

Azriel sat for the next hour sitting in the center of Cronk Karren as the rain poured down on his head. With every dark thought, he raised his fist to the sky, releasing peals of thunder. He glared at the sea, churning the water into swells that crested and broke against the cliff, reaching heights that sprayed him with salty foam.

Suddenly a voice rang out behind him.

"Desist!" she shouted, and the rain abated and calmed to a soft drizzle. "Azriel, you will tear this island apart!" Amaryllis glared her disapproval.

"How did you know I was here?" he asked, irritated.

"By now, don't you think I would know the difference between a natural storm and a magickal one?"

Azriel scowled up at her. He was about to rise when Felisa leapt from behind a boulder and sailed gracefully through the air. She landed on Azriel, pinning him to the ground.

"Boy, you're really stupid sometimes," she giggled.

"Yeah? What would you know about it?"

"More than you think. You're acting like a baby. Did you enjoy your little tantrum?"

"Oh, bugger off, Felisa."

"Enough!" Amaryllis snapped angrily. She clapped her hands, and in an instant he found himself transported along with Felisa and Amaryllis to her home. A fire blazed in the hearth and a kettle bubbled merrily over the flames. "Here, get out of your wet clothes and put this on." Thrusting a robe in his hands, her manner was less than amiable. Azriel excused himself and returned quickly, dressed in the warm, comfortable robe. He sat in the chair by the hearth and scowled as he stared into the hearth.

Amaryllis sat opposite him in the other chair while Felisa, having returned to her feline form, curled up by the fire. "Azriel, do you think you're the only one who has ever had to live with disappointment?"

"You don't understand!"

"Oh, really!" Amaryllis answered with sarcasm. She doled out a bowl of hot porridge and thrust it brusquely into his hands. "Eat." She ordered. "Now I want you to shut up and listen." Azriel arched an eyebrow. "What you need to realize, son, is that life isn't always pretty. We all hide parts of our past that should never see the light of day. We all have our nasty little secrets, you included."

"Yeah? Well, I never killed anyone." Azriel countered.

"Do you think murdering someone is the worst thing a person could do? What about betrayal or indifference, treason or maybe unforgiveness?"

"Those are hardly the same."

"We're all murderers, Azriel. Every time we ignore the suffering of others, we murder. Every time we allow poverty or injustice to continue, a part of the world dies. One doesn't have to use a blade or a gun to kill. We murder with our thoughts and words."

"Nothing you're saying makes any sense to me."

"Azriel, there are degrees to everything. You're not entirely innocent either. I know you have your own hatreds."

"No I don't, at least not enough to kill someone."

"You're lying. I know you've thought about it." Amaryllis smiled grimly.

"Yeah, like who?"

"What about that boy, Eddie?"

"Are you actually defending that creep?"

She laughed lightly, "See, you hate the boy without knowing anything about him."

"I know enough!" Azriel snapped. "He's mean, arrogant, and stupid, and he's hurt Camille on several occasions. And why are we even talking about him?"

"Because you have allowed yourself to become blinded by your hatred of him. Have you ever wondered why he is the way he is?"

"I really don't care!"

"That's my point, Azriel. You judge without knowing. That makes you as bad as a murderer."

Azriel fumed with her accusation. "What does any of this have to do with my mother?" He stood, ready to leave the room.

"Sit down!" Amaryllis ordered. "I'll tell you what this has to do with! You judge Abelene without knowing the truth, just like you judge that poor boy. Now let me show you something."

Amaryllis removed an old black cauldron from her pantry and filled it with water. She placed it before Azriel and waved her hands over it, intoning an incantation. "Now look. Think of your home."

"Why my home?"

"Damn it, Azriel. Look and see!" Amaryllis glared at him, annoyed by his stubbornness.

Grumbling, he gazed at the still water until images began to coalesce and take shape. It was afternoon in Harden Lake. The eaves of his house dripped from the autumn storm. The walkway leading to the porch was drenched with mud-laden puddles, and the heavy rain beat upon the roof, typical of mountain weather in October. Azriel didn't see the point of all this and was about to voice his annoyance with such a useless exercise when he suddenly noticed movement under the overhang. Peering closer, he saw that Eddie had seated himself on the porch swing with his head bowed. He appeared to be waiting and looked out into the street.

"What the heck is he doing at my home? What is he up to?" Azriel fumed.

"Be quiet and observe." Amaryllis muttered.

Eddie stood and removed a note from his pocket. That's when Azriel realized that Eddie didn't look at all well. He seemed haggard and haunted. His eyes had a wild and tortured appearance like that of a hunted animal. Eddie stuck the note between the door and the jamb, then left sadly, muttering to himself. He hopped onto an old motorbike and made his way through the woods. Taking the path that led past the high school, he continued for some time until he rode into the driveway of a run-down double-wide trailer home.

Azriel scratched his head. None of this made sense. Eddie had always boasted about his rich father and all the cool things he had, yet this seemed to be the worst part of town.

Eddie unlocked the door and stepped inside only to find his mother had passed out on the couch. An empty bottle of bourbon lay on its side atop the coffee table alongside a container of pills. Eddie dropped to his knees and desperately shook his mother, trying to rouse her from her stupor.

"Mom! Damn it, Mom, not again! Wake up!" Eddie began to cry with rage. He picked up the empty bottle and threw it with all his anger. It shattered against the wall. He placed his hand on her forehead and held his ear to her lips. In panic he picked up the phone and called 911.

"Please help!" He pleaded. "It's my mom. She's passed out. Her skin is cold and she's barely breathing. Hurry please!"

He hung up the phone and cradled his mother in his arms, weeping. "Mom, please don't die. How long are you going to blame yourself, huh? It's not your fault that Dad left."

"Seen enough?" Amaryllis asked sternly.

Azriel backed away from the cauldron and plopped onto the chair by the fire. "What was that all about?"

"Not everything is as it appears, Azriel. That's the third time this year his mother has tried to commit suicide."

"Will she live?"

"That remains to be seen. Hopefully the paramedics will be in time."

As much as Azriel couldn't stand Eddie, he couldn't help feeling pity for him. The anger that had burned so fiercely a moment ago dulled into something heavier and far more complicated.

Amaryllis sat next to Azriel and took his hand. "There's something you need to understand. I keep my eyes on everything and anyone who has the potential to harm you. Nicodemus charged me to protect you. I've been observing that boy ever since Kita told me of someone prowling around your house. That boy Eddie waits at your house at least once a week for a few hours—always waiting."

"But why?"

"Perhaps that's for you to find out. But I can tell you what I do know. Things have gone badly for Eddie. His father abandoned him and his mother. It was Altais who cruelly used magick to show Eddie his father in the arms of another woman. He used Eddie and manipulated him to set a trap for your mother. When he saw how Altais hurt Abelene, Eddie tried to stop Altais and was rewarded with a broken jaw. Since then, that sad young man has been tortured by nightmares and has been haunted by guilt over what he's done. Compound that by living in poverty with his alcoholic mother. You've actually seen one of his good days. When she isn't passed out, she abuses Eddie, beating him. He takes it because he loves her and doesn't want to hurt her. He just wants her to get well. I know you despise Eddie, but do you think he really deserves a life like that?"

Azriel didn't answer. He stared at the floor, avoiding Amaryllis's eyes.

"I want you to think about that." She said firmly, "and I want you to put all that in perspective while considering your feelings toward Abelene right now. You hate what she did, but now you need to think carefully and consider why she did it."

"I'm sorry. I didn't know." Azriel rubbed his eyes with fatigue.

"I'm not the one you need to apologize to." Amaryllis said gently. "Now use the guest room and go to sleep. You're exhausted."

Chapter 10

The following morning, Azriel awoke to bright sunlight blazing through the window. He dressed quickly and strode into the living room. Felisa scurried about preparing breakfast.

"Where's Amaryllis?" he asked.

"She had to go. There's been an emergency." Felisa answered as she stirred a pot of hot cereal.

"What happened?"

"Rosemary has disappeared. She hasn't been seen since yesterday morning. Mr. Parkins is quite worried."

"What's the big concern? She's usually in the habit of going for a morning swim."

"Yes but this time she hasn't returned, and her boat is gone."

"Maybe I can reach her." Azriel removed the ring from his leather bag of magickal items and placed it on his finger. He reached out, preparing to communicate with Rosemary. Initially, he felt a link forming, but all he received was muffled sound, a sort of bubbling.

"Don't bother," Felisa said. "Amaryllis has already tried." She doled out a portion, and Azriel ate quickly. He thanked Felisa and threw on his jacket.

"Where are you going?"

"I'm worried. I'm going to help find Rosemary."

"Good luck." Felisa threw herself into Azriel's arms and rubbed her cheek against his face. "I'm worried too."

Azriel removed the dream orb from his pocket and implanted an image. Within moments, he found himself by the Fairy Bridge. It seemed like a good starting point. He thought of Pog. Although he knew Eltanin was really Pog, he missed seeing the old troll.

The Fairy Bridge, as usual, was festooned with notes and trinkets attached to the rails—greetings and gifts for the elusive faeries that guarded the short span. Azriel stepped onto the planking, heading toward Castleton. Midway, a plank suddenly disappeared and Azriel plunged fifteen feet into the river below.

"Dammit!" Azriel sputtered as he slapped the water.

"Yer a wanker, ye know!" Pog sat by the riverbank with arms crossed.

Azriel swam over with fire in his eyes. He wanted to kill Pog. "Nice greeting!" he grumbled.

"Aye, ye deserved it, laddie. Ye been acting like a fool."

Azriel glowered at the water.

"Here ye go, laddie." Pog handed him a towel to dry off. "Ye've created quite a stir with yer temper, boy."

"What, I can't be alone to collect my thoughts?"

"That's not what I be talkin' about, ye moron. Yer fit of rage has created a big problem. Rosemary was out in the ocean when ye released that unnatural storm. Now she's missing, ye dolt! Ye need to control yer temper, boy. Don't ye understand that yer far more powerful than you think?"

"I'm sorry." Azriel scowled.

"Aye, ye been doin' that a lot lately, apologizing." Pog shook his head with disapproval and removed a dream orb from his pocket. Within moments, Azriel was transported to the quay at Castleton. He was now sitting in a small rowboat. A bundle of supplies was neatly stacked at the bow of the tiny craft. Pog pushed him off from the dock and called out to him.

"Now I suggest ye go lookin' fer the lady. It's yer fault she's out there. Let's just hope no harm has come to her, otherwise there'll be hell to pay." With an audible pop, Pog disappeared.

Azriel sighed as he began to row. This was an impossible task. How was he supposed to find Rosemary in this vast ocean? Aside from not being much of a mariner, he had no idea where to start.

He rowed for about an hour, when off in the distance, he saw what appeared to be the remains of a small watercraft. Shattered planks of wood bobbed on the waves. He rowed over to the flotsam, noting that the debris had spread over a vast area. Panic began to rise in his throat. The message hit home. This was indeed his fault. The previous night, Azriel had released his rage upon the ocean without any thought of what damage he could do. Now he had what course of action to take to rescue Rosemary. If she was dead, the guilt would rest squarely on his shoulders. Thinking it through, he realized there was perhaps a way he could find her.

Azriel rummaged through his small pouch of magickal items. He removed a small shell and fingered it thoughtfully. He spoke Maera's name. Nothing happened. Frustrated, he rowed further past the debris field and gazed into the water, searching for any other sign of Rosemary. Off in the distance he saw something else floating on the waves. As he neared it, he noticed with a chill that it was a dress, tattered and torn. Worse, he recognized it as an outfit Rosemary often wore. He lifted it out from the water with an oar. Holding it helplessly, he stared at the torn fabric.

"You really did it this time, didn't you?" The voice came from the stern of the boat.

Azriel spun around. Maera stood with hands on her hips. Her crown of pearls dazzled his eyes in the sunlight "I've had all I can do cleaning up your mess." She said with disapproval as she wrung out her seaweed hued hair. She fluttered her fin-like wings in agitation.

Azriel hung his head in shame. "I can't find her."

"Yes, and it's not likely you will without my help."

"So what am I supposed to do?"

"It's obvious isn't it?" Maera smiled.

"No, it's not that obvious at all."

"Well, this is where she went down. So look for her."

"Under water? I don't swim very well so what's the point?"

Maera hummed musically, as she reclined on the edge of the boat hanging her hand lazily in the water. Azriel's eyes narrowed. She didn't seem all too concerned. "You know something, don't you?" He stated with suspicion.

"Uh huh!" She answered somewhat aloof as she lolled, sunning herself happily.

"Well?" Azriel's voice rose in pitch with his agitation.

"Oh here. You've been punished long enough." She reached inside the bundle of supplies at the bow of the tiny vessel and tossed something to him.

Azriel stared at the object, a conch shell, with curiosity. "What am I supposed to do with this?"

"Just blow into it." Maera sighed. She seemed almost bored.

Azriel didn't hide his annoyance. "You're sure taking all this in stride. Aren't you the least bit concerned?"

"No, not really. Rosemary can take care of herself."

"Are you serious? She could be drowned, or worse, eaten by sharks." Azriel's face turned crimson with his anger.

"You don't listen very well, do you, Azriel. Just blow into the shell."

"All right, whatever you say."

Azriel, feeling somewhat foolish, took a deep breath and blew into the conch shell, releasing a pure tone that resonated off the water. He had his back to Maera and said crossly, "Okay, so now what?" He was answered with silence. He looked behind him only to discover that Maera had vanished.

"Great." He muttered.

Just then, he was surprised to see a hand come up and grasp onto the edge of the boat. It was followed by a head popping out of the water. Rosemary smiled broadly at Azriel.

He breathed a sigh of relief. Boy, am I glad to see you. Aw geez—You're naked!"

Rosemary giggled impishly. "Oh, Azriel, don't be such a prude. Would ye help me into the boat?"

He blushed, trying to avert his eyes as he clasped her hands and pulled her in. But in shock, he stared, mouth agape, as he realized that from her waist down she was covered with blue-green iridescent scales and sported an elaborate tail.

"You're a mermaid." He stammered.

"Well of course I am, you silly twit. You knew I was an undine."

"Yes, but I thought you told me you would never be able to return to the ocean. You said that too much time had passed, that you would always be human.

"I guess I was wrong. Now would ye hand me that towel and blanket?"

Azriel reached behind and grabbed the bundle. He thrust it at Rosemary, eager to cover her nakedness. She wrapped the blanket around her body, completely covering her tail, and began drying her hair.

"So what happened?" Azriel asked with wonder.

She replied, "An interesting thing occurred yesterday afternoon, quite remarkable really. Ye see, Azriel, the little beastie ye brought to me from the desert outgrew his tank. Poor thing was miserable, lookin' all sad, like he just wanted out. So I packed me a lunch, wrapped Percy in a wet blanket, and rowed out to sea so I could give me pet a proper home. It was a beautiful afternoon on the water, sun shinin' bright, me getting' all emotional as I prepared to say goodbye to Percy. Then, out of the blue, a storm, the likes of which I never seen before—arose out of nowhere! Er, ye wouldn't know anything about that, would ye, Azriel?"

He hung his head, staring at his feet with a guilty expression.

"So there I was, with waves churnin' about me, crashin' over me head like doomsday had come upon me. Then, a mighty breaker came rushin' toward me and capsized me poor little boat. Of course, Percy was quite happy to be back in his element, but things didn't fare so well fer me! Even though I'm a powerful swimmer, I thought it would be the end of me since I was so far from land. The storm got worse, lightning and thunder crashin' all around me, and if that wasn't bad enough, the ocean was churning up all sorts of debris. I got me foot tangled in an abandoned net and got dragged down beneath the waves. Poor Percy also got tangled in the bedeviled thing. I tried to release him and myself, but we got pulled down deeper and deeper."

Azriel was captivated by the story. "So what did you do?"

"Hmm, well, Percy was fine, even though he was tangled, him being a lungfish, don't ye know. But I was in a mighty pickle; soon, I wouldn't be able to hold me breath and I figured I was a goner! I said me goodbyes and when I could no longer breathe, I opened my mouth and inhaled the water ready to face me doom and let the sea take me. Ah, but then a remarkable thing happened. The moment I gave myself to the sea, my tail grew back and I began to breathe normally, see?"

Rosemary pushed aside her hair. Three slits behind each ear attested to the fact that her gills had returned. She continued to dry herself off and began to dress under the blanket. She tossed it aside, now wearing a simple dress. She had also returned to her human form and crossed her shapely legs.

"So in retrospect, it appears as if yer gift of that dried up old fish from the desert was a message of sorts. I just didn't realize what it was until after the fact. Ye see, Azriel, as soon as Percy breathed in water, he became alive again to the ocean. Same fer me, I suppose."

Azriel stammered, "Wait a minute. I remember you telling me that if you remained out of the water for more than a day, you would thereafter remain human—that you could never go back. So what's up with that?"

She nodded in agreement, "Aye, I guess me mother lied."

"Why would she do that?" he asked, annoyed. "Seems a lot of that's going around lately."

"Aye, she probably lied to protect me, to keep me from straying too far. Just like Abelene lied to protect you, Azriel. Ye were terrible mean to her. Ye should have given her a chance to explain herself."

"Yeah, I guess you're right," he said with remorse. "I should talk to her as soon as possible."

"Aye, indeed. Now perhaps we should return. I suspect a few people are worried about me."

Azriel was about to man the oars when another hand grabbed at the tiny boat. Another face popped out of the water and smiled. She had features similar to Rosemary's. Azriel smiled back. "Are you Rosemary's sister?"

"No, son. I'm her mother." She turned to her daughter. "Are you leaving so soon? You haven't been back but a day."

"Indeed, mother, but I'm needed on land. There's too much work to do. Things have become dangerous for magickal creatures like us—and like Azriel."

"Like Azriel you say," She looked at him critically. "What are you, son?"

"Ferrishyn."

"Ahh, I haven't seen one of your kind for many years. Is Eltanin still alive?"

"Yes, ma'am."

"Then would you convey my greetings to him when you see him?"

"I'd be happy to."

"Good, tell him Cleadora sends her love and would like to speak with him at his earliest convenience. It's important."

"Mother, are ye planning some mischief?" Rosemary crossed her arms.

"No, dear. As queen of my people, I am concerned for their safety."

"Very well, I'll tell him myself."

"Good." Cleadora smiled. "Now next time don't take seventeen years to return home. I was so worried."

"Then perhaps ye should have told me the truth in the first place!" Rosemary scowled.

"I was only trying to keep you safe, daughter, like any mother would."

Rosemary scowled. "Aye, but yer lie kept me away for so long. Ye could have done better scarin' me with some boogeyman tale!"

As they bickered, Azriel tried to act busy, examining the oars, anything to ignore the family squabble. Rosemary giggled. "Look, mother, we are making Azriel uncomfortable."

"You're right. Now don't be too long. We have much catching up to do."

With that, Cleadora upended and headed back to the depths, slapping her tail against the water to grace Azriel and Rosemary with a good splash.

Azriel put his back to the oars and headed to Castleton. "So you're a princess." He stated.

"Aye."

"Why haven't you told anyone?"

"What would be the point? I'm content enough to be who I am. I don't need a title. Now hurry up with that rowin' and stop dawdling. I'm sure me father is worried sick."

"Yes ma'am." Azriel sighed.

Remaining at Castleton wouldn't have served any other purpose, so Azriel prepared to return to Caer Wylusung. He waited for Rosemary, who busied herself in her storage closet looking for something. Azriel sighed with impatience. "Is this going to take long?"

Her voice was muffled from behind the door. "Hold yer horses, Azriel." The sound of clutter and boxes dropping clattered through the room as Rosemary shifted the vast amount of stores in her possession. Azriel walked into the next room just in time to see an avalanche of boxes tumble over Rosemary. He helped her up from the ground.

"Are you all right?" he asked, amused.

"That hurt a bit, but I'll get over it." She held a dusty old box and handed it to Azriel. "Here, I think you'll have use for this."

Azriel opened it and found an old book. He lifted it out of the carton and opened the cover. It was blank. No text was written on any page. He fanned through the bound paper with a quizzical expression.

"What is this?"

"It's magickal."

"Yeah, but what is it for?"

"I don't know. Eltanin told me to give it to ye. He said ye would need it later."

"For what?" Azriel didn't hide his impatience.

"Don't know that either. I'm just the messenger."

Azriel shrugged and placed it back in the box.

Rosemary gathered a few more things and tossed them in a cloth sack along with the book. She hefted the bag over her shoulder and smiled. "Shall we go?"

"Are you coming with me?"

"Aye. I'm not needed here for a while—and Nicodemus needs me."

"Why, what's happening there?"

"There's a problem with Halimah."

"Why didn't he tell me?"

"Why indeed. Didn't you have enough on yer plate? Ye can't solve everything, Azriel."

He removed the dream orb from his pocket and prepared to shift back to Caer Wylusung.

"Not yet," Rosemary warned. "First we must retrieve Amaryllis and Felisa. I need their help."

Within moments they stood in Amaryllis' living room. She and Felisa were already packed. Amaryllis also had an old chest in her hands and tossed it to Azriel.

"What's this?" he asked.

"Healing potions." Amaryllis answered. "Now let's go. Halimah's in trouble."

"Is she sick?"

"No, it's nothing like that. She's under a spell. She placed herself into a magickal trance and can't be awakened."

"Why did she do that?"

"Wish I could say. But it's nothing we can't handle."

The castle was atwitter with activity. Maggie hurried to Halimah's room; arms loaded with cold compresses. Camille waited by the door wringing her hands visibly worried. When she saw Azriel, she flew into his arms in tears and held him tight. Then she released him and punched him hard in the arm.

"Ow, what was that for?"

"That's for making me worry. What the hell were you thinking, just disappearing like that?"

"Could we talk about this later?" Azriel scowled and rubbed his arm.

"You're not getting away with this, Azriel. We have some rules to discuss. That's the last time you leave me in the dark!"

Nicodemus cleared his throat to get their attention. "Perhaps you can have your domestic quarrel later. There are more urgent matters at hand."

"Yes," Amaryllis said in agreement. "Camille, Julia, and Maggie, you're needed here. Perhaps you'll learn a thing or two. Azriel, Jasper, and Albert—go away. We ladies will handle this."

The girls followed Amaryllis and Rosemary into Halimah's room and closed the door behind them.

Halimah lay prone on the floor. Her body shook and cold sweat covered her face. Amaryllis knelt beside her and placed her hands on the girl's temples to assess her condition. "Oh, dear. She's in deep. This will be difficult. First we must lift her carefully onto the bed."

The five women lifted Halimah and placed her gently on the mattress. Touching her, however, disturbed her trance and she began to spasm uncontrollably. They had all they could do to keep Halimah from hurting herself. Rosemary ordered quickly, "Hold her down—keep her immobile!"

Maggie and Julia pressed down on Halimah's legs while Rosemary and Camille held her shoulders still, but her chest still heaved, nearly lifting Halimah off the bed. Rosemary commanded as she struggled to keep Halimah down. "Amaryllis, you know what to do!"

The sorceress opened the chest she had brought and rummaged through the various vials and potions until she found the one she needed. Uncorking the bottle, she pried Halimah's mouth open and poured the liquid down her throat. The girl's spasms ceased immediately.

"What was that?" Camille asked, breathless.

"A sleep potion."

"That doesn't make sense."

"It would seem counterintuitive, but putting Halimah deeper into her trance will protect her body and allow me in. I have to guide her out. Now watch and learn."

Amaryllis lay down next to Halimah and gathered the girl into her arms, holding her tight against her breast. Rosemary, meanwhile, removed a small brazier from the sack she brought and lit powerful incense. She placed it at the foot of the bed, then handed each woman a black candle and lit them. "Now you must repeat after me." She intoned a chant. "Soma Placidus, Quiesco Reverto."

Rosemary and Camille on one side of the bed, Maggie, Julia, and Felisa on the other began to repeat the chant in a slow cadence while Amaryllis prepared to enter Halimah's mind. Rosemary handed Amaryllis another vial. The sorceress drank it down quickly and held Halimah tight. She shuddered once and fell into a deep sleep.

Rosemary found herself in a dreamscape of unimaginable horrors. All around her seemed the aftermath of a horrible cataclysm. Everywhere flames engulfed the remains of what was once a beautiful oasis. Monsters and demons arose from a roiling field of lava. As she drew closer to observe, she saw what appeared to be a cloaked man, his hands raised in triumph, summoning the spawns of hell from the eternal pit. They climbed out from the abyss and pursued Halimah with all intentions of devouring her. She vied desperately to defend the inhabitants of the oasis, casting spell after spell to destroy the fiends. She gasped with exertion as she released lightning bolts and plasma spheres upon the demons, but their numbers kept increasing. Rosemary placed herself in the midst of the battle. Halimah shouted out as Rosemary began to repel the monsters with a banishing spell. "They are too many! They are killing my people!"

"Halimah, it's not real! Someone has taken hold of your mind. You must control your fear and face your enemy!"

"But I don't know who it is!"

"Face him and you will!" Rosemary commanded. She held her hands out and repelled the foul beasts with blinding light that emanated from her palms. The creatures now held at bay, Halimah called out. "Come and face me, dark sorcerer so I may see your face!"

The robed figure turned and roared with laughter as he lowered his hood. In his right hand, he held a dagger and in his left a flaming whip. As he flicked the whip, it crackled with thunder. His eyes blazed red and his gaping maw was lined with fangs for rending flesh.

"Puny mortals, do you wish to challenge me?"

Rosemary stood firm and thrust Halimah behind her. She opened her robe and held out the talisman she wore around her neck. The Ankh blazed with holy light, and the archdemon shrank back from its power.

He growled in pain. "I know you, Lady Rosaluna, sorceress and witch. Do you think you can defeat me?"

"By the blood of most ancient Osiris and the life force of Isis, I command you to reveal your name!"

The creature struggled against the compulsion, but Rosemary's command overpowered the demon. She increased her hold on him until he roared his name. "I am Abraxas, demon lord of the desert."

"Who has sent you—who is your master?" Rosemary compelled him.

"I answer only to Rastaban!"

"He holds you bound?"

"Yes. I destroy as is his will!" He groaned with frustration. "I must kill Halimah!"

"You will not. She is under my protection!"

"I must!" Abraxas bellowed.

"Is this your will?"

"No, it is the will of Rastaban."

"Why! I adjure you—speak!"

"She is a danger to my lord! She is a seer and diviner and has seen too much!"

Abraxas struggled against Rosemary's binding and howled in pain.

Rosemary paused to consider the demon's plight. He was in agony, but not by her doing. Rastaban held the creature enslaved to his will. She approached Abraxas cautiously.

"Demon lord, what is *your* will?"

"I wish only to be free."

"And if I free you from your bondage, would you still pursue Halimah?"

His eyes shone with a glimmer of hope. "No lady, I would return to my realm and find rest. But you don't have the power to release me."

"You underestimate me, Abraxas. I am no mere mortal as you have assumed. I am an undine, a magickal creature like you. I want your word-bond as a lord: if I free you, no harm will come to Halimah or her people."

"Yes, you have my oath. I want only to be at peace and to be left alone."

"Then I will free you. But there may come a time when I will need you to aid me. I do not compel but only ask."

"I will help you if you have need. I give you my blade as a promise." Abraxas handed over his dagger to seal the oath.

"Done!" Rosemary intoned. "Show me your bonds."

Abraxas lifted his robe to reveal his ankle. An iron manacle was adhered to his scaled flesh, and a cruel spike held it in place, scabbed over by the creature's blood. Rosemary held the dagger out, pointing at the wound. "In the name of Salacia, mother of all undines, I give you release, Abraxas, demon lord of the desert." Where she pointed, cool, refreshing water bubbled up from the parched earth and bathed the creature's feet. When it touched the manacle, it suddenly dissolved and fell away. The flesh around his ankle was cleansed and healed of its festering wound. The demon breathed a grateful sigh of relief.

"It is done," Rosemary said solemnly.

Abraxas bowed formally and intoned. "You have my gratitude, Lady Rosaluna. When the time comes, I will fight with you against my enemy, Rastaban. He has much to answer for."

"Then I release you, friend demon. You are free to go."

Abraxas, demon lord of the desert, nodded and without a word returned to the deep pit he had opened. The creatures and monsters he had summoned followed behind him. When all had returned to the abyss, the portal sealed shut.

A serene calm settled over the desert landscape and Halimah breathed a sigh of relief. Rosemary, however, crossed her arms and stared at Halimah with disapproval. "There's only one thing I would like to ask ye. What were ye thinkin'?"

Halimah stammered, "I—I was trying to help Azriel. I was searching for the Clave to see if I could locate the whereabouts of Abelene."

"You are a powerful seer—yes—but what ye did was foolish and headstrong. Rastaban is a very powerful wizard—far stronger than you. What you attempted should have been a group effort. Now you have put us all in danger, ye have. If Rastaban was able to find ye, he could quite possibly find the rest of us."

"I'm sorry," she sniffled, "I didn't know."

"There are ways to protect ye. It just won't be easy. Now let us return."

"Wait." Halimah paused and thought for a moment. "Did you just make a deal with a demon?"

"Aye."

"Isn't that dangerous? How do you know you can trust him?"

"I don't, but..." she sighed, "He did give me his oath-bond. Even for a demon that is a binding agreement he must honor. And besides, I did him a kindness he will not soon forget."

"But he's a demon!"

"True, but a grateful one. I have struck a blow against the clave. Should the time come, Abraxas will rally to our side. When doing battle, divide and conquer is always a good plan. Abraxas was held against his will and will not soon forget that Rastaban held him captive. If our enemy is his enemy, then it makes us friends—sort of." She smiled ruefully. "When in war, one must use the weapons ye have, even if they are poor ones."

"I suppose..."

"Now I want yer promise that you will never attempt something so foolish again. When ye have a plan, either consult Eltanin, Nicodemus—or me! Is that clear?"

Halimah hung her head in shame. "Yes, Lady."

"Good. Let us go then."

The transition was quick and Halimah awoke in Rosemary's arms, surrounded by her friends. It took a few moments to reorient herself and she looked up smiling with embarrassment. "I guess I created quite a stir."

Amaryllis glowered down at the girl and was about to speak when Rosemary stopped her. "Ye don't need to berate her, sister; I've already read her the riot act."

"Good." Amaryllis glared at Halimah.

Rosemary took Amaryllis by the arm. "Come, we need to talk. The rest of you can go now and give Halimah a chance to rest after her ordeal."

"Wait." Halimah whispered in her weariness. She watched as the room was cleared by all but Rosemary and Amaryllis. She fixed her eyes on the sorceress.

"Rosemary, I thought you said none of it was real."

"Oh, it was real enough."

"Then you lied?"

"No."

Halimah sighed. "It's either real or it isn't. How can it be both?"

"Are your thoughts real, Halimah?" Rosemary smiled.

"I'm not sure."

"Think about it. You're real, aren't you? The thoughts you think are composed of energy, right. In the quantum, magickal world, energy is also matter, which is real. So in a manner of speaking, your foray into the dream world was real, see?" She removed the dagger Abraxas had given her from the pocket of her dress. Halimah gasped with wonder. "So understand, Halimah. If that demon had killed you in your dreams, then you would have died in the mortal world. That's why you should never do something so stupid again."

"I promise I won't, but there is something you should know."

Rosemary and Amaryllis stared at her waiting for her to continue.

"I tried to see into the clave, into Rastaban's mind. He set Abraxas on me to repel my efforts, almost to my end. I guess I would have died if you hadn't rescued me, Rosemary. But for a brief moment, I caught a glimpse of something—a landmark." Halimah yawned and laid her head on her pillow. She mumbled with fatigue, "We might be able to locate Abelene with what I have in my head."

164

Chapter 11

"Mom?" Azriel cleared his mind of all extraneous thoughts and waited for her response. The laboratory was dimly lit by a single candle. He focused on the flame until he felt the link begin to form.

"I am here." He heard the words in his mind, tentative, almost frightened.

"Mom, I'm sorry I shut you out."

"I'm sorry too. I should have told you."

"Why didn't you?" Azriel's heart ached.

"How could I tell you, Azriel? I have lived with this pain and guilt for eighteen years. How could I tell my son that I murdered his father?"

"Was there any other way?"

"No. If I had stayed, your father would have taken you and had you killed. He was so afraid of your destiny—afraid of losing power—he went insane. If I killed him and stayed in Aralia, I would have been executed by men loyal to your father. Fleeing Aralia and becoming exiled on Earth was the only way I could protect you. It was my duty as your mother. I'm so sorry to burden you with all this."

"I understand, Mom. At least now I do. I was so angry. I didn't know what to do. I needed to think."

"I know," Abelene said sadly.

"I haven't been a good son. You being all alone there—it's terrible."

"I haven't exactly been alone."

"Yeah, about that…"

"Don't be angry with me, Azriel. I can't bear it."

"But you're stuck there with a monster!"

"Charlie isn't a monster."

"Charlie?" he retorted, chagrined.

She countered, "It's as good a name as any, and you're wrong about him."

"Are you actually defending him—the Dragon of Death?"

"He's not what you think, son. There is kindness in him—more than you realize."

"Mom, don't get too attached. You know I must face him in battle."

"Don't be so sure about that. Yes, you must face him, but not necessarily in battle."

"Then for what reason?"

"That I can't tell you."

Azriel squelched his temper. "You know I have the dragon's heart scale and Errin-lil has been awakened."

"Yes, I know, and so does Rastaban. Its awakening was felt around the world. Azriel, Rastaban is your enemy, not Charlie."

"I'll do what I have to do." Azriel scowled.

Abelene sighed. "There are many things you must accomplish first. There is time for what you think you must do."

"Mom, why are you being so evasive? Can't you just tell me what I must do?"

"You will know when the time comes. Now I must go. Rastaban is coming to bother me again. He can't discover our secret. I love you, son."

Before Azriel could respond, he felt their connection sever. He couldn't help worrying about Abelene. She seemed to be in such a vulnerable position, but he also knew that the spectral pyramid prevented Rastaban from harming her physically. He just hoped that she was strong enough to thwart Rastaban's mental attacks.

Rastaban descended the flight of stone steps to the deepest chamber. Abelene quickly sat and quietly placed another stitch into the tapestry she had been diligently working on.

"Plotting, Abelene?" Rastaban smiled glibly.

Abelene's manner was aloof. "Whatever do you mean?"

"Don't be so coy, lady. You don't seem to be at all bothered by your—situation."

"Should I be? I have everything I need here, don't I?" She placed another stitch in the ornate arras she had fashioned, ignoring him. Rastaban examined the three-paneled triptych and smirked. The first scene depicted the Clave in a battle with Azriel and the Order of the Ankh. The second panel portrayed the dark dragon of death holding Rastaban in a death grip while Azriel faced him holding Errin-lil aloft. In his other hand he cradled a strange object. The other panel was hidden from Rastaban's scrutiny.

"Very lovely work, Milady, but completely wrong. I would call it wishful thinking."

"Careful, wizard. Prophecy is seldom wrong."

Rastaban chuckled softly and broke out in mocking laughter. "It is you who are wrong, Abelene. Azriel has become more visible to me now that he is immortal. Not only that, but…" he hesitated for effect. "You see, lady, one of his mates—a sorceress—a lovely young lady by the name of Halimah made a fatal mistake. She tried to see into my mind. Such a puny effort." He sighed dramatically. "Of course I could never let that happen, so I sent a demon to kill her."

Abelene placed another stitch and placed the tapestry on the table, unaffected by his words. This, in fact, was old news for she had already conferred with Rosemary and knew the outcome.

"So tell me, Rastaban, was the demon successful?"

"I have held Abraxas bound for a millennium. He does my bidding and never fails me."

"Hmm, I see. And why are you telling me this?"

"Very simple, actually. I'm winning. I will destroy each and every member of your pitiful Order." he gloated, "even if I must destroy them one at a time. It's inevitable."

"And your point?" Abelene's eyes narrowed with cold hatred.

"Ah yes, my point. You can still join me, Milady. Bring your son to my side and together, we can rule this world!"

Abelene laughed lightly as if viewing the antics of an unruly child. "For one so wise, it astounds me that you could be so blind."

Rastaban suddenly raged at her. "No, Abelene, it is you who are blind. I only wish to preserve your son. Otherwise I will have to kill him, and you will watch him suffer and die."

"Such arrogance. Threaten all you want, wizard. I will never join you, nor will my son. Leave me now. I grow weary of your putrid words. You're vile!" She turned her back on him and resumed working on her needlecraft.

"Be warned, Milady. I grow impatient. In the end you will join me." Rastaban turned on his heels and left the chamber.

"He *does* get tiresome, doesn't he?" Charlie yawned, his huge mouth agape. He then stretched, finding a new position. "So Lady Abelene, what news from the outside world?"

"Oh, the usual. Azriel has finally figured a few things out. He's not angry with me anymore, a demon tried to kill Halimah, and Azriel still wants to kill you."

"Oh, is that all?" Charlie sighed with boredom.

"He's still confused."

"Well then why don't you just set him straight?"

Abelene searched for words. "It's a funny thing about prophecy, Charlie. If I try to coerce Azriel onto what we think is the proper path, it could set things awry. It's best not to interfere too much."

"You do know that if he threatens my life, I will not idly sit and let it happen. I will have to defend myself."

"I do know that, but you also must know that I would defend my son from harm, even though we are friends, Charlie."

"Alas I know that as well. Let's just hope that it will never come to that, Milady."

Eltanin sat across from Azriel, sharing a light lunch, simple fare consisting of cheese and brown bread. They ate silently, both lost in their thoughts. Finally, after wiping his mouth with the sleeve of his robe, Eltanin spoke.

"It's time, Azriel."

"Time for what?"

"Your powers are almost fully realized. You've created the Lapis Occultus and have learned the names of the elementals. It is time to release them." he said with a matter-of-fact shrug.

"I know, but where do I start?"

"Ah yes, where to start. A few things have occurred, Azriel, which perhaps eluded your comprehension. For one, you were given a book by Rosemary. It's quite ancient, you know."

"No, I didn't, but it's virtually useless. It's blank."

"That's because it hasn't been activated yet. When you arrive at the truth of things, what you need will appear. The trick is in knowing what you need."

"Convenient." Azriel muttered.

"Another thing, Azriel. It is no accident that Halimah is among us. It was I who requested that she be brought here. She has a gift that will come in handy. Hers is the gift of vision. Albert is quite astute as well, that is, if we can keep his mind off Halimah and more on the work at hand."

"Oh," Azriel snickered, "so you noticed that too."

"Oh yes. He's quite smitten. I would like the four of you to work on finding the locations of our wayward Elementals."

"Who's the fourth?"

"Why Camille, of course. Between the four of you, I believe you to be quite capable of solving the riddle."

"What about Jasper and Julia?"

"Oh, I have a job for them as well."

"And what would that be?"

Eltanin chuckled. "Don't worry about them. You have enough to think about right now."

"You're not kidding. My head hurts."

"Hmm, I suppose it does. Maybe you need a little time off." Eltanin gave Azriel a shrewd look. "Magador misses you. Perhaps you two should spend a few hours together. Go flying. See the sights."

"Somehow I think you have an ulterior motive."

"Me, Azriel?"

"You always have something up your sleeve."

"Whatever are you talking about? Oh, wait a minute. Let me look!" Eltanin surreptitiously yanked at the sleeve of his robe and made a great show of peering inside. Suddenly, he extracted a garishly colorful bouquet of paper flowers.

"Well, would you look at that! There was something up my sleeve all along!"

Azriel stared at him. "You're enjoying this far too much."

Eltanin chuckled at his own cleverness. Azriel heaved a sigh and shook his head as he exited the room.

"Ah, better late than never." Magador said when Azriel emerged from the steps at the apex of the tower. He stretched his wings and fluttered them restlessly.

"What's your problem now?" Azriel shot back.

"Cousin, I'm bored."

"Sorry. Why don't you singe some rabbits or something?"

"I've eaten." The dragon grumbled. "And I've discovered that hawk doesn't quite agree with me. It's a bit gamey."

"Since when have you gotten so particular?" he challenged.

"You know nothing of my dietary needs. We dragons actually have a rather sophisticated palate." Magador retorted, clearly offended. "I really could use a cow right now. I'm starved."

"Oh, stop whining." Azriel said.

"I'd like to go hunting—and I'd like your company." Magador sniffed at the air. "Hmm, I think there's a herd of buffalo about thirty miles west of here."

Azriel sighed. "Oh, all right. I could use some diversion." Mortimer suddenly appeared and smiled eagerly. He buzzed around Magador like a pesky insect.

"I suppose you'll want to come too?" Magador grumbled.

Mortimer nodded with gleeful delight.

"Well I guess it's agreeable, that is if it's all right with Azriel."

"I have no problem with it," Azriel answered as he mounted Magador's back. "As long as he can keep up."

Magador flexed his wings and launched himself into the sky. Soon he soared high above Caer Wylusung and circled, searching the terrain below in a wide arc. At this point, Azriel used his dragonsight, linking his thoughts with Magador. With the sudden freedom, he felt elated. "You're right, Magador. I've missed this!"

"Yes, it's quite wonderful."

Mortimer buzzed alongside and managed to keep up, but only barely. Magador prepared to execute a swift ascent when he hesitated. "Er, cousin, have you put on weight?"

"Um, no. Why do you ask?"

"You feel heavier than last time." Magador craned his neck and looked behind him only to discover that Mortimer had decided to hitch a ride. Magador glared at the little gargoyle. Mortimer grinned guiltily and shrugged.

"Why, you lazy sloth! Get off!" With a vicious flick of his tail Magador sent Mortimer soaring. "Use your *own* wings!"

Mortimer quickly recovered and flew alongside, muttering gargoylish curses under his breath.

"And watch your language, or I'll have to scorch you!" Magador snapped. He ascended high above the castle and peered to the west. Azriel already had shifted his vision to dragonsight. By doing so, his ocular sense had increased tenfold. He pointed with excitement. "There! About two hundred of them. It's awfully far away though." The distance, Azriel figured, was at least seventy or so miles away. The buffalo had overgrazed the sparse grasslands and were already moving further north to the highlands and to greener foraging.

"I think they're too far, Magador. It would take at least two hours to get there." Azriel said, frowning.

"Maybe, or perhaps not! Hold on tight, Azriel." Magador ascended again and released the full force of his brawn with a bone shuddering descent. With a powerful dive he pulled in his wings, building up speed. Azriel looked down, his stomach dropping. The ground was approaching awfully fast. He was about to panic when unexpectedly he felt a jolt of inertia. It seemed as though the air itself had shattered and reconstituted. For reasons he could not explain, their position had shifted and they were now a mere fifty feet above the raging herd of buffalo. Magador extended his talons and nabbed a straggler, lifting it off the ground. The herd began to stampede toward a ridge. Magador swiftly blocked their way, shifting them away from the precipice.

Once satisfied that the buffalo wouldn't destroy themselves, thus devastating Magador's food supply, he reached down and bit the struggling creature on the neck, quickly killing it. With ease, he swooped, circled, and made a soft landing, dropping the carcass beside him. Magador immediately went to work disemboweling the animal, then began to gorge himself. Not to be a total hog, he tore a chunk of flesh from the beast and handed it to Azriel.

"What's this?" Azriel asked, eyeing it warily.

"Why, it's lunch!" Magador answered with his mouth full.

"But it's raw."

"Cousin, don't be such a bother."

Azriel stared at him.

"Oh, all right," Magador sighed. He held up the haunch of meat and released a flame, scorching it until it was cooked well enough for Azriel's taste.

Content, they sat feasting when Azriel finally asked the all-important question. "So, Magador, how exactly did we get from there to here?"

"Why, I shifted, or blinked, or whatever you want to call it."

"I don't understand."

"My, Azriel, you really don't know a thing about dragons or yourself, for that matter."

"So what do you do, shift time and space?"

"It's sort of like that. You merely think yourself to the place you want to be."

"And you just suddenly appear there?"

"No, cousin. It's more a matter of knowing you're already there. It's merely knowing that everything is One. Once you know that time and space are irrelevant, you can move anywhere you want. The trick is in knowing where you want to go. You can't blink to somewhere you've never been or haven't seen; otherwise you could find yourself in deep trouble. You could theoretically wind up blinking inside a solid mountain."

"Yeah, I guess that would be bad."

"No, Azriel, it would be worse than bad, you would wind up dead. We dragons do have an advantage though," Magador said between bites. "We have all the memories of the ones before us. So realistically, there's practically nowhere I haven't been."

Azriel nodded with understanding. "So you've been to Europe?"

"Not me personally, but Maragog was. Had to leave, of course."

"Why?" Azriel picked at his teeth, waiting for the answer.

"Oh, England was such a bother! Knights with their errands and quests, You know—slay the dragon, win the maiden." Magador replied, his voice laced with boredom. "Disgusting, really. Mother charbroiled more knights than she could count. And that armor made it far too easy. Kept in the heat, as you can well imagine."

Azriel laughed. "Yeah, spam in a can!"

"Finally she couldn't take it anymore. She was much happier in China."

"China?"

"Why, of course. Dragons are practically worshipped in China. We're considered quite lucky."

Azriel thought, weighing the sudden insight he'd had. "Magador, would it be possible to blink over to Aralia?"

"No, it's far too dangerous. Mother tried once and it nearly killed her. She was relying on her grandfather's memory of Aralia, but too much had changed. She couldn't calculate distance properly and wound up in the vacuum of space. She almost didn't make it back."

After nearly an hour, Magador finished most of the buffalo before he was finally sated. By this time, Mortimer arrived winded and scowling. He dove from above and attacked Magador, biting him on the rump. Of course, dragons were immune to gargoyle venom, but it hurt nonetheless. He turned and faced the raging creature squarely. Mortimer stomped his feet, gesturing wildly, nearly foaming at the mouth.

"It isn't my fault that you couldn't keep up!" Magador defended his actions with aplomb.

Enraged, Mortimer responded with a series of grunts, squeals and hoots.

"Oh, don't be a pain! You could have asked instead of merely assuming I would carry you."

Azriel interjected, "C'mon Mortimer, don't be sore. He's right. You could have asked."

Mortimer responded with a vicious kick to Azriel's shin.

"Ow! What the hell was that for?" He rubbed at his ankle and glared down at the gargoyle. Mortimer opened his mouth wide and pointed at it, while rubbing his empty stomach.

"Oh, is that all? Well, here then." Azriel was stuffed, so he tossed Mortimer the remaining third of the haunch of meat he couldn't finish. The gargoyle greedily gobbled up the meat, then crunched up the bones, swallowing noisily. Not being sated, however, Mortimer continued eating any remains that were strewn about, including the parts that were not fit for consumption by any normal creature. He even went so far as to gobble up the viscera that had been cast aside, slurping it up greedily while making noises of contentment.

"Ugh! Will he ever stop eating?" Azriel said, turning away from the gory scene with disgust.

"Not likely," Magador replied, snorting. "He'll eat himself into a coma if you don't stop him. It's not his fault, really. It's an unfortunate trait of all gargoyles."

Mortimer polished off the remaining orts of meat and finished by licking the residual entrails from his fingers. He glanced around furtively to make sure he didn't leave anything, not even for the crows and vultures circling overhead.

Azriel crossed his arms and stared down at the creature. "Are you quite done?" he muttered. "I think it's time we get back."

"We have time yet, cousin. There's someplace I'd like to show you." Magador lowered a wing to offer a perch for Azriel to mount his back. "You might as well get on also, Mortimer. It's unlikely you'll be able to fly after gorging yourself."

The little gargoyle, barely able to move past his lethargy, crawled onto Magador and rested wearily against Azriel's back. In moments he was asleep.

"Well, I guess the lazy little lout is going to miss all the fun!" Magador commented as he beat his wings soaring ever higher into the sky. When he gained enough speed, the air began to shimmer and soon he and Azriel were high above a craggy mountainside sparsely dotted by rugged trees that seemed to have resisted the ravages of time. Thanks to the full moon, they were able to wend their way through with the dim light, yet remain undetected.

"Where are we, Magador?"

"In the highlands of China. We are in the Taihang Mountains, quite far from civilization."

"But why here? I can barely see anything."

"Quite simple, really. I've felt a presence here beckoning. And besides, it's better we come under cover of night. We don't want to upset the locals. Now use your dragonsight, Azriel."

It took little effort to shift his sight from mortal to interdimensional. The rocky tor above glistened in the moonlight. The gray granite reflected soft light, and the rarefied air was clean and crisp. Forging their way from the native rock, twisted pines clung to life, wizened and misshapen from the constant abrading wind. Off in the distance on a higher plateau, Azriel noticed an area that seemed to be devoid of life, as if the very trees refused to encroach upon it. Azriel pulled his jacket tighter around his collar to fend off the cold. As the moon fell lower in the sky, the wee hours of morning brought with it lower temperatures. Frigid though it was, nevertheless Azriel was compelled to move forward to examine the strange anomaly. He approached cautiously, his senses telling him that something of enormous power lay dormant within the center of the clearing, as he scaled the rocky earth to higher elevation for a better view. The pines surrounding the open space were intertwined and tangled to prevent passage to the interior as if purposely guarding a sanctuary. It seemed impassable, but when Azriel neared the perimeter and touched one of the elder trees, soft emanations of power passed from his hand to the gnarled bark. Oddly, the closest trees began to tremble and sway. This created a small opening to the interior, and Azriel quickly seized the opportunity to gain entry. Ahead in the center of the clearing, emerging out of the glistening granite stood a tree impossibly ancient. Few leaves clung to life on the contorted branches. What remained of its once lustrous bark now hung down in tatters. Distorted as though straining against a terrible weight, the tree seemed to be in the last stages of life. Its demise seemed imminent. Yet atop the tree a few fruits defiantly clung to the uppermost branches.

Azriel stood staring at the tree. Something about it seemed quite odd, not so much from its age but for its shape. The grain of the bare wood stretched and strained against the weighty burden, crying out against its charge. Imprisoned within the tree, bound for millennia, the imprint of a dragon had shaped the wood. Imperceptible to human eyes, the only reason Azriel was able to see it at all was his keen dragonsight. The creature within the tree appeared to be sleeping in a fetal position.

Approaching the tree cautiously, Azriel had to strain against the power emanating from the ancient tree. It repelled him with each step and movement suddenly became impossible until Azriel backed away. He tried again but still had the same reaction. He began to sweat from the effort.

"Don't Azriel."

Surprised, Azriel turned and faced Magador. "How did you get inside?"

"Cousin, you can be quite dense at times." Magador looked up at the sky and sighed with consternation.

"Oh… yeah… of course." He again forged ahead, the effort like trying to slog through mud. With each step, the approach became more difficult. The closer he came, a ring of argent light became visible and began to surround the tree, blocking it from intrusion.

"It's a trap, cousin. Be careful."

"What kind of trap?"

"I'm not sure, but I wouldn't trigger it if I were you."

"It seems like an energy field. Maybe I can get past it."

"Foolish," Magador replied, "You may be immortal, but you can still be slain by stupidity."

"Then what should I do?"

"First, you might want to determine what is trapped inside the tree."

"It's one of the elementals, of that I'm certain."

"Yes but which one?"

Azriel paused and stared, frowning.

Magador clucked his tongue with annoyance and a wisp of sulfuric smoke escaped from his lips. "Use your logic, Azriel. Could it be fire?"

He thought for a moment, "Well, no. Fire would consume the tree."

"What about Earth?" Magador quizzed.

"No, that couldn't be it. Earth anchors the tree, not the other way around."

"Good. You've eliminated two."

Azriel continued reasoning it through. "And it couldn't be Air, since the tree creates air by converting carbon dioxide to oxygen. Air passes through it."

Magador chuckled. "Very good indeed! I think you're getting it now. So what does that leave you with?"

"Water, of course, which makes sense. Water is trapped within a tree, which gives it sustenance. Without water, the tree would die."

"And there you have it."

"So what should I do now?" Azriel rubbed his chin.

Before Magador could answer, Mortimer buzzed over the circle of trees protecting the sacred glade. Spying the tempting fruit atop the magickal tree, he dove toward it in anticipation of a tasty treat. Azriel cried out, trying to warn him, but the tree erupted with power, throwing off filigrees of sparks. It trapped Mortimer within the puissant field and repelled him. Singed, Mortimer sailed like a cannonball and landed on the ground with a thud. He was momentarily knocked unconscious, but he shook himself awake. He began to stomp his feet with rage and spewed a string of expletives only understood by Magador.

"Well, don't blame Azriel. He tried to warn you."

Amused, Azriel asked. "What did he say?"

"Oh, you don't want to know. Besides, I don't repeat such vile language."

As a result of Mortimer's intrusion, however, a change had taken place. The argent ring of white light was now clearly visible and within it, another ring had appeared closer to the tree glowing with blue brilliance. Azriel gaped in wonder.

The moon descended below the mountain and dawn was imminent. Azriel shivered from the cold. Magador shook out his wings with a suggestion. "There is nothing more we can do here right now without a strategy. I suggest we return to Caer Wylusung and discuss this matter with Eltanin."

Azriel quickly agreed. He was chilled to the bone and welcomed the thought of desert heat. He mounted Magador's shoulder and Mortimer straddled behind him. Within moments they were airborne and blinked back to the castle.

The sun was just setting as they circled and landed on Magador's turret. They were greeted by Camille who stood there fuming with arms crossed.

"Where were you?" Her eyes blazed with anger.

"In China." Azriel shrugged.

"Yeah, right." She growled.

"What's got your feathers in a ruffle?"

"Have you forgotten?"

"Forgotten what?"

"We had a date. We're supposed to be meeting Jasper and Muriel in Castleton in fifteen minutes! Remember? You're supposed to use the dream orb to get us there! Look at you. You're a mess!"

Azriel couldn't hide the guilty look on his face. "All right, give me five minutes." He dashed down the steps while Camille glared at him. She then fixed her gaze on Magador.

"Thanks a lot!"

"You're surely not angry with me, are you?" Magador's tone was one of nonchalance.

"Both of you just fly off whenever you want and never consider my feelings!"

"Well it's not my fault. Azriel never told me he had a date."

"Of course he didn't, because he forgot!"

"Oh, stop being so petulant, Camille. It's not like we were just gallivanting. We were doing something important."

"Like what?"

"Like locating a missing Elemental."

"You found one?"

"Of course."

"Well that's terrific." Camille replied blandly. "But that doesn't change anything." She turned on her heels and stormed down the steps to the main hall.

Magador chuckled lightly to himself as he peered westward with a contented sigh over the Canyonlands below. Atop his rocky perch, sundown was always particularly beautiful. The waning light painted glorious bands of color along the pointed and striated rock. Shades of gold and sienna were punctuated by purple and russet belts of color. It had been a good day and Magador was happy to have lived it.

Gazing outward, Magador spoke quietly. "You can show yourself, Eltanin. I know you're here."

A slippery shape shimmered and seeped from the stone cut wall and solidified into the wizard's form. His expression was one of surprise. "Did you see me, Magador?"

"No, of course not, Master Wizard. Your cloaking spell is quite good. Actually, I sensed you. A dragon is not so easily fooled."

"I see." Eltanin smiled easily amid the friendship of the great beast. "So you were successful, I assume."

"Yes. Azriel is becoming more attuned. His powers will soon be fully realized."

"They should be all realized by now. He is after all, immortal."

"True, but there is still that one thing he doesn't know yet—the one thing that will save him."

Eltanin thoughtfully removed a pipe from his robe and lit it. He puffed a few times as he considered Magador's words. "You may have to force his hand, er...or his wing, as it were, if he doesn't learn soon."

Magador agreed. "Yes, of course. But he has time yet."

Changing the subject, Eltanin asked, "So the elemental is trapped where I said it would be?"

"Indeed, which also begs the question, Eltanin. Why didn't you release it since you knew where it was?"

"It was never appointed for me to do so. Only Azriel has the power to release Salacia from her bondage."

"You do know there are safeguards around her. Azriel will have to be very clever to remove them."

"I wasn't aware of any traps. Did you notice anything unusual about them? Perhaps anything dark that the clave could have set?"

"No, nothing like that. I sense they are a challenge to test Azriel's worthiness. After all this isn't just common magick to be trifled with. Releasing the elementals will also give Azriel power over them. Can he handle it without being corrupted?"

"He had a good teacher. Abelene's wisdom is within him." Eltanin blew a smoke ring. "Allay your fears, Magador. Azriel will not abuse his power."

"It's not Abelene's teachings that concern me, Eltanin. He has his father's blood in him as well."

"True, but it is also my blood. Berrill was an anomaly, swayed by those who feared the future. It was fortunate that Azriel never knew his father. I believe in his goodness, Magador. He won't fail us."

"But how can you be so certain?"

"I guess it's a matter of faith. Azriel knows what's at stake. I have seen that for the most part, his decisions are based on the greater good. If you can trust in anything, you can trust in that."

Chapter 12

Azriel stood in the courtyard with Camille, Albert, and Halimah. They were all dressed in black capes to cloak them and blend into the night. Though it was midday in the Canyonlands it was the darkest part of night in the Taihang Mountains of China. Though it was unlikely they would ever be noticed, one couldn't be too careful.

Nicodemus gave instructions on the best possible way to release Salacia, the dragon elemental of water.

"Consider it a puzzle," he said with a grin. "Certainly it is set up to elude any interlopers or intrusion."

"So where does that put us?" Albert asked.

"Perhaps in a tenuous position, but never forget that Azriel is the key to solving the riddle."

"Nicodemus, where are Jasper and Julia?"

"They have gone to retrieve Rosemary, Amaryllis and Muriel from the Isle of Man. We will locate the next elemental—a scouting mission if you would. Time is getting short, and we need to act soon."

Azriel adjusted the harness holding Errin-lil across his back. It was uncomfortable and felt heavy on his shoulders. Camille was armed as well, with her wand and athame, A leather pouch containing an assortment of potions hung from her belt. Likewise, Halimah came armed with assassin's weapons, mainly poison-dipped daggers, and Albert held an ornate magickal staff.

"Hey Albert, where did you get that?" Azriel asked, eyeing the staff.

"Extra protection. Eltanin loaned it to me."

"Cool! What does it do?"

"I'm not sure. Eltanin just said that if the need arises to tap it on the ground three times."

Azriel shrugged and nodded. "Well, I guess we should get going."

"Not just yet." Nicodemus removed an old watch attached to a gold chain from his pocket and checked the time. Shielding his eyes, he peered up at the sun. He tapped his foot impatiently as he checked his watch again. "Blast!" he grumbled. "They're late."

"Can we go yet, Uncle Nick?" Azriel asked.

"No, not yet. Amaryllis is going with you. She knows more about elementals than anyone I know. Oh, here they are."

On the far side of the courtyard in the center of the stone-etched pentagram, Jasper, Julia, Muriel, Rosemary, and Amaryllis blinked into view. Jasper held a dream orb in his hand and grinned.

"Hey, Jasper, you're getting pretty good at that!" Azriel grinned back.

"You're late!" Nicodemus blustered.

"Sorry, Uncle Nick, but we had to be careful. Amaryllis thinks her home is being watched. She had to place a spell of protection over it before we left."

"He's right, Nicodemus," Amaryllis strode to the forefront. "I've had the disquieting feeling that the Clave has been sneaking around. One can't be too careful." She planted her feet firmly and held onto a delicately wrought scepter crowned with an alabaster lotus flower. Azriel examined the magickal item.

"What is that, Amaryllis?"

"I have had this for over 6000 years. It is the scepter of Isis."

"Cool! What does it do?"

"It preserves life—and it has other uses. It's the preferred weapon of the goddess."

"How did you get it?"

"Enough chit-chat." Nicodemus groused. "It's time for you to go."

"Yes, right!" Azriel smiled sheepishly. He removed the dream orb from his pocket and imprinted the vision from his memory. The substance of reality shifted and in moments they all found themselves at the periphery of the magickal glade. However, it was not what Azriel expected. He and his companions suddenly crouched into a defensive posture. Strange and monstrous creatures surrounded the ancient tree and now there were five concentric glowing circles of color protecting it.

Camille grabbed Azriel's arm nervously.

The closest to Azriel, guarding the first ring, was perhaps the strangest creature Azriel had ever seen. He had the body of a man, but that was where the similarity ended. For one thing, he was blue. He had a beaked nose and the wings, claws, and largish eyes of an owl. He held a huge drum in one hand and a hammer in the other.

Behind him, guarding the next glowing ring was a woman—at least the upper half of her. From the waist down she had the coiled tail of a serpent.

The third ring was protected by what was unmistakably a bird. Though fabulously colored, it had a fierce visage and stood on one leg.

Beyond that, the second ring was inhabited by a golden-scaled creature that in Azriel's opinion looked much like a cross between a fish and a dragon.

Finally, guarding the innermost ring was a creature that had no equivalent. It most resembled a unicorn, having but a single horn above its brow, but it had a white mane beneath a head that was more like a dragon's. Its graceful body was that of a stag, yet it had the tail of an ox. It was not a very large creature, but overall its demeanor was the most mystifying.

Azriel drew Errin-lil from its scabbard. Following his lead, Halimah drew her dagger, and the others fell into a defensive position. However, the first monstrous creature facing Azriel spoke calmly.

"There is no need for weapons here, Son of Luminance."

"Who are you?" Azriel spoke, his sword still unsheathed.

"We are the guardians of the tree, and what is captured within it. You are here not for a test of weapons, but for a battle of wits. If you are found worthy, then you may pass."

"Do you have a name, dread creature?" Azriel dared to ask.

"I am Lei Gong, guardian of thunder."

"Yeah, right."

"Do you doubt me, Son of Luminance?" Suddenly, Lei Gong pounded his drum with the hammer. Lightning peeled across the sky above, though no clouds were present. It was accompanied by an ear-splitting thunderclap. The concussion nearly dropped Azriel to the ground.

"Okay, I believe you!" Azriel bowed formally in the presence of the god, and sheathed his sword. "What must I do then?" Azriel ventured.

"You are to be tested for wisdom. If you are found worthy, then you will have dominion over the elemental trapped within the tree. If you are not, then you will be turned away."

"How do I know you're not being controlled by the Clave?"

Lei Gong chuckled. "A valid question." He cast his gaze behind Azriel at Halimah. "Seeress, what do your senses tell you?"

Halimah stared back at the creature and stroked her chin as she thought. She allowed the emanations from each magickal being to pass within and through her. "Azriel, they are neither good nor evil. They serve but their own purpose. Also, their appearance is not their true form, but only a representation of their nature, based on the legends of the locals here."

Azriel felt more at ease and faced the god. Lei Gong nodded formally. He said, "You will be challenged with five riddles. If you answer correctly you will proceed to the next ring of power. If you fail, one of your companions will be turned to stone."

Behind Azriel, Camille blanched. "How is that in any way fair?" she shot back.

"No one ever said it was fair, Lady of Light. It is what it is!" Lei Gong bellowed.

Albert glanced at Rosemary. "This sucks," he muttered.

"Shush, Albert. This is important."

Lei Gong continued. "You may confer with your companions, but use your opportunity wisely. Remember, with each wrong answer, one gets turned to stone. Are we agreed?"

Azriel glanced at Albert and Halimah, and sighed. They nodded. Rosemary and Camille followed suit.

"It is agreed." Azriel conceded.

With his acceptance of the challenge, the outer ring suddenly changed from white to red. Lei Gong planted his feet firmly and posed the first question.

"What walks with four legs in the morning, two legs in the afternoon, and three legs in the evening?"

"You're kidding, right?" Azriel grumbled, but the guardian just fixed his gaze upon the young man. Behind Azriel, Amaryllis giggled.

"That's an easy one, Azriel. It's the riddle of the sphinx."

"Yeah, I know what it is, and I also know the answer." Azriel turned to Lei Gong and replied confidently. "It's a man."

"Explain, son of Luminance."

"The day you speak of is a metaphor for the lifetime of a man. In the morning or infancy of a man's life, he crawls upon his hands and knees. In the afternoon, he is in the prime of his life and walks upright on two legs, but in the evening, in the twilight of a man's life, he is old and infirm and requires a cane to support his steps—thus three legs."

"You have answered wisely." Lei Gong suddenly transformed his appearance into that of a noble elder. He stood erect in white silk robes and a golden cap. His ancient face was adorned with a mustache that draped below his chin. His eyes lit up when he smiled. "You may pass, Son of Luminance." The elder god touched the ring of power and it suddenly dissolved away. Lei Gong stood aside and let Azriel advance to the next ring.

He stood before the next guardian. She slithered over to him with sinewy grace. From her waist up, she was actually beautiful, but the lower aspect of her, the long, serrated tail of the serpent, made her somewhat frightening.

"I am Nu Qua, and I maintain order here and in the heavens. I guard over the four cardinal directions so one, if he is wise, may always know where he is going. To the mariner, I give hope in the night; for the horseman, I maintain the path of the sun so he may follow it to his destination." She smiled graciously and Azriel felt more at ease. "Now, Son of Luminance, are you ready for the next challenge?"

"Ask, lady guardian."

The ring of light turned from yellow to red and glowed ominously.

"Here it is," Nu Qua posed. "At night they come without being fetched, and by day they are lost without being stolen."

Azriel puzzled over the enigmatic question, rubbing his chin with frustration.

"Am I allowed to confer with my companions?"

"You may, Azriel, but remember, these questions are for you, not for them. They are a test of character. Your companions will pay the price of your failure."

Azriel muttered with frustration. He knew these riddles were in a way, a test of logic. He crossed his arms and glanced at his friends. Albert shrugged apologetically. Thinking, Azriel wrestled with the answer. What was there at night and lost by day? Baffled, he looked up at the night sky and mumbled to himself.

It was clear and crisp, high up in these mountains. The rarefied air made the stars appear particularly bright. To the south, Azriel could see Orion, perhaps the most recognizable of the constellations. The answer suddenly dawned on him and he smiled slyly.

"I know the answer, Lady."

"You may speak it, son of Luminance."

"The answer is *stars*!"

Satisfied with his answer, Nu Qua smiled. Her serpent's tail fell away, and she now stood on slender legs. She wore flowing silk raiment of deepest red. The ring she guarded dissolved, allowing the way to the next ring. Nu Qua strode over to the side and joined Lei Gong.

Azriel stepped forward and confidently approached the next ring. So far, the challenge had been easy—a walk in the park! The next creature he faced was a bird, perhaps only two feet tall from its head to its singular leg. Covered with blue, grey, and white feathers, it hopped forward on its one leg to face Azriel. It wasn't nearly as terrifying as the first two, but Azriel would not make the mistake of underestimating the creature. For its size, it radiated tremendous power.

"I am Shang Yung. I herald the coming rains. I am the teacher and guardian of irrigation and water management. In olden days, the City of Ch'i was in danger of being destroyed by flood." Shang

Yung piped, its voice a warble. "There, I flew down and alit on the shoulder of the Prince of Ch'i. He had sought council with the great Confucius for a way to save his city. I taught him how to create a system of drains, conduits, and canals. In this way, the Prince of Ch'i saved his city from destruction."

The rain bird flew up and landed on Azriel's shoulder. "Are you wise enough to solve the next riddle?" Shang Yung chirped, and playfully yanked at a lock of Azriel's hair with its beak.

"I'm as ready as I'll ever be, I guess."

The fabulous bird flew back to perch on the azure ring it guarded and screeched. The ring now glowed red. Shang Yung extended its wings to display its colorful plumage and cried out.

"I never was, am always to be,
No one ever saw me, nor ever will.
And yet I am the confidence and hope of all,
Who live and breathe on this terrestrial ball."

Azriel was stumped. He wasn't surprised the riddles would get more difficult with each passing. True he could confer with his companions, but he would only get one shot at this. If he got it wrong, someone would pay the consequence. He stared at his friends and back at Shang Yung.

"That's it? You're not going to give me even a little hint?"

The colorful bird preened its feathers and shrugged, "You can always come back tomorrow. We will still be here."

From behind him Camille called out. "Azriel, I think I have the answer."

"Well, I hope it's a good one because I'm baffled," he said and walked over to confer in a tight circle. He glanced at Camille, "So what are you thinking?"

"Well, it's something that's never seen, but it's the hope of all, right?

"Yes,"

"I think the answer is Knowledge."

"I don't know. I'm not sure it fits," Azriel countered.

"Think about it, Azriel. No one sees Knowledge, but it's always there for those who seek it. Without knowledge, there is no hope for tomorrow. People would just remain stupid."

"Sounds logical enough," Azriel nodded.

"No, it doesn't." Halimah countered. "It doesn't quite fit with the first line, Azriel. I think we must be more precise. The first line is 'I never was, am always to be.' The way I see it, Knowledge *always* was there from the beginning for the discovering. If it's always to be, then it hasn't gotten here yet. I think your logic is flawed, Camille."

"She makes a good point," Albert said in support of Halimah.

Camille became defensive and proud. "I think my answer makes perfect sense. It wasn't there in the beginning. People began to learn things and got smarter with each new discovery. My answer is the right one." Camille insisted.

"I'm inclined to agree." Azriel said. He turned and strode toward the third ring and Shang Yung, who waited there.

"I have the answer." Azriel said with confidence.

"Speak it then, son of Luminance."

"The answer is Knowledge."

The magickal bird shook its head sadly. "You have answered incorrectly." A surge of power left Shang Yung and settled over Camille. She immediately congealed into stone.

"Hey," Azriel snapped, "why did you do that?"

"You did agree to the rules of the game, Son of Luminance." The bird said calmly.

"Change her back!"

"I cannot," Shang Yung piped, "maybe you should think about it and come back. There is always tomorrow."

"Is she going to be like that forever?"

"That's up to you, Azriel."

Enraged, Azriel rejoined his friends. "This sucks!" he growled.

Amaryllis took Azriel by the shoulders and gave him a gentle shake. "Put away your anger, Azriel. This is not the time for it. Anger will cloud your logic."

"What should I do?" He gently touched Camille's stony cheek.

"Answer the question correctly. That's all you can do. It would help to go over everything from the beginning. What clues are there?" Amaryllis instructed.

"Doesn't seem to be much." Azriel sat on the ground in a huff.

"I never was and always to be," Halimah repeated the first line of the riddle thoughtfully. "What can that possibly be? What would not be there yesterday but would be there tomorrow?"

"Yeah, but we have to fit it in with the next line," Albert added, "No one ever saw me, nor ever will."

"Right, so it's also something unseen, but always will be. It speaks of the future then?"

"Don't forget the third line," Amaryllis added. "I am the confidence and hope for all…"

"This is impossible!" Azriel grumbled. "Maybe I should take Shang Yung's advice and come back tomorrow. Perhaps I'll do better with time to think about it."

Azriel glowered at the ground, defeated. They all sat in silence, trying to piece it all together. "Wait!" He brightened, "That's it! It makes perfect sense now. It's all about the future! No one can see it, it doesn't appear in the past, and everyone has hope for it."

Azriel arose quickly and strode over to the Shang Yung. The bird still roosted on the third ring. It had its head tucked under a wing. Its chest rose and fell as it napped. Azriel coughed a few times to get its attention. Shang Yung fluttered awake.

"The answer is *Tomorrow*!"

"You have answered wisely!" The fabulous bird stretched its wing, as the third ring dissolved. Shang Yung swirled into another shape—that of a young adolescent girl. She wore a blue silk robe and her long black hair was decorated with a spray of feathers. She smiled brightly and said, "You may proceed to the next riddle." She bowed and joined Nu Qua and Lei Gong.

Now there were but two rings and two remaining riddles to solve. Azriel warily approached the scaled creature and bowed respectfully.

"I am Yu Lung." The creature spoke in a whisper. Though very much like a golden dragon, its arms were finlike and his head was that of a giant carp. Though grotesque to behold, the creature graciously crossed its fins over its heart in greeting. "Young Master," Yu Lung continued, "I am the guardian of the student, and of knowledge. When one advances from apprentice to adept and finally to a Master of one subject of study, I bless with wisdom. The question remains as to whether you are truly a Master. I must test your knowledge, son of Luminance."

"You may ask. I am ready." Azriel looked behind him at Camille transformed into stone. He couldn't help feeling inadequate and responsible for her dilemma.

"A word of wisdom, Azriel," Yu Lung offered. "Do not allow circumstance to cloud your mind, for all circumstance is merely an illusion of your making."

"Thanks, that helps." Azriel muttered, then winced.

"Very well. Here is a riddle."

I am free for the taking through all of your life,
Though given but once at birth.
I am less than nothing in weight,
But will fell the strongest of you if held."

Azriel gaped at the fish creature, incredulous. Another impossible question. He wanted to ask for help from his friends, but if he did and answered incorrectly, another would be turned to stone. Again, he looked behind and noticed that Amaryllis and the others were in a heated discussion. He headed over to listen. Albert was arguing his position. "Look, it has to be one's name. That is given to you when you are born. It's also free all your life. It also doesn't weigh anything."

Azriel considered the argument. It sure sounded logical. But Amaryllis countered. "It may fit the first three lines, but it doesn't work for the fourth line. You can't hold a name, nor would a name drop you to the ground."

"Nor is a name free for the taking. It is a thing given." Azriel added, taking Amaryllis' position.

"So the logical step would be to start at the beginning," Halimah said. "What is at the very beginning but birth?"

"Wait," Amaryllis said, "why don't we look at a birth—yours, Azriel."

"How can we do that?"

"Are you forgetting, Azriel. I was there. I attended to Abelene during her time of travail." Amaryllis glanced at Yu Lung, and the creature nodded his approval.

"So how does that in any way help?"

"Just watch."

Amaryllis lifted the scepter of Isis and whispered an incantation. The Lotus flower began to glow and suddenly projected an image. In wonder, they all watched as Abelene, her legs covered with a blanket, strained to push her baby out into Amaryllis' waiting hands. Abelene clutched at the sheets and screamed, giving one final push. Amaryllis now had baby Azriel in her arms. She carefully turned him over and gave a sharp smack on his little bottom. He gasped his first breath and began to wail. Amaryllis deftly cut and tied off the umbilical cord.

Halimah stared in awe and giggled, her eyes moist. "Oh Azriel, you were such a beautiful baby—and you had such a cute little bum!"

"Oh, please." Azriel moaned. "This is so embarrassing."

The projected image went blank and Amaryllis smiled. "So what happens at birth, Azriel?"

"Well, you come out of your mother and then you get smacked on the butt!"

Albert laughed.

"All true," Amaryllis agreed. "Then what happens?"

"You cry—no wait! You breathe!" Azriel filled in the blanks applying it to the riddle. "Hmm, free for the taking all your life, given once at birth, it weighs nothing, and if you hold it, it will drop you like a stone!" he said, excited. "Thanks Amaryllis."

Azriel strode over to the waiting guardian.

Yu Lung asked, "Have you an answer, Son of Luminance?"

"I do! The answer to the riddle is *breath*!"

"You have done well. You have learned that it is good to take wise counsel, but you have also learned that not all counsel is wise!"

Yu Lung bowed and transformed into a young man with a cheerful face. He wore a purple robe lined with gold. As he joined the other guardians of the tree, the second ring dissolved to allow passage to the final ring.

Azriel approached the final ring, and the creature suddenly began to prance around the ring with what could only be described as unbounded joy. It reared once in salute and began to speak.

"Son of Luminance, thus far you have proven yourself in this most celestial game. You have but one more challenge."

"Do you have a name, Great One?"

The creature nickered. "I am Ky-Lin; some call me Yin-Yang, for I embody the balance of all nature. Within me dwell the five elements, and the five virtues."

"The five virtues?" Azriel inquired.

"Yes, these are the qualities that define the upright man. They are Benevolence, Justice, Courtesy, Wisdom, and Faith. One can spend a lifetime studying these virtues and never become a master of them. But fear not, Azriel, for you are well on your way toward understanding. You have mastered the elements of water, fire, earth, air, and that of metal—the divine quintessence from which was born your immortality. Ours is an auspicious meeting for I do not appear to anyone who is unworthy, but only to those who are virtuous."

"I've never really seen myself as virtuous," Azriel said humbly.

"A man is judged by what is in his heart, not the attainment of worldly wealth and pleasure. You have chosen the difficult path instead, one that will heal this world of rigid science and heal the Magickal world of its mortal wounds by reuniting the Yin with the Yang. Much like me, I am the unity of masculine and feminine and thus I am in equilibrium—perfect balance."

"I think I understand."

"That is well, Son of Luminance, thus I will ask you the final riddle. Solve it! Learn it, and it will guide you in your every endeavor."

Azriel nodded, ready for the challenge.

> "What is greater than the gods,
> worse than evil,
> the poor have it,
> the rich require it,
> and if you eat it, you die!"

Ky-Lin posed, then said gently, "This question you must answer alone. You may have no help, for in answering it correctly, you will gain tremendously in wisdom." The creature turned to Azriel's companions, and a soft radiance emanated from its horn. They were suddenly frozen, as if time had stopped. At the same time, Camille was reconstituted from stone to mortal flesh, but like the others she was still immobile.

"What have you done?" Azriel wasn't angry, for he sensed the creature's benevolence.

"Do not worry, Azriel. They are unharmed. As you have already suspected, time has slowed for them, so you may solve the riddle at your leisure." Ky-Lin sat before the ring and touched his horn to the ground. A bowl of fruit appeared there. "You must be hungry. Eat and contemplate, then give me your answer."

Azriel was indeed hungry. He picked up a piece of fruit and ate while he considered the riddle. The fruit was exotic and perhaps the most delicious thing he had ever eaten. It was so scrumptious that he was nearly moved to distraction. Azriel had to force himself to stop eating so he could solve the question.

What could be greater than the gods? Could it be the universe? Azriel pondered. No, that couldn't be it. The gods created the universe. A creation is never greater than the creator. He sighed with frustration. What about evil? What's worse than evil? Azriel could think of nothing. The poor have it, the rich have need of it, and if you eat it you die! He examined the next three clues. What possible thing could the poor have that the rich require? And what about eating it that would kill you? Could it be poison? No, that's not it at all. Azriel mused and growled. Neither the rich nor the poor would want poison. Azriel dismissed that answer.

He tried several more answers and none of them fit. Azriel thought of things more esoteric, such as death or life, beauty,

Magick, but nothing seemed to work. Every possible answer he could conceive of wound up a big fat zero—nothing!

Azriel paused in his thinking and suddenly began to laugh at his own stupidity, tears springing to his eyes. He chuckled for a few more minutes and wiped the tears from his face with his sleeve. Now that he knew the answer, it was so obvious and profound in a way. He picked up another piece of the delightful fruit and gave pause while he ate. There was obviously a lesson here and a piece of wisdom if one took the answer to heart. He stood and approached Ky-Lin.

"Have you an answer for me, Son of Luminance?" the creature nickered.

"I do!" Azriel smiled with confidence. "The answer is *Nothing*! Nothing is greater than the gods, nothing is worse than evil. The poor have nothing, the rich require nothing, and of course if you eat nothing, you'll die!"

"You have proven yourself, Azriel, and you have gained in wisdom!" Ky-Lin touched his golden horn to the final ring, and it dissolved away, allowing access to the tree.

Like the other four guardians, Ky-Lin transformed into a human figure, but was barely visible. He was a being of radiance, and it was hard to tell whether he was male or female, as his features were soft and feminine. He spoke with a high musical voice. "The key to releasing Salacia is now yours, Azriel. Your companions are welcome to approach, but there are three who are not present that should bear witness to the reawakening. I shall call them."

Azriel heard a tone like a soft chime resonate in his subconscious, just beneath the level of hearing. First Amaryllis and Camille cautiously came forward and joined Azriel. When Albert and Halimah came forward to examine the enigmatic tree, the naiad, Maera, was with them. Her fin-like wings kept her aloft and she smiled, pleased with Azriel's progress. Soon after, Eltanin arrived with Lady Rosaluna. Eltanin placed the dream orb back into his pocket.

"Well done, Azriel!" he beamed.

"Don't congratulate me just yet. I still have to release Salacia."

"Don't fret, Azriel. It seems you have done the most difficult part. The rest of it should be easy."

Maera and Rosaluna came closer and examined the gnarled tree. It appeared twisted and distorted with age, as if the magick it contained was the only thing keeping it alive.

Ky-Lin smiled affably at Maera. "Yes, queen of Naiads, you have sensed the truth of it. This tree has held the spirit of Salacia for untold years. If Azriel had not come now, Salacia would have been lost to us, for the tree is at its last moments of life." He turned to Rosemary. "Princess of the Undines, you must spread the word when you go back to the sea that Salacia has returned!"

Azriel examined his next challenge. A circle of quartz crystals, the purest white, surrounded the base of the tree. They jutted from the ground in various lengths and thicknesses almost appearing like a regal crown. Only one of the crystals was different. It radiated the deepest sapphire blue, and bound the rest of the crystals together.

Azriel's brow furrowed as he considered the crystals embedded around the tree. There didn't seem to be any particular order in which they were placed. They seemed almost natural, except the blue sapphire. It had been carved into a shape—a perfect inverted triangle. Power radiated from its core and energized the remaining circle of crystals.

Ky-Lin explained. "Do not puzzle over the stone, Son of Luminance. You have merely to remove the stone from the rest and you will see."

Azriel did as instructed. The sapphire crystal separated easily from the others and a soft tremor suddenly emanated from the ground, spreading beneath their feet. Having been held together as if the sapphire were the binding glue, the surrounding crystals began to vibrate and fell away into piles of sand. As they disintegrated, the ancient tree, held together by magick for millennia, began to decay and crumble into chaff. A moist wind from the south gusted through the glade, finishing the job of releasing the Elemental Dragon that had been trapped within. The poor creature looked small, weak and near death. Her breathing was labored as she struggled for life. The scales of her wings were tattered and bare patches of white skin shone through. The creature stumbled toward Azriel and lay at his feet.

"This isn't right. She shouldn't look like this," Azriel looked down with pity. "What should I do?"

Lady Rosaluna crouched to her knees and cradled the dying creature in her arms. She stroked Salacia's crested head and noticed that there seemed to be an impression in the dragon's forehead.

"Azriel, give me the sapphire. I think I know what to do."

He handed it down to her and Rosaluna examined the stone. It was the right shape and would fit into the impression on the creature's head. She carefully placed it over the mark and it seemed to jump from her fingers and embed into Salacia's skin. The dragon, now empowered, suddenly reared and began to expand in size, throwing Rosaluna to the ground. Azriel helped her to her feet as they all watched in awe as life crept back into Salacia's body. She shimmered with blue radiance as her magnificence filled the sky. Stretching her massive wings, Salacia flapped them a few times and a gentle warm rain graced the companions. She roared with pleasure and her breath smelled of the ocean. Looking down at Azriel, her jeweled eyes, also deep sapphire, shone with gratitude. As health returned to her body, her iridescent scales took on all the combined colors of ocean, river and stream. She hovered above and spread her wings, looking down at Azriel.

"My brother," Salacia's voice sounded like waves crashing on the shore. "You have freed me and I thank you. I will heed your summons when you have need. Now I must return to my place in the south."

"But you will be seen by all. How will you protect yourself?"

Salacia laughed. "Few can actually see me in this body, and you only see me in a form you can understand. For the rest, I am manifested in the rains, the oceans, and the mighty waterfalls, but even they won't recognize me. The Ferrishyn have always treated me with reverence. Man, however, has been my enemy. In my physical absence, he has poisoned me and poured his filth into me believing I was dead."

Azriel suddenly felt afraid. "Are you going to punish them for their neglect?"

"I do not need to. Man punishes himself, and he will do so until he learns. Allay your fears, son of Luminance, for they will not see me, nor will they see you for what you are. Like me, you are merely a shadow of your true potential. That can be said for your companions as well. Though all of them are mortal, there is something hidden far grander than mere appearances."

"I don't understand."

"Of course you don't, and you're not necessarily meant to, at least for now." Salacia smiled. She then turned to Eltanin. "I remember you, Arch Wizard. We elementals have paid dearly for your mistake. True, we agreed to take on the burden if only to save humanity, yet they have still not learned, nor have they ever acknowledged our sacrifice."

"They never knew what took place, mighty Salacia. Much of humanity prefers living in darkness."

"Nevertheless, dear Wizard, the time is soon upon you when you must pay for your meddling. We, the elementals, have upheld our end of the bargain. Soon it will be time for you to uphold yours."

"Yes, for that I am prepared."

Salacia nodded and turned her gaze on Azriel. "I must bid you farewell for now, brother."

She flew into the sky, and her wings obscured the sun, casting a deep shadow onto the glade. They watched as she soared higher and disappeared behind a cloud. As she did, the five immortals, guardians of the tree, turned and bowed deeply to Azriel.

Ky-Lin spoke for them all. "Son of Luminance, we have fulfilled our purpose here and now must return to our own realms. We thank you for our release of service and wish you good luck and good fortune. Be well."

The five suddenly dissolved and disappeared.

"Well, that's one down and three to go." Albert shrugged. Eltanin turned to him and sighed with exasperation before dealing him a glancing smack to the back of his head.

"Ow, what was that for?"

"For being glib! You speak as though this was a walk in the park. It was anything but easy."

Resentful, Albert rubbed his head. "Geez, now I know where Nicodemus gets it from."

The companions all laughed at Albert's expense and prepared to return to Caer Wylusung.

Chapter 13

Kita, as was her habit, prowled through the woods surrounding Azriel's home in Harden Lake. Remaining hidden, her ears perked. There it was again, the sound of a mountain bike. She watched as the boy parked his riding machine and dismounted. He looked particularly bad this time. A haggard expression haunted his face as he strode up the three steps to the porch. He tapped on the door a few times and, in despair, sat on the porch swing as was his habit every week—always the same.

Waiting—always waiting.

Hermes crouched by Kita's side. "Mother, should we get rid of him? I'm in the mood for a good chase."

She chuckled. "No, Hermes. Eltanin told us not to harm the boy."

"Why does he do it, mother? Every week he comes here with the same result. It's madness."

"I think the boy *has* gone mad. Isn't it obvious he feels remorse for what he's done?"

Hermes paused. "I think I actually feel sorry for him."

"Perhaps it is time to resolve this matter." Kita licked her paws as she thought. A ring of communication had been secured around her neck with a rugged chain. Nicodemus had given it to her with orders that she be his eyes. Kita purred three times in short succession, and the ring began to glow.

"Master Nicodemus?"

He responded at once. She heard his voice clearly in her mind.

"What is it, Kita?"

"That boy is here again. Should I chase him out?"

"No, that's not necessary, but it is time to get to the bottom of all this. I am sending Azriel."

"When?"

"Now. He and Camille are with me. We're having lunch."

Kita heard Azriel's muffled voice through the ring. He was decidedly unhappy with having to deal with Eddie. "Do I have to, Uncle Nick?" Azriel grumbled. "The guy's a pain!"

Nicodemus replied. "Look, it's obvious the boy will not leave until you face him. Give him a chance to explain himself."

"I'd rather roast in hell."

Camille chimed in. "Azriel, I'll go with you. Nicodemus is right, even though I despise Eddie, there must be a reason he keeps coming to your house."

"Fine." Azriel cursed under his breath. "Maybe Kita should just eat him and be done with it!"

Kita chuckled. "Nicodemus, would you inform Azriel that I can hear everything."

"Yes, Kita, he's on his way."

Azriel used the dream orb and translocated to his home. Camille whispered as they walked from the backyard to the front porch. "I don't like it any better than you do, Azriel, but he obviously has something he needs to say. Why else would he be coming back every week?"

"Beats me. This better be important."

They walked to the front and stood, waiting for Eddie to acknowledge them. He had his head down. When he looked up, his eyes were red-rimmed and moist. Camille was shocked at his appearance. Eddie was dirty and unkempt. His normal bulk had melted away. In fact, he looked gaunt, like he hadn't eaten in weeks. But it was his eyes that evoked pity. Wild, haunted, and troubled, he had the look of one who had been hunted and barely escaped capture by a horde of demons. And it wasn't too far from the truth, either. With Azriel's dragonsight, he noted that a swirling, dark mass surrounded Eddie. He knew what it was. It was the handiwork of the Clave. A curse had been cast upon Eddie, probably by Altais, meant to torture and wreak havoc to his mind.

"What do you want, Eddie? Haven't you caused enough trouble?"

"Azriel, I…" Suddenly Eddie began to convulse and threw himself to the ground. He began to scream and flail his arms as if trying to fight off something terrifying. He curled his arms around his head, trying to protect himself.

"Azriel, you have to help him," Camille cried out.

"I don't know what to do."

"Maybe a banishing spell."

"Okay, we'll both do it!"

Azriel took Camille's hand in his and grasped his amulet with the other, calling upon its power. In unison, they began to chant:

Demons of torment, creatures of night
I cast thee out, far from my sight.
Go back to the darkness to boil and burn
I banish thee now to never return!

With an unearthly shriek, a dark mass suddenly lifted from Eddie's body and turned on Azriel, trying to capture him, but Azriel called upon the elements and the amulet erupted with blinding light, sending the evil force headlong into the ground.

Eddie began to weep with relief. Shaking, he arose to his hands and knees then sat on the porch swing, hanging his head in shame.

"Azriel..."

"Eddie, why are you here? You've been prowling around my house for weeks. Why?"

"Because you're the only one who can help me."

"After what you have done? Why should I help you?"

Eddie rubbed at his temples in misery. "You're right. There's no reason why you should, not after all the things I did to you and Camille."

Azriel stared at him fuming. "You also helped lure my mother into a trap."

"I'm so sorry." Eddie's eyes welled with remorse. "If I could take it back, I would."

"Why, Eddie? What did I ever do to you? What did Camille do?"

"Nothing," he replied miserably. "I guess I was just jealous of you."

"Of me?" Azriel retorted.

"You don't understand. You have a good home and a mother who loves you. You always seemed happy and content." Eddie paused. "Is your mother okay?"

"She's missing. I haven't seen her since the day the Clave took her."

"The Clave?"

"Yes, they are a group of very powerful wizards, and the worst evil the magickal world has to offer. Your buddy Altais is one of them."

"He's no friend of mine. You saw what he did to me, Azriel. He broke my jaw because I defied him."

"It's the way of the Clave, Eddie. They thrive on cruelty."

Eddie became introspective. "That nice old man you were with somehow fixed it. That was the first time anyone treated me with kindness without wanting something in return. It got me thinking that maybe I backed the wrong horse."

"You speak of Eltanin. He's the most powerful wizard that has ever been."

"And you know him."

"He's my great-grandfather... sort of."

"The whole thing made me realize that there's a whole world I know nothing about."

Camille interjected, "You have no idea..."

Azriel sighed. "Look, Eddie, I can appreciate you wanting to apologize, but it doesn't change anything. Besides, that's not the only reason you've been hanging around here, is it?"

"No, it isn't. After everything happened, Altais came to find me. He wanted me to do something horrible, but I refused. He tortured me! He..."

"What did he want you to do, Eddie?"

He looked Azriel in the eyes and swallowed a few times. His chest rose and fell with ragged breathing. "He wanted me to kill you—or at least capture you. He gave me this."

Eddie removed a small object from his pocket. It was a perfectly shaped, translucent pyramid. It glowed slightly with power. Azriel backed away. "He then put a curse on me and said I would be haunted by demons until I completed my mission."

Eddie held the crystal pyramid out to him. Azriel knew what it was. The Carcer Eternis emanated dark magick.

"So that's why you are here—to kill me?"

"No, you misunderstand. I want to help you," he pleaded.

"Why should I trust you?"

Eddie smirked. "Yeah, I suppose I wouldn't trust me either, but you have to believe me! Altais won't leave me alone! At least you foiled some of his plans by breaking the curse he put on me. But there's something more, Azriel. I think he did something to my mother. She's gone off the deep end. Now she's in a state asylum. They keep her locked up in a rubber room, so she won't hurt herself. Now they won't even let me see her."

Camille spoke. "Eddie, we know a little bit of what happened to your mother, and maybe we can help. But how can you, in any way, help Azriel?"

Eddie answered, "One time Altais took me to this place. It was weird. He dragged me through a mirror, and we were suddenly in this fancy room. I think it was their headquarters. Then I met this guy, Rastaban, and he took me to a chamber below ground, really deep in a cavern. He had a black dragon imprisoned in one of these!" Eddie fingered the Carcer Eternis. "Seriously, it was a friggin' dragon!"

Camille repressed a giggle. If he only knew.

Azriel thought. Perhaps Eddie could be useful. He had information that could help locate the Clave's lair. Eddie waited for a response while he fiddled with the tiny pyramid.

"All right. I'll trust you for the moment. First things first." Azriel removed a leather pouch from his pocket and opened it.

"Drop it in here."

Eddie complied.

Azriel smiled ruefully. "That thing is not a toy. It's made with very dark magick. In fact, its use is forbidden to any decent wizard."

Just then Kita and Hermes loped up to greet Camille and Azriel.

Eddie cowered against the house and paled. "Mountain lions! Don't let them eat me!"

"They won't—unless I tell them to…" Azriel snickered.

Eddie's eyes widened further. "That's not funny, Azriel."

Kita sat on her haunches and regarded the terrified boy. She spoke in a low growl. "Brother, this is the one who injured me with that flying stick."

Eddie rambled, "I'm sorry—I'm sorry! I'll never do it again."

"Okay, Kita," Azriel chuckled. "I think he's sufficiently frightened." He turned to Eddie. "I need to speak with Eltanin and my Uncle Nick before I make any decision about helping you."

"Wait! Are you leaving?" he said with rising anxiety. "Take me with you!"

"Ahh, I don't know."

"Azriel, I can't go back home. Altais will find me. He'll know that I betrayed him again. He'll kill me!"

Azriel sighed. "Just wait here. I need to discuss this."

Away from Eddie, Azriel conferred with Camille, Kita, and Hermes.

"I don't like it," Camille whispered, "I still don't trust him. How do we know he's not a mole?"

"Much as I don't like the guy, I believe him. I think he's been put through hell by the Clave, and I think he knows how badly he screwed up!"

Hermes added, "If he gets out of line, I can always bite him!"

"That will be enough, son," Kita scolded.

"And besides," Azriel continued, "Eltanin will want to speak to him. If he's hiding anything, Eltanin will know. Are we agreed?"

"Yeah, I guess." Camille scowled.

As they discussed the matter at hand, from the porch, Eddie kept staring at Azriel. There was something not quite right about him—something just beyond his perceptions. He seemed different from the last time Eddie had seen him. When Azriel approached after having arrived at a decision, Eddie stopped him. He squinted and walked around Azriel examining him.

"Okay, this is going to sound weird, but did you get a dose of radiation or something? You're glowing!"

Azriel crossed his arms and peered suspiciously at Eddie. "You shouldn't be able to see that, Eddie. Most mortals can't."

"What are you telling me? You're immortal?"

"There's a lot you don't know, Eddie. I'm taking you to a safe place, but the form of travel is something you've never seen, so don't be scared, okay?"

Azriel removed the dream orb from his pocket and implanted an image. Camille took his hand, but Kita and Hermes leaned against her to make contact. Azriel instructed Eddie. "Just place your hand on my shoulder and hold on."

The effect was instantaneous. Eddie gasped wide-eyed at the courtyard of Caer Wylusung. It was deserted, other than Mortimer, who perched lazily on the closed gate. Curious, he flew over to examine the newcomer. He scratched his head, puzzled. He had seen this one before, but where? Then Mortimer suddenly remembered and glared at the boy, cursing and spitting with agitation.

"Calm down, Mortimer. He won't hurt anybody. He's here as my guest!"

Magador silently swooped down behind Eddie and stared down with interest, towering over the unsuspecting young man.

"Mortimer's very agitated, cousin. He believes you have finally lost your mind bringing this criminal here."

Nearly frozen with fear, Eddie slowly turned around, afraid to see what spoke. It was obviously large. The shadow it cast had completely blocked out the sun—and it seemed to have enormous wings. Eddie trembled and risked a peek.

"Dragon!" he squealed. He ran for the first thing that would offer some protection, squeezing himself beneath a stone bench. "Oh crap! Oh crap! Oh crap!" he bawled. "Don't let him eat me!"

Magador looked down and tilted his head with amusement, baffled by the newcomer's odd behavior. "Cousin, I do believe your guest has suffered a mental break." He reached down, removed the stone seat, and carefully placed it aside. Eddie cowered with his hands over his head. Magador then lifted Eddie by his jacket and placed him on his feet amid his cries for mercy.

"Honestly," the dragon huffed, "your behavior is quite unbecoming for a young man of your age. You act as though you've never spoken to a dragon before!"

"I haven't!" Eddie's voice squeaked.

Azriel chuckled. "Hey, Magador. How's your day going?" He scratched behind the dragon's crest.

"Probably better than yours. Who is this *person* you have brought?"

Azriel eyed Eddie critically. "To be honest, I'm not really sure who he is anymore. That's why Eltanin will want to speak to him."

Albert and Jasper walked into the courtyard, but when Jasper saw Eddie, he charged forward, ready to deck him. Camille intercepted, holding him back.

"Leave him alone, Jasper. Eltanin wants to have a word with him."

"You have got to be joking. You're actually defending him? I just want one shot!" He clenched his fist.

"Jasper, let it go. I promised Eddie he would be safe here."

"Safe!" Jasper's face reddened. "Maybe we're not safe. You're nuts bringing him here!"

"Maybe, maybe not. Eltanin will figure that out!"

"I seem to be hearing my name thrown about." Eltanin entered quietly and stood casually beside Azriel. He wore his ritual dark robe and held his staff, stroking his beard thoughtfully, considering Eddie. "What do you have to say for yourself, young man?"

Eddie gulped, lost for words.

"Oh, come now, son. I'm not going to punish you. I just want to speak with you." He turned to Azriel. "Let me have the pouch."

Eltanin looked inside and cocked an eyebrow. "It's a good thing you didn't touch it, Azriel. It's keyed to trap you. These things are very specific."

"Yes, I figured that."

"There's only one wizard I know who can create the Carcer Eternis besides me. I see Rastaban has been quite busy." Eltanin scowled. He considered Eddie. The boy was unkempt and filthy. His clothes looked as if they hadn't been laundered for a month—and he smelled bad.

"First things first." Eltanin mused. "There is a bathroom and shower inside the castle—use it! I will have some clothes laid out for you. Please put your old clothes in this." Eltanin snapped his fingers, and a cloth sack appeared. "Then you will take them up to the tower where Magador will incinerate them forthwith! Next you will eat a good lunch. When you are ready, Azriel will show you to my study. Is that clear?"

Eddie gulped with apprehension. "Yes, sir."

Eddie showered meticulously. Hot water was a luxury he hadn't had since his mother had been admitted to the state hospital. The power to the double-wide had been shut off, and food had become scarce. If not for at least the shelter of his run-down home, Eddie might as well have been considered a transient. For all intents and purposes, Eddie felt homeless and abandoned. He thought of Azriel. Eddie had hated him throughout his schooling, had been a bully, and had even resorted to near-criminal behavior, and yet Azriel saw fit to trust him, even after all he had done. Eddie let the hot water soak his skin and leaned against the stone wall of the shower. "How could I have been so wrong?" he wondered aloud. "I was such a prick!"

Like absolution, the hot water washed away not only the grime on his skin, but the animosity he had felt his whole life. These people were kind and caring. Sure, they used magick, which Eddie had been taught was evil, but they weren't evil! There was a goodness about them that Eddie found disconcerting. He wasn't used to it.

After showering, Eddie found a stack of clothing neatly laid out on a bench outside the washroom. There was a new pair of pants, a shirt, shoes, socks, and an unusual green robe. He could not know the robe was that of an acolyte of the magickal arts. He shrugged and dressed quickly. As instructed by Eltanin, he stuffed his old clothes into the cloth sack. When he exited the lavatory, Mortimer was waiting outside the door. He motioned to Eddie and led him up to the turret where Magador waited.

"You can toss that over there, young man." Magador pointed to a blackened section of floor. He belched out a controlled flame and quickly reduced the sack to a pile of cinders.

Though Eddie was still frightened, he couldn't help but remark with respectful awe. "Cool!"

"Actually, it's quite hot. Now, if I were you, I would go downstairs and eat. You're going to need your strength when Eltanin questions you. A word of advice: Don't lie. Master Eltanin will be able to see right through you."

"Do you know who I am?" Eddie asked.

"Of course I do. You're the young man who has caused so much trouble for Azriel," Magador stated as a matter of fact.

"And yet no one wants to kill me?"

"What purpose would that serve?"

"I don't know—revenge?"

"Revenge is a waste of time and energy, and it also never quite satisfies. It would serve a greater purpose for you to understand who we magickal beings are, and why we do what we do. Now go eat some lunch. Eltanin is waiting."

Eddie found the massive dining room and stared agape at the table laid out with more food than he had ever seen in one place. It was like a Thanksgiving dinner amplified. Azriel, Camille, Jasper, Albert, and Julia were at the table eating, along with other people he didn't recognize. Azriel introduced Rosemary, Maggie, and Halimah, then Nicodemus and Amaryllis. Eddie was amazed to see so many varied and exotic faces, and smiled sheepishly. Oddly, no one there eyed him with suspicion but instead welcomed him to the table.

"Geez, Azriel, do you eat like this all the time."

"No, we just figured you were probably hungry. Ever have rabbit? It's pretty good. Mortimer's an ace at nabbing them."

"Mortimer?"

Azriel pointed to the end of the table where the gargoyle was half-buried in a bowl of food. Muffled sounds of gobbling and slurping filled the hall.

"Don't mind him. Mortimer's table manners are atrocious, but he's really pretty sweet once you get to know him."

"I'll take your word for it." Eddie grimaced. He helped himself to a heaping plate of food and ate until he was sated. Not much conversation took place, as it was awkward and uncomfortable having Eddie there. Thankfully, Eddie was at least comforted that no one there treated him with contempt. When he was done, Azriel showed Eddie to Eltanin's study.

Eddie tapped on the door, and Eltanin ushered him to a desk situated to the side of a massive study. He walked gingerly, letting his eyes adjust as the room was barely illuminated by candles placed haphazardly in every available free space. Everywhere Eddie glanced, he saw piles of books, strange lab equipment, and various other arcane paraphernalia that defied definition. On Eltanin's cluttered desk sat a human skull that doubled as a candleholder. Beside it, a sizeable crystal ball perched upon an elegant gold pedestal. Eddie suddenly felt fear, but it wasn't the same as the terror he had experienced facing Rastaban. It was more a feeling of respectful awe.

"Edward Allen Breck, I have been observing you for quite some time now."

Eddie gulped.

Eltanin continued. "I see everything. I know more about you than would bring you comfort."

Eddie stammered. "But...how?"

"I'm a wizard," Eltanin said with a touch of humor. "It's my job to know, and my duty to protect those I love."

Eddie squirmed uncomfortably. "What do you want from me— why have you brought me here?"

"Edward, you have been the victim of misinformation. Everything you've learned over the years about this world and about magick in general has been in error. It's not entirely your fault. Most people of this world walk about in ignorance, completely unaware of the power they have over themselves. It has been purposely designed that way to keep people passive and controllable. Everything humans do is meant as a distraction to keep them from thinking—from learning the truth."

"I don't understand," Eddie replied. "What do you mean?"

Eltanin smiled warmly. "Son, there are two worlds we live in— that which you see and that which is hidden. Only by applying oneself to study and observation can the hidden become transparent. You have been led to believe that Azriel is your enemy because you know so little of him, and what you know has been tainted by your own prejudice. It is the way of this world that reality is often misunderstood."

"Master wizard, I know I screwed up big time, but what can I possibly do now to make it better?"

"You've already taken the first step. You are here, are you not?"

"But what good does that do?"

"Your mind is beginning to open, son. That's the first step to changing your perceptions. For example, there has been animosity between you and Azriel for many years. Your anger has blinded you to friendship, and yet, Azriel is not entirely innocent either. He has also become blind to your potential. He has only seen you as a rotten kid who likes to hurt people."

"Yeah, but that hasn't been far from the truth."

"That may be so, but I can see promise in you. I think you and Azriel would benefit from friendship." Eltanin sighed. "Edward, there are things you don't know. Azriel carries with him a burden you couldn't possibly imagine. Although he appears strong and confident, he needs friends just as much as you do." The old wizard nodded knowingly. "More on that later." He removed the crystal pyramid from the leather pouch and placed it on the desk. "Do you know what this is, son?"

"No, not really."

"This is the Carcer Eternis. It is made with dark magick."

"What does it do?"

"It's an eternal prison because it has no beginning or end. Not to worry, I have neutralized it. It cannot harm Azriel anymore. It needs to be embedded with a specific name. Azriel's name was written upon it." Eltanin hesitated. "You have seen one other like this one before, haven't you?"

"Yes."

"And what you saw within it terrified you."

Eddie nodded.

"What you saw, Edward, was the Dragon of Death. The Clave has held it captive for twenty thousand years. Soon Azriel must face him. And he will need your help."

"Me? There is no way you could ever get me to go back there. I'd rather die!"

Eltanin sagely folded his hands over his chest. "Edward, there are some things far worse than death. Take your mother for instance. She is in a perpetual nightmare, some of it her own doing; some of it by the dark designs of the Clave."

"What did she ever do to them?"

"Nothing. They are using her to get to you. You see, Edward, when Altais brought you to their lair, he made a fatal mistake. You now have knowledge that can lead Azriel to them. If Azriel can find them, he can defeat them."

"So why didn't Altais just kill me when he had the chance?"

"To be honest with you, Edward, that's as much a mystery to me as it is to you. Rastaban is very smart. There must be something you have or perhaps something you know that makes you valuable to them just yet. This we need to explore. On the other hand, the Clave thrives on the misery of others. They did not need to kill you but simply drive you mad. In that they nearly succeeded. After all, who would ever believe a peculiar boy telling stories of wizards and dragons?" Eltanin chuckled.

Eddie looked down at his feet. "Master Eltanin, would you help me get my mother out of that horrible place?"

"I have no intention of leaving her there, son. Between Azriel and myself, we will bring her here, but we can't do it alone. We will need your help as well."

"Anything you ask," Eddie's eyes glimmered with hope.

"There is more to tell you. You need to know why all this has happened and why Azriel is the key to everything. I'd like to tell you about a world known as Aralia..."

Nearly three hours had passed, when Eddie emerged from Eltanin's study, pale and badly shaken. Eltanin had just told him a history he could never have imagined—that of a shattered world split in two and of a destiny to reunite the worlds into one again.

In a rare moment of relaxation, Azriel was sitting by the hearth, surrounded by his friends, laughing. Beside the cheerful fire, they were playing a game of Monopoly. He had his arm draped around

Camille's shoulder, cheering her on. He had already lost, having discovered a ruthless side of her he had never seen before. Now she was wiping the board with Albert. He had just landed on Boardwalk and was whining about the rent.

"Here, that's everything. Hope you choke," Albert grumbled.

Camille giggled. "Oh, don't be such a sore loser. You should have listened to Halimah when she told you not to sell me Park Place."

Halimah's eyes twinkled as she began poking Albert in the ribs. "Sore loser! Sore loser!" she teased as he tried to wrestle her hands away amid everyone's laughter.

Their bantering suddenly ceased when they noticed Eddie watching them. After his time with Eltanin, Eddie's eyes were troubled by the knowledge he now had. He approached gingerly, not quite sure he was welcome or even worthy of joining them. He faced Azriel squarely.

"Azriel..." Eddie shook his head. "I wouldn't want to be you for all the money in the world!"

There was an uncomfortable silence as everyone glanced at each other, but they all suddenly broke out in laughter at Eddie's expression. Julia slid over on the carpet to allow space for Eddie to sit. He joined them and stared at the game board. "Are you still playing?" he asked.

"No, I think we're pretty much done," Julia smiled. "Camille kicked our butts. Watch out for her, Eddie. She can be mean and vicious."

"I'll consider myself warned." Eddie glanced at them. "I guess this must be weird—me hanging out with all of you. I haven't exactly been nice to any of you."

Azriel replied. "Everyone changes, Eddie. The truth has a way of doing that."

Eddie nodded.

"So what did Eltanin tell you?"

"Everything." He paused. "Hey, you're really from another world?"

"Yeah, I guess. But I was born here."

"Eltanin offered to teach me how to use magick."

"Sounds dangerous," Jasper commented.

"Don't listen to him, Eddie." Julia said. "It's only dangerous for my brothers because they're in the habit of making things blow up!"

Eddie smiled. "Cool!"

"First things first." Azriel said, changing the subject. "I spoke to Eltanin. We have a plan to get your mom out of the hospital. Have you been there—seen where they've locked her away?"

"Yeah." Eddie replied and frowned. "But now they won't let me visit. Those idiot doctors say my presence is preventing her recovery. Do you believe that?"

"No, it doesn't make sense. I wonder if something else is going on."

"Yeah, me too." Eddie stretched and yawned. "Azriel, I'm really tired. Is there somewhere I could crash?"

"Sure." Azriel motioned to Mortimer. The little gargoyle flew over. "Would you show Eddie to the guest room?"

Mortimer placed his left hand over his belly and bowed. Eddie rose and said goodnight, then followed Mortimer upstairs to the second floor. Waiting until they could no longer hear his footsteps, Azriel addressed his friends.

"So, what do you think?"

Julia spoke out. "I'm amazed. He's actually nice when he's not being a jerk."

"Yeah, but I'm still not sure he can be trusted," Albert added.

"There must be a reason Eltanin wants me to help Eddie rescue his mother." Azriel said, pondering.

Albert thought, then replied. "You could always say no."

"That's true, but I have to trust Eltanin's instincts. I guess what it all boils down to is choice. I have the power and the wits to help. If I do nothing, Eddie would have just cause to hate me. If I do help him out, at best, he would become a loyal friend, though I'm not sure how I feel about that. At minimum, he would owe us a debt of gratitude."

"So either way, we're stuck with him." Jasper mused.

"The thing that bothers me, though, is that he and I have been enemies for so long, I really can't imagine him being my friend."

"I don't think you're being fair. Give him a chance," Julia said defensively.

They all turned and looked at her.

"You're not actually taking his side, are you?" Camille jabbed playfully at Julia's arm.

"No..." She answered awkwardly. "I just think that anyone deserves the chance to change for the better. Don't you remember how shy you were, Camille, how you didn't think anyone could like you?"

"Yeah..." she answered defensively.

"The truth is, Camille, in the beginning, I thought you were just being a snob! I thought you didn't talk to us because you thought you were better than us."

"Really..." Camille's ire began to rise.

"Look, all I'm saying as that everyone's perceptions of you were completely wrong. Once we got to know you, nobody here could do anything but love you, particularly Azriel." She smiled impishly.

Halimah giggled and teased. "I think maybe you're kind of sweet on Eddie."

"No I'm not!" Julia's cheeks reddened. "Although now that he's cleaned up his act and lost all that weight, he's really not so bad looking."

Camille screwed up her face. Albert and Jasper chuckled.

"Okay, so are we agreed then? Do we give him a chance to prove himself?" Azriel asked.

Everyone nodded, though Albert and Jasper did so grudgingly.

Mortimer opened the door and allowed Eddie entry into the room. He quickly lit all the candles in the sconces to provide adequate light. Eddie looked around and blinked, not believing his eyes.

"Wow!" he gasped. The room was more than just cozy. It was opulent. The cut-glass window was slightly ajar and moonlight flooded in, adding to the splendor. Tapestries and paintings hung from the stone walls, and beautiful stones, both natural and carved decorated the dressers. Central to the room was a four-poster bed with a thick mattress. Eddie felt the brocaded bed spread and pushed down gently. He grinned with delight. The room was fit for a king.

As beautiful as the room was, it was chilly. The desert air had a tendency of cooling off considerably at night, and Eddie shivered. Mortimer motioned to the hearth, and Eddie nodded. Soon the little gargoyle had a comfortable fire blazing.

Eddie watched as the creature moved about the room, making sure it was properly equipped. "Hey Mortimer, you're the creature that bit me and turned me into stone, aren't you?"

Mortimer smiled innocently.

"Not that I blame you. I was wrong you know, and I deserved it."

The little gargoyle shrugged and flew to the foot of the bed as Eddie changed into the night clothes laid out on the bed.

"Mortimer, I was wrong about a lot of things. I'm sorry."

He flew closer to Eddie until they were face to face. He reached out and tenderly placed his hand over Eddie's heart and nodded. Then he ruffled the boy's hair.

"You're actually a neat little guy. Thanks, Mortimer."

Like before, Mortimer bowed cordially and let himself out of the room. Eddie sighed with contentment and laid his head down on the pillow. The bed was soft and comfortable. A finer bed he had never experienced. Soon he was fast asleep dreaming of good things. It was the first peaceful night Eddie had in several months.

Michael Anthony Cariola

Chapter 14

"It happened just the way you predicted, Lord Rastaban." Altais smiled gleefully, "Azriel took the bait. He now harbors that boy, Eddie, and soon we will have him right where we want him."

Rastaban sat at the head of the conference table, stroking the smooth mahogany surface as he nodded. Giausur, Edasich, and Thuban watched him closely, waiting for him to respond.

"My Lord?" Edasich probed. "What say you?"

Rastaban held up his hand to forestall any further inquiries while he thought out the next phase of his dark plan.

"Azriel is becoming predictable," The lord wizard chuckled. "Such a soft, bleeding heart, that he would take in an enemy. No doubt he will try to free the boy's mother, and when he does, we will be waiting. Thuban, I commend you. Insinuating yourself into the hospital as an orderly was brilliantly executed. Have you kept the woman completely under your control?"

"Yes, my Lord, but if I may, this plan makes me nervous. He has avoided capture thus far. Azriel seems always to be one step ahead of us. He is as elusive and crafty as Eltanin was. It almost seems as though the Arch Wizard is back from the grave!"

"Be at peace, brother. Eltanin is long gone. Think of our plan as double indemnity. If the boy wizard evades our capture when he comes for the woman, she will surely lead us to where he is hiding. You do have the tracking spell in place as I requested?

"Yes Lord Rastaban. It's subtle, so the possibility of detection is quite remote."

"I see—good. We may finally get an answer to that which has had me so thoroughly mystified."

"And what would that be, my Lord?" Edasich asked.

"The boy's elusiveness. I'm not surprised that he has grown remarkably in power. Certainly he's a worthy adversary, but there seems to be an unseen hand guiding him."

"Perhaps you shouldn't have killed Nodus so soon, Lord Rastaban," Giausur interjected. "I suspect he knew something and you silenced him forever before he could reveal it. He died laughing at you."

Rastaban's face darkened. "Your fears are unfounded. Nodus was becoming erratic and tiresome. He was a liability to all of us. Be careful, Giausur, that you don't become a liability as well."

"Never, my Lord!" Giausur said quickly, but his eyes narrowed spitefully as Rastaban turned away.

"Now it may be true that the boy wizard grows more powerful. There are indications that Salacia has been found and raised, and only Azriel could have done it. That is evident in certain anomalous events occurring throughout this planet. In the past month, both the Sahara and the Gobi deserts have seen record rainfall. If this keeps up, the deserts will retreat and become green again. Many rivers polluted by the negligence of man have suddenly and inexplicably begun to clear. Yes, my friends, the Elementals are being raised one by one. This is detrimental to our plans. People are beginning to have hope again. Should this continue, we will lose control over them." Rastaban fumed. "We cannot abide this anymore. It is time we resort to more persuasive measures. Azriel's numbers are growing and more flock to his cause. I'm sure you have felt it!"

"Indeed I have," Altais responded. Magick was nearly dead on this world, save for our own Magick. Our manipulations caused the Inquisition and the witch hunts. We were nearly successful."

"Yes, but now people are learning not to be afraid. If they realize their potential, our task will become more complicated," Thuban added.

"Perhaps we should bring in reinforcements to foul Azriel's plans. Abelene has taught him well, and he is obviously aware of his destiny. I think it is time to raise Lilith from the underworld."

Giausur paled. "Do you think that wise, my Lord? It's well known she cannot be trusted. She serves only herself. She would just as soon betray us if it would serve her own ends."

"True, my brother, but her goals and mine are the same. Perhaps we may benefit from mutual cooperation. And besides, if I summon her, *I* control her!"

"My Lord," Giausur asserted, "are you forgetting that it was you who vanquished her to the underworld in the first place?"

"Of course I haven't, brother. But she would be grateful for her release..."

"...or vengeful," Giausur replied quickly. "She defied you the first time, which is why you defeated her. Don't forget, my Lord, that she wanted to usurp our power and wield it herself."

"And if I may add," Thuban interjected, "In the absence of the Dragon of Death, Lilith has taken control of the underworld. What would she benefit by aligning with us?"

"Brothers, you have no imagination!" Rastaban chuckled. "Consider an alliance between the dark forces of the underworld and the Clave. Together, we would be invincible against anything Azriel and his pathetic Order of the Ankh could throw at us. Mark my words, Thuban. A war is looming on the horizon. Should Azriel succeed in reuniting Aralia and Earth, we must have a contingency plan. We will have to turn the world against him. Through such turmoil, humanity and Elvinkind will turn toward us to save them from annihilating each other. We would be their saviors."

"So what do you propose?" Edasich asked.

"A sacred union between the lovely Queen of the Underworld and myself."

The Clave was stunned to silence.

"My lord! You will place yourself and us in danger!" Thuban responded in horror.

"Tut, tut, Thuban. You overreact." Rastaban said with an obsequious smile. "An agreement has already been made—an oath sealed in blood. Lilith and I have come to terms." Rastaban motioned to the far corner of the chamber. "Lilith, come, my dear!"

They all turned as one and stared with curiosity at the bookshelf filled with old tomes and magickal scrolls. They stared back at Rastaban as if he had lost his mind. There was nobody there.

"Come, Lilith, don't be shy."

Atop the shelf, a blue iridescent butterfly crept forward and alit. It floated gracefully from its perch and landed on Rastaban's arm.

Suddenly it swirled and morphed into a golden-haired woman. Voluptuous and dressed in red and black lace, she wore a golden headdress in the shape of an owl with outstretched wings that encircled her head. She was stunningly beautiful in a sensuous and seductive way, but there was wildness in her eyes that hinted at danger and the threat of oblivion.

Her lips twisted into a smile that sent waves of longing to the wizards in the room, but also chilled their hearts with icy fear. Her voice was sultry as she rested her hands on her shapely hips. "Hello, boys," Lilith smiled faintly. "Did you miss me?"

Abelene placed the finishing touches on the tapestry she had designed. She knew that someday it would hang triumphantly in the great hall of Aralia. It would attest to Azriel's future victory over the Clave. Though she could not claim the castle as her ancestral home, by rights, it was Azriel's inheritance. In a little less than a year, Azriel would ascend the throne and rule his homeland. The thought certainly brought Abelene a sense of exhilaration, yet it also caused her grave concern. He would ascend as king of Aralia in a changed world, one in which Magick and the technology of man would be forced to cohabitate. But could they? The fundamental differences between the two philosophies could easily lead to war. Men had certainly fought over less. She could only hope that Azriel would have the wisdom to prevent such a terrible outcome. Abelene decided not to think about it. Worrying would serve no purpose anyway. No one could predict the result of merging the two worlds. Without question, the topography of the merged planets would be dramatically altered— the flora and fauna as well. Earth had not seen magickal creatures for twenty thousand years. In human memory, such creatures as dragons, griffins, gargoyles, unicorns—they were all dismissed as merely legends or old wives' tales. Worse, if anyone did confess to seeing a dragon, that person's sanity would be in question. Such sightings would fall into the category of UFOs or the paranormal, and such notions would never be entertained by reasonable men. As Abelene thought about this, she grimaced. How, indeed, would humanity react to a magickal world when mankind clearly had a history of being shortsighted in so many categories?

"You seem to be quite deep in contemplation, Milady," Charlie interrupted Abelene's train of thought.

"Honestly, Charlie, I would welcome some diversion right now. The future looks so uncertain."

"Oh, I wouldn't say that. Azriel will succeed."

"It's not that," Abelene mused. "Sometimes I think we would all have been better off if Azriel had been kept completely unaware. Perhaps it would be safer if the conjunction of both worlds would pass unnoticed by all."

"Not to correct the imbalance? No Abelene. That would be wrong for so many reasons."

"But think about what will happen when both worlds merge. Every scenario I envision ends in conflict and destruction. I fear for the future, Charlie, and for the life of my son."

"Let it unfold as it will, Lady Abelene. Besides, we have far bigger concerns."

"Oh?"

"I believe Rastaban has finally lost his mind."

"But we knew that, Charlie. No sane man would do the things he has done. His mind has been twisted—corrupted by his lust for power and control."

"Well put, Lady Abelene, but I speak now of an even more ominous danger. Are you familiar with one named Lilith?"

"The legends of Aralia speak of her."

"What do you know of her?" Charlie probed.

"Human legends tell of her, but the history of Aralia is far older. Eltanin, as you know, was the first wizard of the old world. He had been empowered by the Dragon Elementals. They imbued him with all the powers of life and creation. They gave him the knowledge of all the rituals, both of light and darkness."

"That is true, Abelene. I was present at his infusing as well. He had earned the right to the secret knowledge, for he was the first to recognize the hidden potential in all living things, animate and inanimate. From him, all other sorcerers, wizards, and witches were taught. Yet there were some things that he kept hidden—that should still remain hidden."

"Indeed," Abelene said, and picked up where Charlie left off. "As I recall the story, Eltanin had a bright, promising student, this Lilith we speak of. After learning all she could from Eltanin, she became the most powerful sorceress that ever lived. She betrayed Eltanin and was eternally banished to the underworld for her disloyalty."

"Well that's a watered-down version of the story and, only half of it." Charlie sighed heavily. "You see, Lady, Eltanin became enamored with his young student. She was bright and beautiful beyond what would be considered reasonable for any woman. In truth, he loved her, and it was his love that blinded him to the truth. That has always been Eltanin's flaw, you see."

"Loving deeply isn't necessarily a flaw, Charlie." Abelene couldn't hide her indignation. She caught herself and wondered why she had become so cross with the great dragon.

"I see I touched a raw nerve," Charlie chuckled. "People do the strangest and most foolish things for love, sometimes even to their own deaths."

"You seem to have a rather low opinion of love."

"I've just never had much use for it, Lady Abelene, particularly in my line of work. It would most certainly cloud my judgment, just like Eltanin's mind had been deceived by Lilith's charms. Eltanin broke the first law of wizardry, a law that he himself had put into place. She had attempted a spell that almost killed her. In his grief at the prospect of losing her, Eltanin gave Lilith the gift of immortality, thus cheating me of her soul. She had never earned the right, and to make matters worse, Eltanin was blind to the darkness that dwelled in her heart. Compounding her immortality with her gift for sorcery, Eltanin thought that, as equals, they might be wed, but she betrayed him and almost imprisoned him, as well as the Clave, so she could wrest power from them and rule Aralia. At that remote time, Rastaban had not yet been turned to darkness. It took the combined efforts of Eltanin and the Clave to send Lilith to the underworld. In my absence she has crowned herself Queen of the Underworld. She is solely responsible for being the mother of demons and all other manner of foul beasts and lords of corruption. I will have to clean house when I finally return to my domain."

"Charlie," Abelene said, rubbing her scalp, trying to understand the connection, "Why are we discussing this at all? Is there something I'm missing?"

"Sadly, yes, Milady. Rastaban has released her from the Underworld and seeks to forge a union."

Abelene paled.

"Of course, it is in her nature to betray. At the first opportunity, mark my words, she will deceive Rastaban. But before that time, she poses a great threat to Azriel and all that he loves. Her powers are formidable, and to make matters worse, she has the gift of sight. Eltanin's secret is no longer safe."

"Will she harm Azriel?"

"No, that is not her way of doing things. In truth she's a coward, but she will do everything in her power to interfere with Azriel's success through distraction and deception."

"Then I must contact Azriel as soon as possible," Abelene scowled.

"That would be wise, Milady."

Abelene pondered their conversation. "Charlie, may I ask you a question?"

"Of course. I always welcome your inquiries."

"Are you capable of love?"

"That's a difficult question. I suppose I can love in my own way, but you must understand, Abelene—love would be painful for me. Consider what would happen if I became enamored with someone. Eventually, that person's number would be up, so to speak. I would be reluctant to do my duty and take that one's soul. If I failed in my duty due to my own personal feelings, I could upset the perfect balance forged from the beginning. It is better for me not to become emotionally attached."

Abelene laughed lightly.

"Lady," Charlie asked, slightly offended. "Are you mocking me?"

"No, my friend. It's just that it's the first time I've ever heard you lie."

"Lie?" the great dragon uttered with a bemused expression.

"Well either to me or to yourself."

"What are you saying, Abelene?"

"Well, it's just that you love me, don't you?"

If it were possible for a dragon to blush, Charlie would have. Instead, he tapped his foot impatiently and squirmed.

"Come on, Charlie. Admit it."

"Well," he replied in a huff. "You are quite lovely, and I am… well… fond of you, Lady."

Abelene smiled her victory. "I suppose that is the best I can expect from you, Charlie. But that's okay. Your secret is safe with me."

Charlie scowled. "And I will not tell a soul just how thoroughly conniving and manipulative you are, Lady Abelene."

Chapter 15

"Eddie, this is important," Azriel instructed. "You need to focus every detail you can remember into the dream orb. The more details we have, no matter how insignificant they seem, the better chance we'll have of getting into the State Hospital."

"Where should I start?"

"Try to think of a place in the hospital that would be kind of deserted. Is your mother alone or roomed with others?"

Eddie started to panic. "Azriel, I don't know. The doctors there have moved her around a few times. The last I heard, she was in a catatonic state. She's completely retreated into herself. No one can reach her."

Nicodemus strode up, wearing an overcoat. "It's never going to work using a clandestine approach, Azriel. A more direct approach will be necessary in this circumstance." He removed his coat and, to Azriel's surprise, revealed a gray suit and tie, a badge pinned to his chest identifying him as hospital staff.

"Doctor Nick Stevens?" Azriel smiled wryly. "Do you think it will work?"

"Of course it will work with a little luck and perhaps a glamour spell. The nurses will think me quite charming. Now Eddie, do you remember what the outside of the hospital looks like?"

"Yeah. It's pretty hard to forget. It looks like something straight out of a horror film." Eddie directed his thoughts into the dream orb and soon an image coalesced within the crystal globe. Nicodemus peered into the orb as the representation began to clarify. The edifice seemed to have been built in the early twentieth century, judging from the structural design. Typical of American institutional architecture of its time, it resembled a prison more than a hospital. Gray and uninviting, it had barred windows and a central tower that brooded over the stone courtyard below. A wrought iron fence surrounded the compound to keep away intruders and to prevent escape from its deranged patients. Indicative of a time when mental health was in its infancy and treatment bordered on medieval torture, Azriel cringed at the sight of the place as they were transported beyond its gates.

"Okay, now what?" Azriel whispered.

"Well for one thing, both of you need to look a bit older." Nicodemus formed a few hand gestures with a flourish and Azriel suddenly sported a well-trimmed beard and mustache. Eddie now donned a mustache and a pair of wire-rimmed glasses that certainly gave him a pronounced scholastic look. They were professionally dressed as well. On their jacket pockets hung I.D. tags that identified them as interns.

"Now, my doctors in training, shall we proceed?"

Nicodemus led the way up the steps to the main foyer where they were greeted by the attending nurse. A thin, frail woman in her sixties with graying hair and a chiseled nose, rose, flustered at their approach. She spoke in a clipped nasal voice. "Doctor… er…" She glanced at his tag. "Er yes, Doctor Stevens, you are aware that it is after hours?"

Nicodemus spoke with authority. "Of course I am, nurse Vandersnoot. I would have arrived here sooner if not for engine trouble. Forgive the inconvenience but I am here to see a patient; Jessica Breck is her name."

"Oh, that one." Nurse Vandersnoot replied with annoyance. "She's unresponsive, Doctor Stevens. You're wasting your time."

"Madam, it's my time to waste." He retorted indignantly. "May I see her charts, please?"

The nurse grudgingly handed over the charts and Nicodemus flipped through the pages as he muttered to himself. "It's no wonder that Mrs. Breck hasn't shown improvement. Locking that poor woman away, pumping her full of sedatives and antipsychotics is no way to treat a mental disorder. This hospital's license should be revoked! As a matter of fact, I will be ordering a full inquiry into the substandard practices of this institution when I return to the State Department of Health."

Nurse Vandersnoot stammered. "Sir, we're underfunded and understaffed. We do the best we can."

"Madam, your best is not good enough. I will observe the patient now. Where is she?"

"Room 219, sir."

Nicodemus shot her a wry smile. "Thank you for your cooperation, madam."

Once out of earshot, riding the elevator to the second floor, Azriel commented. "Uncle Nick, you sure laid it on pretty thick, didn't you?"

"I had to appear convincing, didn't I?"

"Yeah, I suppose…"

"Listen both of you. We're not through this yet. I'm sure Nurse Vandersnoot is checking my credentials right now. When she discovers I'm a fraud, things are going to get rather interesting. I hope you're up on your spells, Azriel. Edward, did you bring the items I gave you?"

"Yes sir. They're right here in my pocket."

"Good. Let's go."

The dimly lit corridor seemed to go on forever as they searched for room 219. They rounded a corner and were accosted by two orderlies.

"Halt!" one said barring the way. "This floor is restricted."

"I'm a doctor, you fool!" Nicodemus growled.

"You're an imposter. No self-respecting doctor would come here after hours." The man reached up to a security panel mounted to the wall when Azriel released the first spell that came to mind. "Arto Agitus!" he waved his hand and the orderly's movement suddenly ceased, frozen in stride. As to the other, Nicodemus intoned the single word, *Reducto*, and the other orderly was reduced to barely a foot tall. Eddie couldn't help but laugh at the helpless expression on the orderly's face. He picked him up and dropped him into a nearby trash can.

Nicodemus walked past, but not without saying, "Don't worry too much, little man. It wears off in about an hour."

They found room 219 and made entry. Eddie was shocked at his mother's condition. She was strapped to the bed by her wrists and ankles. Unconscious, her face was pallid, creased with stress.

Eddie began unbuckling the restraints and called to her gently, though his face was red with anger at his mother's treatment.

"Bastards! Why are they doing this to her?"

Nicodemus said with compassion, "Now's not the time, Edward. We need to leave this place immediately."

Eddie lifted his mother into his arms while Azriel removed the dream orb from his pocket. As he was projecting the image of Castle Wylusung into the globe, a concussion blasted them to the floor. Eddie nearly dropped his mother but quickly lay across her, protected her body with his own. "What the hell was that?" he shouted.

Altais suddenly appeared among them and looked down at Eddie. "I see you switched sides."

"Yeah? Well screw you!"

And look who we have here. Why, it's Azriel. What a pleasure. I can't believe my eyes—Nicodemus himself! I thought you were dead!"

"Sorry to disappoint you, Altais, but I'm very much alive. Here, I believe this belongs to you. Nicodemus released a fireball from his hands and watched as it struck Altais' body. But the wizard, anticipating the move, shrugged it off as if it were nothing but a nuisance. He returned the volley with a salvo of plasma spheres. Nicodemus repelled them with a magickal shield. "Tecum!" he shouted. The protective shroud covered Eddie and Azriel as well.

While prone on the ground, Azriel faced Eddie and whispered. "Do you remember what to do?"

He nodded and smiled deviously. He reached into his pocket and removed two little balls the size of marbles. "You ready?" Azriel smiled and took hold of Nicodemus' ankle while Eddie held onto his mother. Nicodemus and Altais continued to exchange magickal blows, neither gaining the advantage, but being thus occupied, Altais didn't notice that Eddie had rolled the two balls under his feet. "Genero Flamma!" Eddie invoked the simple spell. Thick smoke billowed up and Altais' pants caught fire. Amid the distraction, Azriel activated the dream orb, and they vanished while Altais slapped at his burning legs in frustration.

Relieved to be back in the castle, Eddie placed his mother gently on the bed while Camille and Maggie tended to her. Jessica was still unconscious, but no longer catatonic.

Nicodemus lifted her eyelids and scowled. "I expected as much. That so-called hospital was keeping her enslaved in order to lure us, Azriel. And it's obvious who is controlling things there. The Clave's grasp has become far-reaching."

"Uncle Nick," Azriel replied. "You knew something was going to happen, didn't you?"

"I had my suspicions. One must think three moves ahead, just as in a game of chess. I knew it was possible that Eddie, by way of his mother, was being used to set a trap."

Eddie threw up his hands. "I didn't know anything about it!"

"Of course you didn't. You're blameless here. Oh, and by the way, good job on the Flamma spell. Surprisingly, you're a quick study, Edward."

"Thanks. I never thought I'd be doing magick."

"Brace yourself. There's a lot more to learn." Azriel smiled.

Nicodemus continued to examine Jessica and placed his hands on her temples, sensing her mental state when Eltanin tapped gently on the door.

"I will need to examine this woman," Eltanin stated. Everyone moved aside to allow the wizard through. He sat beside her and placed his aged hand on her forehead.

"Hmm, this is troubling. It seems her memory has been blocked."

"The Clave?" Nicodemus asked.

"No…something else. From what I am sensing, this poor woman had gone through a terrible ordeal. Whatever it was caused a total loss of memory. She is also not what she seems."

"What do you mean?" Eddie asked defensively.

"I would say there is more to your mother than meets the eye, Edward. How much do you know of her life, son?"

"There's not really much to tell. She never spoke of her childhood. She met my father when he was an EMT. She was in some sort of accident, but she says that she doesn't remember what happened. My father thinks it was a hit and run. Mom was cut up and bruised pretty badly, but that's all I really know. Dad often said that my mom had to rebuild her life from there. When she was found, she had no ID and no one knew where she came from. About a month after they met, they married.”

“Puzzling.” Eltanin mused as he brushed her golden hair aside and examined her features. He glanced at her ears and arched an eyebrow. “I will attempt to unblock her memory. First she must drink this.”

Camille lifted Jessica and supported her from behind as Eltanin poured a small vial of a glowing yellow liquid into her mouth. He stroked her throat to force a swallowing response.

“What is that?” Azriel inquired.

“It’s a cleansing potion. It will remove all effects of medication from her body. The result should be instantaneous.”

Eltanin then began to chant, his words almost inaudible. Azriel thought he heard the words ‘Renovo Memoria’ and other phrases he couldn’t translate. Suddenly, Eddie’s mother began to spasm, arching her back as if fighting off a demon. The tremors intensified requiring Camille and Maggie to hold her down to prevent injury. The woman suddenly bolted upright and began speaking in a language Eddie had never heard before. Eyes wide with terror she squeezed Eltanin’s hands.

“Sema tem cariha te Abelena! Tarah tem semija te Abelena!”

Azriel’s jaw dropped in shock. The woman was speaking the Aralian tongue, but what made it stranger was that she was asking for Abelene.

Eltanin answered her. “Hume’ ladien, tiu ner somiste geniat leume.”

“What is he saying?” Camille asked.

“He’s telling her that she needs rest.” Azriel answered breathlessly

“How do you know?”

“She’s speaking Aralian.”

“How’s that possible?”

“It could only mean one thing—she’s from Aralia.” Azriel turned and glanced at Eddie. “No... it can’t be.”

“Quiet, both of you,” Eltanin ordered. “Give this woman some time to realign her thoughts. Her past is returning and needs to adjust and mesh with her time here on earth.”

"On Earth?" Eddie shouted in panic.

"Son, I think your reality has just dramatically changed." Eltanin turned and stared into the woman's eyes. "Good. I think lucidity is returning."

First she appeared disoriented; then a look of comprehension—like fog lifting from an ocean—lit up her face, she turned and stared at Eltanin.

"Where am I?"

"You are safe here, under my protection."

"Where is *here,* and who are you?"

"You are at Castle Wylusung, and I am known as Eltanin."

"*The* Eltanin—the Arch Wizard of Aralia?"

"Yes, Jessica."

"Jessica... I took that name for a time, but that is not my name."

Eltanin arched an eyebrow. "And what *is* your name?"

"I am Elsinore. I need to speak to Lady Abelene."

Eddie blustered, "Mom, this is craziness!" He turned on Eltanin. "I thought you said that stuff you gave her would make her better."

"Edward, be at peace. There is much to tell." Elsinore said gently.

Eddie looked at his mother fearfully. She never called him Edward, and her speech was more refined, even her bearing was far more sophisticated than her normal demeanor.

"Mom, I don't understand."

"Son, much of what I have to tell you may frighten you and you won't understand everything, but we are in good company. Finally, I feel I am home."

Eddie's brow creased with incomprehension.

After allowing the revelation to sink in, Azriel finally asked. "Lady, are you Elsinore, cousin to my mother Abelene?"

She smiled. "So you are the one—the heir to the throne of Aralia! That means Abelene was also successful in crossing over to this world!"

"Yes, she was. I know the circumstances that led to her hasty departure—why she fled Aralia. But tell me, Lady Elsinore, why did you follow her here?"

"Yes, this I must tell. After Lady Abelene's disappearance, the kingdom was given over to chaos and anarchy. I did what your mother told me to do, Azriel. I married Elrid, Captain of the Guard and took the throne as Queen Regent in your stead, waiting for your arrival. This was unacceptable to your subjects for I am not of House Ferrishyn, but of House Gorlyn, like your mother. Seizing an opportunity, Houses Varn, Porin, and Telynech conspired against Houses Ferrishyn and Gorlyn. Elrid tried to rally the people to defend the city, but many had already joined the rebellion against us. We were vastly outnumbered when they came to storm the castle. Elrid fell defending my honor." Tears welled from Elsinore's eyes. "It has been said that House Porin in particular had always resented House Ferrishyn for the maiming of King Flen, and though cooperative with the alliance of Houses for hundreds of years, they always hoped for an opportunity to practice vendetta against Ferrishyn for the grave insult to their house. When the attack came, the rebel houses not only destroyed the city but killed many of our own people, even those who had sided with the rebels. The throne was toppled and is now occupied by these brigands. King Storak of House Porin set up his son, Prince Hallet, as surrogate king of our beloved city. House Ferrishyn has been exiled. Knowing that I would never escape the city without losing my head, I recreated the spell your mother had fashioned to cross over to this world. But I was never as adept as Abelene, and though I managed to escape, the crossing over was so terrifying that I lost all memory of Aralia."

Azriel pondered Elsinore's story. He remembered how Abelene's crossing had nearly driven her insane. If not for the gentle ministering of Nicodemus, she might not have regained her sanity. But Elsinore had no one to meet her on the other side. It was then no wonder her memory had been completely erased by the dangerous spell.

Elsinore turned to Eddie. "Son, there is more to tell."

Eddie just stared at his mother, trying to allow the story to settle into his mind. It was too much to absorb already. He stood mute with astonishment.

"Edward, before your father became an entrepreneur, during his college days he worked as an EMT. When he found me, I was brought to a hospital where he never left my side. I had total amnesia and had to learn to speak and live among the humans on this world. Your father protected me and loved me for a time, but there was one thing he could never resolve. The fact is, Edward, that you are not his son. When I was found by your father, I was already a month pregnant with Elrid's son—you, Edward. So you see, like Azriel, you are not of this world."

Eddie sighed heavily and stared at Azriel. He scratched his scalp in consternation. "You realize what all this means, don't you?"

Azriel couldn't help but laugh at the irony. "Yeah—we're cousins."

Elsinore lay back down on the bed. Fatigued from the flood of returning memories, she suddenly wept. "Azriel, I'm afraid there's not much of a kingdom left for your return."

"Don't worry about that. You need to rest."

Eddie sat next to his mother and stroked her hair affectionately. She smiled sadly at him. "Son, I'm sorry to lay this burden on you and I'm sorry for all the terrible things I did to you. I wasn't in my right mind. I would have told you about all this had I been able to remember."

"It's okay, Mom. You just get better. I'm here if you need me."

She took his hand in hers and soon nodded off to sleep.

Azriel rubbed his brow with dismay. It was so much to absorb and his head hurt. He turned to Eltanin. "Grandfather, what is the likelihood that Elsinore would wind up living in Harden Lake?"

"The chances are rather remote. It does suggest a higher order. Perhaps the gods have a stake in all this as well. I sense their hands at work, meddling with the course of history. Lady Elsinore's amnesia was a blessing of sorts. It has protected her from being detected by the Clave."

Eddie climbed the stairs to the tower and took a seat on the wall. He stared up at the moon. There was much to think about, and he needed this time alone. Everything he ever believed had been in error. He, like so many others, had lived in ignorance of the truth. The whole theater of humanity went about its daily routine, oblivious to events that had shaped the world. And all this—the rending of one world into two—had been so under the radar, so to speak, that it had been blotted from human memory. No one on Earth would ever believe that such a thing had taken place. In the few days that Eddie had spent at Castle Wylusung, his grasp on reality had indeed changed. Now Eddie wasn't quite sure who he was, and it left him feeling unsettled.

"Be careful. It's a long drop from here." Julia had climbed the steps to think as well, and was surprised to find Eddie there. She smiled tentatively. "Do you need to be alone or would you like some company?"

He looked at the stars pensively, and didn't respond.

"It's okay, I'll leave you be."

"No, wait. Please stay," Eddie said apologetically.

"It's an awful lot to grasp, isn't it?" Julia said tenderly.

"You sure got that right. I'm not even sure who or what I am anymore."

"Well, of course the word is out that you and Azriel are cousins. My brothers had a great time with that. They laughed for hours. Azriel's taking it pretty well though."

"Yeah, I get it. How do you erase years of animosity. Think of it, Julia, Azriel and I are related—second cousins! What exactly does that make me?"

"Well, that would make you Ferrishyn, of course." Julia grinned impishly.

"I'm not even sure what that is!" Eddie grumbled.

"Well, as Azriel tells it, that would make you Elfin. See, there's really not much difference between elves and men, except that you're wired differently. Oh, and there's this, too." Julia reached out to brush Eddie's hair away from his ear to peek, when he pushed her hand away, suddenly embarrassed.

"Stop it! What are you doing?" he said, a bit annoyed.

"C'mon," she giggled. "Just a little peek!"

Eddie sighed and grimaced. "If you must."

"There's the clincher," she stated proudly.

"I don't like showing my ears." Eddie groused. "They're weird looking."

"Not for a Ferrishyn. Azriel hides his too. He has the same pointy ears. That's proof positive that you, Eddie, are Ferrishyn and that Azriel is indeed your kin."

"Wow. All this stuff just blows my mind, but the funny thing is that I kind of like it. And now that I'm getting to know Azriel better, he's actually okay."

"And you're not so bad yourself, Eddie, that is, when you're not being such a jerk."

Eddie snickered. "Yeah, I guess I deserved that." He hesitated, suddenly feeling penitent and a bit shy. "Hey Julia, if I was ever mean to you, or insulted you or anything like that, I'm really sorry. Truth is, I think you're okay—I always have."

"Apology accepted!" Julia smiled winningly.

They both heard footsteps coming up from the tower and Azriel rounded the corner.

"I thought I'd find you up here."

"Hello...cousin. Man, that feels so weird to say." Eddie shrugged. "How did you know I was up here?"

"I passed Magador in the courtyard. He seemed rather put out, and grumbled something about needing a proper place to sleep. This is where he likes to roost."

"Oh, sorry."

"Don't worry about it. Magador just gets a little grumpy sometimes."

"So what do you want?"

"I have something I'd like to show you. It might help to put a few things into perspective."

The three left the turret and descended the stairs. Azriel led them to his room. Upon his entry, Errin-lil, mounted on the wall, began to glow faintly.

"Cool sword." Eddie commented.

"Yeah, remind me to tell you about it sometime. Here this is what I wanted to show you." Azriel lifted a large tome from his dresser and placed it on the bed. He had a page bookmarked and opened to it. The mystical symbol of the eye was embedded into the page.

"What is it, Azriel?" Eddie asked.

"This is the Book of Aralia. It describes all the history of our world. It's also magickal. It will display images from the past. There's one I want you to see."

He placed the crystal plate over the page and invoked a word. "Truth!" Azriel commanded.

Eddie watched, amazed as an image projected up from the page. It was a scene in which Azriel was familiar. Abelene was locked in a tower, imprisoned against her will. Outside the door two guards kept watch to prevent escape. A cloaked and hooded woman strode up with a tray of food, and, as was customary, the guard ran his fingers through the food to check for any weapons, but the food was laced with a powerful poison that absorbed into the man's skin. He began to convulse and died foaming at the mouth. The other guard drew his sword, ready to run the woman through, when an arrow flew from the far end of the hall piercing the guard's heart. Her rescuer, followed by two other men, marched up. The captain spoke as Elsinore lowered her hood. Elrid dropped to his right knee in respect.

"Are you injured, Lady Elsinore."

"I'm fine, Elrid. Please help me open this door."

Elrid, Captain of the Guard, extracted the keys from the dead man's belt and unlocked the heavy oak door with a loud click. Elsinore flew into Abelene's arms.

"Milady, we are here to release you." Elrid bowed. Elsinore spoke quickly. "My Queen, please turn so I can get that cursed thing off your neck."

The magickal device had been designed to prevent Abelene from invoking any spells. If she attempted to use magick, it would shrink, choking off Abelene's breath. Lady Elsinore used a strangely shaped key to unlatch the collar from Abelene's neck and threw it away from her with disgust.

Abelene smiled at the captain. "Elrid, you're my hero!" She then turned to Elsinore. "Thank you, my cousin." Abelene embraced her with gratitude. "You took an awful risk."

"I could not let you rot in here. I swapped clothes with your chambermaid. No one ever suspected."

"Come, Milady," Elrid said. "We have an escape route."

"Not until I find my husband. I owe him that."

The scene played out to completion, displaying Abelene's confrontation with King Berrill and her ultimate escape from Aralia.

Abelene stood in the center of a room, surrounded by seven full-length mirrors. Strapped securely from a harness to her back was the stolen Errin-lil and she cradled the Book of Aralia in her arms. Sounds of battle bled through the doors and someone shouted from beyond: "The king has been murdered! Find the assassin!" Suddenly there was a pounding on the great door.

Elsinore was frantic. She embraced Abelene in tears. "Milady, you cannot delay. You must go now!"

The pounding and shouts behind the door grew louder.

"I wish I could take you with me, my cousin." Abelene wept. She took Elrid's hand. "My loyal friend, flee the kingdom and keep Elsinore safe. Marry and protect her! When all is safe, protect the throne. You and Elsinore must rule in my stead."

"I am your servant, Milady. You have my vow."

"You must all stand back now," Abelene ordered. She stared at Elsinore with tears in her eyes. "Farewell, dear cousin. I will always remember you."

The images ended as they always did, with Abelene being blasted through all seven mirrors and disappearing.

When the images receded back into the book, Eddie sat stunned, still staring at the empty space where the reflections had been.

"Cousin, there's a reason I wanted you to see that. That is who your mother and father are. Elrid was a hero. He saved Abelene. You should be proud!"

Eddie straightened up and stood facing Azriel. "I am." So overcome with emotion, he fell onto Azriel's shoulder and wept.

Azriel was stunned at first but then embraced his cousin and smiled.

"We're not enemies anymore, Eddie. We're family."

Eddie wiped his eyes. "You have my word. Whatever it is you're embroiled in, I will always have your back."

Azriel grinned and clasped his cousin's hand. "It's all in the book, Eddie. You need to know the world you come from. Not all of it is pretty, but it will certainly give you a sense of who you truly are. Any time you're ready, the book of Aralia is yours to use."

Chapter 16

"It would seem events are beginning to escalate. Everything is coming together more quickly than I would have thought." Abelene said thoughtfully to Charlie. She had just spoken to Azriel through their usual telepathic link. So far, the Clave had been none the wiser to this form of communication.

"So if I understand correctly," Charlie pondered, "Your cousin Elsinore has been here for eighteen years; her son is that boy who has given Azriel so much trouble, and neither you, nor the clave had any knowledge of it?" He chuckled. "Oh, this is rich—rich indeed!"

"Actually, in retrospect, it's all beginning to make sense... in an odd way."

"How so, lady?"

"Well, you know the circumstances of my capture. The boy, Eddie, had sided with Altais, truly unaware of the evil with which he was aligned. It's a pity how easily a lost boy can be lured into darkness. Altais had used him to get to me. Charlie, when I saw Eddie's face and the guilt clouding it, I took it very personally. I chided him as I would my own son. I think at that instant, Eddie knew he had made a grievous mistake. Of course, I didn't know at the time that he was of my lineage, yet something inside me perhaps recognized him as family."

"It would seem, then, that the boy serves some yet-unnamed purpose. You saw him in your visions and recorded it on your tapestry."

That's true, Charlie, but I still don't have a clue as to what his significance is. Do you have any insights?"

"Hmm," Charlie scratched behind his crest thoughtfully, "Only this: there are no coincidences. All this is much bigger than you and me—even bigger than Rastaban and Eltanin. An unseen hand is manipulating events to bring about a great change. It must be very important—perhaps a grander design undetected by all.

Interesting, when you consider that the Great Mother Dragon has never before interfered in the lives of elves and men."

"Then it's possible that Rastaban and the Clave are merely pawns to bring about an end." Abelene chuckled darkly, "Somehow that brings me great comfort."

"Alive? Nicodemus is alive?" Rastaban marveled.

"I wouldn't have believed it had I not seen him with my own eyes." At a loss, Altais spread his hands helplessly. "He has grown more powerful. Sad to say, we were evenly matched."

"So you let Azriel escape." Rastaban's face darkened; his eyes narrowed dangerously.

"I wouldn't exactly say I let him. I was surprised by the boy—Eddie. He used magick to aid in their escape."

"I told you when you first started using the little fool he would become a liability. You should have killed him as I suggested. You're becoming soft, Altais!"

"My lord, I must protest. It was impossible to predict that he would align himself with Azriel and his crew. Neither could anyone have foreseen that Nicodemus would have survived all these years. He escaped your far-reaching sight did he not?" Altais argued. "With all due respect, my lord, perhaps it is you who underestimated that human wizard's cleverness."

Gentle footsteps sounded in the chamber. "Boys, boys!" Lilith scolded. "You quarrel like children. True, Nicodemus is quite clever..." She smiled seductively. "But he is not invincible. You were just unlucky. When you destroyed his stronghold five-hundred years ago, he should have been killed. He just managed to outsmart you. I think it makes the game so much more interesting!"

"And your point, Lilith?" Rastaban held his temper in check.

"Oh, don't be such a boor, darling." Stroking Rastaban's cheek and pressing her voluptuous body against his, Lilith cooed, "Now that we know he's alive, we can find him again—and destroy him. You were simply operating on the wrong assumption. Find him, and we find Azriel. Find Azriel, and we can annihilate the entire Order of the Ankh!"

"And how exactly am I supposed to do that, my love?" he snapped, frustration sharpening his voice to venom. "Nicodemus has eluded my notice for five hundred years."

Lilith tittered mischievously. "That's because you think like a man. Perhaps you should leave the spying to a woman. After all... I do have my ways."

In the wee hours of the morning, Castle Wylusung lay deathly quiet. Azriel awoke before dawn and sat in bed, thinking. At least Abelene was now up to date on the latest events. But now there were new complications. Azriel was now fully aware that Lilith had been summoned from the Underworld. Though he knew something of its implications, he wasn't quite sure what it would mean to Eltanin, except the archwizard had locked himself away in his study and would receive no one. One thing was certain: Eltanin had been badly rattled by Elsinore's appearance.

Azriel decided he had waited long enough. He crept up to Eltanin's chambers. From behind the locked door, he heard the Master muttering to himself and the crackle of old parchment being shuffled through. He tapped gently on the rugged old door.

"Grandfather, I've brought you some tea. I need to speak to you."

"Azriel, is that you?"

"Who else would call you grandfather?"

"Yes, of course. How foolish of me." The deadbolt slid back, and Eltanin opened the door. "Come, Azriel. Sit. We must discuss the dark matters of this world."

Eltanin accepted the tea gratefully and sipped at it gingerly. Azriel couldn't help but notice that Eltanin's hands shook slightly.

"Grandfather, what has you so disturbed?"

Eltanin rubbed his troubled brow. "Ah, Azriel, I have grown old and blind."

"I don't understand. No one could have guessed that Lady Elsinore would have crossed over to this world."

"Yes, but I should have! I should have sensed her passage through time and space. Such powerful magick should not have escaped my notice. The energy from such a spell would have left its mark. There was nothing in the prophecies or in the book of Aralia to suggest she would play any part in this. I am at a loss to determine what her presence here means."

"Maybe it doesn't mean anything." Azriel shrugged. "Did you ever consider that maybe we were lucky that somehow she escaped detection by you and Rastaban? She could have been captured by the Clave and used for their dark purposes."

"I don't know, Azriel. I think that perhaps I am being punished by the gods for meddling into what was their domain."

"Grandfather, you don't really believe that, do you?"

"I do, son. Some things are better left to the gods. I had no right to interfere with the course of events when humans arrived on Aralia. There had to have been some as of yet unnamed purpose for their appearance. It was arrogant for me to think that I knew better than the great Mind of the Universe."

"Second-guessing yourself only leads to doubt and confusion. A wise man once told me that."

"Oh? And who was that?"

"You, Grandfather... or Pog... either way, it was you who said it."

"Maybe you shouldn't listen to me. My meddling has done irreparable damage to the course of history. None of this would have been necessary if nature would have been allowed to take its course. And you would not be in such mortal danger with the monumental task you must complete. It was I who set you on this course."

"Grandfather, I don't blame you, nor do I accuse you. Things are what they are. There's no use pointing fingers—even at yourself. It's not going to change anything. Besides, I need you. As to Lady Elsinore, I'm sure her purpose here, and Eddie's for that matter, will make itself known."

"When did you become so pragmatic, Azriel?"

"I learned it from a very wise man." Azriel smiled with affection but then his face sobered. "There is something else you should know, Grandfather."

"It sounds serious."

"It is. Abelene told me of a thing that will no doubt be cause for concern. Where she is being held captive has offered her a unique opportunity to see into the mind of the Clave, that is, with a little help. The dark dragon, it would seem, knows what Rastaban has been doing. Though the Dragon Lord is separated from his realm, he knows the comings and goings of those under his dominion."

"Get to the point, Azriel." Eltanin said impatiently.

"Rastaban has released Lilith from the Underworld. This she couldn't have done on her own. Only Rastaban had the power to do it."

Eltanin was stunned to silence. He peered out the window of his study and reflected on this unfortunate tidbit of news.

"Grandfather?" Azriel said with concern.

Eltanin sighed heavily. "That is ill tidings. She is one woman I hoped never to see again."

"That I fully understand. My mother has told me a little of what happened."

"Azriel, you cannot fully grasp the scope of her betrayal. It was many years ago, when I was still a young man of eighty. I had studied at the feet of the Elementals and believed I knew every secret of the universe—of Aralia itself. I was steeped in nature's hidden lore. I had solved the mystery of the Lapis Occultus. To put it plainly, I thought I was at the height of my power. I knew everything... except the workings of my own heart.

"At that time, there were few good wizards left. Worse, anarchy reigned—evil warlocks, and one powerful sorceress named Morta. The world lay in the grip of festering malevolence, and the people lived in constant fear of the wicked rising against them. As the foremost among them, I left seclusion and challenged Morta to magickal combat. When that fateful day came, we began to battle on the plains of Shenach. "For two days we fought—rending the earth, leveling mountains, turning rivers from their beds.

Azriel's brow rose. "Two days?"

Eltanin nodded.. "The devastation drew the people in droves to witness the battle. Their hopes were that I would rid them of the evil that held them bound to servitude. After two days, however, I was at the end of my strength. I could not hold out against Morta, for she was strong and mighty with wicked power. But then a strange and wonderful thing began to happen. The people, so close to being freed, started to hope. "They cast off their fear and poured their strength and magick into me. United, we surged with renewed vigor—and Morta was defeated, cast down into the abyss."

"I have read this before," Azriel stated. "It's in the Book of Aralia.

"That's true," Eltanin nodded. "And as you can well imagine, I was now targeted by the remaining evil lords of Aralia. But the people had a taste of victory. "Other great wizards joined me—Rastaban, Edasich, Thuban, Nodus, Altais, and Giausur.

"Rastaban was the first to join me and together, we marched on Triondor to defeat the warlock, Lord Korloth. Shortly after, we formed the Clave of Wizards to solidify our power. Draconis, as it was named became the ruling council to guide the people. In order to serve the people, we searched all the provinces for the most talented of sorcerers, when a young woman came to the attention of the council. Lilith was tested and found to be naturally gifted in more ways than one. She wielded magick in ways no one had ever seen—without formal training. And she was the most beautiful, most beguiling woman I had ever met. I should have seen the danger at once, but I was blinded by her beauty. I never saw the darkness that festered in her heart. I never saw her vanity and her lust for power."

Eltanin heaved a sigh. "Her presence created division and jealousy among the Clave, mostly because of me. I favored her and fell blindly in love with Lilith. I was a fool, savoring her sweet words of admiration and praise, when in fact it was ambition that drove her to my arms. She used me—feigned love to steal my secrets. If not for the warning in my heart, I would have revealed all of them to her."

"Grandfather, Abelene told me you gave Lilith immortality. Is it true?"

Eltanin muttered, "Sadly, yes. She attempted a spell even an experienced wizard would fear to try. But in retrospect, I believe she planned to fail. She knew my heart better than I did. As she lay bleeding, dying in my arms, against all wisdom, I gave her the Lapis Occultus."

Azriel's stomach tightened.

"Soon after, she began to change—selfish, greedy, cruel, heartless. Lilith began to delve into dark forbidden Magick—spells that warped and distorted the natural order of the universe. By that time, I had banished her from Aralia. She, however, was far from defeated. There was still a vast evil threatening the land. It was Lilith who used her charms to gather them all under her wing. It was her plan to march against me and the free peoples of Aralia. "Through forbidden magick she created demons, devils, and all manner of fell creatures. She raised an army of undead and bent them to her will. To this day, even in earth legend, Lilith is known as the mother of demons."

Azriel interjected. "I read in the account that you had raised an army of twenty thousand free people and met the evil lords at the Grey Wastes."

"Yes, and it was Lilith who led a horde of evildoers against us—they followed her banner. We were vastly outnumbered and the people felt the cold grip of fear clench around their hearts."

Azriel smiled. "True, but yet you still defeated them by raising the Elementals."

"Alas, you're right, Azriel. But don't forget that the evil warlocks had raised the Dark Elemental of Death. It would have been to our ruin, but the Elementals of Earth, Water, Fire and Air merged their powers to create the Quintessence—the ultimate power that transcends time and space. It was that day, by the way, that your destiny became fixed in the stars, Azriel."

"I'm not sure I understand."

"You will in time."

Azriel shrugged. "So what happened to Lilith and her army?"

"Well, that you know, Azriel. They were utterly obliterated and Lilith was captured—but she could not be killed since I in my foolishness had given her immortality. Instead, with the help of the Clave, she was bound and cast into the Underworld."

"So if Rastaban has released her, what does it mean?"

"Only one thing. War. And she will seek vengeance upon me."

"Then why not just hunt her down?"

"It could be my death, Azriel. She was nearly equal to me twenty thousand years ago. Now she has aligned herself with the Clave. Believe me when I tell you, it's only a matter of time before she finds me. Not that I fear death. I have lived too long… but there are still things I must finish before I can rest."

"Grandfather, you're not going to die. I have faith in your shrewdness and power."

Eltanin smiled fondly. "You, my progeny, are a kind and noble young man. I promise I won't die before you fully come into your power."

Azriel looked down at his feet. "That's not what I meant."

Eltanin laid a gentle hand on his shoulder. "I know what you meant, son."

The following morning, the breakfast table buzzed with chatter. Eddie now felt more at ease with his new friends and practiced a spell that Julia and Elsinore taught him. For all his life it had never occurred to him that he might possess natural magickal talent; in fact, he had never even entertained the idea. But Eddie, after all, was Ferrishyn, which gave him an advantage over ordinary humans. It was, however, necessary to clear the cobwebs of doubt from his mind. Like Azriel had years earlier, he needed to unlearn many concepts he had always accepted as absolutes and begin thinking in terms of the intangible, for it was in the indefinable that magick became possible. It was therefore no surprise to anyone that, when releasing his spirit animal, it was a charging bull—fearless and proud.

Elsinore strode in with a plate of waffles, smiling proudly. "Bravo, Edward—Bravo!"

Eddie smiled and blushed. "Thanks, Mom. Why don't you show me your animal spirit?"

"Oh," she laughed lightly. "It's been so many years. Maybe another time."

"Oh, come on, Lady Elsinore." Camille prodded. The others joined in, cajoling her to comply.

"Oh, all right." She smiled and sighed. With a quick flourish of her fingers, a soft mist coalesced into an image of a graceful, slender animal.

Eddie scrunched up his face. "Mom, really? A weasel?"

Elsinore replied somewhat wounded. "Yes—a weasel, more properly an ermine. Ermines observe silently, analyze situations and solve puzzles with ease. Never underestimate an ermine. It can strike and steal when you least expect it—so don't mess with me, Edward."

"I'll consider myself warned!" Eddie replied with a touch of fearful respect, but then he smiled broadly at Elsinore. He liked this new version of his mother—fearless and poised.

Azriel strode in with a heaping plate of food and went immediately to work ravenously wolfing it down.

"Hungry, are we?" Amused, Camille asked lightly, amused.

"Hey, give me a break," he said with his mouth full, "I've already been up for four hours."

"Where were you?"

"With Eltanin."

"Anything we should know about?"

He hesitated. "No… not really."

Camille examined his face. She had known him long enough to know when he was holding something back. She forced him to meet her eyes. He reached under the table and gave her hand a gentle squeeze—a signal to ask him later when they were alone.

Camille sighed and stood from the table. "Well, I guess it's time for me to begin my training."

"What are you talking about?" Azriel asked somewhat puzzled. "I thought we were going on a hike today."

"No, you are. Actually Magador has been trying to get your attention for the past two days. He's in a rather foul mood. He seems to think you've been avoiding him."

"That's nonsense. It's not like I haven't been busy."

"Well, maybe you should take that up with him." Camille shrugged then turned to Halimah. "Shall we?"

"Wait a minute—where are you going?" Azriel scowled, feeling a bit put out.

Halimah intervened. "Don't be so protective, Azriel. I just think it's about time Camille and Julia learn how to defend themselves. Sometimes magick isn't enough."

"And this was your idea?" Azriel asked gruffly. "What does Nicodemus think of all this?"

"Actually, it was Grandfather's suggestion." Halimah turned to leave but then stopped and crossed her arms. "What is it about you *men* who think that you're the only ones who should know how to fight?"

Julia held her hand to her mouth to hide her laughter, as she followed Halimah and Camille out of the room.

"What the hell was that all about?" Jasper asked.

Azriel glanced at the door where the girls had just exited. "Damned if I know."

Jasper and Albert then stood, about to leave.

"Hey, where are you guys going?" Azriel asked.

Albert grinned deviously. "Jasper and I are working on something with Nicodemus."

"Really? And when were you going to tell me about it?" Azriel glared at them. He was beginning to feel abandoned by all his friends.

Albert spread his hands, gesturing. "C'mon, Azriel, you got things to do, so do we!"

"Fine. Keep your secrets." Azriel groused and headed toward the tower.

"Hey, Azriel, do you mind if I tag along?" Eddie asked.

"Sure—why not!"

When they reached the top of the staircase, Eddie and Azriel found Magador. His back turned to them, he glanced sullenly over his shoulder, then lowered his head to the cold stone floor and sulked. "Well, it's about time," he snapped.

"What's your problem now, Magador?"

"Me? Oh, I have no problems," he answered with feigned aloofness. "I can just stay up here all by myself, thoroughly ignored, while the entire world falls apart around me."

"Oh, don't be such a crybaby. I was busy."

"Hmm, Yes—too busy to say hello. How are you doing, Magador? Are you feeling all right, Magador? Are you having a good day, Magador?" He sighed. "No, I could be dead and rotting up here, and no one would care in the least."

"Oh, good grief!" Azriel moaned. "Must you be so dramatic?"

Eddie snorted, trying not to laugh at their bickering. "You two sound like you're having a lover's quarrel. Should I leave you two alone?"

"Oh, shut up, Edward," Magador said testily.

"Yeah, shut up, Eddie." Azriel agreed.

"Now, if you had bothered to visit with me, Cousin, you would have known we have something important we must do."

"And what would that be?"

"Somewhere we must go." The great dragon stretched his crimson-tipped wings.

"You're being awfully vague, Magador. Where are we going?"

"Southwest, I think. And don't ask me who we are going to see—I don't actually know."

"Then how do you know we're supposed to go anywhere?"

"You know, Cousin. You're awfully dense for a dragon…"

"Here we go again…" Azriel grumbled.

"…we dragons, if we are keen and perceptive, can sense when we are being summoned. If you had your wits about you, you would have felt it two days ago."

"Is this really important?" Azriel asked impatiently.

"Only someone with powerful magick can summon our kind. It must be important indeed."

"How do you know it's not one of the Clave trying to draw us out?"

"I would know the difference. I have felt no evil intent. Now, are we going to argue all day or are you going to mount my back?"

"All right then. Let's get going."

"Well, it's about time." Magador shifted to allow Azriel onto his back.

Eddie looked on longingly as they prepared to leave. "Hey Azriel, do you think it would be okay if I came along?"

"It's not up to me. It's up to Magador."

"Oh, I suppose I could handle the extra burden," Magador groaned tragically. "You're welcome to join us, Edward. Perhaps you'll have more appreciation for my abilities than your neglectful cousin."

Azriel's shoulders slumped, and he heaved a sigh. "Do you ever stop complaining?"

"Perhaps I would if I didn't feel so ill used all the time."

"All the time, Magador?" Azriel retorted as he mounted the dragon's shoulders.

"Well... most of the time," Magador replied grudgingly. He heaved off from the tower and was quickly aloft.

Eddie released a whoop of glee. "Awesome!" he shouted.

"Yeah, it is pretty cool!" Azriel laughed. Somehow, even through all of Magador's grousing, being airborne was the most pleasurable thing Azriel ever experienced.

"Hey Magador," Eddie called out. "Do you know where you're going?"

"I'm just following my nose, Edward."

They banked to the left and caught a thermal, sending them higher, granting Magador the luxury of resting his wings. He barely had to flap them to maintain his speed and heading. Southbound, they continued for about an hour when Azriel finally asked, "Magador, why don't you just blink over to the location? Wouldn't it be faster?"

"Yes, it would, but I don't want to risk losing the beacon. It's very faint. Besides, I wouldn't want to give Edward a heart attack on his first ride."

They flew on for another hour. As the sun set in the west, Magador slowly descended toward the wide desert expanse. The mesas and buttes had been carved by millions of years of ancient winds. The ochre-red gut rock stood as a mute reminder of long-vanished mountains. In the waning light, they seemed to glow with ruddy fire. The sun now below the horizon, the outcroppings of rocks quickly shifted from magenta to deep purple. Stars began to emerge as last light departed from the sky to be replaced by velvet blackness. Such was the swift pace of change in the desert.

Eddie looked up to the sky, and his breath caught in his throat. "Wow! I've never seen stars like that!"

"Yes they do seem particularly bright tonight," Magador replied. "There is magick afoot." He corrected his course and headed toward a small hidden cave illuminated by a fire from within. "There! There is our destination!" The dragon said proudly. He alit before the cave and swiftly folded his wings, allowing Azriel and Eddie to dismount. They heard a voice from inside the cave—frail and ancient.

"Come! Come in, my friends, so we may commune. Many thanks to you, great dragon, for hearing my summons and bringing the one who will usher in the great cleansing of the world."

"Why don't you show your face so we may see you?" Azriel challenged.

"I cannot, for if I leave here, I will vanish before I can complete the task for which I was appointed."

Azriel and Eddie cautiously peered into the cave and saw an old man sitting before an inviting fire. The desert had rapidly cooled and the fire seemed to beckon them forward.

"Please, please come in and warm yourself," the old man smiled graciously. Several teeth were missing and he appeared almost a caricature of an ancient Indian. Dressed in a loin cloth and a woven fiber shirt, he wore beaded jewelry of agate and turquoise.

They sat, and Azriel cleared his throat. "Who are you, sir?"

The old man cackled with glee. "Perhaps the more fitting question might be: who *were* you?"

"Okay. So who were you then? Medicine man—chief—holy man?"

"No, just a man. In life, my name was Yukiuma. I have waited for you a long time, Son of Luminance. See the truth of it." The old one pointed to a recess in the cave barely lit by the fire. Nestled within, the dry bones of a skeleton sat cross-legged, slumped over in death.

"How long have you waited?" Azriel asked.

"Hmm… lost count." Yukiuma gave a toothless smile.

"So what has brought me here, grandfather?" Azriel ventured to ask.

"A dragon." The old man laughed. Eddie chuckled too. The old man's laughter was infectious.

"That's not quite what I meant."

"Of course it wasn't. Allow an old spirit to play a little. I am here to tell you a story."

"You waited all this time just to tell me a story?"

"Some stories are too important to leave behind. Before you hear it, though, we must drink together so your minds will be open." Yukiuma nodded in the direction of another hidden recess of the cave. Two tiny creatures emerged. Miniatures of men, they were dressed like ancient warriors. Their faces were severe and painted with tribal patterns. Each carried a bowl and placed them before Azriel and Eddie.

"Who are they?" Azriel asked.

"These little fellows are Po-okonghoya and Palongahoya, Po-ok and Pal for short. They are the war gods of the Hopi, my people. Po-ok and Pal are the grandsons of Spider Woman."

"Who is Spider Woman?" Eddie inquired.

"She is the creator of us all and everything there is."

Azriel commented. "Magador might disagree. He would say the universe was created from the first egg of the Great Mother Dragon."

"What's in a name, eh?"

"Point taken." Azriel shrugged.

Yukiuma continued. "Po-ok and Pal are part of the story. Drink so you may receive it."

They both looked down skeptically at the cups placed before them. Eddie was the first to lift the cup to his lips but instinctively backed away from the nasty aroma.

"Ugh! It smells terrible."

"Ah! I remember. Yes it does." The old man muttered. "But, nevertheless, you must drink it. It would be better if you just gulp it down."

Azriel and Eddie complied. Almost immediately, Eddie held his hand to his lips, followed by Azriel. "Cousin, I think I'm going to be sick!"

"Me too!" Azriel bolted to the mouth of the cave and vomited. Eddie couldn't keep it down either; he crouched beside Azriel and puked his guts out.

"Do not worry, my young friends. Your reaction is quite normal."

"Well thanks for the warning," Azriel grumbled.

He flopped by the fire and immediately a buzzing began in his ears, followed by hallucinatory flashes of color before his eyes. The air was suddenly alive with music, and the fire began to dance spectral images. The flames became blazing dragons darting about the cave. Ghostly shapes began to transform beside Yukiuma. Three Native women appeared. The first was ancient and shook rattles as she chanted. The next woman was matronly and beat a drum in a slow, compelling rhythm. The other, a young maiden, played an ancient song on a wooden flute long since forgotten by human memory.

Yukiuma began to narrate.

"Many years ago, the People were troubled by the wind. It blew and blew all the time. The soil eroded from their fields, and the People tried to plant their crops. The wind tore the soil away before the seeds could germinate. My people were sad and worried, fearing they would starve. They made offerings of many prayer sticks to the gods, but the gods did not hear the pleas of the people.

"Many a council was held by the elders in the sacred Kivas. The elders smoked their pipes and discussed the dilemma, debating why their gods had sent such a strong wind against them. After a while, they decided that they would ask the Kachinas—the war gods Po-okonghoya and Palongahoya—his younger brother, to help them."

The tale was interrupted by Po-ok and Pal. They leapt about whooping out war chants. Yukiuma smiled, tolerating their interruption. He continued.

"When the war gods came as summoned, they demanded to know why they were called. The Hopi elders said that they needed help. Something must be done to the wind. The Kachinas said yes, they would help the people.

"They told the men to stay in the kiva and offer many prayers. Po-ok and Pal asked their wise old grandmother, the Spider Woman to help still the wind. In response she made some sweet cornmeal mush to take along on their journey. Of course they knew who the wind god, Yaponcha was and where he lived—a few days' journey near the Sunset Mountain. He dwelled within the big cracks of the black rock.

"The kachinas returned to the elders with the cornmeal mush. The elders had ready for Po-ok and Pal the ball which they always liked to take along to play wherever they went. Bows and arrows had also been made for them, because it was much like going on the warpath. The arrows were made of bluebird feathers which were considered most powerful in those days.

Po-ok and Pal set out for the San Francisco Peaks. The old men followed them as far as the Little Colorado River and there they sat down and smoked their pipes, waiting.

"The little warriors went on and on, playing with their ball. They reached the home of the Wind God, Yaponcha, on the fourth day. The Wind God lived at the foot of Sunset Crater in a great crack of the black rock, through which he breathes and does so even to this day. They threw the many prayer sticks the old elders had made into the crack and quickly took out their old grandmother's sticky cornmeal mush. With it they sealed up Yaponcha's door.

"Now the wind god was awfully angry, and he blew and blew, but he could not get out. The Kachinas laughed, pleased with themselves and went home."

Azriel experienced the tale not merely a telling; he saw through the potion-induced vision the actual journey the little warriors had made into the black rock of the mountains.

"Soon the people in the villages began to feel that it was too hot. The air became warmer and warmer every day. Down in the elder's sacred meeting place, it grew so hot that the men came out and the people came from their houses. They stood upon the housetops looking toward the San Francisco Peaks in despair to see if any clouds were heading their way to bring cooling rains. But there wasn't even the smallest of clouds to give a pleasant shadow, nor a breath of cool air, and the people thought that they would die from the relentless heat.

"Desperately they called the Kachinas again and begged them to go back to Yaponcha to appease the angry god. The elders made many special Pahos—prayer sticks as offerings of peace to Yaponcha. For the heat was much worse even, than the wind. And so Po-ok and Pal agreed to see what could be done to make things better.

"On the fourth day, they arrived at the house of Yaponcha and they took council together, deciding that the best thing to do would be to let Yaponcha have just a little hole opened, just enough to let him breathe, but not large enough for Yaponcha to escape. Po-ok and Pal removed some of the cornmeal mush, and right away a cool wind came out. A little white cloud appeared and went over across the desert toward the Hopi towns.

When the Kachinas returned to the villages, everybody was happy and relieved and has been ever grateful. Ever since that time the winds have been just right—just enough to keep the people cool without blowing everything away.

To this day, my people offer prayer sticks to the Wind God, Yaponcha, in thanks and with gratitude."

As Yukiuma finished his tale, Azriel and Eddie both drifted off into a narcotic sleep. The old man stood and looked down on the sleeping boys, then at Po-okonghoya and Palongahoya.

"Please look after them, my friends. You have been good company for these many years, but alas my task is finished. I may finally rest."

The three women also arose. The old crone, the matron, and the maiden merged into one and began to glow with the brilliance of the moon. She smiled adoringly at Yukiuma. He nodded graciously to the woman saying, "Thank you Great Mother Spider Woman for opening their eyes." Yukiuma suddenly transformed into the blazing golden light of the sun. Spider Woman took his hand and together they vanished into the night.

Chapter 17

For a moment, Eddie couldn't remember where he was—or whether the old man, the spirits, and the story had been nothing more than a dream. Groggy and dizzy, he blinked against the thin gray light creeping into the cave. The fire had burned down to cold ash. The air smelled of dust and smoke. Azriel still slept beside him, curled against the stone. The first light of dawn seeped in, revealing more of the ancient cave. It seemed as if it hadn't been used for many years. Indeed, the dry bones of the old man were seated, propped up in a deep recess. Before the skeleton sat earthen bowls, their contents long since gone by time and decay. The placement of the items had the appearance of funerary offerings. Obviously the old man had held some importance to his tribe.

Something else caught Eddie's eye. To the right and left of Yukiuma's corpse, two wooden figures stood as if protecting him. Oddly, they were attired in clothes and wore the tribal patterns that the creatures Po-ok and Pal had donned the previous night. Eddie rubbed at his temples and moaned in pain. His head throbbed terribly from whatever it was he had ingested the night before.

He looked at the cold ashes of the fire and then at the mouth of the cave. Eddie decided to let Azriel sleep and ventured outside. Magador was just finishing eating a fresh kill.

"I hope you don't mind. I was rather hungry."

An unfortunate buffalo had become Magador's breakfast. A particularly nice cut, however, was resting on a sizable rock.

"I managed to save a piece for you and your cousin." Magador belched out a controlled flame onto the rock and soon the steak began to sizzle.

"Wow, pilot and cook! That's great, Magador." Eddie smiled.

"Why thank you, Edward. It's wonderful being appreciated."

Sleepy-eyed and yawning, Azriel emerged from the cave. "I thought I heard talking out here. How did you sleep, Eddie?"

"All right, I guess. Strange dreams, though."

"Yeah, me too." Azriel winced. He had a raging headache.

"I actually slept remarkably well. Of course you would know that if you had bothered to ask, Cousin," Magador added with pointed sarcasm. "But then again, I'm just a dragon, so it's not necessary to ask *me* how I slept."

"Oh, hi Magador. Sorry… sort of a weird night."

"Humph." Magador turned his back on Azriel. "Your breakfast is on the rock. Sorry there's no silverware," he added in an acerbic tone.

"Hey, Magador," Azriel said contritely, "I didn't mean to ignore you."

"Of course not. You never mean to do anything. You just do things without thinking."

"That's not fair. I told you we had a strange night."

"Well fine then—what did you learn?"

"I think I know where the Air Elemental has been imprisoned. It seems the old man had been waiting for me for quite some time to tell me. It's in a place called the Sunset Mountains." Azriel removed a piece of meat, now well-cooked from the rock and bit into it. "Thanks, Magador. This is tasty."

"So how do you expect to find these mountains?" Magador asked.

"I just figured you would take me."

"Well you figured wrong. There you go, assuming. I haven't a clue where that is."

"Really, I thought you knew everything—dragon memory and all that."

"My memory is just fine, cousin. But none of my ancestors have ever been to the place."

"That does present a problem, then, doesn't it?" Eddie interjected. He had just finished his portion and licked his fingers, wiping the remainder on his pants.

"I guess we'll just have to figure it out," Azriel mused as he peered back at the cave. He craned his neck and scratched his head, puzzled. The two wooden figures now stood at the entrance to the cave. Azriel was sure he hadn't moved them.

"Hey, Eddie, did you take those wooden dolls from the cave?"

"No, why would I?"

"Weird." Azriel walked to the entrance and looked down at the Kachinas. "I think we're supposed to take them with us."

"You sure?"

"Reasonably so." He picked them up and studied them. As he was about to place them back on the ground, with a flash of light, they suddenly transformed into Po-ok and Pal. Po-ok immediately stabbed Azriel's hand with his spear.

"Ow! Crap!" Azriel snarled while Eddie laughed at him. The two tiny warriors scrambled onto Magador's back and stood looking at Azriel. Their stance was one of impatience. Pal pointed to a mountain range in the distance. Po-ok looked at his brother and smiled deviously. He removed a golden ball from a hidden pouch and hefted it into the air. With remarkable skill, he tossed the ball skyward, then as it descended, swung his spear, whacking the ball in the direction of the mountains. When it landed, a deafening peal of thunder shook the ground.

"I think we're supposed to follow." Eddie suggested.

"Good idea." Azriel agreed.

"I haven't even had time to digest my breakfast," Magador grumbled. "And I hate flying on a full stomach." He sighed. "Well, let us go then."

Aloft, they watched with fascination as the two brother warriors darted from place to place at remarkable speed. The game, it appeared, was to see who could hit the ball the furthest. Every time the ball landed, it was accompanied by an earth-shaking concussion. The louder the thunder, the more the Kachinas seemed to be delighted in it. This continued throughout the morning until they reached the base of the San Francisco mountain range. The game continued up the steep slopes of the rocky crags. Po-ok and Pal scrambled up the slopes and back down into valleys and crevices formed of black rock spewed forth in ancient days from long-dormant volcanoes. Toward midday, the tiny warriors suddenly ceased their play and pointed to a deep depression scarring the rock. It was much like a crater blasted from the earth. Po-ok and Pal stood rigidly and planted their spears firmly into the ground. Like before, there was a sudden flash of light, and they transformed back into the wooden dolls that had guarded the remains of Yukiuma.

Magador alit beside them. Azriel and Eddie slid from his shoulders and surveyed the terrain. He peered down into the crater and noticed that, dead center in the depression, a cone-shaped rock, black as onyx, jutted from the volcanic earth. Conspicuous by its lack of any feature and the dull grey gravel around it, Azriel decided to investigate. Followed by Eddie, they half climbed, half slid down the slope. Amused, Magador watched from the rim of the crater as Azriel stumbled and flipped over a few times before landing at the bottom. Dusty and slightly bruised, he brushed off the grit. Eddie extended his hand to help Azriel to his feet.

"That wasn't fun," Azriel griped while he glared up at Magador. The dragon was beside himself with laughter.

"Hey Magador, glad I can keep you entertained." Azriel's voice was thick with irritation.

"You'd have far fewer problems if you had wings, cousin!"

"So you've said before."

The boys headed toward the black rock jutting from the grey lava field. Most of the surrounding pebbles were pumice—lightweight but horribly abrasive. Eddie jerked his hand away. Meanwhile, Azriel circled the jutting boulder a few times. Two things caught his attention. First, a fissure in the rock that, except for a small opening, seemed sealed with pale yellow lava, as if it had bled from the stone itself. From the vent, a steady stream of air flowed. The other thing he noticed was something half-buried at the base of the huge rock—symbols of some kind. He began clearing the rubble away. Eddie joined in until they were fully exposed.

Around the base were glyphs that circled the black stone. Fashioned of bronze, only one glyph emanated a blue glow. Above them, however, were alchemical symbols of which Azriel was familiar.

Eddie asked, "What are they, Azriel?"

"They're runes of some kind, but they're nothing I've ever seen before."

"They are dragon runes," Magador answered. He had swooped silently down into the crater and sat on his haunches by Azriel's side.

"Are you sure?"

"Well, of course I'm sure. I'm a dragon, am I not?" Magador shot back testily.

"So what do they say?" Eddie inquired.

Magador examined the runes and scratched at his crest for a moment before responding.

"Interesting. It says: I am Anvindr, guardian of the winds. Place me within the fire and I shall burn. Merge the Fire, combine the Water, and Earth shall release Æther."

"What is that supposed to mean?" Eddie's brow creased.

"It's a riddle of alchemy." Azriel scowled. "Why does it always have to be a riddle?" he muttered to himself. He then crouched and pointed at the symbols above the dragon runes. "See this triangle? That represents fire." Azriel explained. "Now this triangle is reversed, with the point facing down. It looks like a cup—that's why you know it represents water."

"Yeah, I sort of get it, but what about these two?"

Azriel smiled. "This one looks like the first, point up, but with a horizontal line crossing a third of the way down the triangle. That one's air. And this one looks like the symbol for water, with the point facing down, but as you can see, it has a line crossing the triangle a third of the way up from the base, which represents earth."

"So what are you supposed to do with them?"

"I'm not quite sure, but I have a suspicion." Azriel turned to Magador and pointed to the glowing blue rune. "What does this one say?"

He chuckled, "Why, that's the elemental's name: Anvindr!"

"I kind of thought so."

"Honestly, cousin, it's really quite a travesty that a dragon your age could be so illiterate."

Azriel let the comment pass and contemplated the rune bearing Anvindr's name. An inkling of an idea crossed his thoughts and with hesitation, he reached out to touch the rune. Suddenly Po-ok and Pal blocked his way with threatening gestures, alternately shaking their spears and jabbing menacingly at Azriel.

Eddie said, "I don't think they want you to touch it."

Azriel sat down and faced the Kachinas. "I'm supposed to free Anvindr. I know the rune has something to do with it."

In response, Po-ok and Pal stood rigidly and purposefully crossed their spears blocking Azriel's access to the rune. Azriel pressed his lips together and exhaled with exasperation.

"If I place the rune within fire, it will burn, right?"

Po-ok nodded. But then Pal upended his spear and scribed a few squiggly lines in the dirt. Next to it, he drew a straight line with the same wavy lines going up from it vertically.

"Wait! I get it!" Eddie said enthusiastically. "That's water and next to it is fire."

"Well, that doesn't make sense. Water would only put out the fire. We need fire to release Anvindr."

Magador chimed in. "No cousin, you need both."

"Well one thing I know for certain is that there's no water here for miles. We need water." Eddie added.

"Good point." Azriel smiled.

"At least you now know where the Elemental is. We can always return tomorrow with water." Magador suggested.

As the dragon finished speaking, Po-ok and Pal congealed back into the wooden Kachina dolls that housed their spirits. Like before, their spears were crossed to protect the rune.

Azriel smiled down at them. "Thank you, my friends, for guarding over Anvindr. I'll return as soon as I can."

"Shall we go, cousin?" Magador lowered his wing to allow easy access for Azriel and Eddie.

When they alit in the courtyard, Castle Wylusung was in chaos. Camille shouted at Mortimer as he savagely chased a tiny owl around the main hall. The pygmy owl tried desperately to escape the gargoyle, but Mortimer anticipated its every move. If it swooped toward the ceiling, Mortimer blocked it. When it dove toward the main gate, he intercepted it. Amid the shouting,

Mortimer had the tiny creature cornered and pinned it to the ground.

Julia and Albert tried to pull Mortimer off the frightened bird when he turned on them. He snarled, baring his teeth, as if he might attack.

Jasper turned to Azriel and gestured helplessly, "I don't know what has gotten into him. He's gone nuts!"

"Mortimer, what is wrong with you?" Azriel blustered. "Let that creature go—now!"

The gargoyle shook his head and hissed at Azriel as if he were a total stranger. He turned back, staring at the quivering owl. He had his claw extended while it struggled beneath his feet. Low snarls rumbled from his throat as if the creature was his enemy.

Amid the fracas, Eltanin emerged from his study.

Master Eltanin, I've never seen Mortimer act this way," Camille cried, sobbing for the terrified bird. At Eltanin's appearance, however, the tiny owl began to screech, struggling frantically to escape.

The master wizard's eyes narrowed as he assessed the scene. This wasn't predator against prey. Mortimer was outraged—acting as if he were protecting his pack. The owl still pinned in Mortimer's grasp, the gargoyle breathed heavily, ready to kill. He looked up at Eltanin.

"Do it," the wizard ordered.

With one quick motion, Mortimer nicked the bird with his extended claw. The pygmy owl instantly congealed into stone.

"Good work, Mortimer." Eltanin rubbed Mortimer's head in praise and removed the frozen owl from his grasp.

Eltanin carried the stone owl to his lab and retrieved a wire cage from one of the shelves. He returned and thrust the bird inside. Mortimer flew onto the table and stood beside him, growling at the cage.

"You did well, Mortimer," Eltanin said.

"Well?" Camille hissed. "That was completely barbaric. He terrorized that poor creature. Now look at it!"

"Young lady," Eltanin scowled. "Things aren't always what they seem. Sharpen your wits."

"What's so dangerous about a little bird?" Jasper asked.

"Usually nothing." Eltanin scowled. "But consider Mortimer's reaction. Something's not right. I have a suspicion…"

"Well what do you think it is?" Azriel posed the question.

"I'd rather not say. Now if you all would leave me be," Eltanin said firmly.

Throughout the next day, Azriel continually checked on Eltanin, peering into the study. The old man sat rigidly by his desk, taking neither food nor drink. He merely stared at the pygmy owl, brow knitted in disquiet, waiting for the inevitable. Mortimer's handiwork would soon wear off, and then the old wizard would know for sure.

Camille strode up beside Azriel and peeked into the study. "Is he still at it?"

"He hasn't moved at all," Azriel said with a shrug.

"This is too weird. How could a little bird be such a cause for alarm? And it's so cute!"

Azriel's eyes widened. "Shhh! Look, it's moving!"

Bit by bit, the owl's feathers transformed from gray stone to tawny brown speckled with white. With one swift motion, Eltanin reached into the cage and seized the struggling bird. He produced a dagger from his pocket and laid it on the table beside the bird. It began to screech, attracting Jasper, Albert, and Julia from the other room. Halimah also rushed in and held her hand to her mouth in horror.

Eltanin rounded on the bird. "Reveal yourself, foul demon!" He snatched the dagger from the table and held it to the struggling creature's throat.

Azriel had to hold Camille back as she tried to rescue the bird amid the others' protests.

Camille gasped. "No, don't hurt it! What has it ever done to you?"

"Get out, all of you—now! This is none of your concern!" The old wizard thundered. Frightened by the old man's anger, they quickly fled from the room. He brusquely motioned with his hand, and the door slammed with a resounding thud.

"How rude!" Camille shouted through the closed door.

The tiny creature continued to struggle in Eltanin's clenched hand.

"Reveal yourself, demon, or I shall remove your head!"

The owl began to screech pathetically.

"I'll do it!" Eltanin's fury rose. "If you know who I am, then you know not to take my threats lightly." Suddenly, with a blinding flash, Eltanin found his hand around a woman's throat staring into a pair of sultry blue eyes. He whispered with contempt.

"Lilith."

He jerked his hand away as if she carried a disease.

"You still remember me." Lilith smiled seductively and stroked his cheek. "I'm touched."

Eltanin couldn't hide the pain in his eyes. He had hated her for centuries, yet seeing Lilith still young and beautiful stirred his heart with unwelcome memories. Once, many years ago he had loved her. His passion for her had nearly destroyed his world. With forced control, he removed her hand from his face.

"You betrayed me," Eltanin whispered. "Tell me Lilith—did you ever love me, or was it all a ruse to gain power?"

"I loved you in the beginning, I suppose." She smiled tenderly. "That was a long time ago." Her eyes became distant as she recalled her time with him. "But as I became more adept, I grew to love power more than any love I felt for you."

Eltanin laughed bitterly, "Those might be the first honest words I've ever heard from your lips, my dear. I taught you most of my magick, but sadly, there is something you never learned. Power, my dear, is highly overrated."

"Oh, I wouldn't say that," Lilith purred. "I have found it quite to my liking."

"Then you've learned nothing. The allure of power only leaves one empty. It never satisfies. The more you attain, the easier it slips through your fingers. In the end, you lose it—and usually with a painful plunge into despair."

"Oh, I've been to the abyss, Eltanin," she spat. "You and the Clave put me there, Remember? But now I've returned."

"Yes—and it's quite obvious who brought you back, and with whom you've allied yourself."

Lilith chuckled lightly, "Oh, Eltanin, don't be such a boor. You could return to the Clave at any time and resume your rightful place as head of Draconis. I could help you."

"Your kind of help, I don't need, Lilith. The Clave has outlived its usefulness. Rastaban and the Clave—my former brothers—have corrupted the pure power from which they were made. And you, my dear, have also corrupted the pure power that I gave you. That is a mistake I have had to live with for untold years. Your deeds have become legendary—or rather, infamous—mother of demons, and all that is unholy."

Lilith chuckled. "True—all true. Of course, you know that I can't allow your progeny, Azriel, to complete his task."

Eltanin's face reddened. "If you touch a hair on his head, I will destroy you, Lilith."

"You don't have the power anymore, Eltanin. You've become weak. Useless. And as you well know, I cannot be killed. I'm immortal, thanks to you."

"I wouldn't be so sure, Lilith. There are always ways around magick—things you never learned. Traps. Back doors. Secret passages."

Lilith scowled, enraged. It seemed as though Eltanin was trying to provoke her. "Old man, you don't want to mess with me. You'll lose."

"Don't underestimate me, girl. I didn't teach you everything."

Suddenly Lilith clawed her hand and thrust it forward. Bolts of lightning burst from her fingertips, blasting Eltanin across the room. He rebounded off the stone wall. Nearly unconscious, he rose and glared at the sorceress.

"So it is combat you desire," Eltanin sneered. "Then so be it. Don't say I didn't warn you." Focusing downward, he began to scribe arcane sigils in the air. The castle walls resonated and shuddered with the power he released. It attracted the attention of everyone in the dwelling. Nicodemus came running into the room along with Halimah. Dressed in protective armor, they had been sparring, practicing swordsmanship to sharpen their skills. Azriel and Camille watched in astonishment as thorny vines erupted from the stone floor. Eltanin thrust his hands forward and the lethal vines darted toward Lilith, twining around her body. She burst into flames. The vines fell away like chaff in the wind. A moment later she resumed her normal form and smiled wickedly.

"That was a good trick, Eltanin. Perhaps you'll like this one!" With a sudden gesture, a crystal sphere, which sat on a pedestal by Eltanin's writing desk levitated from its stand and flew into Lilith's hand. She smiled deviously.

"You wouldn't destroy my gazing ball, would you?" Eltanin sighed with exasperation. "It was a gift!"

"No, my old friend, just a simple transformation!" She savagely threw the orb with all her strength. It shattered against the wall. The fragments instantly transformed, swelling into monstrous stone creatures. They resembled men in the fact that they had two arms and legs. But that was where the similarity ended. Their misshapen heads were devoid of eyes and what barely passed as mouths were great gaping maws lined with crystal teeth shaped like daggers. Their clenched fists were like mauls, ready to crush anything in their path.

"Stone golems, Lilith? Really?" Eltanin's voice was filled with disdain. The hideous creatures, however, did not attack Eltanin but instead filed out to assault the observers in the adjoining room.

The battle began. One golem immediately charged Julia, but Halimah intercepted with sword raised. She struck at the creature, but her sword merely glanced off its body. It swung its arm and nearly crushed Halimah's skull, but she was too quick—ducking, rolling, and regaining her feet. Nicodemus called out, "Granddaughter, no conventional weapon can kill a golem—you must use magick!"

Camille was pursued by a golem. When it nearly overtook her, Azriel intercepted. He understood alchemy and noted that the golems were fashioned from sandstone. Strong acid would melt them back into sand.

"Fundo!" He shouted as he thrust out his hands. Vicious streams of green liquid shot from his palms and splattered the golem. It howled with an unearthly roar and dissolved into a heap of sand.

"Use the Fundo spell." He shouted at his friends. Jasper, Albert, and Maggie began melting the golems where they stood, but there were too many—they kept coming. As they dissolved, the sand piled higher, making it increasingly difficult to move. One golem lifted Julia off the ground. She screamed as it began to crush the life from her. Eddie charged recklessly to her defense, casting a salvo of plasma spheres at the creature's back. It wasn't enough to harm it, but it served as a distraction. It dropped Julia and turned on Eddie. He scrambled between her and the creature. The golem charged, diving toward Eddie, threatening to crush them both. Eddie reacted immediately by shielding Julia with his body and rolling them both from the monster's path. It struck a glancing blow, shattering Eddie's arm. He howled in pain.

Albert called out to Eddie, "Shield yourself!"

Sprawling next to Julia, he had barely enough strength to mutter the spell.

"Tecum!" He gasped through the agony of his broken bones. A transparent shield rose over him and Julia before he passed out. Jasper and Albert quickly began to work together in tandem. From either side of the golem, they shouted "Eradico," unleashing a destructive concussion that pulverized the monster into dust.

With each golem destroyed, the sand piled higher. Soon they wouldn't be able to move. There were still four golems remaining, and with their destruction, the defenders would all be buried in sand. Nicodemus had to think fast. Pronouncing a destructive spell, he blasted the south wall outward, spilling the sand into the courtyard. Freed from the sand, Azriel, Camille and Nicodemus quickly dispatched the remaining golems. From the adjoining room, however, Eltanin still battled Lilith. She released a scorching volley of fireballs that merely glanced off his body. He returned the onslaught with such intensity that Lilith was nearly overwhelmed. But with arrogant flair, she caught the last plasma bolt and prepared to hurl it back at Eltanin. She heaved it with all her strength, but it wouldn't fly—as if glued to her hand. She tried to shake it off, baffled that it wouldn't move.

"Wha...?" She knitted her brow with confusion. Lilith's eyes widened. The ball of energy had concealed something far more lethal. In her hand rested a tiny translucent pyramid—the Carcer Eternis.

"You wouldn't!" She hissed at Eltanin as the magickal device grew from her hand to imprison her.

"Oh no, my dear, I've done something far worse—at least for you."

The prison continued to grow, shattering the nearest wall until half of it settled into the courtyard. It was furnished with everything Lilith could ever need while she remained imprisoned within its blue, transparent walls.

"What could be worse than the Carcer Eternis?" she raged. "Eltanin, this is beneath you to use forbidden magick."

"That's true, my dear," Eltanin beamed, "but you see, I didn't fashion this prison. Your friend, Rastaban, created this one in an attempt to capture Azriel. Rastaban used Azriel's cousin to lure him into this trap. Let's just say I've made a few alterations. Pity I had to use it on you. It was truly meant for Rastaban." The old wizard turned to leave the room.

"Wait!" Lilith's voice rose in desperation. "You're not going to just leave me here."

"Well, of course I am!"

She screamed her rage and frustration at Eltanin's obliqueness. "This is cruel, Eltanin."

"No crueler than you have been. I'll make this easy for you, Lilith. This is not what you have wrongly assumed is the Carcer Eternis. It is something far more subtle. It is the Carcer Letalis Perpetuus. You may stay here forever, or you may choose to leave."

"Well that's not much of a prison then." She laughed at Eltanin as if he were nothing more than a fool. She strode to the periphery of the prison, about to step through.

"Careful, dear." Eltanin warned. "You see, I haven't told you everything. Should you choose to leave these walls, you will lose something very dear to you."

"Oh, and what would that be?" She sneered.

"Your immortality."

"You wouldn't," she gasped.

"I already did." He shrugged. "Not only that, my dear, but the effect is permanent. You can never become immortal again. The Lapis Occultus won't work on you. As to any other effect it may have on you, I'm really not sure. I've only done this once." He beamed a boyish grin.

"What do you mean?" She growled.

"Well, I'm just not sure if you will retain your loveliness or if perhaps you will be turned into a decrepit, ugly old hag. You might even crumble into dust. After all, you are over twenty thousand years old, are you not?"

He turned and left the room.

"Eltanin? Eltanin!" In panic, Lilith called out after him. Left to herself, she heaved a querulous sigh. Resigned, Lilith sat on the richly embroidered divan, contemplating her dilemma.

Afterward, Caer Wylusung resumed its normal routine. Most of the damage done was magically repaired, other than the part of Lilith's prison that still protruded from the north side of Eltanin's study.

Eddie awoke disoriented after having slept for the entire day and night. Eltanin had mended Eddie's shattered limb and restored it to soundness, but it was still remarkably sore. When he opened his eyes, the room was half-lit by an oil lamp. Eddie was surprised to find Julia seated on a chair next to his bed. She was slumped over, having succumbed to fatigue. She apparently had watched over him the entire time he had lain unconscious. He gently took hold of her hand.

"Hi." He smiled sheepishly. Julia's eyes fluttered open and she yawned. Looking down at him, she smiled. "Hi, Edward," she whispered.

Wincing, he flexed his arm, testing its movement.

"Your arm was broken in a few places. Eltanin fixed it." Julia assured him.

"Glad I don't remember much. Are you okay?"

"I'm fine. I've got a few nasty bruises, but I'll live, see?" Julia lifted her shirt slightly to reveal her midriff. The golem's handprint was clearly visible in the bruises. She paused and looked down at her feet. "Edward, you were really brave. That thing could have killed you, but you saved my life."

"You would have done the same for me, right?"

"Yeah, I suppose, but I was so frightened. That was the side of magick I've never seen before. It has always been fun learning spells and using them in practice, but that was the real thing. Do you still want to stay with us?"

"Are you kidding? I'll never return to who I was. How could I? I'm in for the long term, and I'll always have your back, okay?"

"Okay," she whispered, swallowing down her fear. Julia's eyes welled up with gratitude. "Thank you, Edward." She reached down and gently kissed Edward on the lips. When she stood, there was a faint blush to her cheeks. She turned to leave.

"Wait." Edward grinned and pulled her back by the hand. He returned the kiss, this time with more passion. She gasped with unexpected emotion welling up inside. "I have wanted to do that for a long time." Eddie smiled, surprised at himself.

"It's okay," Julia awkwardly suppressed a grin, "I liked it."

"Feeling better, are we?"

They both looked up guiltily as Elsinore strode into Eddie's room.

"Hi, Mom," Eddie said quickly and straightened up.

"Edward, don't act so self-conscious. It's quite all right to steal a kiss from time to time, particularly from such a pretty girl."

Julia blushed further.

"I'm very proud of you, Edward." Elsinore nodded and smiled. "You behaved valiantly and showed your true character."

"I didn't really do anything, Mom, except get my arm broken."

"…and save Julia," she added. "You've inherited your father's courage, and the valor of your bloodline."

Eddie looked down uncomfortably.

"Are you feeling well enough to get out of bed? Your cousin would like you to go with him today. He's returning to release Anvindr from the mountain. I understand you were quite helpful."

"Not really, but it was a pretty neat adventure."

Nicodemus strode in. "Well, your adventure has only just begun. Good morning, Edward."

"Morning, Uncle Nick."

"Edward, I have something for you. It's been in my possession for a few thousand years, and now I want you to have it. It will bring you luck and give you strength." Nicodemus handed a small wooden box to Eddie.

Upon opening it, Eddie's eyes narrowed with curiosity. Attached to a golden chain, a small silver horn hung from an ornate mount. "What is it, Uncle Nick?"

"It is the tip of the horn from the Bull of Minos. He was a ferocious creature that guarded the labyrinth. Though somewhat dimwitted, he was strong and fearless—like you were yesterday— er, not the dimwitted part, of course. Wear it for protection."

"Thanks, Uncle Nick."

"Now you must dress, eat your breakfast, and meet up with Azriel in the courtyard within an hour."

Azriel was ready to depart when Eddie strolled up. He was surrounded by Jasper, Albert, Julia, and Halimah. At their feet were a few glass jugs of water. Eddie noticed also that at the far end of the courtyard, the base of a shimmering blue pyramid protruded from the wall, surrounded by stone rubble where it had broken through. A beautiful woman stood within the structure, arms crossed, staring menacingly at the group.

"So who is she?" Eddie asked, pointing with his thumb.

"Lilith." Azriel answered. "She may look pretty, but as Eltanin warned, she's entirely evil. Best that you avoid her."

"Why doesn't Eltanin just kill her and be done with it?"

"It's not his way, Edward. Besides, he probably has some plans for her. Eltanin doesn't always tell me everything." He removed the dream orb from his pocket and implanted the image of the San Francisco Peaks and the crater in which Anvindr was imprisoned. Azriel added, "Since we know where the Elemental is now, we can go there immediately. If we get stuck, I know exactly who to ask for help. Are you all ready?"

As one, they touched the orb and were transported to the base of a mountain. Looking down, they saw a scree-strewn crater, and in the very center, a volcanic cone jutted up like an angry fist holding a prize. Scrambling down, they came face to face with Pook and Pal. They immediately transformed from wooden dolls into their human form. They nodded with approval when they spied the jugs of water carried by all present.

"So now what?" Jasper asked.

"I think I'm supposed to remove this rune and place it in the symbol for fire, but after that, I'm not really quite sure. That's why I brought this." Azriel removed two tiny objects from his pocket. He held up a gray cube and a small metal wand. With purpose, he struck the wand against the cube and produced a respectable spark. A new member now floated among the companions.

"Hello, son of Luminance," Fieré beamed with a smile. Scantily clad in raiment of fire, sparks flew from her wings as she hovered before him.

Eddie's eyes widened. "Wow, she's beautiful, Azriel!"

Julia, suddenly jealous, smacked Eddie in the arm. Halimah held her hand to her mouth, suppressing a giggle.

"Ow! What the hell was that for?" Eddie rubbed his arm.

Fieré giggled impishly. "Your thoughts aren't very nice, Edward. My fire never goes out! I am Fieré, queen of the Drakes." She turned to Azriel. "Why have I been summoned?"

"Do you know where we are, Fieré?"

"Of course. Anvindr has been imprisoned here for untold years."

"I am here to release Anvindr, but I don't know how to combine the elements of fire and water."

She laughed with nonchalance. "But of course water and fire could never be combined. They are opposites."

"Yet this riddle here says to do exactly that."

"Then you misunderstand, Son of Luminance. Tell me, what is stone, from where does it spring?"

"Well that's easy, it is from the element of earth."

"Good! Now, does rock change if you, let's say, heat it up?"

"No, it might change shape, but it is still the same element."

"Excellent, we're almost there, Azriel." Fieré grinned.

"Now would the heated rock change if you poured water upon it?"

"Well, no." Azriel scratched his head. "It's impenetrable."

"Yes it would!" Eddie interjected. "It would probably crack!"

"There!" Fieré beamed. "Listen to your cousin!" She giggled and suddenly vanished.

Azriel shrugged and looked around at his friends. "Well here goes." He reached for the blue glowing rune that signified Anvindr's name. Surprisingly, reaching for it caused the rune to float into Azriel's hand. As instructed by the riddle, he placed it into the alchemical symbol for fire. The rune jumped from his hand and snapped into place. Oddly, it changed color to shimmering yellow and filled the triangular depression. A subtle change took place, imperceptible at first, but they all felt it. The sensation of heat began to emanate from the stone. Soon it started to glow—deep red at first—but then it blazed orange and morphed to bright yellow.

Azriel suddenly felt a sharp jab in his foot. He looked down and Po-ok was motioning with his hands as if to say, "What are you waiting for?"

"Everybody—now!" Azriel shouted. As one they poured the jugs of water over the blazing stone. With an ear-shattering concussion, the stone suddenly split open and released a geyser of steam. They were all thrown back by the blast. Some received a few cuts and bruises by the flying shards of stone. The ground beneath them began to quake and tremble. Azriel feared the earth would open up and swallow them where they stood, but he held his footing and watched the marvel taking shape. The column of steam started to expand, filling the sky, ever widening. The mist began to congeal, taking shape—first a pair of gossamer wings then a massive golden, nearly transparent body, and then the crested head of a golden dragon. Anvindr stretched his wings and towered over the companions. His breath was as sweet as a cool spring day as he roared in triumph.

Anvindr looked down at Azriel with eyes that glowed golden as the rising sun. "Brother," he said. "I have awaited your coming and thank you for my release!"

"It is my honor to do so, Anvindr, Ruler of Air," Azriel answered formally. Po-ok and Pal now stood by Azriel's side. The Kachina dolls that had housed their souls were burned by the fire and reduced to ashes. The gods of thunder now stood taller than Azriel. Pal held out the transformed rune in his hand. He spoke in a powerful voice that resonated through the canyon. "My friend," he said. "As you have freed the wind god, you have also freed us. My brother and I are grateful. We will grant a boon in your time of need. For now, take this stone and complete your task."

Azriel received the stone and held it up to the light. Triangular, a horizontal line was inscribed a third of the way from the base. It glowed golden as he offered it to its rightful owner. Anvindr bent low so Azriel could place the gem into the great Elemental's forehead. It adhered with a loud click.

"Thank you, Brother." Anvindr sighed with relief. "There are yet two of us to release from bondage, but I must warn you, Son of Luminance, that the time grows short. My Sister, Lagina-Tierra, languishes and grows weak. It is urgent that you finish your task, for the time of the conjunction draws near."

"Great Elemental, I do not know where she is hidden. It will take time to locate her."

"This I know, my Brother. That is why you must heed my words. There is a place surrounded by four rivers, two, most ancient, flow with life-giving water. Two have long since vanished, when once the world was destroyed by flood. In a barren valley hidden by four mountains that mark the cardinal directions, you will find a place where the blood of the earth freely flows. But I must caution you, Son of Luminance. The way is perilous and inaccessible to men who would exploit its riches. Should it be found, then the earth will die, for it is the heart and navel of the world and its life-blood. There you will see where my sister is imprisoned. I have been able to maintain my strength through the eons, but Lagina-Tierra has not been as fortunate. The destruction that man has waged upon this planet has taken its toll upon her. If my sister is not released soon, this world will perish before you can save it. You have one among you familiar with the terrain." Anvindr fixed his eyes on Halimah.

"Accept this gift. It will hide you from those who would prevent you from completing your task for that land is hardened by war, and the men there are suspicious of strangers. The way is dangerous."

As Anvindr spoke a silk bag floated down from the sky and landed at Azriel's feet.

"What is this, Anvindr?" Azriel was about to open it.

"Save it for when you need it, my brother. It holds within its dark interior a Mirage to hide you from unsuspecting eyes. Use it sparingly, for it can only be used once a day by invoking my name."

"What will you do now?" Azriel asked.

"My time has been long overdue. There is much to heal in the world. In many places, the air is unbreathable. It must be cleansed. Now, Son of Luminance, I must take my leave. I will return when you summon me. That time shall be soon."

Chapter 18

In a fit of rage, Rastaban swept the contents of his conference table onto the floor. Goblets and a decanter shattered. He stomped them underfoot as he continued his tirade.

"My lord, what has you so upset?" Giausur asked.

"Upset? Upset doesn't even begin to describe what I'm feeling. I am surrounded by incompetence."

"My Lord?" Thuban stuttered, fear in his voice.

"The Air Elemental has been released," Rastaban muttered through gritted teeth. "Of this I'm sure. Azriel—Son of Luminance," he spat with a sneer, "has been busy. Have you seen the news? Mysteriously, the smog over some of the most polluted cities has blown out to sea! The ice caps have stopped melting. If this keeps up, the world will become healthy again!"

"Are you sure, my lord?" Altais strode in.

"Where have you been?" Rastaban demanded.

"Searching. It seems Azriel covers his tracks well."

"Bah!" he growled, waving a dismissive hand. "Have you seen Lilith? She should have reported back to me by now."

"No, my lord, I haven't."

"It's time to interrogate Abelene. She must know something."

"It's a waste of time, Rastaban. She won't betray her son."

"We will see." The wizard scowled and headed toward the chamber below.

The iron door creaked and groaned as Rastaban pushed it open. His hurried footsteps echoed through the cavern but slowed as he heard music coming from Abelene's prison.

He hid in the shadows, listening intently to a lilting tune. Abelene sat on a brocaded chair playing a lute. The ancient melody, a ballad from Aralia, rose and fell, swelled with passion and then faded into a whisper. It stirred such longing that it tugged at Rastaban's heart.

"That was lovely, milady," Rastaban said as he emerged into the light.

"Well, for the first time, we agree on something." The dark dragon looked down at Rastaban, eyes flashing with malice. Abelene suppressed a giggle and stood to face the wizard.

Rastaban waved his hand, and a comfortable chair appeared by Abelene's prison. He sat and faced her. Likewise, from the inside of the transparent shield, Abelene motioned and the chair slid over. She sat and faced Rastaban. "What brings you here today, Rastaban? More verbal jousting?" She absently tuned a string and began playing again. She was ready for psychological warfare; the tune she played was meant to confuse and confound. Its effect made her opponent more pliable and honest. The stress creasing Rastaban's brow softened, and he became more relaxed in the chair. He sat transfixed until the tune ended. Smiling, Abelene placed the lute by her side.

"So what do you wish to discuss today, lord wizard?"

"Your son, of course."

"Indeed." She smiled.

"He has released another Elemental."

"Yes, I have sensed it."

"Why, my Lady?"

"Certainly you're not that obtuse, Rastaban." Abelene answered with all sincerity. She knew it would do no harm at this juncture to be honest; in fact, she hoped it would frustrate him even more. "Rastaban, if the Earth and Aralia are to be reunited, it will be easier for all concerned if Earth is healed of its wounds. The reintegration of both worlds is inevitable, as prophecy has foretold. You rage against it, you plot and create strife, but in the end all your efforts will come to naught."

"I still have influence, Abelene," he responded with self-assurance. "I can still set the nations at war with each other. Humans have always existed in a precarious balance; it doesn't take much to push them over the edge. I have done it before, and I will do it again. It is actually quite easy. Create shortages of essentials, and the greed of men will drive them into turmoil."

"Hmm, what you say is true, Lord Wizard. Continual conflict has prevented humans from reaching their true potential. That is the thing you have feared all along, isn't it?"

"You are perceptive, Lady Abelene, but have you considered this? If the worlds shall reunite, it will not be peace that Azriel will inherit. No, my lady, it will be all-out war between the users of Magick and the builders of technology. The two philosophies are diametrically opposed. They cannot exist side by side. My way is the better one. Keep the worlds separated and prevent the destruction of both!"

"No, Rastaban, keep the worlds apart and both will fade into oblivion. Aralia and Earth are shattered worlds; magick is fading and technology is destructive. I know you have felt it. Together, they must learn to coexist; otherwise it will spell the doom of both the Human and Elfin races. That is why the remaining two elementals shall be released. With each one freed, the Earth heals. The destruction brought about by man is reversed. The oceans are stabilized and clean, the air breathable again. The soil, laid waste by neglect, shall again bring abundance, and fire shall purge the world of disease. It is a second chance for all of us. This you must see!"

Rastaban paused to consider her words. He needed to make Abelene see reason. He knew she could exert influence upon her son. Any mother would do so. "Milady, I propose a truce. I propose that Azriel become part of the Clave. With his power and influence, we may avert all-out war. You must speak to your son."

Abelene laughed lightly, "Even if I could, you fail to see the obvious. Azriel *is* the head of Draconis. With Eltanin gone, and Azriel his direct heir by inheritance, he, in fact, is the leader of the Clave! With Eltanin's death, you took that position by default. Would you move over to let Azriel lead? I think not. Oh, Rastaban, you are too invested in your position to ever let it go, and Azriel will never be swayed away from his true destiny." She sighed. "But the point is moot. As long as you keep me imprisoned, I cannot speak to my son."

Rastaban chuckled heartily and waved his finger at Abelene as if scolding a child. "You are naughty, Abelene, and a terrible liar. I have sources, and I happen to know that you are in daily conversation with Azriel. I have made the mistake of underestimating human magick. Nicodemus taught you well, Abelene!"

"Ah." Abelene didn't bat an eye. "I suppose it was inevitable that I would be found out, but it doesn't change a thing. Azriel will never join you."

Rastaban was about to respond when he heard the chamber door open and felt a gust of air from above.

"Who's there?" Rastaban called out.

"It's… It's me, my Lord."

"Lilith?"

"Yes, I must speak with you."

Rastaban turned to Abelene. "We will continue our conversation another time, Lady Abelene. I must take my leave."

He rose and climbed the stairs to the dwellings above. When Rastaban entered the main room, the lights were dim. A figure hid in the shadows.

"Lilith, why do you hide?"

"I am not myself, My Lord."

"Come into the light."

When she approached, Rastaban was shocked at her appearance. Lilith's hair was speckled with gray, and her once perfect face was now creased with wrinkles.

"What has happened to you, my love?"

"I have been stripped of my immortality. I am now mortal."

"Who did this to you?" Rastaban raged.

"Eltanin!" she wept.

"Impossible!"

"Not impossible—he's outmaneuvered you." She accused. "You doubted all these years that he could be alive."

"Where is he?"

"I can show you, my Lord." Lilith wiped her eyes.

"Yes, indeed you will, my dear Lilith. And I shall avenge you!"

"I wouldn't be so sure, Rastaban. Eltanin is more powerful and clever than ever, and his progeny, Azriel, is no slouch either." She hissed. "The Son of Luminance is building his own Clave, my Lord. They are young, but they are robust and eager, albeit inexperienced. While I kept Eltanin occupied in Magickal battle,

Azriel and his minions managed to defeat an onslaught of stone golems. Stone golems! Do you understand? Do not dismiss the boy so readily. But if we are to attack, it must be done with expediency while they are not expecting it. They must be destroyed utterly."

"But now that you have escaped, they will expect it." Rastaban's face darkened.

"Not just yet." She smiled wickedly.

My dear?" Rastaban tilted his head.

"Before I left, I fashioned a simulacrum of myself. To their knowledge, I am still imprisoned."

Lilith suddenly noticed movement by the chamber door and growled. She hurled a fireball at the creature, and it scurried away through a crack in the wall.

"I hate rats!" She hissed through gritted teeth. "Honestly, Rastaban, you should clean this place up."

"Don't be petulant, my dear. Rats are the least of my concern. But you are right. It is time to attack. Assemble your demons."

Down below, in the chamber of imprisonment, Abelene crouched on her knees as close to the magickal field as she dared. Opposite her, a gray rat chattered and squealed while she listened intently.

"Thank you, my little friend," she said and smiled. "Sorry about your tail." The creature screeched indignantly as it licked the scorch marks from its fur. The tip of its tail was bent at an awkward angle. Abelene added, "I would fix it if I could. You know that."

The creature chattered a few moments more and scampered away, disappearing into a small crack in the cave wall.

Abelene stood, fear shadowing her eyes.

"What has you worried, Lady Abelene?" Charlie asked.

"Azriel and the others are in immediate danger. Rastaban now knows where he is and is going to attack. I must warn them."

Abelene needed to calm herself and send a telepathic message to Azriel, but it wasn't their usual time. If he was engaged in something, he might not hear her. Nevertheless, she lay on her bed and did her best to clear her mind. Down below, in the chamber of imprisonment, Abelene crouched on her knees as close to the magickal field as she dare. Opposite her, a gray rat chattered and squealed as she listened intently.

"Thank you, my little friend." She smiled. "Sorry about your tail." The creature screeched indignantly as it licked the scorch marks from its fur. The tip of its tail was also bent at an awkward angle. Abelene added. "I would fix it if I could. You know that."

The small creature chattered a few moments more and scampered away, disappearing into a small crack in the cave wall.

Abelene stood, fear shadowing her eyes.

"What has you worried, "Lady Abelene?" Charlie asked.

"Azriel and the others are in immediate danger. Rastaban now knows where he is and is going to attack. I must warn them."

Abelene needed to calm herself to send a telepathic message to Azriel, but it wasn't their usual time. If he was engaged in something, he might not hear her. Nevertheless, she lay on her bed and did her best to clear her mind. As she began to project her thoughts outward, a thumping resounded through the chamber. It began softly, then increased in volume. Soon it grew so loud that Abelene was forced to cover her ears. She knew what was happening. Rastaban was using any form of distraction to prevent Abelene from contacting her son. As the volume and vibrations grew, Abelene cried out in despair. The sound became painful. She could neither block it out nor could she magically dispel the noise.

Charlie, watching her agony, roared in outrage. As a guardian, however, he had the ability to project his image like his brother and sister elementals could. He was not easily confounded by such disturbances.

Azriel was in the great room of Caer Wylusung, making preparations to release the next Elemental when a shadow began to coalesce, seeping up from the floor.

"Greetings, my brother." Charlie projected the full magnificence of his image.

Azriel sighed, annoyed by the intrusion. "Really, this is not a good time."

"You must listen, Azriel. Caer Wylusung is under attack. It is coming soon."

"Why should I believe you? My mother could have told me."

"No, brother, she cannot. Rastaban is attacking her with sound, which prevents her from reaching you. I am doing this for her."

"Why," Azriel countered, "what have you to gain by helping us?"

"My freedom!"

"How do I know this isn't some form of trick?"

"Brother, listen to me! Lilith has escaped from Eltanin's grasp. She has told Rastaban where you are!"

"Now I know you're lying. She is still here. Look and see!"

Charlie stomped his foot and roared. "Are you so easily fooled, Son of Luminance? Her image is merely an illusion meant to deceive. Test it for yourself."

Azriel strode into Eltanin's study and examined Lilith. Trapped within the transparent shield, it was unlikely she would have left at the risk of her life. She was sitting at a desk with pen in hand, writing into a book. Azriel stood before her and cleared his throat.

"Lilith, I would like to speak to you."

She turned, smiled, and then went back to writing in her book.

"Azriel, what are you doing here?" Eltanin had just entered his chamber.

"I am testing something. The Dark Dragon was just here. He said the castle is under attack and that Lilith is leading the way."

"Impossible," Eltanin smiled confidently. "She's right here, aren't you, my dear."

Again, Lilith turned and smiled, then went back to writing in her book. Azriel stared at her suspiciously. Why didn't she say anything?

"Lilith, I want to ask you something." Eltanin probed. As before, she turned and smiled, then went back to scrawling on the open page.

Azriel narrowed his eyes. He picked up the closest object he could find, a teacup, and hurled it at Lilith. It passed through her and shattered on the floor. She turned and smiled.

Eltanin paled. "Quick! Gather everyone together! Hurry!" he ordered.

"Where are we going?"

"There is only one place I can think of where we cannot be traced." Eltanin answered. "Now that Rastaban knows I'm alive, he will want to meet me in magickal combat."

"You're not afraid, are you? You could kick his magickal ass!"

"Perhaps, but now is not the time. It must be a time of my choosing." He turned and called out, his voice resonating through the castle. In moments everyone met in the courtyard. Magador flew down from the tower with Mortimer. Kita and Hermes also trotted up. When everyone was gathered, Eltanin made the announcement.

"Soon we will be under attack." Everyone's faces sobered. "You must gather your things. Take only what is necessary. Remember your Reducto spell. My experience with the Clave is that this castle will not remain standing. Be back here in five minutes."

"Damn!" Nicodemus grumbled. "You heard what he said! Now let's move."

They all scrambled to their rooms. Azriel strapped Errin-lil onto his back and shoved all his magickal items in a cloth sack. He had a fair collection of spellbooks and wouldn't be able to carry them all. With the reducto spell, he was able to shrink them down to a manageable size. All his belongings now fit into a small wooden box. It was the same with Camille. She was the first to return to the courtyard. The Cunninghams were next. Mortimer prodded Muriel and Jasper along, much to the boy's annoyance. Julia looked visibly worried until Eddie and Elsinore strolled up with their belongings in hand. Next to arrive was Nicodemus and Eltanin. In short order, they managed to remove all essentials from the castle and store them in impossibly small sacks. Finally, Azriel arrived, with Halimah trailing behind.

"So where are we going?" Camille asked, but before Eltanin could answer, a concussion shook the castle. The tower exploded with a blinding light. They all had to scramble to avoid being pulverized by falling rock.

"We must go now!" Eltanin removed his dream orb from a pocket in his robe. Everyone made contact and was immediately transported to the Fairy Bridge outside Castleton. From there, Eltanin snapped his finger and the group was now standing around the entrance to his former home. He had resided here for centuries in the guise of Pog. Azriel smiled, remembering the place.

"We are not yet at our destination," Eltanin remarked and then looked up at Magador. He cleared his throat uncomfortably.

"You, my friend, do present a problem however."

"And what would that be?" Magador scowled down at the wizard.

"Well—your size! You couldn't possibly fit through the door."

"Couldn't I just fly there?"

"Not where we're going."

"Then what do you propose?" Magador snarled.

"I must shrink you. It's only temporary of course." Eltanin replied affably.

"I refuse!" Magador raged. "I am not a toy to be played with."

"Magador, it's the only way. The portal through is cramped even for a normal sized man. You can't get through any other way." The old wizard reasoned.

"This is preposterous!"

"Trust me. It won't hurt. The spell will wear off in an hour."

"Fine, then." Magador sighed, clearly unhappy.

With an apologetic shrug, Eltanin removed a wand and waved it toward Magador. "Reducto!" he commanded. In moments, Magador shrunk in size until he stood a mere ten inches tall. Julia gasped with delight. She quickly snatched him up from the ground and held him in the palm of her hand.

"He's so cute," she bubbled.

Magador bit her on the thumb and she howled in pain. Mortimer thought the whole incident particularly amusing and chortled merrily while pointing at the tiny dragon. In a rage, Magador bellowed a searing flame and scorched Mortimer's stubby tail. He hopped around howling as he slapped at the flames. "This is thoroughly humiliating," Magador raged in a tiny squeaky voice and flew onto Eltanin's shoulder. "I will not forget this, wizard."

Though everyone was amused, they dared not laugh for fear of hurting Magador's feelings. It didn't take a stretch of the imagination to assume that Magador would be in a particularly foul mood when he returned to his normal size.

Eltanin guided the group to a massive tree. At the base, between two gnarled roots jutting from the ground, a dirt path nearly indiscernible from the rest of the terrain led to a small door. They had to crouch to gain entry. Eltanin led them through a confusing labyrinth of rooms, passed through the library that Azriel recognized, then through a corridor that led to another door. Azriel rubbed his chin thoughtfully and peered at Camille, finally understanding what the old wizard had in mind.

"Wait, Grandfather. Wouldn't it be wise to warn them?"

"Er… yes. Indeed!"

Jasper asked, "Eltanin, what is this place?"

"It is a bridge between worlds. When Earth and Aralia were torn asunder, this place was created in an instant. Try to imagine it as the glue that binds them together. Within that dimension resides all magick and possibility, which is why you must control your thoughts at all times while inside its boundary. What you imagine can become very real so you must remain disciplined at all times. There is something else you must know. Time works differently here. A day will pass in this in-between place, but only ten minutes will pass on Earth. That buys us a certain advantage over our adversaries, since it will give Azriel more time to prepare. Now, follow me."

Eltanin opened the door to allow passage. Azriel and Camille had been there before and knew what to expect, but the others were wide-eyed with wonder. The enchanted world was rich with beauty, like something from the most magnificent dreams of man.

The rise they stood upon looked down upon a valley. Azriel recognized the gazebo from his last venture here. Surrounding it were colorful tents now erected with delicate streamers at the top, one tent for each of them.

Azriel glanced at Eltanin. "How did these get here?"

"I *thought* them up." The old wizard smiled. "All of you will need a place to stay."

"Why not a castle?" Camille asked.

"Nothing permanent can stay here. It is ever-changing and shifting according to desire. That's why, lovely as it is, it can also be dangerous, so watch what you think. You must think only honest and good thoughts. The food here will also make you transparent to one another."

Azriel laughed. "Yes, both figuratively and literally."

Having been duly warned, they each found a prospective tent and began unpacking their belongings. By the time they emerged from their dwellings, Magador had returned to his normal size. Feeling humiliated and grumpy, he now lay beneath a sprawling shade tree, brooding. Azriel strode up with Camille, hoping to soothe Magador's bruised feelings.

"Would you like to fly the countryside?"

"I wish to be left alone."

"Aw, c'mon, Magador. If there was any other way to hide you here, don't you think Eltanin would have figured it out?"

"That's not the point, cousin. I resent fleeing with my tail between my legs like a coward. I would have preferred to fight!"

"We could have been vastly outnumbered."

"It was cowardly. I'm surprised at Eltanin. I thought he had more spine than that."

Azriel shook his head. "It wasn't cowardice, Magador; it was wisdom. Rastaban is powerful and aligned with Lilith. Even though she has lost her immortality, she can still raise a horde of demons. We were not prepared to fight that."

"It might be as you say, cousin, but have you considered that Rastaban is not beneath unleashing his evil throughout the planet? This will have dire consequences. Humans are not prepared to battle magick."

"I'm sure we will return when the time is right. Eltanin is addressing the issue as we speak."

"Well, he'd better hurry, then. We may not have a world to return to."

"I think your concerns are unfounded, Magador. Rastaban is after Eltanin and me. He considers humans beneath him, and a waste of time."

"Well I hope you're right. Nevertheless, I resent waiting here. My talents are being wasted."

"We will have our day, I promise you." Azriel smiled. "Here, I know just what you need."

From beyond the rise, Magador heard mooing. His stomach began to rumble. "Thank you, cousin. I am rather hungry." He spread his wings and flew over to investigate. Azriel and Camille watched as Magador disappeared beyond the ridge. They heard the sound of scuffling and a pathetic bellowing, then silence. Camille began walking in the same direction to satisfy her curiosity, when Azriel pulled her back.

"You probably don't want to see that. Trust me, it's not pretty." Turning away, they found Eltanin and Nicodemus deep in conversation.

Azriel asked, "So what are our options?"

Eltanin answered sagely, "You must wait one day and return to the other side. Only ten minutes will have passed there. This will give you plenty of time to prepare and release the next Elemental. The attack on the castle will still be taking place. Rastaban will think we are fighting back."

"But there's nobody there. Surely he's not that stupid." Camille retorted.

Eltanin chuckled. "No, actually he's quite clever. Let's just say that I left a few surprises. Nicodemus and those Cunningham boys have set a few traps as well. Actually, they're quite good at pyrotechnics. The castle will defend itself. He will think I'm still there. The key is to out-think your opponent, dear. He will never suspect that we are here. In fact, it's unlikely he knows this place even exists."

"But I thought you said he was really smart." Camille replied.

"True, but in all my years of knowing him, I learned that Rastaban has always thought of things in terms of black and white. He was never able to see the middle ground. That was always his flaw. I will use that flaw to our advantage."

"Grandfather, I was thinking…" Azriel said, rubbing his chin. "If this world is a bridge between Aralia and Earth, wouldn't it be safe to assume that a portal is located somewhere that would take us to Aralia?"

"That's a good observation but unfortunately, I never found it. Besides, when the worlds are reunited, the ritual must be done on Earth right where the devastation first occurred, and you know where that is."

"Right, Cronk-Karren, the remnants of the Temple—all that remains of the Heart of Aralia."

"Yes, but first things first. You must release Lagina-Tierra. Halimah, Camille, and Nicodemus will accompany you. While you are gone, I will instruct all who remain here. There are still a few spells they need to learn. When on your journey, pay attention to what Halimah has to say. She knows how to read the desert, so trust in her senses. Camille also is unusually perceptive. Trust her intuition."

Camille smiled proudly and took Azriel's hand.

"I think I can handle this on my own." Azriel retorted. He didn't wish to put them in harm's way and wanted to protect them. He would never forgive himself if Camille was injured in any way.

Eltanin sensed his thoughts. "You may be powerful, Azriel, but it is folly to think you don't need help. Wisdom is in knowing when to accept assistance."

"I just don't want Camille and Halimah to get hurt. Anvindr said it was dangerous."

"And so it is. But don't underestimate Camille and Halimah based on them being women. They have more strength than you realize."

Camille took Azriel's other hand and faced him squarely, staring into his eyes. "I'm going and there's nothing you can do about it, so get used to it!"

Five wizards surrounded Caer Wylusung. Rastaban led the frontal assault with Altais and Lilith by his side; Giausur, Thuban and Edasich attacked from the rear.

Examining the structure, Rastaban grimaced. "Let's just see what kind of mettle our adversaries are made of."

His assault, not to be taken lightly, he gave the signal. The wizards in tandem released a firestorm upon the massive citadel. Wave upon wave of fireballs fell from the sky, engulfing the castle. Oddly, though, the attack merely glanced off a protective shield and dissipated.

"Very clever, Eltanin." Rastaban smiled, enjoying the game. "Let us see if you can handle this!" He, along with the Clave sent plasma missiles at the foundation of the structure. Upon impact, they deflected away from the structure and randomly flew back in all directions. One missile bounced back in the direction from where it came. Rastaban, Altais and Lilith had to dive for the ground and take cover. It exploded twenty feet beyond them and blasted a crater into the native rock.

Lilith snarled, "This is a waste of time, Rastaban. The castle is magically protected. We need to destroy the shield first."

"You are absolutely right, my dear." Rastaban stood and brushed off the dust from his robe. He did a quick survey of the area until he found what he was looking for. A few yards away he noticed a lizard sunning itself on a rock. He scrambled to capture the creature and held it in his hand, stroking its head.

Rastaban directed the spell onto the lizard. "Creo Multi!" he whispered and opened his hand. The creature trembled and suddenly another lizard popped out from the first one. From two, they multiplied into four, then eight. Soon there were too many to count.

"Reperio!" he directed toward the teeming horde of lizards. In a frenzy, they scattered to the outer walls of the castle. As they approached the perimeter of the defensive shield, though not visible to the naked eye, they began to climb upward, clearly defining the scope and breadth of the protective sheath laid out by Eltanin. It defined a bowl of power over the entire castle and courtyard.

"Good! Very good." Rastaban chuckled. "We shall break your defenses, Eltanin!"

He directed another spell at the lizards covering the magickal shield. "Novo!" he shouted. "Change—transform!"

The lizards, one by one, began to morph into giant ants, but with a difference. They were composed of steel with razor sharp pincers. As one they began to chip and gnaw into the shield as if it were made of cheese. Sparks flew from their forceps-like teeth and the protective spell surrounding Caer Wylusung began to unravel. With such destructive force, the shield collapsed and the steely ants fell to the ground, forming a great heap. With nothing to destroy now, they located their next target and headed toward the wizards with all intention of tearing them to shreds.

Wide-eyed with fear, Lilith spread her hands and shouted, "Reddo!" The effect was instantaneous as the ants began to click together and merge until there was just one. The steel creature shook and writhed, magically restored to its former state as a lizard. The offended creature hissed at Rastaban and darted away to find a rock to hide beneath and brood.

Rastaban, pleased with the result, called out toward the castle. "I have broken your defenses, Eltanin. Come out and face me!"

He was answered only by silence. Enraged, he kicked a rock and sent it sailing. "Eltanin, you're a coward. Prepare to meet your doom!"

Imperceptible at first, the wizards heard laughter. It rose in volume until it echoed through the canyon. It rang of mockery.

"Who is that?" Rastaban growled under his breath. He headed toward the castle gate.

Altais stopped him. "Do you think it wise, my lord?"

"Probably not, but no one makes a fool of me."

Altais followed along with Lilith. Giausur, Thuban and Edasich remained behind to guard the gate against any intrusion or unseen trickery. Meanwhile, the laughter from inside the castle grew in volume and verged on hysteria.

Rastaban entered the main hall cautiously and was surprised by the most bizarre sight he had ever seen. Sprawled atop a massive mound of food sat a rather rotund creature. Its skin was neon purple with yellow spots. With stubby legs and a reptilian tail, the creature seemed much like a dragon without wings. It continued to laugh and pointed at Rastaban while he wiped mirthful tears from his eyes. He picked up a bunch of grapes and stuffed them in his mouth as he giggled with juice dripping down his cheeks. He spoke as he chewed. "Boy, you guys are a bunch of nitwits."

Irritated, Rastaban suppressed the urge to strike the creature with a lightning bolt, but he needed information. "And why would you call us—nitwits?"

"Well, what kind of idiot attacks an empty castle?"

"Empty!" Rastaban roared. "Where is Eltanin!"

"Hmmm," the creature mused, "Eltanin... Eltanin... nope, can't say I know any Eltanin."

"Then how did you get here?" Altais posed the question.

"By portal...I think." He scratched his head. "Allow me to introduce myself. I am Meep! That's short for Maniacal Epiglotic Explosive Polymorph! That's me!" Meep burst into riotous laughter as he lay on his back kicking his legs with delight. "And look at all this wonderful food!" he bubbled. He picked up a leg of lamb and sloppily devoured it in a few seconds. He threw the bone by Rastaban's feet.

The wizard simmered. "If you came by portal, then who brought you here?"

"Don't know." Meep shook his head, "Nice old man, though. Tall, gaunt, very kindly, wore a robe...and he gave me all this food and told me to watch the castle. By the way, who are you?"

"I am Rastaban, Arch Wizard of the Clave." He was quickly losing his patience.

"Oooh, sounds important." Meep picked up a pie and shoved it, tin and all into his mouth. Cherries and juice dripped down his jowls onto his belly. As he ate, his stomach seemed to grow larger. "Mmph, mmph, Thish ish jush deelishush!" He swallowed noisily and erupted with a resounding belch that shook the walls.

Lilith grimaced. "Ugh, what a disgusting creature!"

Meep glared at her. "Hey Rastaban, who's the cow?"

"Cow!" Lilith raged. "Why you..." She curled her fingers into a claw and released an energy bolt. It struck Meep squarely in the chest and his head exploded, but oddly, two grew back in place of the one.

"That stung!" the right head said.

"Yes I would agree—and it was very rude, wouldn't you say, Meep?"

"Yes, for sure. Y'know I always wanted to talk to myself."

"Absolutely, Meep. Talk about a split personality!" Both heads bellowed with laughter.

"Enough!" Rastaban clenched his fists.

"Sorry," both heads responded sullenly and merged back into one. Meep continued to stuff his face with more food. He pulled a roast chicken from beneath his butt and devoured it, slobbering with grunts of satisfaction.

"Now, I'll ask you again. Where is Eltanin?"

Meep replied, his mouth now filled with several raspberry tortes. "I told you before, ulp, ulp," He smacked his lips as his belly expanded even further. "He's not here. Maybe he went to another dimension, maybe even to mine. The food's quite good there, y'know."

"And what dimension are you from?" Altais asked blithely.

"Lemme see," Meep held out a hand and began to count. "Uhh, one, two, three, four, five. Oh dear, out of fingers." Three more suddenly sprouted from his palm. "There we go, six, seven, and eight. Yep that would be it!" Meep said proudly. "Eight dimensions from here. Quite disturbing, by the way, to be roused from your sleep and dragged to another realm, not that I mind, though. The food here is terrific!" The creature picked up a barrel of mead, upended it, and drained the entire keg, soaking himself. His belly grew even larger as Meep squeezed out a rancid fart. "Uh, pardon." He said, not the least embarrassed.

"Ugh, this is a waste of time." Lilith fumed and covered her nose and fanned the air.

"Yes, but it's my time to waste." Meep smiled as he gobbled down another roast chicken. He managed to devour most of the food as he continued to expand. "Matter of fact, that nice man who gave me all these yummy goodies told me to waste as much time as I could." He finished the remainder of the food and licked his fingers. "That being done, there's only one more thing to do. That is to go home." Meep grinned, "So I guess this is goodbye!"

Suddenly, Rastaban heard a strange rumbling and the floor beneath him began to quiver and shake. A grim look of realization clouded Rastaban's face.

"Eltanin be damned!" He muttered. "Run."

"What?" Lilith asked.

"I said, RUN!"

But before they could respond and turn away. Meep suddenly exploded with a resounding concussion. Rastaban, Altais and Lilith were covered head to toe with gobbets of undigested food. The impact knocked them off their feet and they sprawled on the floor, slipping and sliding as they tried to regain their footing. The walls of Castle Wylusung began to shudder and quake. Several explosions shook the castle in a magnificent display of pyrotechnics. From the apex of the ceiling, it began to crumble and disintegrate dropping chunks of stone and rubble. Rastaban, Altais and Lilith scrambled with barely enough time to escape the destruction with their lives.

As the smoke and dust cleared, Rastaban glared at the heap of stone where the castle once stood and growled. "I'm going to find Eltanin, and when I do, I'm going to kill him!"

Azriel stared at the old wizard with what amounted to amusement and awe. "You did what?"

Camille and Halimah giggled as they walked beside Azriel.

"Okay, so what you're telling me is that the poor creature just exploded?"

"Oh, I wouldn't worry about it too much," Eltanin chuckled. "That's how they reproduce. They eat until they detonate, and two grow back in their place."

"Weird," Eddie commented. "Where do they go after they explode?"

"Usually back to their own dimension." Eltanin waved dismissively. "They're trans-dimensional creatures, as it were, able to cross with a mere thought."

"And what of the castle?" Camille asked.

"Reduced to rubble." Eltanin shrugged. "It wasn't all my doing, though. Jasper and Albert are quite adept at making things blow up. For that matter it's a minor miracle they're both still alive."

Halimah laughed.

"Grandfather," Azriel mused, "I know it was a great joke to play on Rastaban, but I'm certain he's pretty angry right now. He'll seek revenge if he is true to everything you've told me about him. Doesn't it make him more dangerous?"

"Certainly," Eltanin chuckled. "It's true that he will be outraged. Rastaban never took kindly to being made a fool. He will be dangerous indeed, but also reckless, and a reckless man makes mistakes. At least that is my hope."

"Let's hope you're right." Azriel muttered.

They continued back to the gazebo. Magador flew overhead and landed beside them. He was curious to see what the wizard had planned for them. Eltanin looked at their garb and examined their faces. His gaze went from Azriel to Camille, then to Edward and Halimah. He shook his head. "This will never do." He mused. "Azriel, I need your dream orb."

Azriel handed it over and watched as Eltanin implanted an image.

"This is the path that leads to the caverns where Lagina-Tierra has been imprisoned for millennia. The way is dangerous. Outlaws and brigands live in those mountains and wouldn't hesitate to murder you. Best you blend in and keep that mirage bag of yours handy." Eltanin fixed his gaze on Halimah. "I would say that you are a bit overdressed, my dear."

Halimah wore silk pantaloons and a matching blue blouse that kept her midriff exposed. Around her neck and in her hair hung lavish jewelry that made her appear the tribal princess that she was. Certainly she would be like honey to a bee for any robber wishing to divest her of her jewels. With a flourish, Eltanin performed a few hand movements, and the four found themselves in du- colored frocks and outer robes of dusty brown. They wore heavy boots and their heads were wrapped in white turbans.

Halimah examined herself and a sound of disgust escaped her throat. "These clothes are hideous!"

"They are necessary, my petulant young lady. They will keep you well camouflaged in that rugged place. You will appear as poor travelers and draw no attention to yourselves." He handed the dream orb back to Azriel.

"Now you know what to do."

Azriel rubbed the back of his neck in consternation. "Grandfather, I don't understand. If you already knew the location of the Earth Elemental, why didn't you release her?"

Eltanin heaved a sigh. "This task was not appointed to me, and besides, I am not worthy to complete it. You must understand..." The timbre of his voice lowered with humility. "I was responsible for their plight. Had I not had the hubris to interfere with the destiny of Aralia, it would not have been split into two worlds. Although it was the choice of the Elementals to accept their fate in order to preserve the worlds, it was my meddling that placed them in that position in the first place. I know there is still a heavy price to pay for my part in this. A wizard should never make such grievous errors in judgment."

"But you did what was necessary to preserve humanity, did you not?" Camille asked.

"Yes, my dear." Eltanin shook his head sadly. He suddenly seemed old and frail. "But it was my lack of vision that nearly destroyed Aralia. I am sorry that the task of restoring the worlds has fallen to Azriel. I live with my failure every day. Now it is time for the four of you to leave."

Magador interrupted. He was quite agitated. "Are you going to tell me that we could have come to this in-between place with the dream orb, that it was completely unnecessary for me to suffer the humiliation of being shrunken to the size of a fire lizard?" Magador glared at Eltanin with indignation while Azriel suppressed a chuckle.

"Now, now, Magador." Eltanin could not mask the humor in his voice. "You know as well as I do that there are no fixed points in this dimension. It is ever-changing..."

"Except for this gazebo." Magador pointed angrily with his wing. A puff of sulfurous smoke fumed from his nostrils.

"Umm…" Eltanin held his hand to his mouth and mused. "Good point. I never thought of that!"

"I think your brain has grown feeble, wizard." Magador growled. "I am outraged." Grumbling under his breath, he stomped off and flew over the next ridge to brood.

Watching the dragon depart, Eltanin gestured helplessly and then shrugged. "Well, you had best get going."

Michael Anthony Cariola

Chapter 19

They were nearly bowled over by the intense heat and glaring sunlight. On either side of the narrow path leading down into the gut-rock of the mountain, rugged stone walls rose high above them like a fortification that could likely conceal hidden dangers. It seemed as if nature had sliced open the mountain with a blade. The path was covered in many spots with ankle-wrenching rubble. Certainly they would need to proceed cautiously. Halimah was now grateful for the desert garb, which would effectively shield them from the scorching heat and the abrading wind blowing through the crevice. Still, they needed to shield their eyes from the sand and dust.

The narrow corridor led downward. Far ahead it darkened to where the small band couldn't see past a certain point.

A faint clatter echoed up the stone passage.

All four froze.

Halimah raised a hand and crouched low, listening. Voices—distant, guttural—carried upward through the narrow defile, followed by the scrape of boots on gravel.

"Outlanders," she whispered. "Scavengers or brigands. They use these cuts through the rock to ambush travelers."

Azriel's pulse quickened. There was nowhere to run and nowhere to hide. The corridor was too narrow.

"Don't move," he murmured, already reaching into his mirage bag.

From within, he withdrew a small fold of gauzy fabric that shimmered like heat above desert sand. With a practiced flick, he spread it across the stone wall beside them. The air rippled. The light bent.

Where they stood, there now appeared only broken rock and shadow.

They pressed themselves flat as footsteps approached.

Two rough-looking men passed within arm's reach, blades at their belts, scanning the passage.

"One way down," one muttered. "No one stupid enough to take this path."

They moved on.

Only when their voices faded did Azriel release the breath he'd been holding. The mirage dissolved like morning haze.

Eddie blinked. "Remind me never to leave that bag at home."

They were now at an opening that led into the mountain. It had a slightly foul odor.

Eddie peered inside and shuddered. "I don't like it, Azriel."

"That's your fear speaking," he replied.

"It's still scary." Eddie muttered.

Azriel pointed. "We will take this one, agreed?"

No one spoke, but Eddie peered into the rough aperture and suddenly the hair on the back of his neck bristled. Azriel sidled against the rockface until he reached the entrance, but as he was about to step in, Eddie placed his hand on Azriel's shoulder.

"Cousin—no!" he swallowed noisily. "Not that way. Something feels off."

"Why? The way to the other entrance looks too dangerous."

"This one just feels wrong." Eddie replied, eyes wide with fear.

Azriel smiled with assurance. "Don't worry, we'll be all right."

"I mean it, Azriel. My gut tells me we shouldn't go in there. I don't know why. It's just a feeling." Eddie said with vehemence.

Azriel held down his annoyance. "You're just afraid. Shake it off."

Eddie stared down Azriel, his eyes intense. "Look cousin, when I found out we were kin, I promised you that I would always have your back. Now this is me having your back. Don't go in there!"

"Edward, I respect that, but you're forgetting that I'm in charge here. This is the easier way in. I'm sure of it."

Eddie held down his temper and muttered forcefully, "Yeah, maybe too easy!"

Camille interrupted. "If you want my opinion, which by the way, you didn't bother to ask, I think that perhaps we should listen to Eddie."

"Not you too!" Azriel scowled. "How the hell are we supposed to cross this bottomless pit?"

"Carefully, I would think." Halimah chimed in. "I agree with Edward. I don't think we're supposed to go in there."

"Then you all can wait out here." Azriel exploded, red-faced. "I'll go by myself."

Eddie clenched his fists. "I swear, Azriel, you're not going in there, even if I have to sit on you."

Azriel was about to unleash an abrasive retort, when he heard a voice calling from above.

Magador swooped down with reckless speed and alit on the ledge. "Thank the Mother I got here in time! I come with a message."

Azriel stared at Magador, waiting for him to continue. He spread his hands. "Well?"

"Yes, of course. Poor old man—I think he's getting senile. Eltanin forgot to tell you not to go into the first tunnel."

"Why not?"

"He said an unspeakable horror lies dormant within those chambers. Things will not go well for any of you if you awaken it."

"What things?" Azriel grumbled.

"Let's just say it would be very bad," Magador countered.

Eddie, Camille, and Halimah turned and glared at Azriel.

He, in turn, stared back—mostly at Eddie—with a sheepish grin. "I guess I owe you an apology."

Camille pressed her lips together and fumed. "No, I'd say you owe us *all* an apology. Just because you're immortal and bulletproof doesn't mean that we are!" She turned away in a huff.

"Hey Camille..." he called after her helplessly.

Eddie snickered, "Want me to talk to her?"

"No, that would only make it worse," Azriel sighed. "Well, we know which entrance is the right one. Um—thanks Eddie. Now the problem is how to get there."

Magador spoke, somewhat offended. "I could bear you across even though you didn't think to ask."

"I didn't want to assume."

"Well I appreciate that, cousin, though I must say that you're a strange sort of fellow."

"How so?" Azriel bristled, annoyed.

Magador rolled his eyes with exasperation. "Well it just seems to me that you often want help when you really don't need it, yet there are times like this when you clearly need help and don't bother to ask for it!"

Eddie burst out laughing.

Azriel grumbled under his breath. "Well, thanks for that astute observation, Magador. Shall we go across?"

"Yes, cousin." Magador sounded a bit smug, which annoyed Azriel even more. "But perhaps I should take the ladies first. Come, Camille; Come, Halimah."

The dragon extended his wing so they could mount his shoulder and flew easily across the chasm to the other side. He returned to carry Azriel and Eddie, but Eddie hesitated. "Thanks, Magador." He stroked the great dragon's flank.

Magador chuckled. "It is my pleasure, Edward. Come, dragonriders!" He winked at Eddie. "Imagine what your friends would say!"

Eddie winced. "My old friends left me a long time ago. Besides, they would never believe it. Sometimes I'm not sure I do."

"Well, Edward, if you don't mind me saying, you've proven yourself a good friend to all of us here, and perhaps that's the only thing that truly matters."

"Thanks. That means a lot, particularly from you."

Magador left them right by the entrance to the cave that led into the heart of the mountain.

"And here I must leave you." Magador smiled in the manner of dragons and bowed. "I suppose you can handle it from here, cousin."

Azriel held back a sarcastic barb at Magador's patronizing tone.

Upon entering the passageway, the temperature dropped dramatically, but it didn't even come close to Camille's frostiness toward Azriel. She didn't bother waiting for him to take the lead. She and Halimah walked ten paces ahead. Though Azriel could make out only a few words of their conversation, by the tone, he could tell Camille was not at all happy. He thought he heard words like 'jerk' and 'idiot,' but decided not to fuel the fire with a comment or a rebuttal. He knew he had been wrong and hated the fact that he very well could have placed all of them in terrible danger. Eddie, to his credit, said nothing and let the whole matter pass.

As the path widened, Eddie finally asked, "Azriel, why does Magador always refer to you as cousin?"

"I don't quite know. Somehow Magador has it set in his brain that I'm a dragon, as improbable as it may seem. We've had many quarrels over this, and yet he refuses to relent. I've given up trying to convince him otherwise."

Eddie chuckled. "I don't know, maybe he's right!"

"No, the whole thing is ridiculous."

"That's not what I mean. Since being introduced to the magickal world, I've noticed things are never as they seem. What people perceive as reality often isn't even close to the truth."

"Yeah, I suppose. Trust me though; the likelihood of me sprouting wings is really quite remote." Azriel smiled.

As they continued their descent into the heart of the mountain, the path widened until it opened into a great chamber. It was dimly lit with an unearthly glow, yet there were no torches on the rocky enclosure. That's when Azriel realized that the rocks themselves glowed with an eerie luminosity. As their eyes adjusted, the glow took on different hues of phosphorescence—brilliant blues, greens, and oranges, punctuated the soft white light with dazzling color. Halimah gasped with delight. "It's beautiful!"

Camille agreed. "It sure is pretty." For the moment she forgot she was still furious with Azriel and asked him, "So where do we go from here?"

He scanned the chamber and noted that at the far end there seemed to be an opening. It carried the faint aroma of crude oil. Azriel pointed. "There, I think."

He was about to proceed when suddenly the four were surrounded by smallish creatures that had emerged from the walls. They slid out like misty water and congealed into ghostly forms; however, there didn't seem to be anything threatening about them. They were the size of children with largish round heads and long limbs that ended in hands and feet that appeared more like delicate tree roots. Their bodies had the pasty appearance of mushrooms, yet they glowed with green luminescence. Their large, wide-set eyes were red and piercing, but oddly none of them had discernible mouths.

One of the larger beings approached Azriel. "You must be tested before you may pass."

The creature did not speak, yet they all heard its voice clearly in their minds.

"Who are you?" Azriel asked.

"We are the Greenlings. We protect and serve the Mother."

Azriel nodded. "We have come to give the Earth Mother release."

"That is well, for she is near the end of her endurance." The Greenling said, "Yet you must be tested for truth." As the creature spoke, several others came forth bearing four polished chests. The golden caskets were carried by staves, slid through two rings on each side. Four Greenlings, one on each corner, bore the strange boxes on their shoulders and laid them before each of the companions. Camille looked down at hers and suddenly felt apprehensive. Eddie and Halimah shared the same sentiment, but Azriel, used to being tested, merely glanced at his chest and then back at the Greenling.

Camille asked, trying to squelch the quaver in her voice. "What's in it?"

The Greenling answered. "Fear."

Camille backed away from the chest.

"You must face your most difficult challenge, which is to confront yourself and see the truth. How you respond will determine your true character."

Eddie blanched. "What if I fail?"

"There is no pass or fail. There is only truth. You must look inside." The Greenling concluded.

They all felt a compulsion to look down as the chests as they magically opened. At the bottom of each chest was merely a mirror. Halimah peered into hers and saw her own reflection. Azriel, Camille and Eddie did as well. As their reflections stared back at them, there emerged from each chest a puff of dust that surrounded their faces. Paralyzed, they each fell into a deep trance as the cloud of spores transported them through to the realm of dreams.

Halimah found herself amid a crowd of people from her Bedouin tribe. Her view was blocked and she had to push her way through to see what the stir was all about. It seemed as though they were heaping honor and praise upon a woman at the forefront. When she finally managed to get a better view, Halimah was stunned to see herself lounging upon a divan. This version of her wore an intricately embroidered robe, the best her people had to offer. Her head, wrists, and neck were bedecked with priceless jewels to match the finery she wore. Yet for all her opulence, this vision of Halimah felt wrong. She held her head up with pride and the slight sneer of disdain spoke of haughtiness, as if her people were now somehow beneath her. They all were behaving as though they were subservient to this elevated princess. Soon she was joined by her half-sisters, who brought trays stacked with cosmetics and perfumes. One held up a mirror while another took delight in applying the make-up. Another applied henna in an intricate design on Halimah's hands. The princess primped and preened, so immersed she was in her vanity. "Oh, Hali, you're so beautiful!" her half-sister said.

"Of course I am. I must be beautiful for my people."

The people surrounding her dropped to their knees and bowed as one. "Praise Princess Hali, the most beautiful, the most gracious and kind!" They all shouted in unison, but upon closer scrutiny, Halimah noticed that their faces did not match the cries of adulation. No, if anything their faces hid contempt and their eyes shone with fear.

"Yes, yes. Thank you, thank you." She sounded bored and dismissed them with an imperious wave of her jewel-bedecked hand.

The crowd of worshippers dispersed with haste. Halimah tried to move out of their way, but they didn't even seem to be aware of her presence. She thought she would be trampled, but several from the crowd walked through her. That was when Halimah realized that she was a ghost to these people, or maybe it was the other way around. Perhaps these were ghosts from some possible future. Halimah turned and stared at this future version of herself with disgust.

Just then, the curtain moved aside and Albert slipped in. "May I enter, my Princess?" He was dressed in the ceremonial robes of a first-rate wizard. Obviously, this future Albert would be highly accomplished as a sorcerer.

Princess Hali yawned with boredom. "What is it this time, Albert?"

"I only wish to prove my love for you, my princess." He smiled, though his face appeared weary and sad. This was clearly not the first time he had tried to woo the princess. Albert carefully removed a soft, delicate rose from his sleeve. Halimah gasped at its beauty, but the princess rolled her eyes with disdain. "Really, Albert, is that the best you can do?"

"My lady," Albert said, wounded. "This is a Midas rose and exceedingly rare, though not as rare as your beauty."

"Must you flatter, Albert. It gets so tedious." She sighed with an indifference Halimah would never have believed her future self capable of displaying.

The princess motioned and a vase appeared. "Just put it in there." She muttered as if the golden treasure wasn't worth her notice.

Albert placed it in the vase and turned away, his face stricken with sadness. His shoulders sagged and he left the tent brokenhearted.

Halimah spun on her heels, tears in her eyes for Albert's pain. She couldn't understand how the future princess could reject him with such cruelty, particularly since Halimah had lately grown quite fond of him. She clenched her fists and raged at the princess, "You heartless bitch!"

The princess turned and stared at Halimah; her lips curled into an arrogant sneer. "Oh, it's you. I thought I killed you a long time ago." She broke out in mocking laughter.

"You are not who I am." Halimah pointed at the princess with anger. "What has turned you into someone so cold and indifferent?"

"Turned? I've always been inside you." The princess said with scorn. "I have always been stronger and more powerful than your pathetic compassion and false humility."

"No! That's a lie." Halimah raged. "Love is not weakness. Sometimes it is far more difficult to love than to resort to hatred."

"Who needs love?" the princess smiled seductively, "I am beautiful and charming. I can manipulate anyone to get what I want."

Halimah's eyes hardened. "You're a fool. You think your people love you? They don't love you; they fear you, and in secret despise you for what you've become. I reject you!"

Hali laughed with derision. "You can't reject me. You and I are the same."

"Oh, no we're not. I would never have treated Albert with such contempt. He is kind and gentle and I care for him!"

"Ugh, he's so common. He is not worthy of us."

"You mean *you*!" Halimah spat. "I do not judge him based on his social status, but by what is in his heart. The truth is, you are not worthy of *him*!" Halimah was now nose to nose with her counterpart. She suddenly swiped the mirror from Princess Hali's hand and directed an incantation at it. "The inside is on the outside! Reveal!" She then thrust the mirror at Hali and forced her to look at herself. "You think you're beautiful? Well, take a good look at what you really are!"

She stared at the mirror in disbelief. Reflected back at her was a face she did not recognize: matted hair, bald in places, framing a hideous visage creased with scars and festering sores. Her eyes were those of a viper, yellow and venomous. Jutting from her cruel mouth were fangs for tearing the flesh of her hapless victims. As the princess peered into the mirror, the images from the mirror began to manifest on her own body. She now stank of putrescence and decay. Her once beautiful body was bent and twisted with a debilitating malady and her once perfect hands became gnarled and ill-formed. The sores and cankers covering her arms, legs, and face were deep abscesses that burst and began to ooze with vile-smelling pus. Her fine clothing became rotted rags that hung from her twisted form. She wailed in terror, "What have you done to me?"

"I have done nothing but show you what you are. You have done this to yourself!"

The princess collapsed to the floor and began to weep over her demise—over the wretch she had become.

Halimah stood over her with arms crossed. "It would seem you have a decision to make and but one choice."

Eddie found himself in what appeared to be an old vaudeville theater. Plush seating faced an ornate stage with deep scarlet curtains draping to the hard maple wood floor. Surrounding the stage and throughout the theater were intricate carvings of mythical creatures—centaurs, unicorns, minotaurs, and satyrs. Atop each gilded column, fabulous birds and dragons peered down at the audience—except Eddie was the only one present.

As he waited, the lights dimmed and the curtain opened. At center stage stood a large cage, more like a jail cell. Within that cell, Eddie saw himself chained, with a manacle on each wrist, allowing only the slightest movement.

As Eddie gaped, wondering about the meaning of such a spectacle, he heard laughter from either side of his seat. Surrounding him now were the ghosts of everyone he had ever known—old friends and lost acquaintances. Two rows ahead Eddie noticed the phantasms of his former friends Bernie, Dirk and Cory. Like in the vaudeville days of old they pointed at the cage, hooting with laughter. They joined the audience in mocking the helpless victim, tossing rotten fruit and vegetables.

Stage left, a spotlight suddenly came on. Seated on a couch, Eddie's stepfather and mother were in the heat of an argument.

"All you ever do is heap ridicule on the boy." Jessica spread her arms, exasperated.

"He's fat, lazy and stupid." He looked at his watch. "And I don't have time for this. My flight leaves in two hours."

"Tony, he loves you! He needs your attention, not the things you bring back from Tokyo."

"It's the best I can do."

"Oh? Did you notice the last thing you gave him is still in the box on his dresser? He's grown wise to you, Tony. He doesn't want your gifts. He wants his father's attention."

"Father? I'm not his father and he's not my son. Perhaps if he had my genes, he wouldn't be such a loser."

"You bastard!" Jessica broke down and cried.

Tony continued his tirade despite Jessica's tears. "He spends half his time in detention. He's constantly getting into fights, and he doesn't give a rat's ass about his grades. You deal with him. I'm done!"

He stood abruptly, grabbed his briefcase and overcoat and left without a backward glance. Weeping, Jessica walked over to the liquor cabinet and poured herself a double.

Eddie called out from his cage. "Mom, I'm sorry! Please don't blame yourself!" As he called out, he began to regress in age. He now appeared to be about ten or eleven years old.

The lights faded to black and the audience erupted in riotous laughter. They continued to heap scorn on the caged boy. When the stage lights rose again, Eddie was at the corner sandwich shop waiting for his friends. Cory, Bernie and Dirk were supposed to be meeting him for lunch and then they would go to the movies together. Eddie looked at the clock and noted with impatience that they were over an hour late. The movie was supposed to start in less than twenty minutes. Dejected, he finally rose from his seat and paid for the malted he had ordered. He figured that they forgot and he would just go to the movies by himself. The theater was a quick jaunt around the corner, so he still had plenty of time.

Eddie strode up to the window and purchased his ticket, but when he entered the lobby he noticed that Cory and Dirk were waiting by the candy counter while Bernie was ordering a cola. Seeing Eddie, they suddenly looked guilty and embarrassed.

"Hey guys," Eddie said. "I thought we were going to meet at the luncheonette."

Cory and Dirk glanced at each other. "Yeah… about that," Cory muttered. "Look I don't know any other way to put this, Eddie. We just don't want to hang out with you anymore. It's like all we ever do is listen to you obsess over your problems. You get us in trouble all the time and you have no ambition. We just don't want to hang out with a loser."

As the scene played out, the caged boy began to cry. He lost another few years and, due to his diminished size, slipped from his shackles and flopped onto the floor. The audience howled with laughter and continued their tirade of throwing garbage onto the stage. Eddie stood in his seat and clenched his fists in rage. "Stop it." He bellowed. "This isn't the least bit funny!" But being merely ghostly apparitions, they were oblivious to Eddie's protests.

The scenes on stage continued to play out events in Eddie's life. Each failure and humiliation—each moment of helplessness and scorn—chipped away at him until Eddie was reduced to a mere child of two. He lay in his cage, squalling in anger and pain.

The audience continued to jeer, wildly casting their scorn upon the wailing infant. Eddie turned his back on them to face the damaged, broken child within the cage.

Camille's transition left her floating for what felt like a long time. Surrounding her on all sides stretched a beautiful countryside vista, and beyond it a blue ocean where boats bobbed lazily on gentle waves. A crowd of people awaited her arrival. Their arms were raised to receive her as she alit to the ground.

Camille looked around in wonder. Everyone she had ever loved was there. Closest to the center, her mother and father stood facing her with love and adoration. Her eyes welling with tears, Camille cried out to them, "Mama…Papa? I've missed you so much!" They smiled with understanding, and Camille rushed forward, arms outstretched to embrace them. No sooner had she touched them than they suddenly vanished before her eyes. Stricken to the heart, she called out piteously as her eyes filled with tears. "Mama? Papa?"

As they faded from her sight, the world seemed to grow dimmer. There were others. Her aunts Pen and Daffie beckoned to

Camille, but when she approached, just like her parents, they vanished as well. The assembly of her loved ones soon began to disperse in the same fashion. With each disappearance, her world grew darker and more dismal. After a time, the only ones left were the Cunninghams, Halimah, and Azriel. Jasper and Albert with Julia between them, held hands and faced Camille. Her voice quivered with fear and panic. "Please, please don't leave."

They smiled sadly, then, like the others, slowly and inevitably, faded from view. Halimah stared at Camille and then covered her head with a shawl.

"And you? Will you also leave me?"

Halimah bowed her head with sadness. She turned and walked away, fading into the darkness.

Azriel was now the only one who remained standing before Camille. He was the only source of light in Camille's darkening world. But as he held out his hand to her, his radiance began to fade.

"Please, Azriel. Don't leave me alone. I'm afraid." Camille's voice cracked with her rising terror.

Azriel, his expression one of remorse, gently reached out and touched her cheek. But when his hand made contact, he dissolved into the ground leaving Camille in utter darkness.

She whispered her pain, "But I love you..."

Consumed by terror, dreading the dark and her profound loneliness, Camille sank to the ground and curled into a ball. Helpless and frightened she began to sob uncontrollably.

Lightning streaked across a dismal, cheerless sky. Azriel found himself facing a colonnade that led to a marble-hewn throne. The seat of Aralian royalty beckoned him forth, daring him to take his rightful place as king of his country. Gingerly, he approached the throne, but hesitated to sit. Suddenly, amid peals of thunder, the specter of a man appeared and solidified upon the throne of Aralia. King Berrill sat in all his majesty, an expression of arrogance on his face. He stared down at Azriel with condescension.

"The throne is mine. Aralia is MINE!"

"That would be impossible." Azriel planted his feet firmly on the ground. "You're dead!"

"Of course I'm dead." Berrill snarled. "Your mother made sure of that!"

"Then it seems we're in agreement, Father."

"Don't be so cocky, boy. I still live inside of you. After all, you are my son."

Azriel shook his head with disdain. "Yes, I am your son—a son, by the way, that you would have killed had my mother not killed you first!"

"So you know about that. Your mother is a murderer."

"That depends on your point of view. She saved my life and most likely her own as well. You're the murderer, Father."

Berrill chuckled. "Eh, perhaps." His manner became more amiable. "I've sentenced more men to death than I can count." He waved a finger. "But your mother—a clever woman, that one. She was the only person I could never outmaneuver. If you want some fatherly advice, then here it is. Never trust a woman."

"There is nothing I want from you, Father. You gave up the right of counsel when you tried to have me killed. The throne of Aralia is mine by rule of succession. My destiny has already been set and is proceeding according to plan. The worlds will be reunited as prophesied."

Berrill tapped his fingers together thoughtfully. "Ah yes, the scrolls of Eltanin. Would you place your faith in the ravings of a dead lunatic?"

"It might come as a surprise to you, father, but Eltanin is far from dead. He has been in hiding since the cataclysm that tore the worlds apart. And, by the way, he is far from mad. Merging the worlds to one will restore magick in all its potency to Aralia."

"To hell with Magick!" Berrill raged. "Have you given the slightest thought to what uniting the worlds will do? Do you think it will bring peace—order? No, it will bring chaos!"

Azriel paused to consider his father's words. Over the past few years, all his thought and energy had been dedicated to the problem at hand—getting all the pieces in order to bring about the ritual at the proper time and place. Yet there was always the underlying fear within his soul that the problems facing him after the ritual would be far greater than the ones before. Many things required consideration. Could the proponents of magick and the users of technology even coexist without leading ultimately to war and extinction for both humanity and elf-kind? Would it even be possible to teach humanity the benefits of magick and the ways of peace?

King Berrill chuckled on his throne. "Ah, you see it, don't you, boy?"

Azriel scowled up at him.

"So what are you going to do, son?"

Azriel pressed his lips together with determination. "I will do as I am supposed to. I will complete the ritual, and I will assume the throne of Aralia."

"And what then?" Berrill's eyes were cruel as they bore into Azriel's.

He looked down feeling lost and powerless. "I don't know."

"Well that's not good enough, boy." The king said with scorn. "You're too soft—too much like your mother."

Azriel's head snapped up in anger. "My mother is wise and noble."

"She is stubborn and pigheaded!" Berrill erupted. "She knows the risks of the ritual. It damn near destroyed Eltanin. Are you more powerful than he?"

Azriel paled as doubt began to creep in.

"Ah, she didn't tell you that, did she?"

Azriel defended Abelene. "She didn't have to. I know the risks. I have read the Book of Aralia from cover to cover. I also know that over the years the line of Eltanin—particularly house Ferrishyn—progressively became weaker and more depraved. Your father, Aldorag, tried to bend Errin-lil to his will, using it to feed his lust for power and his greed." Azriel slid it from its scabbard and held it high. "This sword turned on him and it destroyed him. And you were no better. The Ferrishyn line is all but ruined. You had the opportunity to heal the division between the great houses and reunite the kingdoms through the power and magick of Errin-lil. Instead, you squandered it for fear of losing what was left of your kingdom to me. How weak! How craven the Ferrishyn line has become that a father would be jealous of his unborn son."

King Berrill bolted from his throne and bore down on Azriel. "I'll show you weak!" He unsheathed the sword at his belt and raised it over his head, ready to smite his son.

Halimah looked down at the princess—the part of herself that if allowed license, would become a monster. Though she felt no love for the wretch, she nonetheless felt a small measure of compassion. It made her realize how easy it was for a person to lose sight of what truly mattered.

The ruined princess looked up at Halimah, tears streaming down her face, and whispered, "Will you destroy me? Then what are you waiting for?"

Halimah paused for a moment as the princess sobbed. She answered softly. "I cannot destroy you without damaging myself, since you are such an integral part of me. I will allow you to live, but you can never dominate me."

Hali stood and faced Halimah with a glimmer of hope in her eyes. As she rose, all the ugliness and disease left her. Like a mirror image, she faced Halimah and smiled. "I think I understand now."

Halimah replied, "Yes, it is not a crime to be beautiful, but to let it consume oneself feeds the monster we all are capable of becoming. Hali, we are more than that. Beauty must shine from within; otherwise, we are no more than an artificial shell."

Hali nodded. "Then must I disappear?"

"No, of course not. You will live within me and…" She smiled slyly. "I will let you out from time to time; after all, we don't want to be ugly old hags, either."

Halimah embraced her counterpart and allowed Hali to merge with her. Like liquid, she flowed gently into Halimah's body. When she was whole again, the room suddenly dissolved from view, and Halimah found herself back in the cavern. She lay on a carpet of soft moss. Looking to her left and right, she saw Eddie,

Camille, and Azriel also unconscious under the spell of the Greenlings.

Eddie sprinted from his seat and climbed up the stairs to the stage. He turned and glared at the audience. With a voice of command he shouted out to them. "You will not torture that child anymore, do you hear me? Be gone!" Eddie made a broad swipe of his hand and the entire assembly of spectators vanished into wisps of vapor. He was now alone to face the caged infant.

With purpose, he strode over to the pen and sought to unbar the door, but he found it locked and chained. The shackles were formidable and he didn't have a key. Eddie grasped at the chains, trying to break them, but they were beyond his strength. He sat before it and paused to consider the dilemma. Inside, the child shuddered and sobbed, pressing his little body against the bars, trying to disappear. Eddie's heart surged with compassion for the child, and found it a strange feeling. Throughout his entire life, he had never loved himself—only felt contempt and disdain for his weakness and ineffectiveness. This was new and freeing in a way, but he was still unable to reach the caged child.

"Hmm, what would Azriel do? How would Camille handle this?" Eddie rubbed his brow with frustration. "No, what would I do? What would this new Edward do?"

Eddie smiled slyly. "Of course," he spoke aloud." I have something I never had before! I have friends! I have a mother who loves me—and I have Magick!"

Eddie spread his fingers and waved both hands with authority. He spoke the spell of release. "Solvo!" he intoned.

Not only did the locks and chains fall away, but the cage imprisoning the child melted into the floor. With compassion, Eddie picked up the quivering child and held him to his chest. The little boy shook in his arms and cried on Eddie's shoulder.

"Shh, shh, no one is ever going to hurt you again." He rubbed the little boy's back, gently calming him until he ceased quivering and began to breathe easier. Soon the child cuddled up to Eddie and fell asleep.

Eddie felt a gentle hand on his shoulder. Startled, he spun around, his eyes wide.

A man faced him and smiled warmly. He was dressed in fine leather jerkins and highly polished boots. A breastplate with the white dragon crest of Aralia covered his chest. Draped and clasped across his shoulders was a beautifully embroidered cape of midnight blue. On his belt hung a sword with a golden hilt carved into a dragon's head.

Eddie's eyes widened with recognition.

"I'm proud of you, Edward." Elrid grasped Eddie's shoulder and gave it a gentle shake.

"Father?" he stammered.

Elrid nodded gravely. "Son, I'm sorry I could not be there for you. I fell in battle before you were born."

Eddie choked back tears. "I know. But I also know that you died bravely and with honor defending Aralia."

"Aye, it is as you say. It is well that you have learned the truth of things, son. Had you been raised in Aralia, you would have known sooner, and your childhood wouldn't have been so troubled." Elrid sat in one of the stage set chairs and motioned for Eddie to sit as well. "To use an expression from your world, you were dealt a lousy hand, but that can never be used as an excuse ever again."

"I know, Father."

"I have a command for you, Edward." Elrid smiled proudly. "You must always defend your cousin. Soon he will be King. As I was Captain of the Guard, so shall you be. You come from a long and noble family tradition. It was my duty to defend the throne of house Ferrishyn, as my father did before me, and his father did before that, and so on. Certainly trust the strength of your arm, but more so trust what is in here." Elrid placed his hand over Eddie's heart. "If you listen to it, you will always act with valor and honor."

Eddie smiled. "You have my promise, Father." The child in Eddie's arms stirred a bit and sighed with contentment before settling back to sleep. Elrid stroked the little boy's head with tenderness.

"It is time for me to go, son. Always know that I will be with you in times of doubt. Just look within your heart and you will find me and the strength of all your ancestors. Be proud of who you are!"

I am—and I am proud of you, Father, as I will always be."

"Oh, and one more thing," Elrid smiled candidly. "Always take good care of your mother; honor her courage and sacrifice, and…" he averted his eyes with regret. "Tell her I miss her." Elrid bowed solemnly and saluted Eddie with his sword before vanishing from the stage.

Alone and in the dark, Camille's soul shrank in fear. She sat immobile, unable to rally her courage. The pervading darkness bore into her and filled her with such a sense of dread that she wrapped her arms around her legs, whimpering. Terrified, she remained in this state for some time, rocking back and forth and sobbing her anguish. Suddenly, though, she felt something inside her snap, and her heart began to swell with anger.

Camille quickly rose to her feet, fists clenched, and raged at the darkness. "No! I will not succumb to this fear. I am better than this!"

She remembered her magick and held out her hand with purpose.

"Flamma!" She invoked. A few inches above her hand, a flame appeared. It did little to dispel the night, but it brought her comfort and the trembling in her heart waned. Standing alone, Camille began to feel empowered. Oddly though, she heard voices—faint whispers that seemed to be absorbed by the inky blackness. In the distance—or perhaps closer for she could not gauge how near or far—a tiny flame suddenly appeared, then another. In moments, they multiplied one by one until she was surrounded by twelve tiny flames in a circle. Then they grew brighter to reveal faces of women she had never seen before. She now saw that the twelve women held lanterns that cast a warm glow over her surroundings. The women, ranging from a youthful girl not much older than Camille to an elderly crone, wore soft dove gray robes and were crowned with silver circlets. Each crown bore an emblem on the forehead—an upturned crescent moon. Their faces were indistinct until one approached Camille and held out her hand.

She spoke gently. "You are in good company, my daughter. You have conquered your fear."

"Mother?" Camille's voice trembled.

"Yes." She smiled and embraced Camille.

"Mother, you look different."

"Of course." She stroked Camille's cheek. "This is my true form, unencumbered by the tragedies and hardships of life."

Another woman came forth and took Camille's hand. Middle-aged, she was tall and elegantly handsome, as one who had aged gracefully. "Camille," she said, "I am your grandmother. Though we have never met, I have always been with you. In fact, we who are assembled here have always looked out for your welfare."

"Who are all these others?" Camille asked.

"We are a coven of twelve, your ancestors from the beginning of our magickal line that leads to you. You are thirteenth, completing the circle. All our knowledge and wisdom, all our magick, resides within you."

Camille looked up at her grandmother and began to cry. "Everyone left me!"

From the back of the circle, a young woman approached and faced Camille. She was blonde with sparkling green eyes and oddly, her ears had a slight point to them, similar to Azriel's. When she spoke her voice was laced with a thick Scottish brogue.

"I am Emily, first of the line of McElvins. Camille, you have learned the most important lesson you can ever learn. People will always leave you. They are either in your life for a short time so you may learn from them, or they die and move on, as was the case with your mother. Nothing is permanent; everything changes. The only one you can ever rely on is yourself. There is a difference, my dear, in being lonely and merely being alone. And you are alone, Camille, for you are unique in this world. Know that you have not reached your full potential yet, but you will, as it was ordained to be. In your heart beats the power and wisdom of the ages, for you are thirteenth of our line, unbroken since the time I came into my fullness as a witch. We have remained hidden throughout the years, which was fortunate. Our line had survived the persecution and the burning times of witches. With each generation our power has grown until the fullness of it now resides within you."

Camille's expression became solemn and she glanced at Emily. "Might I ask you a personal question?"

"Of course, my dear."

"Are you Elfin?"

She giggled. "Probably. The story, as my mother related it to me, is this: One day, she was gathering herbs in the woods when she saw a gnome run across her path. Well everyone knows if you catch a gnome, he will grant a wish! She was so close to catching it when suddenly there was a dazzling light. Being of a curious nature, she went closer to investigate the marvel when a man stepped through the light. He told my mother that he was from the magickal realm and that he wanted to give her a great gift. He took her by the hand and led her through the portal of light. She saw many marvels that day, castles of the purest white, lush orchards of golden fruit. She always spoke of how this man had seduced her and made love to her on the velvet green carpet of the meadow. Not that she was unwilling, mind you." Emily's eyes sparkled with mischief. "He told her that henceforth one of our powerful line would help reunite the world of magick and the world of men by sacred union. Regretfully he also told her that he could never see her again, but he would leave his mark upon her and all who would come after." Emily pulled down her robe to partially reveal her breast. There was a mark in the shape of a heart. Camille pulled aside her shirt and examined her own mark, smiling.

"I always wondered about that!"

"So there it is!" Emily smiled back. "Nine months later on the feast of Samhain, I was born to my mother, and henceforth took the name of McElvin. Now before we leave we must give you a blessing."

The twelve women, ancestors all, surrounded Camille in a circle. Placing their hands on her head they poured their magick and power into the girl until she was energized, charged with her full heritage.

Emily invoked the blessing. "You are the culmination of our line. Receive the power preordained for you to receive. Be the link that will unite the magickal world with the world of men. Be the queen you are destined to be and stand side by side with the Dragon Lord, for together you will forge a new world that will endure and prosper."

The women withdrew their hands. One by one, they all embraced Camille until it was just her mother and Emily, the first of her line.

Camille smiled gratefully. "Thank you, Mother. I think I now understand why you had to leave." They embraced and Camille's mother vanished.

Only Emily remained. Camille asked, "Emily, what did you mean by *Dragon Lord?*"

"No, no." Emily chided her playfully. "Some things are meant to be a surprise. Besides," she giggled. "Why spoil the fun!"

With that, Emily also vanished and Camille awoke back in the underground chamber.

"**You** can't escape me, boy!" Berrill closed in on Azriel. Azriel raised Errin-lil above his head and parried the blow of his father's sword. Sparks flew from his blade when it made contact, and the jewel in Errin-lil's pommel erupted with burgeoning power.

"Ahh, you've awakened the sword, but that won't defeat me! Face it, boy! You don't have what it takes to be king!" He lashed out with a wide swoop, nicking Azriel's arm before he could counter. Berrill raged on. "A king must be ruthless and without mercy. You don't just punish your enemies; you must annihilate them—crush them!"

"That's where you're wrong, Father. You've always been wrong! A king must rule with humility and wisdom, neither of which you have." Azriel blocked a vicious blow and evaded another slice that nearly took off his ear. "A king is a servant of the people, not self-indulgent and prideful."

Berrill erupted with anger and advanced on Azriel. His anger made him reckless, and the king nearly stumbled. Azriel analyzed his opponent. Certainly Berrill was larger and more powerful, but

Azriel being lighter on his feet, had the agility his father lacked. This gave him the advantage. Azriel backed up, putting more space between himself and his father. Berrill raised his sword again to strike and came down hard, threatening to cleave Azriel's skull, but overreached. Suddenly, however, Errin-lil became weightless in Azriel's hand, as though it had taken on a life of its own, infusing him with technique and skill. Becoming one with the sword, Azriel crouched, spun around, and met Berrill's blow with a resounding explosion that rang like thunder. Berrill's sword shattered from hilt to tip, raining shards of steel upon them both. The force of the concussion threw Berrill to the ground. Dazed, he stared up at Azriel with loathing—and a hint of fear. "Errin-lil was mine! Will you now slay me with it?"

Azriel stood over his defeated father, contemplating the victory. He was certain that Errin-lil had fully imprinted itself upon his soul. But he could not kill his father—not when the old man lay prone and defenseless.

Berrill burst out laughing. "See? See! You haven't the courage or temerity to destroy me. Give me that sword and I will show you how to be a true king!"

Azriel nodded. "You're right, father. I can't kill you. I will concede Errin-lil into your capable hands. Strike me down if you will. Let the gods choose."

Taking the bait, Berrill chuckled. Rising to his feet, victoriously he raised Errin-lil high, ready to thrust it through his son.

But suddenly, the sword again erupted with power. The hilt fused to Berrill's hands and began to scorch and burn. Fire built up within the king's body causing smoke to billow from his mouth and eyes. Consuming him from the inside out, Berrill emitted one final, gurgling scream and ignited into flames. Within moments he was reduced to a mere pile of ash, Errin-lil—its power fading to quiescence—lying on the ground.

Azriel cautiously picked up the sword and dusted off the blade before returning it to its scabbard. As he did a massive figure coalesced, towering over him. Though insubstantial and semi-transparent, Azriel recognized the great elemental and bowed low. Lagina-Tierra returned the salutation.

"You have proven yourself the true King of Aralia, Son of Luminance. Wisdom and prudence will often win over pride and ruthlessness. You were wise to recognize the impossibility of reasoning with a madman. Now I must implore you to hurry and release me from my bondage. My strength is nearly at an end. Soon I will no longer be able to maintain my physical form. You will find me trapped beyond the chamber where you and your companions now sleep. Please, hurry!"

Camille was the first to awaken, followed by Halimah. Dazed, they lay there, looking to either side, only to notice Azriel and Eddie also rousing. Disoriented, they all rose to their feet. Staring at Azriel, Camille felt her heart swell with love and relief. Eddie and Halimah also felt elated and unburdened. Laughing, they all fell into each other's arms.

"Wow! We have a lot to talk about," Eddie blurted.

"You're not kidding," Azriel agreed. "But not now. Lagina-Tierra has little time."

One of the greenlings tugged on Azriel's sleeve and pointed to the far end of the cavern. It seemed as if a path had been delineated by rows of strange fungus that glowed with purple and green phosphorescence. Following the greenling's lead, they walked the path to a small fissure in the rock that opened into another chamber. They were immediately overwhelmed by utter darkness. Camille held her nose and nearly gagged. "Ugh! What is that smell?"

A crushing odor of sulfur and rot invaded their senses, and they were forced to back away from the aperture. Halimah replied to Camille's question.

"It's crude oil, and that would suggest the presence of natural gas."

"I guess lighting a match wouldn't be a good idea," Eddie said with a touch of humor.

"This does present a problem." Azriel mused. "We can't go in there without killing ourselves."

"And besides, we can't see a thing," Camille added.

Azriel hesitated. "Well, you can't... but I can."

"Oh, yeah. I forgot about that. So what do you see?"

"She's there—Lagina-Tierra—trapped in a pool of oil, though something else seems to keep her bound."

"So what do we do?" Eddie asked.

Azriel sighed as he considered his options. He could use magick to perhaps blast a hole in the side of the mountain wall to admit light and to release the noxious fumes, but that could risk an explosion if the detonation created a spark to ignite the gases. His experience told him that releasing Lagina-Tierra would likely be relatively easy; the problem would be getting her out of the chamber. Either way, a breach would need to be created for her release.

"I think we need help." Azriel nodded as he came to a decision. Untying the leather pouch from his belt, he removed a few small items: a golden acorn, a feather and a small conch shell. He knew that faerie magick was potent in its own way. Between Paralda, Krinaea, and Maera, they would arrive at a solution. Azriel summoned them and within moments, Paralda, queen of the sylphs was first to arrive. Then the dryad queen, Krinaea, followed by Maera, queen of the Nereids.

Paralda smiled and curtsied primly. "Thou hast summoned us, son of Luminance. What hast thou need of?"

Azriel smiled apologetically. "We need to move a mountain—sort of."

"No small task." Krinaea giggled. "It usually takes millions of years to raise a mountain and millions more for erosion to level it."

"With respect, we don't have millions of years," Camille piped in. "Lagina-Tierra languishes. If we can't release her, she will die."

"Lady of Radiance, we are aware of the Mother's plight. That is why we are here. I must confer with my sisters."

As she spoke, Maera summoned Fieré, and the Queen of Drakes popped into view in a shower of sparks. However, Paralda cautioned her to stay clear of the chamber which held Lagina-Tierra.

The Faerie queens flew a distance from Azriel and conferred among themselves. They seemed to be in a heated discussion, disagreeing on the best course of action to take. Watching them, Azriel began to grow impatient. He strode up to them and crossed his arms.

"Look, I don't mean to rush you, but we're running out of time. Can't you just move the mountain, or at least the top of it?"

Maera answered crossly. "Son of Luminance, we are still bound by the laws of nature. You must be patient."

Azriel sighed and rejoined his companions.

"Well?" Camille asked.

"This isn't going to be easy."

They chatted among themselves while the Faerie queens continued to argue. Finally, after about ten minutes, Maera returned with Krinaea. Azriel noticed that beyond them, Paralda appeared to be trying to comfort Fieré, who had her back partially turned. Scowling, she crossed her arms, clearly unhappy about something.

Maera spoke, though her manner was troubled. "We have arrived at a solution, but you're not going to like it."

"What is it?" Azriel asked.

Krinaea responded. "We must blow the top of this mountain."

"But how do we do that without killing ourselves?"

"Tell me, Son of Luminance, can you create a carcer spell?"

"That's forbidden magick."

"Not for our purposes." She countered quickly. "It need not be a Carcer Eternis, but merely a protective shield. You should be able to dispel the carcer when no longer needed. Unfortunately, the 'tecum' or shield spell would not be adequate."

Azriel grimaced. "Well, I can try."

"There is no *try*; you must," Krinaea countered. She produced a perfect crystal from a concealed pocket and handed it to Azriel.

"Okay, I get it, but then what?"

"Paralda will protect us with a pocket of air. Maera will induce a layer of water atop the oil. I will seal us in the chamber to protect the greenlings, and..." she hesitated, clearly unhappy, "Fieré will ignite the mountain." Krinaea sighed, troubled. "Fieré has the most dangerous part to play. You see, Azriel, although Fieré is impervious to flame, she is not immune to falling debris. She will be unprotected. The blast must be sufficiently large to prevent that."

Azriel was afraid, but accepted. "I need a few minutes alone to produce the spell." He squeezed the crystal in his hand to settle his nerves. Azriel knew this was placing a lot on the line. If he failed, it would not only mean endangering his own life, but everyone else's, not to mention Lagina-Tierra. And then there was Fieré. He would never be able to forgive himself if she wound up dead. Azriel walked off to face Fieré. She sat by herself, arms crossed over her knees, head down.

"Fieré?" he said gently.

She looked up, and her fiery cheeks were lined with tears that flowed like lava from her eyes.

"I'm sorry about all this. Is there any other way?"

"No, Son of Luminance. But… I'm afraid. I seldom know fear."

"Is there anything I can do to help?"

"Probably not."

"Look, this isn't magick—it's science, but it might help. You will be safest at the center of the blast, not at the edge."

Fieré thought about that and brightened. Sparks flew from her wings. "That gives me some hope. Now, Azriel, you must fashion the carcer to protect everyone else."

It took Azriel about fifteen minutes to infuse the gem with the power to expand into a protective layer that would enshroud them from the blast. He returned and stood by Camille's side as everyone gathered closely. Paralda hovered among them with Maera and Krinaea. Sullenly, Fieré floated beyond them, but then changed her mind. She flew over to Eddie and handed him a rather ordinary rock.

"What is this?" he asked.

"It's a Luma stone. You will need that. Just say the word *Lumen*, and it will light your way."

"Thank you, Fieré," Eddie smiled. "Oh, and be careful. We wouldn't want your fire to go out."

Fieré looked down at the fiery raiment covering her nakedness and back up at Eddie. "You are very naughty, Edward." She chided, but it did cause her to smile, and she somehow felt better.

"Art thou ready?" Paralda asked. With their assent, she waved her hands, scribing arcane sigils that glowed blue. They were suddenly surrounded by a pocket of fresh air. It appeared as a faint purple bubble that gave off the aroma of lavender and lilac. Once protected, Maera held out her hands, palms outward, toward the opening to the chamber. Fresh water flowed from her hands and floated above the oil. Paralda aided the queen of Naiads by sending a frigid stream of wind that quickly froze the water to ice, thus giving the companions solid footing.

"You are free to venture in now," Krinaea said gravely.

Entering, they were struck by the enormity of the chamber. Eddie had activated the Luma stone and held it up. The cavern was actually beautiful. Crystals adorned the rock face, and in places, stalagmites hung from the ceiling. Azriel thought it a shame that they would soon destroy it. Moving forward, they found Lagina-Tierra with her head sticking out of a pool of thick oil; however, the newly created ice gave the companions solid footing to approach. The bubble of air settled over her, and the elemental dragon gasped deeply, taking in the fresh air.

She said weakly, "Ah, Son of Luminance, your arrival is timely. I was beginning to think my time was at an end."

Azriel stroked her great head. "We are not out of this yet. First I must protect us."

Camille, Eddie and Halimah huddled close to the great dragon. Paralda, Krinaea and Maera hovered above Lagina-Tierra while Azriel activated the spell.

"Carcer Concisus!" he chanted and held the crystal above his head. It suddenly expanded and grew to surround the group. When it reached its maximum size, it was the signal for Fieré to enter the chamber. She was careful not to flutter her wings, which under normal circumstances would emit a shower of sparks. Instead, she started from the entrance and leapt high, allowing the air currents to let her glide to the approximate center above the Carcer pyramid shielding Azriel and his companions.

She suddenly fluttered her wings, letting go a cascade of sparks to ignite the gas.

The explosion following Fieré's catalyst happened as expected, but no one within the carcer was prepared for the intensity of the blast. Though protected from the eruption, Camille hung on to Azriel in terror. Halimah grabbed Eddie's hand and gaped in horrified awe as the entire chamber became an inferno. She knew, as did all the others, that they would have been instantly consumed by the flames without the magickal protection. The walls began to quake, and suddenly the top of the mountain blasted away like a volcano. Great boulders and shattered scree fell from the gaping fissure above them. Fieré darted here and there to avoid the falling debris. She flew higher through the flames, trying to reach the gaping aperture above, the only safe place from the destruction. She nearly made her escape when a fragment of the chamber wall split off from the rock's face and struck her on the head and shoulder.

Paralda held her hand to her mouth in horror as Fieré tumbled down from that great height and landed at the base of the transparent pyramid.

Krinaea began to cry, for she was powerless to aid her sister until the flames subsided. The companions could only watch in dismay as Fieré lay motionless, so close but out of reach. When finally the gas burned off and the flames subsided, Azriel looked up to make sure that falling debris was no longer a danger. Then he spoke the command to dissipate the spell. Krinaea was the first to reach Fieré, and held her in her arms. She looked at Maera and Paralda and began to sob. "She's cold!"

"What can I do to help?" Azriel asked, trying not to panic.

"She needs a healing fire, as hot as you can make it, otherwise we will lose her." Krinaea ordered.

"Right!" Azriel said. "We need to use the inferno spell, all of us together. Eddie, can you do it?"

"Yes, I'm certain I can." He nodded with assurance as he stepped up beside Fieré. She was beginning to lose her flame, and for all his suggestive bantering with the faerie, he averted his eyes to avoid seeing her nearly naked.

Camille and Halimah joined to complete the circle. On cue, they released the inferno spell upon the injured faerie queen. A blazing column of fire, white-hot, settled over Fi, é. Within the scorching flame, she began to rouse, but it wasn't enough. She whispered in her weakness, "More—hotter, please!" Azriel, as well as the others, poured all their strength into the blaze and nearly scorched themselves, but it was still not enough. Fieré languished.

Trying not to lose his concentration, Azriel called out to Krinaea. "You must summon Magador. We need his flame." Krinaea vanished with a pop and, moments later, returned with Magador.

"Well then! That is quite a decent flame, my friends, but let the expert handle this," Magador said with pride and chuckled. "My, I've never *purposely* scorched anyone before!"

The four companions stepped back to give Magador room, but continued pouring heat into the column of fire. Magador reared back and belched out a directed flame right over Fieré. She gasped with pleasure and stood as if bathing herself in a shower. "Oooh, that's so much better!" she cooed.

Fully restored to health, Fieré stepped out of the flame, glowing with her usual radiance. She stretched and craned her neck as if awakening from a rejuvenating nap. Smiling, she clapped her hands and turned toward Lagina-Tierra. "Well, Azriel, it's time to release the Mother from her captivity."

Now that the smoke and dust had cleared and sunlight blazed into the chamber, Azriel saw that before the pool of oil holding the elemental captive, there stood a small table with a wand perched upon a pedestal. It was emblazoned with strange runes. Beneath it, set into the table, was a large green emerald, cut into a triangle and beautifully faceted with intricate details so it glowed with rich splendor. Azriel knew the hardest task was done, but it was Fieré who had paid dearly for it. He would not forget, and had something special in mind.

He examined Lagina-Tierra's condition. She looked stronger than when they first arrived. The clean air flowing through the chamber had revived her, but a collar around her neck, attached to four heavy, oil-encrusted chains, still bound her. Azriel knew what to do. He removed the wand from its pedestal, and it immediately began to glow a vibrant green. Without ceremony, he touched it to the heavy chains, and they fell away, crumbling into dust. Lagina-Tierra lifted herself from the pool of muck while Maera summoned a powerful spray of clean water from her hands to wash the oil from the great elemental. She towered over the companions and breathed a long sigh of relief. Bending low, she kept her massive head level with Azriel.

"Thank you, my brother. You have freed me. I can now resume my place in the south. If you would, please place the jewel in my crown." As with the other elementals, a distinct impression remained on Lagina-Tierra's forehead.

"I would be honored, great Lagina-Tierra, but I would like to pass that honor to Fieré. She aided in your freedom—nearly at the cost of her life."

Azriel touched the wand to the gem, and it floated from the table into Fieré's waiting hands. It appeared massive in her arms due to her diminutive size, yet she hoisted it easily and flew to face the great elemental. She bowed deeply and carefully placed it above the indentation in Lagina-Tierra's crown. Like a magnet, it flew from her hands into the recess and began to blaze with blinding light. Empowered, Lagina-Tierra spread her massive wings in a glorious, triumphant stance.

She peered down at Azriel and his companions, then bowed deeply. "You have been my liberators. I am grateful and will not soon forget. Now I have a world to heal!" She fixed her gaze on Azriel. "My brother, you have two more tasks to complete before you face your final challenge."

"Two?" Azriel asked, surprised.

Lagina-Tierra chuckled. "Of course. First, you must release my brother, Pyrrhos. Then you must defeat Rastaban. If you do not, he will impede your path to uniting the worlds—the ultimate challenge. If he lives, the transition will be imperfect and unbalanced. To achieve true equilibrium, he must be utterly destroyed. When this is done, the remaining Clave will crumble. Their petty evil cannot endure. Remember, brother: to kill a serpent, you must cleave off its head. Do that, and the body may writhe, but it will ultimately die."

"There is one other thing," Azriel said as he peered up at the great elemental. "Deep within a cavern unknown to me, my mother Abelene is held captive along with the Dark Dragon of Death. How can I defeat death?"

Lagina-Tierra smiled. "One cannot defeat death. It is inevitable for all, but might I ask, Son of Luminance, why you feel it necessary to defeat my brother?"

"It's been prophesied that I will confront him."

"Hmm," the elemental mused. "Confront, yes. That does not necessarily mean defeat. Keep in mind, Son of Luminance—he is your brother."

Azriel stood stunned. "You too? You also tell me this terrible thing?"

"Is it so terrible?" she sighed. "I speak only the truth." She glanced across the cavern at Magador. "I know it; so does Magador. How is it you cannot see it?"

"See what?" Azriel gestured with impatience.

"Why, what else would that be but the truth?"

"What truth?"

"That you are a dragon!" She laughed at Azriel's dumbfounded expression. "Besides, with your dragonsight—and the knowledge two of your companions carry—you will find the secret place where your mother and the Dragon of Death are held captive. It is time, young Lord Azriel, to fulfill your destiny. The conjunction of the two worlds draws near. You must be prepared and fully endowed with your power."

With that, Lagina-Tierra rose through the massive chimney carved by the shattered mountain and disappeared into the sky.

Azriel stood for a long while, staring at the empty sky where the Earth Elemental had been, confused and anxious over Lagina-Tierra's revelation. He was in no way prepared to accept what he believed impossible. How many times had he argued with Magador about it? More than he could count. He sighed, frustration tightening his chest. "We're done here. Let's go home."

Upon their return, Eddie, Camille, and Halimah went directly to their respective tents and retired to bed. They were physically and emotionally exhausted with much to think about. Azriel did as well, but he was far too restless to sleep. He sought out Eltanin and strode toward the ornate tent erected near the gazebo. He softly called as he stood by the flap, hoping that the old wizard would be awake.

Before he could announce himself, Eltanin spoke softly. "Come in, Azriel. I'm sure you have questions."

Azriel found Eltanin resting in an old rocking chair with his feet propped on a cushioned bench. He placed the book aside and folded his hands in his lap. Azriel noted that Eltanin seemed tired—troubled.

"I assume you were successful in your endeavor."

Azriel didn't answer. He stared at him levelly, keeping his temper in check.

"Why didn't you tell me?"

"Tell you what?" Eltanin responded, amused.

"About the first tunnel in the mountain."

"Oh… that."

"Yeah, that!" Azriel simmered. "I could have gotten everyone killed."

"It was a test."

"Haven't I been tested enough?"

"It's not always about you, Azriel. This was about Edward. I know full well what dangers lurk in that place."

"What does Eddie have to do with this?"

"I had a suspicion that Edward possesses a rare ability. He confirmed it when he tried to prevent you from entering that tunnel. It would seem your cousin is what we call a Sentinel."

"A what?"

"He can sense danger in an extraordinary way. It's a rare psychic gift few wizards possess. With proper training, he will be invaluable to you when you take the throne of Aralia. Sentinels have guarded kings since the First Age."

Weary, Azriel rubbed his scalp. The thought of the near future filled him with such disquiet that he wished his rule as future king could be passed to someone else. "Grandfather," he said, trying his best to sound nonchalant though filled with anxiety. "I have a question."

"Yes son..."

"If rules of succession truly apply to the throne, wouldn't it be more in keeping with legalities that you are, in fact, the true king of Aralia, not me?"

Eltanin chuckled quietly. "Ah the burden of kingship has already seeped into your soul. And indeed, it is truly a burden, Azriel. How I wish I could lift that weight off your shoulders, but alas, the seat of power has passed to you.

It will be difficult enough for you to take your rightful place, for, as Abelene has told you, the five great houses are divided, where once there was peace and unity. And as you know, my reputation has been tarnished by years of myth and legend, grown larger with the passage of time. To the Aralians, I might as well be the devil himself."

"But none of it is true!" Azriel shot back leaping to Eltanin's defense.

"No son, much of it *is* true—at least, from a certain point of view." The old wizard shrugged. "It would have been to my advantage had I someone like Edward to warn me that I was stepping into a trap when I performed that ill-fated ritual."

Azriel stared pensively at the ground. "Grandfather, tell me what truly happened."

"You know most of it, son." Eltanin sighed. "I was betrayed by Rastaban. Completely blinded to his duplicity. Humans suddenly appeared on Aralia. They disrupted the Aralian way of life. Their methods were destructive across the land, yet I found no evil in them—only a difference in philosophy. They could achieve with technology what the Elvin race achieved with magick. But the humans left only destruction in their wake. I was never certain why they refused to learn the ways of the Ferrishyn. The truth is, I believed they were fully capable of learning magick. Rastaban disagreed, however, and convinced me the only way of keeping our people safe was to return the humans from whence they came."

"That was the problem, wasn't it? Did they come from the future or the past?"

"Indeed," Eltanin muttered. "The Clave had woven a spell of deception over me, so subtle I never detected it. Me—the greatest sorcerer of them all!" The old wizard spat the words with self-deprecating sarcasm. "I never considered that one vital question. Had I not taken that course, humanity would have been destroyed."

"Grandfather, I have a concern. Once I complete the ritual, what will happen to the humans? Two planets were derived from one. Just like alchemy, the Two always seek to reunite as One. But suppose humans had come from the future. What were they escaping from? If they are from the future of a reunited Aralia, it would seem they continued with their technology and perhaps created such disaster that they had to flee back to a time where they could start over. Or perhaps it was the other way around. Maybe they had come from our past, from so remote a time that the Ferrishyn have no memory of it. Hypothetically, once humans fled ancient Aralia, their absence allowed the Elfin race to thrive. Maybe they were placed in the plains of Shenach against their will."

"I have questioned the same things, Azriel, and found no answers."

"Then there doesn't seem to be any choice in the matter. The past has already been set and the future is uncertain." Azriel replied wearily.

"Oh, there are always choices—and don't be too sure about the past and future. Remember your lessons in alchemy. When everything is viewed as a whole, it is all One—everything connected, everything tied together, though it appears a jumble of confusion. There may, however, be help when the time is right."

"Oh?" Azriel responded, filled with hope.

"I had Rosemary give you a book. There you will find some answers."

"Grandfather, I hate to break it to you, but the pages are blank!"

"Well of course I know that," he replied somewhat indignant. "I created it!" he lowered his voice, "But I never had the courage to use it."

"You, Grandfather?"

"Aye, indeed. It is the Book of Destiny, and it is not what it appears. It is a most powerful tool," he hesitated, "and quite dangerous—deadly in the wrong hands."

Azriel blanched.

"In truth, it is a time portal. It can be used to observe any moment in history—past, present or future. It will magically record everything you see with perfect accuracy. But herein lies the danger. If you change any part of the book, you can irreparably alter the past or future. That is why I never used it. My actions in the past altered the path of humanity and elvenkind. I cannot be responsible for that ever again. Never. But as for humanity, I believe something—or someone—interfered with human destiny and created the paradox of their arrival in Aralia so many years ago. There may come a time, after the worlds reunite, when you will find the answer to that riddle."

Azriel remained silent for a long while contemplating Eltanin's enigmatic response. Then he spoke. "There's something else, Grandfather."

"What is it, son?"

"Am I a dragon?"

"Who told you that?"

"Well..." Azriel scratched his scalp, piecing it together, "Magador has always maintained that I'm a dragon. I've argued with him often about it. Then Lagina-Tierra said the same thing. I asked my mother once, and she said that as your heir, I carry the spirit of the dragon as my guide."

"That part of it is true. Your family coat of arms has always been the white dragon, symbol of House Ferrishyn's strength and wisdom." Eltanin said proudly. "And of course there is the matter of dragonsight, which you have mastered. Few wizards have that ability."

"Do you have it?"

Eltanin hesitated, then exhaled. "No, I'm afraid not." He straightened in his chair. "This is hard for me to concede, Azriel, but in many ways you have surpassed me. Don't get me wrong. This pleases me more than you know. The truth is: you are powerful enough to defeat Rastaban."

Azriel looked up in surprise.

Eltanin smiled and continued, "Do not doubt it, son. Look at all you've accomplished in so short a time. You've awakened the amulet and released three of the four elemental dragons. You have empowered Errin-lil and created the Lapis Occultus. You are ready. But as to your question—are you a dragon? Honestly, I don't know."

"But you can change into a dragon, right? I saw it."

The old wizard chuckled softly. "Trickery—mere illusion. It's quite a simple matter."

"Oh..." Azriel couldn't hide his disappointment.

Eltanin took Azriel by the shoulders and gave him an affectionate shake. "I don't have all the answers, much as I wish I did. But there is one thing I do know. You have a powerful destiny—one that will unfold as you continue to grow."

Chapter 20

When he awoke from a much-needed rest, Azriel exited his tent, surprised to find the place atwitter with activity. Friends he hadn't seen in a while were busy preparing tables for breakfast. Apparently, Eltanin and Nicodemus had been busy rounding up every member of the Order of the Ankh. They must have brought them to the Between Place while Azriel slept. Camille's aunts, Penelope and Daphne, had been brought through from Ireland. They chatted noisily with Rosemary and Muriel as they set a massive table laden with all sorts of breakfast treats. Though they could have relied on magick for the sumptuous feast, they, like Abelene, preferred cooking the old-fashioned way. It wasn't difficult to guess that Nicodemus or Eltanin had magically provided them with all the kitchen utensils they needed. Tending the fire, Mr. Parkins and Billy were loading wood into an old cast-iron stove. At another section of the table, Amaryllis and Felisa quarreled over how much cinnamon to put on the sticky buns they were preparing.

Looking around, it seemed nothing was ready, and breakfast was at least an hour away. Azriel looked around, hoping to find Camille, but she was nowhere to be found. He figured she was still asleep after such a trying day. He noticed, however, Eddie sat with his mother, Elsinore, talking quietly. From the look of it they were sharing an intimate moment, and Azriel gave them a wide berth. Elsinore fell into her son's arms with tears in her eyes. He did happen, though, to overhear some of the details of Eddie's ordeal and found a new respect for his cousin. In another quiet spot, Halimah spoke quietly with Albert. As they chatted, Azriel couldn't help but notice that she held Albert's hand. Smiling, he left them to their privacy. He walked over the rise. The great dragon lay comfortably on the grass, basking in deep conversation with Eltanin and Nicodemus. Azriel noted that Magador was now nearly fully grown.

He strode up and brushed his hand against Magador's golden crest. "Thanks for all your help yesterday." Azriel said with humility. "We couldn't have done it without you."

"Thank you, cousin. It's good to be appreciated." He paused. "I think you and I should go for a flight later. I need to stretch my wings." Magador glanced at Eltanin and smiled subtly.

Azriel noted the exchange and crossed his arms. "All right, what are you two up to?"

"Cousin, you offend me. I have nothing to hide. Why you're always so suspicious is quite beyond me!"

"Really now! You and my grandfather are always having these private chats, and something tells me that I'm the subject of these quiet conversations."

Nicodemus gave Azriel a glancing smack to the back of his head. "Stop being so paranoid! We were merely discussing yesterday's events." Uncle Nick sniffed and smiled. "I think breakfast is ready." Without a word, he turned back to where the massive table was set. Eltanin followed, leaving Azriel alone with Magador. He gave the great dragon a withering look. "I'll deal with you later."

Seated at the table, Azriel sat across from Eddie, Halimah, and Albert. Camille sat to his left and Jasper by his right. The adults sat at one end of the table, which gave Azriel the opportunity to chat with his friends.

"Hey Eddie," Azriel mumbled with his mouth full. "Could you pass the pancakes?"

"Edward," he replied.

"Huh?"

"I said, Edward. *Eddie* is who I was. I'd prefer to be called Edward." Julia, who sat by his side, glanced at Edward proudly.

Azriel examined his cousin's face. There was a hint of pride in his demeanor, and Azriel nodded thoughtfully. "Okay, Edward, it is."

They ate in silence for a few more minutes. Azriel toyed with his food, thinking deeply. Halimah tilted her head staring at him until their eyes met.

"You seem troubled," she probed.

He didn't respond immediately, but finally asked, "Halimah, remember when you went into the trance, trying to probe Eltanin's mind?"

"I'd rather forget," Halimah answered tersely.

"Yeah, I know, but I need to know what you saw."

"Not much, really." She picked at the eggs on her plate. "But there was one thing."

"Yes?"

"When Rosemary released me from the trance, I was lifted out of Rastaban's trap. For a moment, I saw what appeared to be an old, abandoned military shack with one of those old-time radio towers. Oh, and there was what looked like a heliport." She paused. "You know, those red-and-white circles in a cross hair."

Azriel nodded. "What about you, Edward? You were there. What do you remember?"

"At the time I was pretty scared," Edward admitted. "There was this conference table and a huge metal door that led down into a chamber. Altais had brought me there to meet Rastaban. The wizard brought me down to the chamber below, where I saw a black dragon imprisoned inside a nearly transparent pyramid. I know now that it was the Carcer Eternis. One thing did stick out in my mind, though. The dragon had a wound over his chest that bled a little."

Azriel nodded thoughtfully. "Hmm… do you think you could implant those images in the dream orb?"

Camille suddenly squeezed Azriel's hand in panic. "You're not thinking of going there, are you?"

Azriel slipped his hand from hers and rubbed it, wincing. "No—not yet… but soon."

Camille looked down at her plate, pensively. Suddenly, she wasn't very hungry.

"Don't worry," Azriel said with a reassuring smile. "I won't do anything without you guys, nor will I confront Rastaban without consulting Eltanin and Uncle Nick—but I do have an idea."

"So you've finally come." Magador grumbled as though he were tragically bored.

"Aw, come on, Magador. I needed to eat. So where are we going today?"

"Spain."

"Why there?" Azriel asked as he mounted Magador's shoulders.

"Because you have another task to complete. And this time, it is only you who can. You will not get any help."

"Okay…"

"Now, are you familiar with the Rock of Gibraltar?"

"I've heard of it…"

"Across from that landmark, opposite the Strait of Gibraltar, is another peak on the coast of North Africa. These are known as the Pillars of Hercules. Somewhere between the two is where Pyrrhos is imprisoned."

"How do you know that?"

"I've always known. I'm a dragon, after all." Magador shrugged as they went aloft. "And you would know that too if you managed to take your head out of your butt once in a while."

Azriel grumbled, clenching his jaw with annoyance. "Why do you say that?"

"Just shut up and engage your dragonsight while we blink across."

There was a sudden shift of light and a brief rush of cold, then Magador and Azriel were flying above the ocean. "Now what I meant, young master, is that I am getting quite tired of your propensity for delusion. You, cousin, are a dragon!"

"Not this again." Azriel growled.

Magador soared higher and higher, where the air was beginning to grow rarefied. Azriel began to feel lightheaded.

"Um, Magador, could you descend a little?" Azriel looked down. Even with dragonsight, the earth seemed awfully far away. He felt a sudden stab of fear.

"Oh, stop whining." Magador intoned with frustration. "You're a dragon—you can take it."

Azriel exploded with anger. "You're the one who's delusional! I don't know how many ways I can tell you that I'm not a dragon.

Never was—never will be—and I'm damned sick of this same old argument!"

"Oh you are, are you? Well fine then! Get off!" With a mighty heave of Magador's back, Azriel went sailing upward and began to plummet toward the earth. Magador merely banked and followed.

"Are you crazy?" Azriel howled in terror.

Magador flew beside him and answered with nonchalance as Azriel continued to descend, accelerating. "You'll be fine. You're a dragon!"

"I will *not* be fine. I am going to *die!*"

"You can't die. You're immortal—and you're a dragon!"

"Magador—help me!" Azriel screamed.

"I *am* helping you." he said with absolute certainty.

"If I ever get out of this, I'm going to kill you!" Azriel raged.

Magador chuckled. "Oh, stop being so dramatic."

"Dragon, help me this instant!"

"But I told you, cousin, I *am* helping you! I'm helping you become what you were destined to be!"

Azriel continued to plummet, flailing his arms and legs. The ocean drew nearer, as did Azriel's impending death.

"Magador! This isn't funny anymore."

"Of course it is. You just have no sense of humor." Magador sighed with frustration. "The moment you believe that you are indeed a dragon, then everything will be fine."

"Parachute! Parachute!" Azriel hollered, trying to invoke the proper spell, but nothing happened. Panic prevented lucid thinking.

"Dragon…" Magador intoned, goading the boy.

"No!" Azriel screamed, continuing his descent.

"Dragon," he crooned.

"I can't!"

"Yes you can!" Magador urged. "You just need to believe!"

Azriel's impact was imminent, the ocean less than a thousand meters, when he realized it was hopeless. He would plummet into the ocean and the impact would likely kill him and Magador was going to let it happen. He couldn't believe that Magador, his friend and sometime adversary would let him die. It was impossible, not with so much at stake. As the ocean neared, Azriel suddenly had a moment of clarity. Perhaps Magador was right. In fact, he wasn't the only one who had said so. Lagina-Tierra had also insisted in Azriel's dragonhood. What's more, the Dark Dragon had even referred to Azriel as Brother!"

At maximum velocity, Azriel's impact with the ocean was moments away, when in desperation, he spread his arms and finally let go his stubborn resistance and succumbed to his fate. He shouted, "I'm a dragon! I'm a dragon! I'm a DRAAAAAGON!"

Azriel wasn't quite sure when or how it had happened, but he suddenly swooped, and his clawed feet briefly skimming the water. His massive wings caught an updraft and he was aloft, soaring upward with Magador flying by his side. Speechless, Azriel allowed his new senses to surge through his powerful body. He had transformed into a creature of pure instinct. He managed every subtle shift of wind and minute gust of air pressure with the slightest ease. With profound joy in his newfound freedom, Azriel leaned back and roared out a prodigious flame from his throat.

In sheer size, Azriel was larger than Magador. Magador laughed with happiness. "Azriel, I must say—you are a most magnificent dragon."

As Azriel felt the ebb and flow of all life enter his mind, a new awareness filled him to overflowing. It was true that he had learned the dragonsight, but this was different, for now it was ruled by instinct he could never have known in his elfin form. His sight was so sharp he could see below the ocean, down to where Pyrrhos was imprisoned. It was a most clever trap, since the Dragon Elemental of Fire would be extinguished if he ever left his prison. Azriel was filled with a vast sense of knowing. Universal secrets he had only vaguely understood now spilled over within and morphed into a new self-awareness. Not only had he been transformed into a Dragon of purest white, but he now knew why he had long been called along as the Son of Luminance—and why the Dark Dragon had always called him brother. He now knew, because it was all true. Azriel was the equal and opposite of the Dragon of Death. Azriel was the Son of Luminance, the Lord of Light—the Dragon Elemental of Life. With his newfound power, he could transform and become anything he desired—not mere illusion but the reality of substance.

Azriel soared to where the air was thinnest and then pulled in his wings close to his body to descend with bone-shuddering speed, merely for the joy of it while Magador struggled to keep up. Finally, Azriel spread his wings to catch an updraft and settled onto the Rock of Gibraltar.

He and Magador perched side by side peering down into the depths of the ocean.

"Magador, you were right all along."

"Of course I was," he replied with humor. "Honestly, Azriel, you could be quite dense sometimes."

"Yes, I suppose." He answered with contrition. "I now know with certainty that I am a dragon but I'm baffled as to how. I mean, how did it happen?"

Magador thought deeply and then finally answered. "If you're asking me what magick or science takes place in the trans-formative process, I honestly don't know. Just be assured that it happens according to your will. Think about it in a quiet time and all knowledge will assimilate. It takes time, you know."

"Magador, that's not good enough."

"It will have to be for now. Honestly cousin, you have this propensity for over-thinking matters. It was always your destiny from the beginning of time. You are the promised one—the one who was yet to be."

Azriel nodded his massive, jeweled head in contemplation. He peered deeper into the ocean, noting the placement of the giant vault imprisoning Pyrrhos.

"Magador, can dragons swim?"

"Yes, but it's not one of our strengths. Normally a dragon can lift many times its own weight, but unfortunately we're not all that effective in water. With certainty, there are limitations to everything. However, you might want to summon the leviathans. You, after all, have the power of command."

"Yes, yes, that's true!" Azriel swooped down over the ocean and roared out a summons to the leviathans below. With his dragonsight, he noted that they were coiled around the vault guarding the Fire Elemental. Hearing the summons and roused from their slumber, with a great heave, they toiled for some time, but then released the vault from the calcium-encrusted bedrock of the ocean floor. Slowly the vault lifted, dragged up by the massive chain that had held it bound. Soon it crested the waves, held aloft by three leviathans—the ancient wurms of the deep. At least twenty meters in length, their scales sparkled, iridescent in the light. Massive jaws bristled with rows of serrated teeth. They lowered their heads in deference to Azriel, their master—the Lord of Light.

"Thank you, my friends." Azriel bowed with respect as he grasped the great ring affixed to the top of the vault with his clawed feet. With ease, he flew back to the rock of Gibraltar and gently set the vault upon the stone. Examining the great prison, he looked for a latch or trigger to release the door, but it wasn't necessary. The vault began to shudder with an internal struggle, and the door suddenly burst from its hinges. With a mighty roar of freedom, Pyrrhos spread his great wings and breathed in, then exhaled an extraordinary flame. It ignited his wings, and he began to glow red like burnished copper. He bowed low to Azriel and spoke.

"I offer thanks to you, my Brother, for freeing me."

"I am only sorry it wasn't sooner. You must have suffered greatly." Azriel kicked angrily at the great vault, and it tumbled back into the ocean. "You won't need *that* anymore."

Pyrrhos peered down with amusement as the vault caused a great splash and sank back into the ocean depths. "Brother, aren't you forgetting something?"

Azriel stared back at him with blank expression.

Pyrrhos curled his wing, pointing to the triangular depression in his forehead. "My power was lodged in the door."

"Crap," Azriel mumbled, and swooped down to retrieve the gem. Pyrrhos chuckled.

Magador sighed. "He's young yet." They watched as Azriel called back a leviathan. The great wurm dove and returned moments later with a massive red jewel in his mouth.

When Azriel alit back on the rock, embarrassed, he shuffled his clawed feet. "Sorry. I wasn't thinking."

"Well, that's not unusual." Magador rolled his jeweled eyes.

Azriel handed the gem to Magador. "You've been patient with me, cousin. I'd like you to do the honors."

"It would be my pleasure," Magador replied formally. With ceremony, he held the gem aloft and placed it in Pyrrhos' forehead. It adhered with a click, and the great Fire Elemental roared with pleasure. "It is done!" He then faced Azriel. "It is now my time to return to my place in the west. Brother, you have done well. Dragons can now return to the world. Now there is something more you must do."

"Yes, brother, and now I know what it is. I must face our brother—the Lord of Death."

"Indeed." Pyrrhos nodded, then looked up into the sky. "The merging of worlds is nearly upon us. Soon all will be made right."

"I'm not so sure, brother." Azriel shook his pearly crest vehemently. "This is a complicated world. Humans resist change... and the Ferrishyn aren't much different. I'm uncertain whether the two races can coexist when Aralia is merged into one world. I fear there will be war."

"War is inevitable—unless you can bring them together. You have one thing in your favor as king of Aralia—your queen-to-be. She is human and part Ferrishyn."

Azriel glanced up in surprise.

Pyrrhos chuckled. "You didn't know? Thirteen generations ago, the seed was planted by one of your kinsmen—not house Ferrishyn, but house Gorlyn—your mother's house. A young apprentice in the magickal arts had unwittingly opened a portal to this world and planted the seed of magick in your queen's ancestor. That seed has been passed on for thirteen generations and now resides in Camille. She is destined to be a powerful sorceress. A human with magick—that's a potent combination! With her by your side, you will not fail."

"How do you know this?"

"Think, Azriel, and you will know this too."

Pyrrhos bowed formally and lifted into the sky. He roared once and disappeared into the west.

Azriel and Magador blinked back to the cross-dimensional space linking the two worlds. As they soared through the heavens, Azriel noticed Camille standing on a rise overlooking the valley below. Deep in contemplation, her back to him, she was unaware of his presence. Azriel whispered to Magador, "Cousin, I need to speak with Camille."

"I understand. I'll meet up with you later." Magador smiled and banked left. He flew toward a flat plain where sheep were grazing. His belly suddenly rumbled with hunger.

Azriel flew toward Camille and alit soundlessly behind her. So lost in her thoughts, Camille didn't notice at first. Azriel gently curled his wings around Camille in a tender embrace. Seeing the massive wings enfold her, Camille's eyes widened in awe. She spun around and gasped. "Oh, my… you're beautiful, my Lord!" She dropped to her knees and bowed.

"Don't do that. We're equals."

Her face scrunched up with confusion, recognizing his voice. "Azriel?"

"Yes, it's me." With a sudden flash of light, Azriel was restored to his normal form. He held out his hand for Camille to rise. Tenderly, he stroked her cheek. "Have I told you that I love you?" he said with a smile.

Camille's cheeks reddened. "Not lately." Her eyes deepened to a richer shade of blue. "What happened to you, Azriel?"

He took her hand and sat on the lush grass. She sat beside him, leaning on his shoulder, as they watched the activity below. All his friends were engaged in a game of magickal sparring.

"Well, as it turns out, Magador was right all along. I *am* a dragon. In fact, I think I'm the last Elemental—the one who is called Lord of Light. Camille, it's a bit overwhelming."

Camille was suddenly stricken with fear and sorrow. Her eyes welled with tears. "What does that mean for us?"

"It doesn't change a thing. You are—and always will be—my queen."

"You sure?"

"Of course I'm sure. There's something else you should know."

"There's more?" Camille sniffed.

Azriel smiled wryly. "It's not about me—it's about you."

She stared at him, a touch of fear in her eyes.

"Pyrrhos told me an amazing thing …"

"You freed him?"

"Yeah, it wasn't that difficult. Well anyway, he told me you are part Ferrishyn—of house Gorlyn. That's why magick resides in you with such intensity. You're destined to be a great sorceress and will help unite the two races."

Camille didn't respond but went deep into her thoughts. It occurred to her that she had seen the vision of a great white dragon in a protective hold around her in the scrying mirror. That part had come true. But there was the thing that she could never tell Azriel, her looming death. If the first vision was true, then surely the second would be true as well. And her being part Elfin, this she knew as well, for her ancestor had told her it was so.

"Azriel, when we were in the caves and put to the test, I saw my mother and each generation before her to the first of my line. Her name was Emily. She told me a most incredible story."

Azriel grinned. "I think perhaps Pyrrhos told me the same story."

"I at least now know why Magick comes so easily to me. It's been in me all along."

Azriel stared down the valley and suddenly chuckled.

"What?" Camille glanced at him chagrined.

Azriel hugged her tight and gently kissed her on the lips. "You and I? We're going to make a great team."

Chapter 21

It wasn't so much the confinement that bothered Abelene as the boredom. Conversation with Charlie began to grow strained as they were running out of things to talk about. Nevertheless, Charlie was great company, and today they had something spectacular to speak about. Abelene was hardly ever surprised by anything, yet today she stood facing Charlie, Dark Dragon of Death, with her mouth agape.

"I'm most sorry, Milady," Charlie said with delight. "But your son—my brother—has finally embraced his destiny."

"So what you're telling me is that Azriel has become a dragon—a real, live dragon—no illusion."

"Of course. Why do you think he has always been referred to as the Son of Luminance? Now the brotherhood of the High Dragons is complete. This was the necessary event to begin the reunification of both worlds."

Abelene looked down, crestfallen. "I will never be able to embrace my son again."

"Why do you say that, Milady?"

"He's a dragon, and if he's anything like you, I will never be able to hold him in my arms."

Charlie laughed with glee.

"Do you find that funny?" Abelene asked, simmering.

"No, of course not," Charlie chortled, laughing a little more. "It's just that you don't quite understand. My brother is still himself. He can transform anytime he desires, into anything—but the highest form he can take is that of the dragon!" Charlie said with pride.

Abelene gasped, a sudden leap of insight striking her. "Charlie, do you have a human form?"

"Yes I do."

"Show me!" she said, suddenly excited as a little girl.

"I cannot." he answered sadly, pointing to the wound on his chest. "As a dragon, I can bear this wound but as a human it would be mortal. It also prevents me from transforming."

"I'm sorry," Abelene whispered with remorse. "Why didn't you ever tell me?"

"Why, Milady? It's because you never asked."

Abelene held a hand to her mouth and giggled. "Oh, I suppose you're right." She glanced over at the tapestry she had fashioned, now hanging from a rail. The third prophetic panel depicted the four elemental dragons—Charlie, the Dark Dragon, and a magnificent white dragon—in the midst of the ritual that would soon reunite the two worlds. Projected from the heart of each dragon was a beautiful child. The six children held hands in a circle. From the center of their circle, a brilliant beam of light rose to pierce the sky. Abelene now knew the White Dragon was her son! She peered up at Charlie with a shrewd smile. "Now I understand."

"Well, isn't this cozy!" A voice came from the shadows.

Startled by the intrusion, Abelene spun around, but Charlie roared in anger. "You have the nerve to face me, Lilith."

Abelene examined the woman. She was certainly lovely to behold. Lilith's golden hair was coiffed in curls, framing a lively girlish face with soulful blue eyes that seemed almost innocent— but Abelene wasn't fooled. Behind that childlike mask hid a deceitful, ravenous she-monster—a devourer of souls. Upon closer look, Abelene noticed silver streaks in Lilith's hair, and that her beautiful face bore the faint signs of fading youth.

"Why are you here, Lilith?" Charlie growled, a wisp of sulfur escaping his lips.

"Hmm." She shrugged, absently twirling a lock of her golden hair around her finger. "Curiosity, I think. I wanted to meet the mother of the newest Dragon Lord."

"You are quite brazen to face me, my lovely little cheat—and you have much to answer for." Charlie simmered. "I will not be imprisoned forever, and when I am released, I will have to clean house in the Underworld for all the damage you have done. You will pay for that. Eternity is a long time."

"Charlie, what do you mean?" Abelene interrupted.

"Oh, you have no idea what this creature has done! As guardian of the dead, it is my job to provide a place of rest and reflection to all those who pass from life to death. The underworld was once a haven of peace and the portal for those wishing to return to the world of the living. But because of all the destruction, death, and murder she committed, she was banished by the Clave—that is, when they were still useful to the underworld. They were merciful and banished her to the underworld where she could do no harm to the living, rather than consign her to oblivion. But then the worlds were split apart, and I in my weakened state was captured by Rastaban. In my absence, Lilith seized power and set herself up as queen of the underworld."

Abelene glanced over at Lilith, who stood haughtily with her head held high—gloating, mocking—proud of her handiwork.

Charlie continued, "Oh, that isn't all of it, Milady. Oh, no. This lovely creature you see before you—with her evil, twisted little heart—took the lost souls of the underworld and distorted them—warped them into reflections of her own debasement, transforming them into vile demons to do her bidding. The underworld is now a place of suffering. It was never meant to be so. There are now places of torment so horrid I shudder to think of them. It will be a dark irony indeed when Lilith must face the punishments she designed. Such a clever one she is."

"True, all true. But the punishment thing..." She gestured lightly with her fingers. "That will never happen." Lilith cooed as she stepped lightly toward Abelene, dismissing Charlie with a careless flip of her hand.

"You haven't heard a word I've said. Beware, Lilith. The time of reckoning approaches!"

"Oh, don't be such a boor," Lilith sneered, and turned to Abelene. "So here's the great sorceress, Abelene—mother of the Dragon of Life! You do know I will have to destroy him, don't you?"

"What do you want with me, Lilith?" Abelene replied evenly.

"I just wish to engage you in conversation."

"I see." Abelene brushed a tress of black hair behind her ear. "Life with the Clave isn't all you thought it would be. You thought you could control them."

"What do you mean?" Lilith snapped.

Abelene laughed lightly. "Rastaban summoned you from the underworld. That means *he* controls *you*! For a woman of your prowess, that can't be very agreeable."

Lilith hesitated. "No... no, it isn't."

"Of course it isn't." Abelene suppressed a victorious smile. "You and I are powerful women. I *know* what you feel."

Charlie's ears perked up as he listened to their exchange. What kind of dangerous gambit was Abelene playing?

"You could always return to the underworld," Abelene suggested.

"No I can't." Lilith frowned. "Eltanin stole my immortality."

"Oh, Lilith," Abelene spoke as though scolding a child. "That's not how I heard it. To my understanding, Eltanin gave you ample warning. You simply didn't heed it. But that is your way, isn't it—not paying heed?"

Lilith pursed her lips and stared at the floor.

"You broke his heart, you know," Abelene said, her voice carrying subtle inflections meant to manipulate the woman further.

"Who?"

"Eltanin, of course. You were his brightest and most talented student... and his greatest disappointment. Nevertheless he loved you. I think some part of him still does."

"I loved him once."

"Oh, Lilith," Abelene said sadly. "You can lie to me—I understand the need—but don't lie to yourself. After all you've done, you may very well be incapable of love. You will never fully give your heart to anyone. You will never hold a baby to your breast and love unconditionally. You will never have compassion, or empathy, or true kindness—and do you know why?"

Lilith stood rigid, her eyes beginning to tear.

"I'll tell you why, Lilith. It's because you're selfish and short-sighted. You sold whatever love you had in pursuit of power. The one thing you never counted on was the emptiness and loneliness that followed as the consequence of your lust for supremacy. It's like a deep well that can never be filled. Eltanin's love would have freed you. Instead, you chose the way of darkness, Mother of Demons—which enslaved you to evil. Now you can never be free.

When you broke Eltanin's heart, I think you shattered his soul—and your own. He was never the same after that."

Abelene paused and shook her head. "Treasure your mortality, Lilith, and use for good whatever life you have left—if that's even possible. Otherwise, I see you growing old and bitterly alone. For on the day you lie on your deathbed, you will not be filled with memories of love and gratitude. No. You will face your death with fear and regret for all the opportunities you missed."

Abelene shook her head sadly, her voice, nearly a whisper. "No, Lilith, I don't despise you; I pity you. You had it all once, and you gave it away. For all your bravado and bluster, I think you're just a sad, lonely, and miserable little woman."

"Is there no hope for me?"

"There is always hope, Lilith… but I'm not so sure for you. Now I think it's time you return to your master. Rastaban is probably missing you by now. You wouldn't want to keep him waiting. He won't take kindly to you fraternizing with the enemy." Abelene smiled curtly, walked over to her brocaded chair, and sat. She picked up her lute and began to tune the strings. Lilith stared at her indecisively, then finally headed back up the chamber stairs and locked the iron door.

Charlie just shook his head in wonder. "Oh my!" he chuckled. "You *are* good! Bravo. Well played, Milady. You achieved in five minutes what I couldn't have accomplish in five centuries."

Abelene smiled wickedly. "The way to unseat your opponent is to create doubt. She'll second-guess herself now and resent Rastaban if she hasn't already begun to do that already."

"I see. Divide and conquer. An old strategy—and still quite effective."

She sighed, "Perhaps, but maybe—for all I know—I planted a seed of goodness, if that is even possible."

"I wouldn't count on it. I think she's a lost cause."

"No, Charlie, I think you're wrong. Like all of us, she was born innocent. Once, she had goodness in her. Something hurt her deeply and changed her heart—twisted it."

"You have more faith in the living than I do, Milady. But as you know, I must remain neutral in my duties—maintaining the law of life and death—and yet..."

"Yes?" Abelene stood and gave him her full attention.

"Well, it's just that lately I find it more difficult to remain impartial. You have a special talent to look beyond one's evil actions and still see goodness in them. Perhaps it is the thing I love most about you."

Abelene was momentarily stunned to silence. "Charlie... did you just admit to loving me?"

The great dragon suddenly looked flustered. "Milady, what I meant is that I respect and admire you for your qualities."

"Oh, I see." Abelene cocked an eyebrow and suppressed a grin.

"Honestly, Lady Abelene, please don't read too deeply into anything I say!"

She stared at Charlie with growing affection and smiled. "I won't, my dear dragon. And besides, your secret is safe with me." She winked playfully.

Charlie sighed in frustration. "Honestly, Milady, you can be quite exasperating at times."

"I know, Charlie. But sometimes it's my job to do so." She giggled once and returned to her brocaded chair. She picked up her lute and began to pluck out a tune.

After a much-deserved rest, Azriel left his tent and sought out Magador. The dragon lay curled in a ball, resting. Mortimer lay beside him, sleeping lazily on Magador's flank. It was still dark, and the sun was at least an hour from rising. Magador opened one eye and closed it again.

"Hello, Cousin. You're up early."

"Couldn't sleep. There's too much going on in my head. I'm astounded by what I know today that I didn't know yesterday."

Magador rolled over, now fully awake and kicked Mortimer out of the way. The gargoyle grumbled and went back to sleep, fitfully dreaming.

"You were right, of course," Azriel continued. "I am beginning to remember. And now I know there are things I must ask of my friends—the people I love—and suddenly I'm afraid."

"Can you elaborate?"

Azriel looked down pensively. "The two worlds will be in position in less than two months. I am ready, but before that there are things I must do—things I must ask of the people I love. It's dangerous and people may get hurt. How do you risk the people you love—even to the point of sacrificing their lives?"

"In war there is always risk and sacrifice," Magador answered sagely. "One can only depend upon what the other is capable of giving, even to the point of that person's life. You are not responsible for the choices others make; you can only ask. If it results in one's death you must accept that as the cost of war."

"That seems cold and heartless."

"On the contrary, Cousin. If it's not worth the result, then it's not worth the sacrifice. That you must decide. You must ask yourself: what is the cost, overall, if you don't meet the challenge head-on? What will happen if the Clave wins and the worlds are never rejoined?"

"I think we both know that answer. Many more people will suffer or be enslaved, and many more will die. The problem is that most of the world isn't even aware any of this will happen."

"So it's recognition you want." Magador probed.

"No, it's not that at all." Azriel answered, annoyed. "I struggle with the same question I began with. Magick is fading in both worlds. I wonder if we'd be better off without it. It was magick that split Aralia in the first place."

"And it is magick that must reunite it," Magador said quickly. "But you forget something cousin. I... we dragons are a product of magick. Think of all the creatures you've met—like Norga and the Fenadoree, the Ferrishyn and all elvinkind. What about the world of the Faeries and Sprites? They will all fade as will dragons—and even men. It will all be for naught if you do not succeed."

"Then I have little choice."

"It would seem so, Cousin. But I must give fair warning. Do not ask of anyone what you would not be willing to do yourself."

Azriel sighed heavily. "Then I must now meet with Eltanin—and there is something I must ask of him. The unfortunate fact is that I can't be in two places at once. He has the harder job, but only I can do what needs to be done."

Magador cocked his head trying to figure out Azriel's cryptic response.

"Sorry, my friend. This time I do not wish to elaborate." Dejected, Azriel walked toward Eltanin's tent.

As the conjunction drew closer to merging Earth and Aralia, conditions in the between place began to change. The sun was no longer static in the sky but now began to follow the natural rhythm of night and day. The sun was just cresting the mountains, and like every day in the world between, it would be perfect. Birds sang joyfully to greet the morning, but it did little to ease the burden in Azriel's heart. When he approached the ornate red-and-gold woven tent, Azriel was about to announce himself when he heard Eltanin's voice from within.

"Enter, my boy. I've been expecting you," Eltanin said cheerfully.

Azriel pulled aside the flap and stepped inside. Not surprisingly, he found Eltanin and Nicodemus at a small table, drinking tea and sharing a plate of pastries. Eltanin waved his hand, and a porcelain cup appeared for Azriel along with a platter. The kettle lifted off the table obliging itself to pour Azriel a piping-hot cup of tea.

"Sit down, Azriel. Now what's on your mind?"

Azriel didn't answer. He took a sip and returned the cup to the table.

"Come on, Azriel, out with it. I know what happened—and who you are. I always knew but couldn't tell you. Like all your challenges, you had to find out on your own."

"That's not why I'm here, Grandfather. There is something I must ask of you. It's difficult—and dangerous. You might not even survive it. But I know of no other way."

Eltanin glanced at Nicodemus. Uncle Nick set the book he was reading on the table. Nick spoke quietly. "We are in dire times,

Azriel, and time is getting short. We do what is required of us—as you must do."

Azriel sat hunched over, his heart about to break. He peered up at them, tears forming in his eyes, and wiped them away with a sleeve. "I know where my mother is imprisoned—and my brother, Sariel, the Dragon of Death. Between Edward and Halimah, we were able to reconstruct the location of the Clave's lair."

"That's excellent news," Eltanin beamed.

"You might not think so after I tell you what I have in mind. I have a plan—but I need your help to pull it off. I need to confront my brother."

Eltanin nodded. "What would you have of me, my lord?"

"Lord?" Azriel winced. "I'm your grandson—sort of."

"True, but you preceded me. You were always the one who was yet to be. And here you are."

"Well, don't call me lord. It makes me uncomfortable."

Nicodemus chuckled. "Azriel, you will grow into it."

Eltanin smiled. "So what do you require?"

"I need a diversion—but one big enough that Rastaban won't be suspicious. I want you to challenge Rastaban to magickal combat. It needs to be in a somewhere remote—like near Uncle Nick's destroyed castle. He would likely bring the entire Clave with him so he can gloat over his victory."

"It's risky," Eltanin mused, rubbing his chin thoughtfully. "But he won't be able to resist the chance to destroy me. It should buy you time to do what you need. And what is that, by the way?"

"That is yet to be determined, Grandfather. I'll know when I finally meet my brother. That time has always been fated. Do you have a way of getting a message to Rastaban? It can't come from me—otherwise he will suspect something."

Eltanin nodded and smiled. "In fact, I do." He reached into the pocket of his robe and removed a single feather. He held it up for Azriel to see.

"What is that?"

"A piece of Lilith. She'll want it back." Eltanin grinned. "And she will not be able to resist the summoning."

"Good. Let me know when you're ready."

Eltanin waited on the Fairy Bridge spanning the creek that led to the small underground lair that had served as his home for so many years. He held the owl feather aloft and began chanting the summons that would compel Lilith to answer. As expected, a small pygmy owl perched on a tree opposite the bridge and hooted indignantly.

"You can show yourself, Lilith. You have my word that no harm will come to you."

She screeched and alit on the far side of the bridge, swirling into her human form. Prepared, he expected an immediate attack, but to his surprise, she addressed him with civility.

"Why have you summoned me, Eltanin? I thought it would please you to never see me again."

"Would that it were that easy, my dear." He paused and grimaced. "You are still beautiful in spite of your ordeal."

"And you are still a fool." Lilith glowered at him. "I am now mortal, my lord. You took that from me."

"I will not apologize, Lilith. You were too dangerous. Besides," He chuckled and wagged a finger at her, "you know as well as I do, that your immortality was gained by deceit. You used me—oh, yes—you played me, knowing full well I loved you too much to let you die."

"That is true, Eltanin, but not all of it was a lie."

"I wish with all my heart that I could believe you, Lilith, but one's heart doesn't change overnight, and yours has been corrupted by too much time and too little use."

"I met Abelene, my lord." she said, avoiding his gaze.

"Is she well?"

Lilith shrugged. "She is unharmed and I must say, the mother of the Dragon Lord is quite compelling. She could almost convince me to switch sides." She walked over the bridge to meet Eltanin. They now stood face to face.

"You, Lilith? Switch sides? Ah, but that is your way of doing things, isn't it? Like how you betrayed me and the Clave."

"Ancient history, Eltanin, though sometimes I wish I had chosen differently."

"Regrets?" The old wizard took her hand and placed an envelope in her palm.

"No," she smiled sadly. "Hindsight. Your Abelene has a way about her. She opened my eyes to a few things."

"And what would that be, my dear?"

"You don't know, do you..." Her brow creased with realization.

"Tell me, Lilith."

"... why I betrayed you and the Clave?"

Eltanin stood silent gazing into her liquid blue eyes waiting for her to continue. He looked away in pain, not wanting to remember her beauty.

"It was the time of the Imbolc Renewal and the lighting of the Winter Fire. You had promised me that I would be elevated to the Clave. You promised I would sit beside you in counsel." Tears came to her eyes. "You broke your word, and broke my heart. I loved you and hated you ever since. "Why? Because I am a woman—or because I was unworthy in your eyes?"

Eltanin tenderly brushed the tears from her cheeks. "Oh, Lilith, If you had only asked me, I would have told you. The reason is simply that you weren't ready. You were too eager for the power. You didn't understand that being inducted into the Clave, before it had been corrupted, wasn't a privilege—it was a burden of service to the people. If you had only been patient..."

"Twenty thousand years is a long time..." she murmured. "If I had only known the truth... Is it too late to say I'm sorry?"

"It is never too late..."

She looked down at the envelope in her hand. "What is this?"

"I want you to deliver that to Rastaban."

"Why?"

"That is between him and me. And don't try to open it, Lilith. It is magically sealed. The results of your prying would be... damaging. You're much prettier as an owl than as a toad."

"You know I am enslaved to him. I must do his bidding. He summoned me—he has power over me. Rastaban commands, and I must obey. But you could break that summoning. I know you have it in you."

"Yes I could—by killing him—but I won't. It would not serve my purpose… yet. I still love you, Lilith. I just don't trust you."

"Could you ever trust me again?"

"That would all depend on you."

Lilith stroked Eltanin's cheek tenderly. "You look tired."

"I have lived too long."

She nodded, pursing her lips. "I too, perhaps. But I suppose that doesn't matter anymore." She reached up and kissed the wizard gently on the lips. "I will deliver your message. Adieu, Eltanin." She gazed at him for a long moment, then turned away. She suddenly transformed into an owl. With the note in her beak, she vanished into the sky.

Eltanin gazed at the empty air where she had stood and sighed heavily. He, too, mired in the burden of many regrets, wiped a tear from his eye.

Chapter 22

Rastaban sat at the head of the conference table, idly swirling a snifter of Cognac as he read Eltanin's letter. Altais, Giausur, Thuban, and Edasich watched nervously as the Archwizard contemplated its contents. Lilith sat across from him, tapping her fingers, her gaze flicking from face to face as she measured their reactions. Rastaban tossed the letter onto the table and drained the last of the precious liquor. "I was expecting this... but not so soon."

"My lord?" Altais asked.

"Eltanin has challenged me to magickal combat three days hence." He smiled, anticipation curling at the corners of his mouth. "This could be our master stroke."

"What about the boy—Azriel?" Giausur asked.

"We will deal with him later. This, however, is personal."

Giausur countered, "I wouldn't dismiss the boy so readily, my lord. He has grown tremendously in power. He has already freed the Elementals. This world is on the road to recovery. If this trend continues, we will lose our hold on world power."

"You worry too much, my friend." Rastaban chuckled darkly. "I have a plan that will level the playing field. In the end, our boy wonder will not have much of a world to work with. He will not want to unite the worlds when one is so toxic it would ravage the other. Nothing rules a world faster than the threat of its extinction. And remember—we can use human technology against them."

"What does any of this have to do with Eltanin?" Lilith asked.

"Everything and nothing, my lovely little one." He slid the empty snifter across the table in silent command. She obediently rose and poured him another inch of Cognac. "You, Lilith, will be my second in combat."

Smiling, she placed the drink before her master, though she could not hide the disdain in her eyes. She was nobody's slave. "Why me, my lord?"

"Because, my sweet." He toyed with the collar of her velvet gown, then savagely yanked her down until they were nose to nose. He whispered, "My brothers are needed elsewhere. Do not ever question me in front of them again." Rastaban shoved her back, nearly sending her stumbling. Lilith glared at him, murder flashing in her eyes.

Rastaban stared her down with the cold eyes of a serpent until she finally looked away.

"Do you challenge me, girl? The only reason you haven't been banished back to the underworld is that you are still useful to me. That can swiftly change, my dear one."

Rastaban did not so much as lift a hand. He merely held her gaze and whispered a single word in the old tongue.

Suddenly Lilith clutched her throat, unable to breathe. The air itself seemed to tighten like an iron band around her neck. She gasped as her knees weakened, her body on the verge of collapse. Rastaban waited until she was nearly unconscious before releasing his hold.

"You failed me once when you were captured by Eltanin and lost your immortality. Now you are weak. Fragile. Do not fail me again, Lilith. You are to deliver a message. Our precious Abelene is in constant communication with her son. Convey to her that I will accept Eltanin's challenge. Tell her I will meet him in three days."

Holding back tears of rage, Lilith quickly exited the council chamber.

Eltanin chose Nicodemus to be his second for the duel. They arrived ahead of schedule a short distance from the grim ruins of Castle Wylusung. Not a stone remained unturned; so complete was the desolation. Only a part of the foundation still stood intact. Nicodemus stared at the rubble and sighed heavily. "I liked that castle. Pity what's become of it."

"My brother, it's only a castle." Eltanin chuckled and clapped him affectionately on the shoulder.

"But it was my home."

"Oh, all right, Nicodemus. Shall we begin?"

Together, they formed the sigils necessary for restoration and, in unison, intoned, "Refectio Maxima!"

In response, the remains of the castle began to separate, clearing a space. A single stone floated from the heap and settled at the base of the foundation. There was a sharp click as it locked against another stone.

Eltanin smiled, "It will take care of itself, though it may take some time."

A hawk screeched overhead and circled the ruins. Eltanin peered into the sky, shielding his eyes from the midday sun. He noticed an owl circling with it—normally the two would be natural enemies.

"They're here," Eltanin said, his voice uncharacteristically cold.

The two birds circled again and then landed a few yards from Eltanin and transformed.

Rastaban stood side by side with Lilith. He bowed formally to his former master while Lilith acknowledged Nicodemus with a slight nod, though fear lingered in her eyes. In formal combat, only Eltanin and Rastaban would spar; Lilith and Nicodemus were little more than observers sworn to non-interference. They were there to step in only if the other broke that oath. Rastaban's choice of Lilith as his second was particularly cruel to both her and Eltanin, fully aware of their history. He was making an obvious attempt to keep Eltanin off balance and to control—if not outright torture—Lilith.

Rastaban smiled pleasantly—too pleasantly. "Hello, my old friend."

Eltanin enunciated each word with scorn. "Old friend? We were brothers. What you did was unpardonable."

"Eltanin," he said with lazy condescension, "I never asked your forgiveness." He looked beyond Eltanin to the castle. The first layer of foundation had nearly formed and floated into place to complete the first ring.

Rastaban chortled. "Oh, Nicodemus. You were always the sentimental type. Such a very human weakness." His laughter curdled into disgust.

Nicodemus responded in kind. "Perhaps, magician, you could learn a little humanity. It might improve that disposition of yours."

Rastaban growled under his breath at the insult. "Magician? Do I look like I'm here to pull rabbits from a hat?" He flicked two fingers in a careless gesture, and suddenly Nicodemus was transformed into a wild desert hare. Eltanin sighed in annoyance, rolling his eyes. With another idle twitch of his hand, Nicodemus was transformed back. He glared at Rastaban. "Enough of this," Eltanin said. "We did not come here to converse. We are long past words, my brother. Take your best shot!"

"It will be my pleasure!"

With a series of plasma balls and lightning strikes, the battle began.

It began as an itch—an odd sensation settling into Azriel's mind. Away from his comrades, he needed to reflect on the changes coursing through his body. Camille knew he needed space, as did the others. Having transformed into his higher form of a dragon, Azriel flew several miles from the encampment and alighted on the crest of a mountain. He carried a leather pouch containing the crystal and the dragon scale, and Errin-lil hung from a strap across his shoulder, ready for the task ahead. But the sensation of a summoning waxed stronger within him, setting him on edge. This was new, and Azriel didn't know how to respond. He circled the mountaintop until he could sense the direction of its pull. It seemed strongest in the west. Following his dragon instincts, he flew west for nearly an hour until the summons grew so strong he was forced to alight upon another peak. At the apex lay the blasted remains of an extinct volcano, and within—hidden from the outside world—a dazzling light nearly blinded him. He felt an irresistible compulsion to investigate. There was nothing threatening about the light; in fact, it filled Azriel with unexpected peace as he shifted back to his elfin form. The light began to shift, coalescing into something almost recognizable as a living form, though Azriel could not discern exactly what it was.

"Do not fear me, my son." The light spoke gently.

"Who are you?" Azriel asked.

"I am the Mother. The question you should be asking, my son, is who you are!"

The light seemed to radiate an emotion of amusement at Azriel's confusion. She continued. "You were destined from the beginning to bring balance to all existence. You are the one who must restore the worlds to one. You, my son, are the culmination of millions of years of labor in the heavens. You are the quintessence, the merging of fire, water, air, and earth—the very essence of all life itself, but there is a price."

"And what would that be?" Azriel asked, suddenly afraid.

"You are the protector and defender of all life; therefore you are forbidden to deliberately take life."

"Well that seems easy enough."

She laughed lightly. "Your naiveté is forgivable. You must understand, my son, that the ones borne of me must take a certain role and prove themselves worthy. Your brothers and sisters rule over each element, but are all equal and opposite. Your opposite is the lord of death, the gateway to the netherworld as you are the gateway of birth to the living worlds. You may defend and maintain, but killing is forbidden to you, as giving life is forbidden to your brother."

"What if I kill in defense of those I love?"

"You may defend, and if some die as a result, then that is an acceptable consequence, but you may not deliberately murder."

"I have no plans of deliberately slaying anyone."

"Ah, you say that now, my son, but loss and grief can push one to extremity. You will be tested soon. How you respond will determine who you are."

"What would happen if I fell to the sway of revenge?"

"You would prove yourself unworthy. The balance will be shifted toward darkness. Human and Elf will forever be at war. Death will reign supreme over life. The balance would be broken. For one of elemental power, yours is a grave responsibility."

"Then I am truly an Elemental?"

"Not quite. You are a guardian as your brother Sariel is."

"Sariel?"

"Yes, son. That is his true name. He is the guardian of death as you are the Guardian of life. You had a mortal birth thus your destiny is different from that of an elemental. My elemental children are the embodiment of life, so it falls to you to be their protector as well. Although they are immortal in the way of the gods, they can still be damaged beyond repair. You must dispel the ignorance of the races that have hurt this world."

"What about Sariel? Surely he hasn't had a mortal birth."

"True, but he was never born of me to give life. His existence derives from the necessity of death. It is perfect balance. As a guardian he holds as much power as you, but of the Elementals there can only be four. Beware, Azriel. You have all the potential of power, but you are young yet and untested. And you are not immune to being killed. You are immortal, yes, but even an immortal can be slain."

"Mother, I have spent my life in my elfin form. I love a woman. Is that forbidden?"

"No," the light said gently, "It is love that defines you. You may live your life as you choose, but always remember that your responsibility as king and Guardian must always come first."

"It seems an awful lot to juggle." Azriel mused.

"It takes wisdom."

"Could my responsibility as a Guardian ever pass from me?"

"It is always your choice to reach your full potential. You were destined from the beginning. That is why you were put to the test in learning the names of your brothers and sisters, why you needed to learn the secrets of immortality. It was all so you could become something more."

"I never asked for any of this."

"Nevertheless, it is still your destiny to complete. There is something else you should know. It's about the one you love."

"Camille?"

"Yes. She is in mortal danger. What you decide will determine if she will survive her ordeal. Now my son, the time is right for you to put your plan into motion. Eltanin has engaged Rastaban in battle. Go now to meet your brother. You and I will speak again someday."

The cavern was dimly lit by small sconces that emitted weak flames. The reflections danced off the walls, casting deep shadows.

Azriel had realized that he no longer needed the dream orb. His dragonsight was now fully alive within him, and he had easily translocated to the chamber where his mother had been imprisoned. In the ruddy light, two nearly transparent pyramids sat nestled side by side. Azriel stood motionless, sensing the space, testing for any traps. There didn't seem to be any, but he was disturbed by one section of cave rock in which were embedded chains and manacles, spiked racks, and other instruments of cruel torture. In some, the morbid remains of the tortured still lay where they died, their flesh long gone to dust. Only their bones remained. Obviously the Clave's depravities went far beyond mere lust for control. Azriel placed a spell of concealment and silence over himself and strode toward the Carcer Eternis, housing his mother. She lay asleep on a divan. His heart ached to speak with her and embrace her again, but this wasn't the time. Time, however, would be his ally. Empowered by the stone in its pommel, Errin-lil existed outside of time. Azriel unsheathed his sword and touched it to the Carcer Eternis. Like water, he passed through the barrier. He had the power to completely destroy the prison, but that wouldn't serve his purpose yet. With a slight motion of his hand, he whispered a spell over Abelene.

"Soma!"

Her sleep deepened and would keep her unconscious for several hours. No sound, touch, or movement could awaken her. Azriel stood over her sleeping form and gently stroked her face. With affection, he bent down and kissed her on the forehead. "Soon, Mom, you will be free of this place, but not just yet. You're safer in here."

Azriel moved back to the outside perimeter of the Carcer Eternis, fully aware that the prison keeping her in captivity would also protect her from harm in the upcoming battle.

He now stood facing the Dragon of Death. Charlie, as Abelene had often referred to him, lay sleeping, but soon was roused by Azriel's presence. He stood to his full height and faced his opposite. They stared wordlessly at each other until Azriel finally spoke and drew his sword.

"Sariel—my brother. It would seem the time of reckoning is finally at hand."

"Ah, you know my true name. Do you intend to kill me, brother?"

"Not yet, though you know I have the power to end your life."

"Then engage me, Brother. But I warn you—it will not be that easy."

"What I decide depends on you." Azriel sheathed his sword.

"What is it that you want?"

"Will Camille die when we attack Rastaban?"

"Yes."

"You're sure of this?"

"I have seen it," Sariel answered sadly.

"Then I must prevent her from joining us in battle."

"You cannot prevent the inevitable. She will die a more horrible death if you try to prevent it, one in which you can do nothing. Her death is fated."

Azriel's ire rose. "You imply that I can prevent it. Can you elaborate?"

"No! I've already revealed too much."

"But if I kill you, she will live?"

"You may kill me, but that will not abolish the Law of Death. It is immutable—something both Eltanin and Rastaban failed to understand. Another would replace me—the Mother would make it so. So you must choose, Brother. You must trust me."

Azriel wept. Hope now seemed like a hollow pursuit.

Sariel smiled tenderly. "However, there may be a way out of this—a way for you to cheat death, Son of Luminance."

Azriel looked up and read the sincerity in Sariel's eyes. He removed the dragon scale from his satchel and unsheathed Errin-lil, holding both aloft, the sword in his right hand and the scale in his left. With a mighty stroke, the sword passed through the Carcer Eternis and the prison vanished with a flash of light.

"Let me heal you." With his sword back in its scabbard, Azriel held the scale in both hands. Charlie bowed lower to allow Azriel access to his heart. Placing the scale over the wound, it gently settled into the raw tear that had tormented Charlie for untold years. Azriel placed his hand over the spot and allowed his own essence to flow into it, mending the breach that had deprived the Dragon of Death his full power.

"That feels wonderful, my brother. What has changed your mind about me?"

Azriel smiled. "My mother—mostly. She's quite fond of you, and for that I must rely on her judgment and trust that in the end you will aid me."

Charlie looked over at Abelene lying on the divan with sadness and regret. "Soon the endgame will begin, and then I will be free to return to my domain. I will sorely miss her."

"I know. I'm not blind, brother, but there would be no resolution to your dilemma. You both live in different worlds. For her to be with you, she would have to die. Is that what you want?"

"No, Azriel. I wish her a long life. And a long life it will be. Her time of departing this world is a long way off."

"I'm sorry, Sariel. I know it's difficult, but we both have our duties." Azriel removed his sword again and touched it to the manacles that held the dragon by the ankle and throat, freeing him from the clutches of the Clave. The magick dissipated to be absorbed by Errin-lil.

"I am not leaving, brother. I still have a score to settle."

"I know." Azriel smiled wickedly. "That's why I have a plan." He removed a crystal from his pouch and placed it beside Charlie. With a brilliant flash, Azriel transformed into his dragon self. Azriel proudly faced his brother and grinned in the fashion of dragons. "Now here's what I have in mind, Sariel."

"I really prefer Charlie," the dark dragon chuckled. "The name seems to bring great delight to Abelene."

"Okay, Charlie." Azriel whispered his plan as Charlie listened. Soon the great dragon of death had to contain his laughter as he considered Azriel's plan.

"Oh, that's rich! That's rich indeed, but how are we to convince Rastaban that the Carcer Eternis is still active?"

Azriel pointed to the crystal. "Worry not, my brother. Rastaban may be a great wizard, but I'm a better wizard than he will ever be."

Azriel returned to his elfin form and formed sigils over Charlie. The chains that had held him moved back in place, but they were unlocked. Casting a shimmer spell over the manacles, it appeared as if they exuded magick. The spell was so elementary that Rastaban would never suspect it. The shimmer spell concealed the fact that they were unlocked. Azriel then placed his hand over Charlie's heart. It gave all the appearance of a wound that seeped blood.

"Now watch this!" Azriel said proudly. He held his hand over the crystal, and it began to expand. Soon it reached the proportions of Charlie's former prison, identical in shape and size, mimicking the Carcer Eternis that had held the Dragon of Death bound for twenty thousand years.

Alarmed, Charlie cried out, "Brother, do you intend to keep me imprisoned yet again?"

Azriel laughed. "No, not at all. This is not what you think, but if it fooled you, it will certainly fool Rastaban. I call it the Carcer Bogus! It's a fake."

Charlie cautiously touched the glowing wall and his wing easily passed through the shimmer. Pulling it back in, he examined his claws and wiggled them. "Hmm, quite remarkable! I'd say you are a most talented wizard."

"So are we agreed then?"

"You have my word, brother. I will play my part a little while longer." He looked down pensively. "And I will do what I can concerning the other matter."

"Thanks, Charlie. Now I must leave. Rastaban could return at any moment. He will sense my presence, and the plan will fall to pieces."

Azriel turned and was surprised to see Abelene facing him from the other side of her cell, lying casually on the divan, head propped up on an elbow. She smiled deviously.

"Did you think that I would be so easily fooled by a soma spell?"

"Mom, I'm sorry. I just need your patience a little while longer."

"I know, son." She beamed a smile. "I heard everything. It's a good plan."

"Then you're not angry with me?"

"Of course not. I'm proud of you! And, by the way, you're a most handsome dragon! Now you had best leave before you get caught here."

"Soon, Mom, and all this will be over!" Azriel smiled and vanished from the chamber.

Eltanin and Rastaban pummeled one another in rapid succession, their spells colliding midair in flashes of light and thunder. Neither could gain advantage, each countering the other with equal mastery.

Rastaban thrust out his hands and released a barrage of twirling blades that shrieked toward his adversary, but Eltanin deflected them with a sweep of his staff, and the knives clattered harmlessly to the stone.

Without hesitation, Eltanin murmured a multiplication charm. The fallen blades shuddered, rose, and multiplied tenfold before streaking back at Rastaban in a whirling cloud of steel. For every knife he deflected, ten more sprang into being until the storm nearly engulfed him.

"Maxima Reducto!"

At once the blades shrank, dwindling to slivers and then to dust, their weight lost to the wind, which scattered them into nothing.

Eltanin answered with another assault, thrusting his palms forward as a throng of venomous scorpions poured forth and surged toward Rastaban in a living tide. Yet Rastaban merely released a pulse of white-hot plasma, and the swarm ignited midair, falling away as blackened ash.

"I'm impressed, my former master," Rastaban called with dark amusement. "You remain a respectable wizard. But you are still outclassed."

From his pocket, he withdrew a crystal sphere and lifted it to eye level.

"Now... contend with that."

The orb pulsed with a faint inner light and then grew still.

Eltanin waited for the next attack, but none came. Frowning, he extended his senses outward—

—and suddenly his face paled.

"No... Fool. What have you done?"

Rastaban tapped his cheek with feigned innocence. "Nothing so dramatic. Merely a small nudge. The United States launches against Russia, Russia answers England, China answers Korea, Iran answers Israel... such fragile creatures, these humans. It takes so little to send them scrambling toward annihilation."

Understanding dawned like a blow. Across the globe, missiles were already rising, their fiery trails arcing toward distant horizons while counterstrikes answered in kind.

"Rastaban, this is beneath even you!"

"It doesn't take much for humanity to destroy itself," Rastaban replied lightly. "I simply helped them along."

Eltanin closed his eyes and expanded his mind outward until it encompassed the entire world. He saw every trajectory, every warhead, every ticking second. With immense effort, he began forcing them off course, bending their paths upward, away from the earth and toward the waiting sun.

The strain was immediate and terrible.

Sweat beaded on his brow as he fought to maintain control, yet while his concentration stretched thin, Rastaban struck without mercy.

Fireballs, plasma spheres, and lightning bolts crashed against Eltanin's wards in rapid succession. Blows that would have been trivial under normal circumstances now battered him mercilessly, for he dared not break focus.

Burned and staggered, he absorbed the onslaught while still guiding the missiles higher—ever higher—until at last the sky was clear.

Only then did his strength fail him, and he collapsed to the ground.

Rastaban approached slowly, his hands curling like talons.

"And now, my old friend… you die."

From his palms spilled a stream of black lightning, not to scorch, but to drain, to consume, to strip the life from Eltanin's very soul.

Lilith and Nicodemus stood aghast as Rastaban unleashed a relentless barrage of fireballs, plasma spheres, and lightning bolts toward Eltanin, the air itself shuddering with each impact.

Ordinarily such attacks would have been trivial for him to deflect, yet now he could not spare even a fraction of his strength, for all his concentration was fixed upon the heavens, guiding the missiles from their courses and forcing them outward into the cold vastness of space. Each spell struck him unchecked, burning through his wards and battering his body, until the old wizard staggered beneath the assault.

"And now, my old friend," Rastaban said with icy certainty, "you will die."

He arched his back and spread his clawed hands, and from his palms poured a stream of black lightning, not meant to scorch but to drain, to leech the very life from Eltanin's soul.

Lilith felt her breath catch in her throat.

By oath she and Nicodemus were bound to non-interference while the formal duel played out, and for a terrible moment she understood that they were meant to do nothing—meant to stand aside and watch him fall.

Her hands trembled, then slowly curled into fists.

Rage, long buried and long denied, rose within her like a tide.

Before Nicodemus could stop her, she lifted her arms and began weaving sigils through the air, her fingers tracing the ancient forms with desperate precision as she gathered the threads of time itself into her grasp. He moved toward her at once, knowing what such interference would cost, but she caught his eye and shook her head once, a silent plea that needed no words.

Let me do this.

Then she spoke a command.

"Tempus Tardis!" She shouted, effectively slowing time relative to the present.

The black torrent faltered, its terrible current slowing as though forced through thickened glass, sparks stuttering and dying where moments before they had raged. Even Rastaban's movements dragged, heavy and distorted, as though time itself resisted him.

"Quickly, Nicodemus," she urged, her voice already strained. "Help him. Get him out of here."

"Then you must come with us," he insisted.

"I cannot," she said softly. "Rastaban still holds sway over me. If I follow, he will find me, and I will only endanger you all. The spell will not hold him for long. Go—while you still can."

Nicodemus looked at her with naked sorrow, for they both knew what would follow once the spell collapsed. Yet there was no time left for argument. He lifted Eltanin across his shoulders, cast one last lingering glance her way, and murmured, "I'm sorry," before vanishing with the dream orb in a shimmer of light.

For a brief, fragile instant the battlefield stood unnaturally still.

Then time rushed back like a breaking wave.

Rastaban tore free of the spell with a howl of fury that shook the cavern walls.

"You," he thundered. "You robbed me of my victory!"

"I could not stand by and watch you murder him," Lilith replied, her voice hoarse but steady. "If anyone was to defeat you, it should have been Eltanin—not this. So kill me," she spat. "Send me back to the underworld where I belong."

Rastaban approached her slowly, his gaze burning with cold hatred.

"That would be too merciful, my faithless harridan."

Instead of casting a spell, he seized her by the throat with one hand and lifted her from the ground, crushing the air from her lungs as darkness crept at the edges of her vision. When her knees buckled, he loosened his grip only enough to keep her upright, prolonging the torment with deliberate cruelty.

Gasping, she forced herself to meet his eyes.

"So this is what you truly are," she rasped. "Eltanin was right about you. I do not hate you—I loathe you. Go on. Kill me. I dare you."

"No," Rastaban said quietly. "I have something far worse prepared."

Before she could summon even the faintest defense, his fist lashed out and struck her squarely across the jaw, and the world dissolved into blackness as she collapsed senseless to the stone.

376

Chapter 23

Abelene was awakened by the sound of scuffling a short distance from her cell. Enraged, Rastaban threw Lilith against the stone wall, nearly knocking the wind from her lungs. Immobilized by some form of spell, she was unable to counter his attack. With little ceremony, he clamped her wrists and ankles into the manacles hanging from the chamber wall. Lilith's head hung down in misery, unable to invoke any magick. The manacles themselves were inscribed with runes that would prevent her escape as well as dampen any spell she wanted to cast. Her situation seemed bleak and hopeless.

Rastaban strode past Abelene, ignoring her as she stood to confront him. But her voice compelled him to stop.

"Rastaban," She said with a touch of mockery. "If this is how you treat your friends, I pale to think what you do to your enemies."

"Oh, so true, Milady. But she is no friend. She has betrayed me."

"Why does that surprise you? She betrayed you and the Clave over twenty thousand years ago. Does a leopard change its spots?"

"I thought this time it would be different, but that is no matter. I must prepare for your son, Abelene. He will be coming soon, and I must be ready."

"Ready to die?" she asked with feigned innocence.

Amused, he shook his head, "Hardly. It is time to settle scores—the Clave against the Order of the Ankh. We will finally put to rest the future of the world—that is to say, *this* world. Azriel will either join me or he will die. Either way, with him neutralized, the conjunction of the two planets will arrive and will pass; this world will be preserved in the way I see fit."

"Is that how you see it?" Abelene asked in awe. "You truly think that your way will preserve this world? Your way will destroy both worlds, and your overconfidence will also destroy you. You will never defeat my son. He is stronger and more powerful than you, and he has something you will never have."

"Oh, and what is that, Milady?"

"Wisdom."

As was her custom, Abelene walked back to her chair and made herself busy. This was her way of dismissing Rastaban. It also, she knew, infuriated her adversary more than if she engaged him in a battle of wits, in a sense, saying that he wasn't worth her time.

Rastaban, his face red with suppressed rage, left the chamber and locked the iron door.

Now that Rastaban was gone, Abelene rose from her chair and faced Lilith, who was just rousing. The woman shook her chains, trying to release herself, but she knew it was a futile attempt. She read the runes and knew her efforts would be hopeless.

"Why did you do it, Lilith?" Abelene asked with tenderness. As much as Lilith was an enemy, she felt pity for the woman's plight.

"I couldn't watch Eltanin die. He taught me everything I know."

"So in the end, you have a conscience." Abelene stated, nodding her head. "But you must have known it would mean your end."

"True," Lilith said, shaking her head sadly, "I tried to goad Rastaban into killing me so I could return to the underworld where I belong."

"But he didn't take the bait." Charlie interrupted.

"No, my Lord, he did not. Instead it will please him to watch me starve." She held up her manacles. "These are most evil runes. They will maintain my life, denying me death even as I wither away to nothing. Take me, my Lord—please!" She wept.

"I cannot." Charlie said. "It is not your time. Even if I could, you laid waste to the underworld. I would be a fool to do so."

She looked up at the great dragon in misery. "I understand. Instead I will suffer. It is not in the nature of Rastaban to forgive. I just thought you might have a bigger heart."

Charlie answered sternly. "When has having a heart played into anything, Lilith? Where was your heart when you bred demons in my home? Did you have mercy on those you distorted into evil? Think on that, woman."

Abelene was surprised at Charlie's harshness. She had never heard him speak so unkindly. "My lord," she said. "Lilith has taken a good turn. There is hope for her. She saved Eltanin."

"That remains to be seen, Lady Abelene. One good deed doesn't wipe away thousands of evil deeds. Also, Eltanin and I still have a score to settle. I blame him for my captivity."

"But it was not he who captured you—it was the Clave."

"But he summoned me," Charlie snapped.

Abelene countered, "To save the world and to prevent the Clave from destroying humanity. He may have been duped; perhaps he is even a fool, but his heart was in the right place."

"I'm still prevented from interfering in the matter of Lilith, but you're not, so help her if you must." Charlie turned around and sat heavily. His shoulders were hunched as if he were brooding. Surprised at his aloofness, Abelene arched an eyebrow and then turned to Lilith. "How can I help you?"

Lilith hung her head, crying. "I don't think you can. You're trapped here as well."

"Oh, I have my ways." Abelene smiled.

"It's hopeless. I'm hungry and thirsty. Your magick will not work outside of the Carcer Eternis."

Abelene answered slyly, "There are other forms of magick. Watch and see."

Abelene crouched on the ground and whistled a series of squeals and chirps. A few minutes later, a rather large dark gray rat scurried over to greet her. The tip of his tail was bent at an awkward angle. The rat chirped a greeting.

"Hello, little one." Abelene smiled. "Would you grant me a boon?"

The rat chattered in response.

"Yes, little brother, I know she is the one who broke your tail, but she is my friend and needs your help. She is sorry she did that to you."

It squealed angrily, pounding the ground with its front paws.

"I promise she won't hurt you anymore." She turned to Lilith. "Tell him you're sorry. Do it!" she ordered.

She looked doubtfully at Abelene but complied. "Master Rat, I apologize for the damage I did to your tail. I would fix it if I could."

Abelene added, "See, she means it. Now would you and your friends bring her food? She would be grateful to you."

The rat chirruped a few more times then disappeared into a hidden crevice in the rock face.

Lilith stared at Abelene with a mixture of awe and disgust. "You speak… rat?"

Abelene giggled at her reaction. "Of course. They're much easier to reason with than wizards."

"You're a remarkable woman. I see why Rastaban keeps you around."

"It's more my choice than his."

Lilith cocked her head at the strange response.

Abelene added, "I place myself where I can be of the most use."

Lilith's eyes widened with understanding. "You being here was no accident. You let Altais take you."

"Now you get it." Abelene giggled.

Lilith stared at her with humility. "You told the rat that I was your friend. Do you really see me as such?"

Abelene grinned coyly. "There's an old adage that says *the enemy of my enemy is my friend*. You struck a blow at my enemy, putting yourself in jeopardy. I will not soon forget that. Nor do I think my petulant friend over here will either. Isn't that true, Charlie… Charlie?"

The great dragon didn't respond, nor could he. A special task demanded his attention. In a trance, Charlie could not be reached.

Azriel, Nicodemus, and Amaryllis took turns keeping vigil at Eltanin's bedside. He had not stirred from the aftermath of his battle with Rastaban. Azriel had been sitting for at least four hours when Nicodemus came to relieve him. They spoke in hushed whispers.

"Will he return to us?" Azriel asked.

"That is up to Eltanin. The attack on him was vicious. Rastaban used a forbidden life-drain spell on him—not that I'm surprised. He has no scruples."

"Why didn't you counter it?"

"That's the difficult thing about magickal combat. There is a code of honor all wizards must follow."

"Rastaban has no honor," Azriel fumed.

"Lilith was his second. If I had even attempted to intervene, she would have been within her rights to attack me. Like it or not, she is a powerful sorceress. But a strange thing happened, Azriel. She instead attacked Rastaban, allowing me to escape with Eltanin. He almost didn't make it back alive."

"Uncle Nick, I've tried to remedy Eltanin's condition. I've tried everything. I've used a regeneration spell, a vitality spell—nothing's working."

Nicodemus sighed heavily. "I know, son. It's as if Eltanin is resisting all our attempts."

"But I'm the Lord of Light. I should be able to do this."

"That's true, Azriel." Nicodemus placed a comforting hand on his shoulder. "But sometimes death is stronger. Now all we can do is hope."

Eltanin fell into a deep, restful sleep—deeper than he had known in many a year—and surrendered himself to the dream. He awoke rejuvenated, vitality flowing through him. His body was healed of all mortal wounds. He rose from bed and left his ornate tent, walking toward the glade. Oddly, however, he found that all the other tents were gone, as if everyone had packed up and left him alone. Only the Gazebo remained as the anchor for the Place Between.

Eltanin in no way resented them, since he knew that the actions Azriel and the Order must take were crucial to the survival of both worlds. They knew he would be in a safe place. And yet Eltanin did not know how long he had remained ailing in bed. The sun was bright and warm on his flesh, and it felt good. He decided to take a leisurely stroll and walked with no particular destination.

After nearly an hour, he saw someone in the distance he didn't recognize. It was odd that there should be a stranger here. Warily, he approached the man. The stranger was tall and ruggedly handsome, with finely chiseled features, high cheekbones, and a shock of black hair peppered with gray.

He approached, smiled graciously, then bowed with respect. "Do not fear me, Master Eltanin."

"Why should I fear you, stranger?"

"My friend, we are not strangers."

"And yet, I don't have any recollection of you, and I have lived a great many years."

"Indeed you have, and now it is time for you to rest from your labors."

"Ah, I see." Eltanin rubbed his chin, somewhat uncertain.

The man spread his arms as if to embrace the old wizard, but suddenly transformed into a black dragon with jeweled yellow eyes.

"I understand now. You have come for me, Sariel. I am dying."

The dragon morphed back into his human form. "You are not dying, Eltanin—you're already there." Sariel waved his hand and suddenly they were back in Eltanin's tent. "See for yourself."

Eltanin looked at the bed where he appeared to be sleeping peacefully. Somehow he wasn't troubled by it. If anything, he was at peace and eager to see what lay beyond his life.

"Now you may choose," Sariel said amiably.

"Choose what?"

"The nature of your work from here and into the future."

"Are you saying that I may be reborn into another life?"

"That is always an option." Sariel conceded.

"I'm not sure I like the sound of that. I would be reborn into forgetfulness. Everything I have learned and experienced will be gone."

"For most mortals, that would be true, but not for you, Master Wizard. You have as many millennia as some people have years. That is not easily erased. You will return when you are needed many years from now, and you *will* remember. The game is not over."

Sariel waved an arm and the tent disappeared to be replaced by three marble archways, elegant and honed with perfection.

"Now you may choose."

Eltanin smiled like a child as he peeked into each one. All seemed to house a new adventure. All seemed to beckon with a grand invitation. Eltanin peered over at Sariel and chuckled. "They look so compelling, but I think I like this one."

"Then go in peace. You will know when you are needed again."

"Before I do, might I ask a question?"

"You may."

"I was always certain that you would have a score to settle with me for raising you allowing your capture. Do you not wish to avenge yourself upon me?"

"No, my friend. Death is the certainty all mortals must face. You have faced it without fear. And there's another thing…"

"Yes?" Eltanin asked.

"Indeed. There is the matter of Abelene."

"How does she fit into all of this?"

"She has changed me. Abelene is quite a persuasive woman."

"So I've heard."

"Soon I will return to the Underworld. It is what I have desired, and yet now I am reluctant to leave the world of men. I would never admit this to anyone but perhaps you. You are wise and yet you are also a fool. You more than anyone would understand, since I too have become a fool."

"Actually, I don't understand, Sariel."

"I love her." he admitted.

"I see. That is a dilemma. Is not love forbidden to you?"

"Not necessarily forbidden, but not recommended. For once I am in a place that has no solution, and it grieves me."

"Does she love you?"

"She has not come forth and said so, for she has the wisdom to know that such an admission would hurt us both and so it remains unspoken. But all her actions tell me that she does."

"Well, my friend, it would seem you have but three choices. You can try to reconcile both worlds by staying with her while still maintaining your duties. That would be a most difficult choice, for the worlds of the living and the dead cannot be easily reconciled.

"Your next choice would be to give up your godhood and become mortal, but that choice would not be up to you. That can only be granted by the Great Mother Dragon who created you."

Sariel sighed. "That would be impossible, since there is no one worthy to replace me. What is my third choice?"

Eltanin placed his hand gently on Sariel's shoulder. "Perhaps the hardest choice of all, my friend: you can never see her again."

Sariel looked stricken. "My life will become bitter and unbearable. I blame Rastaban for my captivity, and now I damn him for ever bringing Abelene into my presence."

"He has much to answer for," Eltanin answered gravely. "His transgressions are not only against the many people he has murdered, but against life itself. He has distorted this world with unnatural death, not the peaceful release that you offer. I had hoped that I could strike a final blow against him. Is it possible to have a little more time?"

"I understand your desire, but no, it is already done. Your body has returned to dust, and I cannot break the law of death. Besides, that task is not for you, but for my brother, Azriel. He is the one who must heal this world."

"I see. Then I suppose I must leave it in his capable hands." Eltanin placed a hand on the marble archway that led to another world and peered inside with a boyish smile.

Sariel nodded. "Go, Eltanin and take your rest. You will not be bored."

The Master Wizard was about to pass through the portal when he hesitated and held up his finger. "Sariel, with your permission, there is one more thing I need to do."

Azriel found himself by the Fairy Bridge. He sat at the bank of the deep stream, fishing for trout. He knew he was dreaming, since he had no recollection of translocating from the Place Between. A rare break from the turmoil that had become the norm of his life, he sat enjoying the solitude when he heard a plop and a splash.

Several feet away, Pog stood angling with a makeshift old pole, tugging slightly at the line to entice a fish.

"Mornin' laddie!" Pog bowed and smiled broadly.

Azriel felt a surge of relief at seeing the old troll. "Pog! I'm sure glad to see you!"

"Likewise, laddie!"

"I know I'm dreaming, so why are you here?"

"To snag a fish—a big one!"

"Then you must be feeling better."

"On the contrary, laddie. I'm not."

Azriel scratched his head and swatted at a mosquito. "What do you mean?"

"Ah, laddie, yer still a wanker and dense as stone. I've bitten the big one, my boy—kicked the bucket, bought the farm, I'm pushin' up daisies, shuffled off me mortal coil. In other words, laddie, I'm dead as a doornail!"

"You can't be serious."

"Serious as a heart attack, I'm afraid."

"But you can't die. You're Eltanin, the greatest wizard alive."

Pog chuckled. "Aye, ye mean the greatest wizard that ever was. Now *you* are."

Azriel paused and peered into the water in contemplation. "So you've come to say goodbye?"

"Aye, and more. I've come to give ye fair warnin'. The fate of the worlds lies solely in yer hands, laddie. Soon ye will face off with Rastaban. He's corrupt and clever—very clever! He'll use every trick in the book to get at you. Worse, he doesn't want to defeat ye but completely demoralize ye, and destroy ye. It is his way."

"Do you have any other good news?"

"Sarcasm won't do right now, boy. Ye need to listen to me. The other wizards are powerful too. Giasur, Thuban, Edasich and Altais are great, but not as mighty as Rastaban. Draconis is more powerful than it has ever been, but if you cut off the head, the rest of the serpent will die. But do not underestimate Altais. For all his power, he is a coward, which makes him just as dangerous as Rastaban, perhaps even more so."

"So what should I do?" Azriel felt his heart quiver.

"First you must silence your fear. It will not serve ye. By all rights, with my passin', you're the rightful heir to the Clave. That's yer strength, and that's what Rastaban fears most. He has no love for life, but only loves his power. But he will attempt to use what you love most to crush ye.

"Now keep in mind, laddie, that yer friends are most capable wizards and will have yer back, but they're green and untried in battle. You must warn them to be alert and aware of all the subtle tricks the Clave will use. Trust Nicodemus and take his advice when he gives it."

"I will, Pog."

"One more thing," Pog offered, "Lilith has been imprisoned by Rastaban in the same place yer mother and Sariel are kept. Free her."

Azriel stared at Pog as if he were a demon. "Why would I want to do that?"

"I sense that she is a changed woman. You might find in her a surprising ally."

"Why should I trust her?"

"Because, laddie, I do."

Pog suddenly felt a tug on his line. He yanked up and was immediately met with resistance. He struggled, battling the current, and laughed with delight. "Aye, laddie! I've got a big one!" He pulled and reeled one way and then the other. Whatever he had snagged was huge and continued the battle, but ultimately the creature broke water. Except that it wasn't a fish at all. Once the object crested, it floated into Pog's hand. Undamaged, Eltanin's staff glistened in the sunlight. The ornately carved dark wood was crowned with a black orb with a golden inner radiance. Pog unceremoniously handed it to Azriel.

"This belongs to you now. Let it choose who it will, laddie. I fashioned it with the power to give and to take away."

"Life and death?"

"Nay, nothin' quite so profound, but it could come in handy. Er, it'll speak to ye when the time is right, in a manner o' speakin'.

Now I suppose I must be off. Give me a hug there, laddie, would ye?"

They embraced as Pog gently pounded Azriel's back. Pog rested the fishing pole over his shoulder, and without further delay, strode off and crossed the Faerie Bridge. Azriel watched Pog stride toward the dense thicket and disappear into the undergrowth.

Camille announced herself before entering Eltanin's tent. Nicodemus was seated beside the bed, hunched over, his back turned to her. When he turned, tears were in his eyes.

"Uncle Nick, what's wrong?"

He motioned to the vacant bed and shook his head sadly. "Eltanin is gone."

Not understanding, she responded, "Where did he go?"

"Child, he has passed to his next existence."

"You mean he's dead? I thought he was immortal."

"Even immortality has its limits, Camille."

"But where is his body?" she asked, poking through the sheets. Only his robe and clothing remained.

"Well," Nicodemus sighed, "When one has lived as long as Eltanin, it is the essence of Magick that keeps his mortal body alive. When he died and the magick left him, there was nothing to keep his body from deteriorating into dust. It is fitting that nothing remains but memory."

Tears welled up in her eyes. "Azriel will be devastated." She fell onto Uncle Nick's shoulder and wept bitterly. There was more to her grief than Eltanin's passing. Premonitions of her own death were becoming more frequent. Camille wasn't afraid of dying. As a well-tutored witch, she knew her existence would continue. But she also knew the Order of the Ankh would soon face off with the Clave. It would be hard enough for Azriel to deal with the loss of Eltanin, but should she die, his grief would be unbearable. So far, the only one who knew of Camille's forewarnings and her scrying visions was Halimah. So far, the first of her visions had come to pass. Indeed, only a week prior, she had stood upon a hill, lovingly embraced by a white dragon when Azriel had taken that form. Halimah had seen it from below and gasped in recognition. Now only two portents remained. One bespoke of a royal wedding, and another foretold Camille's death. Now she wondered which one would play out. Camille hoped that the one in which she would die was false. Perhaps it was merely her fear that had instigated the vision. Although Halimah had insisted that all the scrying images were true, Camille still could not reconcile in her mind that she could die and still in the end, be married to Azriel to become his queen. It was impossible! One omen *must* be false.

Of course, Azriel knew before entering the tent that Eltanin was dead. Somehow, though, he did not feel sad as one would when knowing the separation from someone you loved was permanent. It was different, knowing Eltanin wasn't really gone but only absent. However, it was the nature of his demise that filled Azriel with a mounting rage for the one who was solely responsible. Rastaban would pay dearly for Eltanin's death. Azriel's growing anger against Rastaban's foul breach of magickal protocol was peppered by his own guilt for even putting Eltanin in such a position. Azriel knew that there had always been the possibility that Eltanin could die, but he hardly believed it could ever happen. Maybe he had been naïve to think that Eltanin would utterly defeat Rastaban. Now Azriel regretted that he had underestimated Rastaban's resourcefulness and treachery. Sadly, Eltanin's sense of decency and his love for humanity had ultimately led to his ruin.

"Azriel..." Camille flew into his arms and cried on his shoulder, but Azriel, though a comfort, could not share in her sorrow. Meeting Pog, otherwise known as Eltanin, in his dream somehow buffered the shock of the great wizard's passing. As he comforted Camille, his friends began to funnel through the tent's opening. They stood around Eltanin's bed in deference to the old wizard's passing. Julia and Halimah were moved to tears. Edward stoically took Julia's hand to offer comfort. Albert and Jasper stood as if at attention. Rosemary, Amaryllis, and Maggie carefully removed the sheets and with reverence gathered up Eltanin's remains, depositing them into a jeweled urn that Rosemary had brought. Azriel stared at the old wizard's vacant bed and at the staff that rested on its pedestal. Gently, Azriel disengaged himself from Camille's arms and lifted the staff off its stand.

Wiping her eyes, Camille asked, "Should you be touching that?"

He shot a quick glance at Nicodemus and then at Camille. "He appeared to me in a dream. That's why I knew he was dead. Eltanin told me it was mine to do with as I pleased, but..." Azriel felt at the shoulder harness that strapped Errin-lil across his back and then stroked the amulet hanging from his neck and winced. "I think I have enough to channel my Magick."

The staff made his hand tingle with its enormous potential. The black orb crowning the staff was held in place by what seemed like a gnarled hand. He hefted it, feeling its weight, then handed it to Nicodemus. "Uncle Nick, keep this for me. You were Eltanin's closest friend. I don't think he will mind you using it in the upcoming battle with the Clave."

Nicodemus took hold of the staff, but it seemed to resist his touch. He nearly dropped it. It felt as though it was melting from his fingers. With a shrug, Uncle Nick quickly handed it back to Azriel. "Much as I would like to use its power, I don't think it was meant for me. It would be useless in my hands, however..." Nicodemus looked at the staff as though giving it considerable thought. He wrapped a towel around his hand and took it from Azriel, then peered at the orb, gauging its reaction. It glowed faintly. Testing, he held it out to Jasper. Not thinking, Jasper grasped the smooth shaft of the powerful staff.

"Ow!" He howled, "It bit me!"

Nicodemus chuckled. "That's because it does not choose you. Perhaps you covet its power too willingly." He then held it out to Albert then to Edward. It showed no reaction. Nicodemus held the staff near Julia, and it reacted with a dull, red glow. "Hmm, not you either. You have too much anger." Julia smiled with chagrin.

"Come, granddaughter." Nicodemus held out the staff to Halimah. It was nearly repelled from his hand. He smiled and shook his head. "It will not attune to you. Camille, come and take the staff."

"It is not for me." She insisted.

"You don't know that, child."

"But it belonged to Eltanin. I'm not equal to it."

"You don't know until you try."

Camille reluctantly held out her hand to take the staff. As she neared the smooth wooden shaft, the black orb began to glow and when she grasped it, the gem erupted with blinding white light. At its touch, Camille began to glow as well. Camille's eyes widened with surprise. The staff began to transmute in shape. The shaft of the staff became a creamy white and the gnarled hand that held the orb shifted in shape to that of a flower. It appeared much like a lotus.

Nicodemus smiled broadly. "It is as I thought. You, my dear, have been called the Lady of Radiance, as Azriel is known as the son of Luminance. You are his counterpart and have been chosen by the staff. It is yours to use and protect. Beware, Camille. The staff has the power to give and to take away. As much as it can heal, it can also destroy. Use it wisely."

"It's time," Azriel said, his tone flat.

Everyone turned and stared at him, confused by his enigmatic statement.

"We need to return to Castle Wylusung to begin our strategy of attack. We are ready and Rastaban will not expect it."

"Are you sure?" Edward blurted.

"Cousin, you've trained with Halimah. How's your swordsmanship?"

Edward shrugged. "Combined with magick, pretty good, I think."

Azriel glanced over at Halimah who nodded enthusiastically. "Does anyone else have any doubts?"

He was answered with silence. "Here's the thing you need to know," Azriel stated. "Rastaban and the Clave use old Magick and are set in their ways, wouldn't you agree, Uncle Nick?"

Nicodemus rubbed his beard thoughtfully and nodded. "I think that's a good assessment."

"Now my mother isn't as helpless as it would seem, and the Dark Dragon—well that's another thing. He is on our side. My brother has a score to settle with the Clave. But the issue here is that we practice a newer form of magick that Rastaban has never encountered. Ours is a combination of elfin and human. Rastaban's Achilles' heel is that he has always underestimated human magick. It's not going to be easy, but I think we can capitalize on his shortsightedness. Ready or not, we need to act now."

Azriel took Camille's hand and left the tent. The staff she held bathed them both in radiant light. Nicodemus followed them with his eyes, marveling. He nodded with pride. Azriel had finally embraced his role as a leader. Right or wrong, he had made a decision. It was very kingly—regal. He mused that perhaps it was the full empowerment of dragon's blood coursing through his veins, but Nicodemus knew Azriel was ready to assume the place of power that had always been destined from the beginning.

Michael Anthony Cariola

Chapter 24

The castle had repaired itself without Eltanin and Nicodemus's presence. It was even stronger than before. The Magick they used continued to exert itself with thicker fortifications and the addition of an underground spring that formed a deep moat. Azriel could not assume that Rastaban wouldn't attack them there, so he prepared for any assault. But it seemed more likely that Rastaban was biding his time, basking in his victory over Eltanin. For that very reason, Azriel would strike first. According to Abelene's report, Rastaban showed no indication that he had ever been aware of Azriel's intrusion. Apparently the Carcer Bogus, as Azriel had named it, had fooled the Archwizard. Still, one couldn't be too certain.

Azriel and Camille stood upon the parapet that encircled the castle. Magador lazed atop the tower, now enlarged to accommodate his massive size. As usual, Mortimer nuzzled against Magador, peacefully snoozing, every so often, his back leg kicking in response to some unnamed dream.

Below, in the courtyard, Halimah and Eddie sparred with blunted swords. Azriel was surprised that, in such a short time, Eddie was on even par with Halimah, which was no easy feat. Her skills were formidable. Eddie—Edward, as he now preferred to think of himself—had truly changed. His demeanor had transformed with the knowledge of his ancestry and the nobility of his family. Elsinore, now that her memory was fully restored, made sure of it. She would gently admonish her son if she saw any sign of him slipping back into his old ways, though that was seldom. Elsinore approached him now with a rather sizeable object wrapped in purple velvet. She smiled at Halimah warmly and apologized, but she needed to speak with her son. Moving away from the others, she found a stone bench in a corner of the courtyard where she and Edward could have some privacy.

"Edward, I'm so proud of you."

He nodded and smiled.

"The message you carried from your father stirred something in me—a memory long buried. As you know, my passage through the Void shattered my mind. I wandered this world half-mad, scarcely knowing who or where I was. Yet even in that state, instinct took hold. I had brought something precious with me from Aralia, something I knew must never be lost. Though my thoughts were broken, my heart remembered what mattered, and I hid it away before the madness swallowed the rest of me.

When I first crossed over, I found myself beside an abandoned church—ruined stone, forgotten by time. Beneath it lay an old crypt. I drifted down into that darkness, and there… your true father appeared to me. He guided my steps, just as he always has. He showed me a broken sepulcher and told me to place the sword within. Sacred ground protects what is laid to rest there. No one would think to look, and no one but our blood could claim it. Last week, while you traveled with Azriel, the memory finally returned to me. I went back… and brought Harrowbane home."

After that, I collapsed—nearly dead, my mind gone. By the time your stepfather found me, I had wandered for miles with no memory of who I was.

Elsinore wasn't above a touch of theatrics. She slowly drew away the velvet and lifted the blade high. Sunlight flashed along flawless steel. Ancient runes shimmered down the center of the sword, and the dragon-headed hilt gleamed with sapphire eyes. As she straightened, something in her bearing changed—the softness of a mother giving way to the quiet authority of a queen.

"Kneel," she commanded.

A bit frightened by her power, Edward knelt obediently. All activity in the courtyard ceased as the others watched in reverent silence.

"Edward, I present to you Harrowbane, the sword of your ancestors. Your father, Elrid, bore this blade in defense of the Aralian throne. I charge you to wield it with wisdom and purity. Do not dishonor it. Wielding Harrowbane grants you authority as Captain of the Guard, second only to the king. This sword will obey your command, for it is no mere steel, but a magickal blade.

For thirty-two generations it has defended the throne. You are now the thirty-third. Bare your right arm, Edward."

Edward obeyed at once.

Elsinore lowered the blade and touched its tip to his forearm.

Fire seared through his flesh, bright and merciless, and he fought the urge to cry out. This was a test of courage. He clenched his teeth and endured. After a few moments, the pain faded to a dull ache. When he looked down, the royal insignia of Aralia had been burned into his skin—the white dragon, wings raised in triumph, encircled by ancient runes etched like living light.

Elsinore placed the sword in his hands. The blade hummed softly, as though recognizing him, and the runes glowed faintly beneath his grip.

"Son," she said, her voice both mother and queen, "this is a sword of truth. No matter how fair a face may seem, it will burn red in the presence of evil and guide your hand against your foe. Use it wisely."

Elsinore embraced Edward and crossed to the other side of the courtyard, where she spoke quietly with Nicodemus.

Meanwhile, Camille and Azriel returned to the tower. She was adjusting to the staff, attuning herself to it—and it to her. She was able now to control its radiance, holding it to a soft glow. Camille had quickly learned that she could channel her thoughts and magick into the staff, and it would respond in kind, amplifying her power into something both wonderful and terrifying. With a swipe of the staff, the surrounding desert bloomed in a marvelous display of color. She stood, pride swelling at her accomplishment, and then, with a thought, the vegetation burst into flames and was consumed in moments. Azriel winced at the sudden destruction.

"Why didn't you just leave it be?"

"I'm just practicing," she beamed. "Besides, it wasn't natural."

"Really?" Azriel smirked. "And a moat teeming with hungry piranha is?"

"Well, one can't be too careful." Camille tried to look innocent, but her wicked smile betrayed her.

Azriel wagged a finger at her. "You know, you have a dark side that's kind of disturbing."

She giggled impishly. "Jasper said a school of piranha can eviscerate a cow in about thirty seconds."

"That's good to know. Maybe we should drop Rastaban in the moat and see what happens."

"Hey, guys." Jasper strode up, Muriel's hand in his. They were both dressed in robes emblazoned with the symbol of the ankh.

"Hey, Jasper." Azriel clapped him on the shoulder. Despite Jasper's broad smile, he appeared worried.

"You look bothered," Azriel said.

"Well, everyone's assembled. Billy and Mr. Parkins just arrived with Muriel." He squeezed Muriel's hand and glanced at Camille. "My mom used the dream orb to bring Penelope and Daphne to the castle. She's getting pretty good with magick. Your aunts are anxious to see you, Camille."

"So what's wrong, Jasper?" Azriel probed.

He hesitated before answering. "Are we truly ready for this?"

"It doesn't matter if we are or not," Azriel said with gravity. "We can't have the Clave interfering in the ritual to reunite the worlds. Rastaban needs to be taken out of the picture."

Muriel grimaced. "Sounds easier said than done."

"So has Abelene contacted you yet?" Jasper asked.

"No, but she will when the coast is clear. She's certain a surprise attack will be the most effective. Uncle Nick agrees. Besides, there is something I must do first."

"And what's that?"

Azriel hesitated. "You're not going to like it."

Muriel pressed her lips together in exasperation. "Well out with it! We don't have all day!" Camille giggled in response.

"Lilith is imprisoned by Rastaban for crossing him. I'm going to free her."

Muriel gasped. "Now I know ye've gone over the deep end. Have ye gone mad?"

"It may seem that way, but my mother assures me that Lilith is a changed woman. She's switched sides."

Jasper scratched his head in consternation. "Yeah, but can you trust her?"

"I don't think I have a choice—and I trust my mother's judgment. She's never let me down before. It's time to gather our forces. Bring every magickal weapon we have. We're going to need them." Azriel tilted his head, as if listening to something.

"What?" Camille inquired.

"It's my mother." Azriel smiled. "It's time. Be ready in twenty minutes." He pulled up the hood of his cloak and vanished before anyone could object.

The cavern was deathly quiet, dimly lit by sconces placed haphazardly along the walls. Though deserted, Azriel knew he needed to remain alert for traps. Though seemingly unguarded, Rastaban might have left snares to warn the Clave of any intrusion. Azriel cast a dampening spell over himself to muffle the sound of his footsteps. He moved like a ghost through the chamber until he faced Abelene.

"Well timed," she whispered. "Rastaban is so certain his hideout is impregnable that he doesn't realize you've already been here. He's grown careless."

"Mom, you should come with me now."

"No. It's best I remain here. Rastaban can't harm me. Save Lilith. In his arrogance, he won't even miss her." She pointed to a spot several feet away. "There she is. Free her and go."

"I'll be back soon." Azriel crept over to where Lilith sat, her back against the wall. Her wrists and ankles were in manacles. Oddly, she appeared to be in fairly good health. Three sizable rats slept by her side. One had a crooked tail.

"Don't hurt them," Lilith whispered.

Azriel nodded. "It's time to get you out of here." He waved his hand and muttered an incantation. The manacles clicked open and fell away. Azriel offered his hand to help Lilith to her feet, but she waved him to silence and cocked an ear, listening.

"One can't be too careful." Before rising, she stroked the largest rat. "Thank you for bringing me sustenance, Master Rat." Now freed of her magickal restraints, Lilith cast a healing spell over the rat, and his crooked tail straightened with a snap. However, her use of magick triggered an alarm. A klaxon blared and Lilith's eyes widened in horror. Though well-intentioned, her spell cost them any chance of a surprise attack. Lilith looked as though she might cry. "I'm sorry, I didn't know!"

Azriel glanced over at Abelene. "That's our cue to leave."

"Don't worry. I'll handle Rastaban. Just go." she ordered. Azriel took Lilith's hand and disappeared.

Within moments Rastaban and Altais scrambled down the steps to investigate. He immediately noticed Lilith's absence.

"Where is she?" He demanded of Abelene.

Abelene feigned ignorance. "Well, don't ask me." She yawned as if she, too, had been awakened from a deep sleep. "Surely you don't think I had anything to do with it."

From the adjoining prison, Charlie began to laugh in derision. "Perhaps, wizard, you underestimated your captive."

"You lie, dragon! Those bonds were magically sealed. They were unbreakable."

"Then maybe, dear Rastaban, your powers have grown weak— and thus your doom is upon you." Charlie laughed with glee.

Rastaban turned to Altais. "Rouse the others. We are under attack! There can be no other explanation."

"That's impossible, my lord," Altais answered quickly.

He snarled. "Just do it!"

Azriel and Lilith reappeared within the pentagram emblazoned at the center of the courtyard. It glowed with power at Azriel's presence.

Lilith smiled tentatively. "You have grown in might. Perhaps you are ready to take over the Clave."

"I don't want the job, Lilith. The Clave has outlived its usefulness, as Eltanin so often said." he retorted.

She hesitated thoughtfully. "That may be so, but you will soon reunite the two worlds. Magick must be harnessed and controlled otherwise chaos will ensue. There are many rogue wizards and sorcerers who will come against you." She took Azriel's hand and fixed her eyes upon him. Azriel read the sincerity in her eyes. She continued. "You will come against Rastaban, but do not underestimate him. You are not just fighting the Clave, but every evil wizard associated with him who has remained hidden in the shadows; those who would prevent you from fulfilling your destiny. He will summon them."

Azriel nodded, taking Lilith's warning to heart. "Listen, I believe you, but we are prepared for him to the best of our talents."

"I can help." Her blue eyes pleaded.

"I want to trust you, but I'm not sure how. It's well-known you have a history of deception and betrayal—thousands of years' worth."

Her smile was mirthless. "I will not deny that, but you must believe me that I am a changed woman. If you don't believe me, test me. You have the power, as a master alchemist, to discern truth. Test my heart." She took his hand and placed it on her chest. By now Azriel and Lilith were surrounded by the members of the Order who had funneled into the courtyard. Jasper held Mortimer at bay, who growled menacingly at the woman. Camille and Halimah glanced at Lilith with distrust but held their tongues. Edward, however, tested his new sword. He gripped the hilt and pulled Harrowbane partway from its scabbard to see whether it glowed red in Lilith's presence. It did not. He glanced at Azriel with a slight nod.

Azriel entered her heart. The first thing he noticed was her independent spirit. Lilith had always, from her youth, resisted being put into a box, being possessed by men who desired her beauty but ignored her astute mind. Eltanin was the first to see beyond her loveliness and recognized her potential as an equal. But she had also been betrayed by her lust for power—her fatal flaw. Though Eltanin loved her, he had recognized that darkness within her and denied her a seat in the Clave. It broke her heart, but her pain went deeper. Lilith had loved Eltanin as well; more than she had ever loved a man. Denying her desire had acted as a poison to her heart and consumed her with hatred. If she wouldn't be granted power, she would seize it on her own. Thus began a series of betrayals of her own heart. She had known all along the unbreakable laws of nature and the alchemy of the universe, but bent it, distorting it to her own will. Azriel, however, saw the truth of it. Every act of evil Lilith had committed, wounded her in some fundamental way. With each act of betrayal, her heart became a chasm of pain, grief, and regret. So immersed in her misery, she could not find a way out. It was Abelene who had supplied the balm of healing by her open-handed offer of friendship and trust. Azriel saw into Lilith's memory the days of shed tears and a desire to make amends for all the damage she had caused to the worlds. He sensed no deception as Lilith's heart was laid bare to him but an eagerness to help defeat the Clave and its minions. More so, her desire for power no longer consumed her. She had learned that power left a bitter taste. It was as easy to seize as to lose it. The trap laid bare, she also knew that Rastaban had been ensnared by it. Once a good and noble man, he had been corrupted by the power he vied to control. Instead it controlled him. Rastaban was a mirror of what Lilith had once been but no longer desired. If anything, she was repulsed by it and seized by remorse so consuming that she wanted to will herself to die in repayment for her transgressions against the two worlds.

Azriel stared into her eyes and no longer felt distrust for her, indeed his heart swelled with compassion. He smiled and shook his head. "No, Lilith. Your death would serve no purpose. Eltanin told me to trust you before he died. This I will do." Azriel paused, visualizing where the robes were stored in the castle storeroom. A dark green cape suddenly appeared in his hand. Smiling, he ceremoniously draped it over Lilith's shoulders. It was emblazoned with the Ankh. "That will keep you hidden from Rastaban's eyes. Come join us in battle."

When they translocated from Castle Wylusung, the chamber unexpectedly blazed with harsh light as Azriel arrived with the entire Order. The combatants stood behind him warily, ready for an attack they knew would be forthcoming. Camille stood beside Azriel with her staff firmly planted on the stone floor. Azriel fully expected an immediate barrage but instead, Rastaban stood waiting patiently with Altais and Giausur at his right. Thuban and Edasich stood by his left. The five archwizards glowed with the potential for destruction.

Rastaban smiled pleasantly and bowed formally. "Azriel, it warms my heart to finally meet the Son of Luminance."

"Well sorry to say, Rastaban, but the pleasure is not mutual. It's time for you to relinquish control of the Clave."

"Ahh!" Rastaban's eyes glowed. "So you are here to replace me? Are you ready then to take your rightful place as the head of Draconis?"

"No! The Clave is obsolete. I am here to disband the Clave."

Rastaban sighed tragically. "Oh come now, Azriel. Let us reason together. You and I could become powerful allies. We could control this world, you and I. Our combined might would be unstoppable."

"That's what it has always been with you—control? Azriel smirked with distaste. "It's an illusion, you know."

Rastaban insisted, "Come, Azriel. Join me."

He shook his head. "You know I can't do that. It was never my destiny. I am heir to the Aralian throne. That makes me your King. Will you concede?"

Rastaban guffawed heartily, the sound of his laughter, cruel. "You have no power here, boy!"

The tone of Rastaban's retort was so much like his father, Berrill, that Azriel's face hardened. It was the same power-driven response he experienced within the dream induced by the greenlings. Azriel knew that there would be no reasoning with the Arch Wizard, not that he wasn't expecting as much.

"Rastaban, you have no idea who you are coming against. Even with all your sorcery, you cannot win." To reveal his true nature, Azriel suddenly transformed into his dragon self and towered over the Wizard. He belched out a flame for effect while Camille looked on proudly. Rastaban stepped back a few feet in shock. This was no illusion. Azriel resumed his normal form. "This is what you will face if you come against me, old man."

"Enough!" Rastaban growled with a wave of dismissal. "I am not afraid of you. I challenge you to formal magickal combat—the Clave against the Order. It is time to settle this!"

"I accept." Azriel strode back to his group with Camille and squared off. The chamber was huge. The five wizards of the Clave gathered at one end where the two Carcer pyramids stood side by side. Their intentions were obvious since the great iron door that led to the caverns above was nearby should they choose to make a hasty exit. But Azriel would have none of it. He would give them no quarter. He whispered something to Camille and smiling, she raised her staff.

"Securus!" she intoned. A glowing beam of light erupted from the staff and the iron door began to burn cherry red. It quickly morphed to white hot, welding and sealing the door shut.

"There will be no escape for any of you!" Camille smiled.

Rastaban raised an eyebrow. The young witch's power was formidable. He would not underestimate her. In response Rastaban released a potent plasma ball at the witch to test her mettle, but Azriel quickly shielded her and drew Errin-lil, parrying the attack. The sword deflected the plasma ball back to Rastaban. It exploded behind him spraying the wizard with shards of rock from the cavern wall. Rastaban chuckled under his breath. Azriel in his inexperience had just revealed a weakness. His love for the girl would make him protect her, leaving him open for attack. That knowledge could be useful.

The Order began to separate, widening their stances to surround the clave, but suddenly there was a rumbling from below.

Abelene, from her prison, had been carefully observing and realized the truth. The Clave was summoning something terrible. She shouted, "Azriel! Guard yourself!"

The rumbling built up in intensity to a high-pitched scream as the stone beneath them began to shatter. A chasm split open behind Rastaban. From the breach poured forth all manner of vile creatures from the darkest pits of corruption. The first to emerge were cave trolls followed by sand gorgons, ogres, demons and devils. But there was more. Seeping out of the shadows, men and women of every race and nationality faced the order. Though ordinary in appearance, it was obvious that they were aligned with the clave. Every manner of evil witch, warlock, wizard and sorcerer stood against them. Azriel paled to realize how many the Clave controlled. This would be harder than he had envisioned, but he also trusted his friends. They were well-trained and disciplined. They spread out in a defensive stance.

Edward moved into position directly across from Altais. Although the purpose was to defend, he had a score to settle with the wizard. This was personal. Albert, Jasper and Julia teamed up as was their habit. Together they were a chaotic force that though often exasperating to Nicodemus as he trained them, would prove an unpredictable weapon.

Nicodemus, Lilith, Penelope, Elsinore, Daphne, Maggie, Halimah, and Mr. Parkins moved to the left of the horde. Muriel, Rosemary, Amaryllis, Felisa, Mortimer and Magador all took strategic positions, but it seemed their defenses were pathetically small. Outnumbered, the outcome looked bleak.

Abelene analyzed both sides; their strengths and weaknesses. Eyes wide, she stared at Charlie. Her eyes pleaded with him to intervene even though she knew he could not. As the angel of death, he had to remain neutral and be the gateway for all souls to pass through to the underworld. He knew this battle would take many lives, and sadly shook his head imperceptibly. He would strike when he could at Rastaban. This was the only interference he would allow himself and even that was risking the wrath of the Great Mother Dragon.

Rastaban smiled with evil glee. "Azriel, you cannot hope to win. Your forces are hopelessly small."

"Not as small as you think!" He formed sigils in the air and suddenly, Paralda, Krinaea, Maera and Fieré appeared, girded for battle. They were joined by the entire force of fairies from their realms. Sylph, dryad, naiad and drake flew side by side in a combined force to battle against evil, for their realms were threatened as well should the Clave's forces triumph.

The battle began. Azriel's forces struck first at the sand gorgons. Experienced with this type of attack, they knew that acid would dispatch the creatures with ease. They were reduced to piles of sand, which Krinaea, directed her sylphs to funnel and whirl to abrading the advancing horde, impeding their progress.

Albert, Jasper and Julia combined their strength to invoke pyrotechnics against the cave trolls. Tough as stone, only mighty concussions would hold them back. Many shattered with the impact as fireball after fireball struck them. Magador flew overhead and belched out bursts of flame against the enemy forces. The cave trolls shrieked in agony as many were scorched. Some crawled back into the chasm to lick their wounds. The demons, however, held back waiting for a signal from Rastaban.

Analyzing the strategy, Azriel rightly assumed that Rastaban had only been toying with them until this point. Something bigger was coming.

Meanwhile Altais advanced on Edward, murder in his eyes. He too had a score to settle. Edward's defection had humiliated him before his leader. Rastaban now questioned Altais' efficacy.

Edward held his ground and brandished his sword. Though not as puissant as Errin-lil, his sword aptly named Harrowbane was powerful in its own right, infused with potent magick. It blazed deep red in his hand. Altais faced him and held out his empty hand with a command. A sword suddenly appeared. A baneful weapon, it gleamed black, embedded with evil curses up and down the blade.

"So it's swords you want, boy." Altais chuckled. "Prepare then to die!"

Edward stared him down with confidence. "It will not be so easy, old man."

Altais nodded and suddenly lashed out with his blade. Strategically, it would not have been a fatal slice. He was trying to nick Edward on the arm. Abelene, watching from her cell realized the truth of it.

She cried, "Edward, beware! The blade's poisoned!"

He stepped back and nodded, never taking his eyes off Altais. "Coward! You have no honor. I was a child when you used me, and I was naïve. But no longer! Guard yourself for truth and prepare to die!" Edward struck hard. With Harrowbane raised above his head, he slashed at Altais. As he fought, the sword felt light in his hand and his arms had a power and vigor he never knew he had. Altais, however, was an experienced swordsman and parried the blow. Sparks flew as their swords crossed. Having trained with Halimah, Edward was proficient and equal to the task.

His strokes were fluid and graceful, like a dance with death. He succeeded in wounding Altais when he nicked the wizard's shoulder, driving him back toward the cave wall. Altais responded by feinting and thrusting back, but it was all a ruse as the sorcerer suddenly released a volley of fireballs. One struck Edward in the chest, knocking him to the ground. With a victorious sneer, Altais stood over Edward ready to thrust the poisoned blade through his heart. But as he raised the sword, he was suddenly met by an assault from Halimah. Having watched in horror, she leaped to Edward's defense. Guarding him, she produced a dagger and thrust it in the old wizard's face slicing his cheek, drawing blood. He fell back in defense, offering Halimah enough time to extend her hand to Edward.

Back on his feet, he smiled gratefully and winked. "Thanks. Good timing!"

The battle raged around him. Jasper and Albert had taken on Giausur and Thuban. For a time they were evenly matched exchanging pyrotechnics in the form of plasma spheres, fireballs and lightning bolts, neither team getting the advantage.

Smiling slyly, Jasper shouted to his brother, "Now!"

They both were masters of illusion. Jasper suddenly morphed into a ferocious bear and used what would naturally appeal to a bear—honey! Lots of it! With a magickal gesture of Jasper's fingers, Thuban and Giausur were suddenly dripping and smeared with the sticky stuff. It was so unexpected that they were both thoroughly unprepared. But that was only the beginning. Albert augmented the attack with a summoning, which was his forte. He almost blew the spell for having to contain his laughter. "Apius Appugno!" Literally it meant, *Bees Attack!*"

The two wizards were suddenly surrounded by a chaotic swarm of angry bees attracted to the powerful scent of honey. Jasper and Albert were nearly doubled over in laughter as the Thuban and Giausur hopped about shrieking as they were continuously stung. They could not escape for wherever they went the bees followed spreading havoc among the enemy forces. Still in the form of a bear, Jasper gave his brother a vigorous high-five. Certainly, it would not kill their adversaries, but it would, without doubt, slow them down.

The battle raged on while Rastaban and Azriel fought and sought every means to outsmart each other. While doing battle, Rastaban abruptly stopped and released a fireball high into the air, like a flare. It was the signal for the demons to attack. They began their slaughter. Watching them advance, Lilith suddenly paled. They were heading straight for her with the intent of tearing her apart. No longer queen of the underworld, she held no sway over them. The demons blamed her for their creation. She had transformed the dead souls into tortured creatures whose only purpose was to destroy.

Lilith, who battled side by side with Rosemary and Amaryllis, turned to Rosemary with a look of defeat. "I'm screwed," She said sadly. "They will destroy me. Then they will destroy you."

"Not so! Stand back, Lilith."

Rosemary suddenly produced a blade from the calf of her boot and raised it high. "Abraxas, Lord of Demons, I summon you!"

They felt a deep rumbling, and Abraxas was suddenly in their midst. He bowed deeply to Rosemary, but then realized who stood next to her.

"You!" he raged at Lilith ready to strike her down.

"Desist! Rosemary shouted. Lilith fights with us. She is not the same sorceress you knew."

"I have not forgotten what she has done to me—to all of us!" he roared.

"Even so," Rosemary reasoned. "Rastaban has all demonkind under his control. But you are their Lord. Only you can turn the tide!"

"Truly, it is as you say. I will do this as you have shown me mercy. But after, my debt to you is paid."

"Agreed!" Rosemary shouted through the din of battle.

Abraxas turned to face the advancing horde and sounded out with a voice of command. "Brothers! Sisters! These are not your enemy." He pointed at Rastaban. "It is he and his minions that control and use you as fodder! I am your Lord!" He scribed arcane sigils in the air, breaking the summons of the Clave. Released from their bondage, they suddenly turned and began attacking the host of evil witches, warlocks, and sorcerers that Rastaban had gathered against the Order of the Ankh.

The massacre began. The demons were nearly impervious to the magick produced by dark forces. Abraxas led the demons to savagely tear the enemy to pieces. Camille and Julia more than once turned away so as not to witness the bloody carnage. In a brief amount of time, the enemy forces were reduced until only Rastaban and the Clave remained. The destruction was so complete that both sides had to stop and gape at the slaughter. When complete, Abraxas faced Rosemary. The horde of demons stood behind him snarling and muttering curses, mostly directed at Lilith.

"My debt to you is paid, Lady Rosaluna. I now ask your leave." Rosemary was about to respond when Lilith interjected.

"Wait," she insisted, then turned to Abraxas. "I made you, Lord of Demons. I have the power to unmake you."

"Lilith, you mustn't. It could kill you," Rosemary warned.

"I am grateful for your concern, sister, but I have much for which I must atone. If I die, then it is fitting." She gave a wan smile. "I have lived far too long anyway." She turned back again to Abraxas. "Will you accept my proposal?"

"I will, but that does not repay the millennia of torture suffered by me and all these." He waved his hand toward the other demons. "We do not forgive what has been done to us."

"I do not ask your forgiveness. I only ask that you depart in peace after I invoke the Charm of Making."

Abraxas nodded solemnly.

Lilith spread her arms wide and began the invocation, a charm lost for thousands of years and known only to two other arch mages—Eltanin, who had taught it to her, and another long ago who perished in the casting.

Anail Nathrock
Uthvass Bethudd
Dochiel Dienve

She repeated the charm several times as her voice took on the timbre of command. But as she did, Lilith began to age. Her youthful appearance gave way to wrinkled skin and her golden hair faded to silver, but she did not waver. Tears streamed down her face as every joint in her body began to burn and ache with arthritic pain. In minutes she was transformed into a stooped-over, spent old crone. She collapsed in Rosemary's arms. But in return for her effort, the demons were no longer. They were transformed into the ghosts of men and women who had lived throughout the ages. Abraxas stood proudly before Rosemary as he appeared before he died ages ago—as a human prince tall and handsome. He stared thoughtfully at Rosemary and Lilith, who languished in her arms.

"Perhaps you have changed, Lady Lilith," Abraxas said solemnly. "I thank you for our release, but I still cannot forgive you." He glanced up at Rosemary. "Lady Rosaluna, we will now depart and find rest in the underworld."

"You are free Prince Abraxas. Go in peace." Rosemary bowed formally.

Abraxas smiled with relief and he, along with all the others, vanished into vapor.

Edward still battled with Altais and was gaining the upper hand. Azriel assessed the situation as Rastaban did. Thuban, Edasich and Giausur were sprawled on the ground along with many other dead. Azriel also noted that many of the Order were also dead. Sadly, Felisa and Mr. Parkins were among the departed. Muriel was badly wounded. Amaryllis sobbed as she held Felisa in her arms, mourning her loss. With a word of command, Azriel dissolved Abelene's prison. "Mother, attend to Muriel."

Stunned, Rastaban's eyes widened. "Impossible! No one has that power!"

"Have you not learned yet, wizard? I do have the power! Do you yield, or do you waste your life? I am not what you think. For I am the Guardian of Life as Sariel is the Guardian of Death, He is my brother. Though I am forbidden to murder, I will defend and will take your life if need be. Test me at your peril, Rastaban!"

The Arch wizard watched in dismay as Edward had Altais backed against the cavern wall. He had his blade poised against Altais' throat. All he need do was thrust when the crafty wizard suddenly chuckled and vanished into thin air!

Rastaban shrieked a curse. "Altais! You coward!"

Azriel smiled, though there was little warmth in it.

"You're alone now, Rastaban. It's just you and me. So what's it going to be?"

The old wizard answered with a low, animal growl and drew his staff inward as though gathering the very marrow of the world to himself. The air thickened around him. Dust rose in slow spirals from the stone floor and the faint light of the chamber guttered and dimmed, as though even the flames feared what he meant to unleash.

Azriel steadied his breathing.

Errin-lil burned bright in his grasp, the blade answering his will at once and filling him with that familiar electric vigor which had carried him through every trial since boyhood. The power coursed through his limbs and set his nerves alight until he could scarcely tell where his own flesh ended and the sword's strength began. All the lessons of Eltanin, all the sacrifices of the Order, all the long roads that had led him to this hour gathered within him like a storm seeking release. This was the moment to end it.

He raised the sword high and called upon the power of the ages, and the answer came in a roaring surge that trembled through the stone beneath his feet.

Rastaban met his gaze—and smiled.

It was not the smile of a cornered foe, nor of a man who had misjudged his opponent, but the calm, knowing smile of one who already understood how the moment would end.

A chill slid down Azriel's spine. Something was wrong.

Yet the power had already left him. Lightning leapt from Errin-lil in a blinding torrent, a spear of white fire meant to strike the wizard where he stood and end the war in a single stroke. In that same terrible instant Rastaban clawed at the empty air and uttered a word that seemed to tear at the seams of reality itself. The space between them folded and warped—

—and where there had been nothing, Camille stood.

Not summoned, not running, but simply there, as though the world had decided she had always occupied that place.

For one suspended heartbeat she stared at him in confusion. Then recognition dawned. Her lips parted, his name forming even as her eyes widened—

—and the bolt struck.

Light exploded. The sound was like the sky itself splitting open. Camille's body jerked as though caught in a storm wind, and then the strength fled her all at once and she crumpled to the stone beyond his reach.

For a moment, Azriel did not understand what had happened. The world seemed muffled and distant, as though he stood beneath deep water. Then the smell of ozone reached him, and the faint curl of smoke rising from her chest.

Suddenly he was moving. He did not remember crossing the distance, only that he was on his knees with her in his arms, his hands slick and trembling.

"No… no, Camille… stay with me… please…"

Her breath came shallow and uneven, each one smaller than the last. Her fingers twitched weakly and sought his face, as though even in pain she wished only to touch him.

"I'm sorry, Azriel," she whispered, scarcely more than air. "I love—"

The words broke something inside him.

"Don't," he begged. "Don't talk like that. We can fix this—we can always fix this—"

But even as he spoke he felt the warmth draining from her, felt that subtle presence that had always been Camille—her laughter, her stubbornness, her light—slipping away like sand through his fingers. Her hand fell. Her eyes dimmed. And she was gone.

The scream that tore from his throat seemed to shake the very chamber.

Behind him came a thunderous crash as Sariel descended and pinned Rastaban helpless beneath his talons, but Azriel neither saw nor cared. The world had narrowed to the still form in his arms and the terrible, unyielding truth that it had been his own hand that loosed the bolt—not Rastaban's, not fate's, but his.

"There has to be a way," he muttered, half mad with grief. "There has to be—"

His fingers found the small golden chest at his belt. The Lapis—of course. The Stone of Immortality. He tore it open with shaking hands.

"No, brother," Sariel warned, his voice heavy with dread. "That path is forbidden."

"I don't care!" Azriel cried. "What use are laws if they let her die?"

He pressed the shining fragment to Camille's lips, praying, pleading, bargaining with anything that might listen.

For a breathless instant nothing happened.

Then her body convulsed.

Her eyes flew open—white, empty, wrong.

A sound tore from her throat, raw and inhuman, filled with agony, and she lurched forward like some dreadful puppet pulled by unseen strings. Azriel recoiled in horror as she clawed and snarled at any who dared come near her, her movements wild and graceless, like something dragged back from a realm where it did not belong.

"Camille…?" he whispered. "What have I done…?"

Rastaban's laughter slithered through the chamber, low and venomous, echoing off the stone like the hiss of a serpent.

"Fool," he mocked. "She cannot live and she cannot die. The only way to release her from her misery is to sever her head from her body."

Each word struck Azriel harder than any blade.

It took Jasper and Albert and the others together to restrain her as she writhed and shrieked in their grasp, neither living nor mercifully gone, her cries filled with such anguish that even the bravest among them turned their faces away. And Azriel could only stand there, drowning in the knowledge that this torment, too, was of his own making.

Slowly—very slowly—he lifted his eyes to Rastaban.

There was no fear left in them.

Only murder.

Errin-lil rose in his grasp, and the ancient blade answered his rage at once, igniting with argent fire until the chamber swam in cold, merciless light.

"No, Rastaban," he said, his voice low and trembling with grief. "I will not kill her—I cannot. But you... you I will deprive of life."

"Brother! No!"

Sariel's command rang out like thunder.

"Think on what you are doing. You are the Guardian of Life. To murder in revenge is forbidden to you. If you do this, you will become like him."

To punctuate the warning, the great dragon pressed harder upon Rastaban, and the wizard grunted in pain beneath the crushing weight of talon and scale.

"Then so be it!" Azriel cried, raising the sword high, prepared at last to end it—to end him—to end everything.

"Think, Azriel!" Sariel boomed. "Look at the man he is. See what you will become."

The words struck home.

Azriel faltered.

The fire along Errin-lil's edge flickered and waned, its brilliance fading into a sullen glow.

A roar of anguish tore from him, raw and broken, and the sword lowered from his hand as though it weighed a hundred stones.

"Then this monster goes unpunished?" he sobbed.

"Oh, I can assure you," Sariel replied, his voice gentler now, "I have a place set aside in the underworld just for him."

"That brings no comfort," Azriel whispered. "My queen is dead, and yet she is not. I cannot kill her."

"There will be no need," Sariel said softly. "Remember what I told you in our last conversation."

He extended a taloned claw, and there, resting in the hollow of his palm, was a tiny golden mote of light, no larger than a spark from a dying ember, yet radiant with a warmth that seemed older than the world.

"Bring her to me," he instructed.

Jasper and Albert, though shaken, obeyed, guiding the struggling Camille toward the dragon.

"But... isn't that forbidden to you?" Azriel asked hoarsely. "Are you not the portal to the underworld?"

"Yes," Sariel replied. "To both questions. It is forbidden. It would seem we have each broken the rules this day."

There was the faintest hint of a smile in the ancient dragon's eyes.

With infinite care, he placed his clawed fingers over Camille's heart and let the golden spark sink into her breast.

For a moment nothing happened.

Then she gasped—a deep, shuddering breath—as though drowning lungs had finally found air.

The soul returned.

But something more stirred with it.

The Lapis Occultus, already within her, awakened like fire racing through dry timber, coursing through every vein and sinew, burning away death, remaking what had been broken. Light gathered beneath her skin, faint at first, then brightening until she seemed almost translucent, as though fashioned from dawn itself.

Unable to bear the radiance, Jasper and Albert released her and stepped back.

Camille threw her head back, not in pain, but in wonder, as life—true life—flooded her once more.

Her eyes cleared, the dreadful white fading away, replaced by that familiar vivid blue Azriel knew better than his own reflection.

The glow slowly diminished and silence fell.

Then she looked at him. Not confused or afraid.

But filled with a depth of understanding and love so profound it stole the breath from his lungs.

"Oh, Azriel..."

She stumbled forward and fell into his arms, clinging to him as though afraid the world might yet tear them apart again.

"Now I finally understand."

"Understand what?" he asked, scarcely daring to hope.

"I've withheld something from you..."

Azriel gazed at her, confusion and wonder warring in his eyes.

She lowered her gaze, suddenly shy, as though the weight of what she must say pressed heavier upon her than death itself.

"You see… I knew I would die," she said softly. "Three years ago, during the Yule celebration, when Abelene taught us the art of the scrying mirror, I looked beyond the veil and glimpsed my own end. I saw it clearly." She swallowed and brushed at her tears with the back of her hand. "I could not tell you. I dared not. Because you would have tried to protect me. You would have abandoned everything—your calling, your destiny—everything you were meant to become… all to save me."

For a fleeting instant anger stirred in Azriel's chest—that she had carried such a burden alone, that she had kept this terrible knowledge from him—but as he looked into her eyes, he understood.

And the anger melted into sorrow.

"You're right," he whispered at last. "I would have done anything to save you… even if it meant the loss of both worlds."

"So you see," she said with a small, wistful smile, "I could not let that happen."

A faint, awkward voice broke the solemn quiet.

"Um… Camille…" Jasper said, squinting. "You're glowing."

Azriel gave the barest hint of a tired smile. "She's immortal now. It will fade in time."

"Well," Rastaban sneered bitterly, "this is all very charming—"

Sariel pressed harder with his talon, and the wizard's words collapsed into a pained yelp.

Camille turned her gaze upon him.

The gentleness vanished from her expression.

What replaced it was something colder, older—something regal.

She did not look away.

"Halimah," she said quietly, "may I have my staff?"

"With pleasure."

Halimah retrieved it from where it had fallen and placed the white wood reverently into Camille's hand.

Camille's fingers closed around it with calm certainty, not in rage or to exact vengeance, but to render judgment.

Sariel's voice rumbled low. "Milady, you must not kill him. As Azriel is the Son of Luminance, so too are you the Lady of Radiance. To take his life would stain you. Besides... I have a fate prepared for him far worse than death."

"My lord," Camille replied evenly, "I have no intention of killing him. Eltanin spoke to us of this staff. It has the power to give... and to take away. There is something I wish to take."

She raised the staff.

Its crown—shaped like a lotus—began to glow with a pale, living light.

Rastaban struggled and writhed beneath Sariel's foot, but could not escape.

As Camille passed the staff slowly over him, a faint shimmer rose from the wizard's body like heat from sun-scorched stone. Threads of light—his stolen power, his hoarded magicks—were drawn out of him and gathered into the crown, where they pooled and flickered like captive fireflies.

The chamber fell utterly silent.

When Camille spoke, her voice carried not as a girl's, but as a sovereign's decree.

"From this day forth, you are stripped of all magick. You may strive and strain and call upon every spell you have ever learned, yet nothing will answer you. You will find yourself weak, powerless, and alone. That is my judgment."

"You have no right!" Rastaban spat, panic finally cracking his voice.

Camille's lips curved into a thin, terrible smile.

"Oh," she said softly, "but I do. Like it or not... I am your Queen. And Azriel is your Lord."

"That's preposterous! You're nothing but a little girl—"

"Silence, old man!" Sariel roared. "It is time for me to escort you to your new home."

He cast a quick wink at Azriel. "Wait here. I shall return shortly."

With that, he vanished in a curl of black smoke.

In his absence, the Order began to gather about Azriel and Camille. Abelene, now freed from her long incarceration, rushed forward and embraced her son, tears streaming freely down her face.

"Oh, Azriel... I am so proud of you."

She drew Camille into her arms as well.

"And you, Camille. You have been braver than any of us."

There followed a round of congratulations—clasped hands, warm embraces, and the hearty backslapping of comrades who had survived what should not have been survivable. Jasper and Albert ruffled Azriel's hair, like boys again, laughing with relief more than mirth. Julia slipped quietly into Edward's arms and rested her head against his shoulder.

Then, quite suddenly, Felisa appeared among them and rubbed her head contentedly against Amaryllis.

"But—you were dead!" Amaryllis gasped and hugged her fiercely, as though afraid she might vanish again.

"Of course I was," Felisa purred. "But I'm a cat, remember? I have nine lives..."

She paused, counting silently.

"Well... eight now. No—wait... seven!"

Laughter rippled through the company, light and welcome after so much darkness.

A moment later Sariel returned, though no longer in the form of a dragon. He stood tall in the guise of a man, broad-shouldered and noble, a shock of thick black hair crowning his stern features. There was something ancient in his bearing still—something unmistakably other.

Abelene regarded him with quiet longing.

Sariel inclined his head to her formally before turning to Azriel.

"It is done, brother," he said with a broad smile.

"What did you do to him?" Azriel asked.

"A fitting punishment. As you can well imagine, I have had many years to consider what should be done with Rastaban when at last I was free. At first, I thought to borrow the punishment of Prometheus—to chain him to the highest peak of Aralia."

"Prometheus?" Camille asked.

"Yes, milady," Sariel replied. "As the tale goes, Prometheus fashioned mankind and, in defiance of the gods, stole fire from

Mount Olympus and gifted it to them. Zeus was enraged. For this crime, Prometheus was bound to a stone in the Caucasus Mountains, where each day an eagle devoured his liver. Being immortal, it grew back each night... only for the torment to begin anew at dawn."

"That's pretty gruesome," Azriel muttered. "What could be worse than that?"

Sariel chuckled softly. "I thought it better that Rastaban experience firsthand every misery for which he was responsible. Over the course of twenty thousand years, he has caused the deaths of millions. I have quickened his mind. Now he shall feel every agony, every torment, every murder, every grief he ever inflicted—one after another. And when it is finished... it shall begin again."

He paused.

"Madness will claim him long before eternity does."

Azriel shook his head slowly. "Creative," he said at last. "I'll give you that."

With the danger past, he finally allowed himself to look fully upon the aftermath of the battle.

Though Rastaban's forces had been shattered, the Order had not escaped unscathed.

Rosemary knelt beside Mr. Parkins' still body, weeping openly while Lilith knelt near, offering what comfort she could.

"He was a good man," Rosemary sobbed. "A stubborn, foolish man perhaps—but good. He found me washed up on the shore and raised me as his own. He never knew I was an undine... silly bloke. Nor did I know I could ever return to the sea."

"I'm sorry, Rosemary," Lilith said gently. "I will help you bury him."

"No, Lilith," she answered softly. "You've given enough. You're too old and too weary for such labor now."

Nearby, Magador stood unusually still, staring down at the ground.

Azriel followed his gaze.

Mortimer lay shattered, broken into pieces like discarded stone.

Magador sighed heavily. "He was rather tiresome," he muttered, "but… I shall miss the little fellow."

"Don't worry, my friend," Azriel said, resting a hand against the dragon's flank. "This, at least, is something I can mend."

He extended his hand over the broken fragments and spoke gently:

"Repario."

The broken pieces, like scattered magnets, began to twitch and slide across the stone, clicking together one by one until Mortimer stood whole again.

The little gargoyle jerked awake with a snarl. He immediately launched into a string of guttural curses in his own rough tongue and, before anyone could stop him, delivered Magador a savage kick to the leg.

"Ow! What was that for?" Magador protested, nudging him away with his flank.

Mortimer continued to rant, waving his fists furiously.

"Well, don't blame me!" Magador huffed. "I warned you not to attack that cave troll. I told you they were immune to gargoyle venom!"

Despite everything, Azriel and the Order of the Ankh couldn't help but laugh as Mortimer carried on with his tirade, indignant as ever.

Azriel's gaze drifted across the chamber—and then he straightened in surprise.

His mother stood apart with Sariel, their hands joined as they spoke in low, private whispers. Tenderly, she brushed her fingers along his cheek and then kissed him with a quiet passion that spoke of long years lost and promises yet to come.

Azriel shook his head. "Oh boy… this can't be good."

Camille punched him lightly in the arm. "What are you saying? Is Abelene forbidden to love?"

"No," he admitted, "but Sariel is. This could get complicated."

"Azriel, leave her be," Camille scolded gently. "Abelene is quite capable of making her own decisions."

"Yeah… I suppose you're right."

Paralda drifted down before them and curtsied with effortless grace.

"My Lord, we thank thee, for thou hast freed us from the threat of Rastaban and the Clave."

Azriel smiled warmly. "No, Queen Paralda. It could not have been done without you and the Faerie realm."

Maera, Fieré, and Krinaea joined her and bowed in turn.

Maera's smile held a trace of sadness. "We have gathered our fallen and now ask your leave, my Lord."

"I am sorry for the losses you have suffered," Azriel said, bowing his head.

"Do not grieve overlong," Fieré replied. "Our kin are never truly gone. They return to the elements and, in time, to us."

"I thank you all," Azriel said. "You are welcome here always."

Krinaea giggled. "Well of course! We wouldn't miss your coronation and wedding."

Azriel flushed with uncharacteristic shyness as his friends gathered to bid the faeries farewell.

Edward smiled at Fieré and gave her a sly wink.

She planted her tiny hands on her hips. "Now, Edward, I've told you before to mind your naughty thoughts!"

"Edward!" Julia smacked his arm.

Fieré giggled mischievously and darted forward, planting a quick kiss on his cheek.

"Ow!" he yelped, rubbing the spot. "That hurt!"

"Of course it did," Fieré replied sweetly. "You've heard the saying—if you play with fire, you're bound to be burned."

With that, she and her sisters vanished in a shimmer of light.

Together they joined Abelene and Sariel, preparing to depart, though Lilith lingered behind.

Abelene, still holding Sariel's hand, glanced back at Azriel. There was something wistful in her eyes—hopeful, almost pleading—that he might understand.

Azriel met her gaze and nodded.

There would be time later for difficult conversations.

For now, there was only parting.

The crowd shifted as Lilith approached. She moved slowly, her age finally catching up with her, yet she bore herself with quiet dignity. When she reached Sariel, she dropped to one knee and bowed her head.

"My Lord?"

"Yes, Lilith."

"My Lord… I ask that you take me now. Let me pass into the underworld."

Sariel regarded her with deep compassion. "Rise, Lady Lilith. Though I would grant you rest if I could, it is not yet your time. There is still work left for you in this world."

"But haven't I paid my debt?"

"Assuredly you have. Yet your part is not finished. You will be needed."

She bowed her head in acceptance and rose slowly.

Turning to Abelene, she clasped her hand. "Thank you, my friend. I have learned much from you. I shall not forget."

"What will you do now?" Abelene asked gently.

"I will go west and rest until I am called again." She glanced at Sariel. "You won't tell me what awaits me, will you?"

"No," he said softly. "But you will know when the hour comes."

"Then I am content… for now."

There was nothing more to be said.

Azriel looked around at his friends and managed a tired smile.

"Well… shall we go home?"

"I would like that," Abelene said brightly, glancing at Sariel. "I'm certain my house is a mess. Would you like to see where I live?"

Sariel nodded and brushed his fingers tenderly along her cheek.

"Then let us leave this awful place," Azriel said.

And as one, Azriel, Camille, and the entire Order vanished from the cavern.

Epilogue

Azriel and Camille stood facing the ocean, watching the waves crest and seethe against the rocks. Cronk Karran, as it was known to the local Manx, overlooked the sea. But they had no recollection in all their history of the Isle of Man that it had once been the foundation for the Temple of Aralia. It was far too remote a time before the shattering of worlds, the memory wiped clean for all but a few. Twenty thousand years ago, it had crowned the Heart of Aralia like a jewel set in stone.

Azriel took Camille's hand and gazed out over the water. "This is where it all began."

"Tell me," she said.

"Well, you know the story. Eltanin was duped into performing a ritual that would have destroyed humanity. Instead, by splitting Aralia in two, he created a place for humanity to survive. The question remains, however, that we still don't know where humanity came from. Did they come from the relative future or the past—and who sent them?" He paused, thinking about what would happen in a month hence when he would reenact the ritual to unite the worlds. Azriel sighed heavily. "I miss Eltanin, and I could really use his wisdom right now."

Camille squeezed Azriel's hand tighter. "Does it frighten you?"

He shrugged. "I'd be a fool not to be frightened."

"Well I think the future looks pretty good."

"How so?" Azriel asked.

Camille clicked her tongue. "Azriel, I love you so much, but boy, you can be dense sometimes. We're going to be married, and I will be your queen, and you will take your throne as King of Aralia."

"You make it sound easy."

"It will unfold as it must. We're not meant to know everything, for example, I saw the portents in the scrying mirror. I saw in order a vision of me embraced by a white dragon! At the time I didn't understand what it meant, but then it happened just as I had seen it. But the next vision I had seen my death! The third vision was the one in which you and I get married. I wondered how both could be true, particularly in that order. But as you see, it happened just the way I saw it. Could I have known that I would be restored to life?"

"I suppose that's true…"

Camille continued, "Remember when you lamented that you would remain immortal while I would age? Could you have predicted the events that happened just yesterday? Azriel, you and I will remain young for a very long time! So the way I see it, the future may be a challenge, but I believe in my heart that it will be wonderful. Azriel, I only see hope for the future."

"That's why I need you beside me as my queen." Azriel kissed her tenderly. "You will keep me grounded!"

"You don't want to be grounded all the time. After all, you're a dragon!"

Azriel was surprised to hear Sariel's voice. He turned around to find Abelene and Sariel, in his human form, had joined them. The look on her face bespoke a joy that she hadn't known for years. Sariel's protective stance told Azriel all he needed to know. The rest, he really didn't want to know.

"Hello, brother." Azriel smiled broadly. "How does it feel to be free?"

"That is a foolish question." Sariel laughed. "It's wonderful, of course. It's even better with Abelene by my side. Er, I hope you have no objections."

"No, of course not, but isn't this dangerous for you? How can you perform your duties as the angel of death and still have time for love?"

"It will be difficult and challenging, but I can't deny what I feel."

"I suppose we both will have to answer to the Mother. You broke the law of death, and I broke the law of life."

"Perhaps. Then let us keep each other's counsel."

Azriel embraced Sariel as a brother. The sun was sinking low, and the sea burned with scattered gold where the last light touched the waves.

Sariel rested a hand upon Azriel's shoulder. "It is time."

Azriel nodded.

They stepped apart and let their higher natures rise. Light bent around them, bones lengthened, wings unfurled, and in moments two great dragons stood upon the cliff—one white as moonlight, the other black as the void between the stars.

Camille and Abelene watched in awe.

Azriel lowered one vast wing. "Come," he said gently.

Camille climbed onto his back, laughing softly as she settled between the ridges of his scales. Abelene did the same with Sariel.

The moon lifted, full and radiant, above the trees.

With a single powerful leap they left the cliff behind.

Wings caught the wind.

Stone fell away.

And together they rose into the night sky, not fleeing the world behind them, but ascending toward the one they would soon restore.

Michael Anthony Cariola

Books by the Author

The Chronicles of Abahrazha Trilogy:

The Singingwood
Arcalian Apocalypse
Children of Prophecy

Shattered Worlds Trilogy:

Gift of the Amulet
Dragonlord
Equilibrium

Summerlands and Other Selected Works

Leo Rising

Echoes of Venus